# REPRESSED

*A Deadly Secrets Novel*

Aug 16

# OTHER BOOKS BY
# ELISABETH NAUGHTON

**Aegis Security Series (Romantic Suspense)**
*Extreme Measures*
*Lethal Consequences*
*Fatal Pursuit*

**Stolen Series (Romantic Suspense)**
*Stolen Fury*
*Stolen Heat*
*Stolen Seduction*
*Stolen Chances*

**Against All Odds Series (Romantic Suspense)**
*Wait For Me*
*Hold On To Me*
*Melt For Me*

**Eternal Guardians Series (Paranormal Romance)**
*Marked*
*Entwined*
*Tempted*
*Enraptured*
*Enslaved*
*Bound*
*Twisted*
*Ravaged*
*Awakened*
*Unchained*

Firebrand Series (Paranormal Romance)
*Bound to Seduction*
*Slave to Passion*
*Possessed by Desire*

Anthologies
*Bodyguards in Bed*

# REPRESSED

## A Deadly Secrets Novel

# ELISABETH NAUGHTON

Montlake
Romance

This is a work of fiction. Names, characters, organizations, places, events, and incidents are either products of the author's imagination or are used fictitiously.

Published by Montlake Romance, Seattle

www.apub.com

Amazon, the Amazon logo, and Montlake Romance are trademarks of Amazon.com, Inc., or its affiliates.

ISBN-13: 9781503936065
ISBN-10: 1503936066

Cover design by Michael Rehder

Printed in the United States of America

*For Jane Droge,*
*a woman who truly knows the meaning of undying love.*
*Aunt Jane, your faith and sacrifice are an inspiration to us all.*

# PROLOGUE

*Go after him.*

Fear pushed her adrenaline up, made her pulse beat hard and fast in her veins. Seth had told her to go home. But she couldn't. Not if he was in trouble. He might need her.

Her feet moved before she even realized what was happening. Crisp air filled her lungs as she rushed up the path and into the trees. She skipped over rocks and limbs, careful not to trip and hurt herself. Her breaths grew heavy and labored. By the time she spotted the cabin through the thick forest, she was covered in a thin layer of sweat.

She slowed her steps. Her pulse turned to a roar in her ears. Her fingers shook as she darted from one tree to the next, trying to stay out of sight, just in case. An eerie orange glow shone from the dirty windows of the run-down cabin. She squinted. Tried to see through the glass.

A crash sounded from inside, and she jumped. Darting behind a tree trunk, she trembled as she peered around the side and searched for Seth.

*Please don't be in there. Please don't be in there . . .*

Another crash echoed, and she jerked back. Wood cracked against wood. Fear gripped her throat like an icy hand. Some kind of fight was happening, but she couldn't see who was involved, didn't know what was happening. Knew she should run but couldn't make her legs move.

The door clanged open. She watched in horror as two shadowy figures pulled another through the space and dragged him away from the cabin.

It was Seth. She knew his long legs and lean frame. Knew that mop of light-brown hair in the moonlight.

She couldn't make out the voices, though. Didn't know what they were saying. And they were moving away from her. Seth kicked out and screamed the bad words that Mommy got upset with her for repeating. Tears pricked her eyes. Something awful was happening. Something awful was happening to Seth.

Her stomach tightened with both fear and indecision. She had to help him. She had to save him. She couldn't let them hurt him.

Her adrenaline surged. She pushed away from the tree trunk and darted through the forest, following the sound of Seth's voice.

*Please, please, please . . . Don't hurt him. Don't hurt my Seth . . .*

Familiarity rushed through her. She'd been through this part of the woods before. Many times in the summer. Careful to stay off the path so they didn't see or hear her, she listened for their voices and ran parallel to their movements. But before she even heard the water splash, she knew where they were headed.

The roar of the falls echoed ahead. Voices mingled with the rush of water. Seth always brought her swimming here when it was hot. The large pool at the base of the falls had always been a place of fun. But these voices weren't having fun. They were angry. Shouting. Yelling. Water splashed again. Followed by Seth's voice once more. Only this time it was frantic. Rushed.

Terrified.

"No! Do—"

Her heart lurched into her throat. Her legs ached, her lungs burned, but she didn't stop. She found the large stream and sprinted along its edge until she reached the falls. Water sprayed in her face, but she swiped the droplets away and gripped the trunk of a small maple tree. The hillside dropped off, opening to the pool thirty feet below.

Voices hollered from somewhere close, but her gaze shot to the ripples fanning out from the middle of the pool and the boy holding a limp body under the water.

The boy pulled the body up out of the water. Dripping light-brown hair caught the moonlight. She squinted to see better. Prayed it wasn't Seth. Gasped when she recognized the lifeless face staring up at the sky.

*No.* A blistering pain lanced her chest. "No! Seth!"

Gravel crunched, but she didn't look to see what had made the sound. Couldn't. Because all she could focus on was the boy holding Seth's lifeless body by the shirtfront in the water. The boy who was now looking up at her with wide, guilt-ridden eyes.

Even though he was thirty feet below, even though she couldn't see much more than shadows and the whites of his eyes, she knew who he was. She'd seen him in town. She'd heard all about the trouble he caused. She'd listened to her parents tell Seth to stay away from the boy.

But Seth hadn't stayed away. And tonight the boy had caused more than just *some* trouble. Tonight he'd taken the only thing she'd ever loved, and in the process, he'd destroyed her entire world.

# CHAPTER ONE

*Eighteen years later . . .*

It said a lot about a person's state of mind when an igloo in the middle of the freezing Arctic looked more appealing than a warm, cozy house.

Samantha Parker flipped off the muted TV documentary she'd been watching with a frown, tossed the remote onto the bed, then balanced on the rickety ladder as she tried—again—to thread the curtain panels she'd bought onto the old rod. The fabric caught on a rusted part of the rod, so she pushed harder. A ripping sound echoed through the room just before the fabric slipped past the obstruction.

"Dammit." Sam turned the rod in her hand so she could see where the fabric had torn. A small gash was visible on the front of the rod pocket.

*Perfect.* This was par for the course for her evening and year. Rising to her toes, she mumbled, "Good enough," and prayed the old ladder held her weight as she placed the rod on the hooks she'd installed earlier and tightened the screws to lock it in place. Climbing down, she scowled up at her work and stepped back.

Not even close to great, but good enough. The red panels matched the red swirls in the bedspread she'd ordered online and hid the crack in the plaster on the right side of the window. No one would be able to see the rip unless they looked closely, but at this point, she didn't even care. She probably should have broken down and bought a new rod, but she didn't want to sink any more money into this old house. Cosmetic updates. That was it. Since her mother's death, all she cared about was making the place look halfway decent so she could pocket a few bucks when she sold it, then get the hell out of town.

She folded the ladder, leaned it against the wall, and climbed back onto her bed. Coming home to Hidden Falls was only supposed to be a temporary thing, but her weeks seemed to be spinning out of control, and the dip in the housing market wasn't helping. She wanted out of this town. Aside from being too small, it was packed with locals who liked to gossip. But more than that, there were just too many bad memories lurking here for Samantha. Too many memories about her brother, her parents, and everything that had happened to rip her family apart.

Images of that cold dark night eighteen years before flickered through her mind. The eerie cabin in the mist, the whispering woods, the roar of the falls. But mostly the screams. So many screams they still woke her in the dead of night. A shiver raced down her spine, but she pushed the images away and forced herself not to think of the past. If she did she'd be sucked back into a vacuum of nightmares she didn't want to relive. And she'd worked so hard to drag herself out of that abyss; she wouldn't go back. She just needed to focus on work. Had to put more effort into selling this house. Only then could she leave this town once and for all and never look back.

The clock on the wall read eleven fifteen, but she wasn't tired yet. Sighing as she relaxed into the mountain of pillows, she bypassed the stack of lab papers she should be grading in favor of her laptop.

Her four-year-old golden retriever, Grimly, whined and tucked his nose under her elbow before she could click the first key, then nudged her arm up.

"Cut that out, you idiot." She shifted her arm away and scanned the links on her screen. "This will just take me a few minutes."

She hadn't taken Grimly for his walk today after school, and she knew he was antsy, but she'd stayed too late at work getting ready for tomorrow's classes, then had come home and tried to do a few of those magical updates her realtor guaranteed would sell the house. Now, she was too interested in looking up the shrink her principal had announced would be observing classes at the high school tomorrow to worry about Grimly's antics.

"Dr. McClane," she said as she typed his name into the search field on her browser. He was probably some white-haired old fart who wore glasses and really bad tweed. That or super slimy in the way only a highly trained emotional manipulator could be. Sam had clocked more than her fair share of hours on a head doctor's couch thanks to her brother's death, and if there was one thing she'd learned over the years, it was that therapists held more power than any other doctor in the medical field. They could lift a person up or completely break them down, but more often than not, they messed with their patients' minds until there was nothing left but self-doubt and paranoia.

Ignoring the unwanted memories that tried to sneak in again, she paged down and stared at a screen full of pictures. Some were taken in a classroom. Some were shot outside at what looked to be a youth camp. But most were filled with faces of kids from all different backgrounds.

Sam scrolled through the photos, reading captions, searching for the slick shrink, and finally stopped on a photo of two men, one old and scraggly, one young and clean-cut, both standing in front of a picnic table with a teenage boy between them.

"Oh, that has got to be him." Sam focused in on the white-haired, wire-rimmed-glasses-wearing, I'll-tell-you-how-it's-gonna-be schmuck on the left and read the caption.

Her brow dropped. She looked back at the picture and read the caption again. "No flippin' way."

Dr. Ethan McClane was the man on the right. The young guy, not the wrinkled judge standing next to a kid he'd referred to Hanson House, a home for troubled teens, where—according to this—Dr. McClane often volunteered during his off hours.

Sure she had to be seeing things, Sam pulled up a new browser window and ran a more detailed search. This time only pictures of Dr. McClane came up, rather than any links to his practice. And yeah, the first picture had been right, but, whoa, it hadn't done the guy justice. He was totally hot—early thirties, thick dark hair, olive skin, a body he obviously took care of, and a smile that could stop traffic.

*He's still a shrink, even if he is GQ material.*

Closing her laptop in disgust, Sam tossed it onto the bed and picked up her green pen and the stack of lab reports. So what if the guy was hot? He was still an unwanted shrink, and she wasn't letting him anywhere near her student Thomas.

She scanned the first lab paper, rolled her eyes at the idiotic answer, and was just about to make a mark when a door downstairs slammed so hard the house shook.

Sam's pulse jumped. Grimly growled and took off for the stairs. Sitting up slowly, she told herself the sound couldn't have come from inside because she lived alone and always locked her doors, but . . .

It sure sounded as if it had come from inside.

Her heart rate picked up speed, and she set the stack of papers on the bed, then pushed to her feet. Barefoot and wearing only thin cotton pajamas, she stepped out into the hallway and peered down the railing to the entry below. Stacks of boxes sat pushed up against the walls, but she zeroed in on Grimly, standing on his hind legs, his front paws braced against the wooden front door, barking like a total loon.

Fear gave way to frustration, then the cold burn of anger. Not an inside door. Probably a car door outside. Those teenagers were messing with her again.

She hurried down the steps, fuming the whole way. First they'd TP'd her trees. Then they'd egged her windows. Last week they'd forked her front lawn, spelling out the word "LEAVE" in white plastic.

As the new teacher on the block, one who expected the students to actually *do* the work she assigned instead of simply goofing off in class, she'd clearly become the target of choice. But if they thought they could push her around, they had another think coming.

She reached the front hall, rounded the corner, and headed for the kitchen at the back of the house. Her purse, keys, and books were just where she'd left them on the counter when she'd come in from the garage. She crossed to them but didn't see her cell phone, and when she checked her purse, it was missing. "Dammit."

Grimly rushed into the room, barking so loudly Sam jumped, and the contents of her purse spilled across the counter. He skidded to a stop at the door that led to the garage, whined and growled, then took off for the front of the house once more, nearly knocking Sam over in the process.

"Dammit, Grimly." Those miserable kids were still out there.

Marching into the office, she grabbed the cordless phone from her mother's old desk and swung back for the front of the house. She side-stepped the half-packed boxes in the hallway, pushed Grimly away from the door where he was going ape shit, flipped the locks, yanked the door open, and yelled, "You don't scare me! You think you're tough? You're cowards. Show yourselves, you little monsters!"

Grimly swept past her, knocking Sam off balance, his frantic barking filling the cool night air. Sam hit the doorjamb with her shoulder and grabbed on with her free hand to steady herself. Pain ricocheted down her arm as Grimly's incessant barking rounded the house.

"Stupid dog." He was going to get her killed with his reckless antics. She stepped out onto the porch.

*Stupid dog . . .*

Her feet slowed, and a space in Sam's chest chilled, bringing everything to a stuttering stop. He *was* a stupid dog. *Just* a stupid dog. And the last thing she wanted was for some juvenile delinquents to think he was dangerous.

Her heart rate shot up. She scanned the shadowed front yard. The lone street lamp to her left illuminated the empty dead-end road. An old oak, devoid of leaves, stood like a decrepit skeleton. Nothing moved at this hour—close to midnight on a Wednesday night.

Grimly's barking grew louder and more frenetic from around the side of the house. Hustling down the rickety front porch steps, Sam ran after him, not even caring that the ground was damp and muddy or that she was barefoot. All she cared about was getting to her dog before those kids did. Breathing heavily, she finally reached the attached garage and spotted Grimly jumping up and down in front of the side door, barking wildly at the grimy window.

"Grimly." Relieved he was all right, she slowed her steps. "Come back here right now."

Grimly continued to bark. Frustrated, Sam crossed to stand behind the dog and reached for his collar. "I said *come on*."

She yanked, but Grimly jerked back and barked even louder. Her hand flew free of his collar. Her foot slipped on the muddy grass. Somehow, she caught herself before she went down. Muttering curses at herself, her dog, at the entire situation, she stood upright, then stilled when she realized what held Grimly's attention.

Red paint dripped like blood down the square window set in the top half of the door. Paint that spelled out the words, "TAKE THE HINT OR ELSE."

Sam whipped around and looked across the open backyard and the dark hills beyond. Nothing moved there either. Only shadowed pine and Douglas fir as far as the eye could see. But the woods were a perfect place to hide, an even better place to wait, and she had no doubt the teenagers making her life hell were out there. Somewhere.

Anger came back, hot and urgent. Childish pranks were one thing, but this was vandalism, and she'd had enough.

She lifted the cordless still in her hand, punched in numbers, and pressed it to her ear. "Yes," she said when the operator came on. "Chief Branson, please. This is Samantha Parker."

The operator mumbled something about the chief being too busy to take personal calls, but Sam barely listened. Will was a close family friend. When she'd come home a few months ago to take care of her mother, he'd told her to call if she ever needed anything, and right now she needed him more than anyone else. He could track fingerprints. Fingerprints would nail the deviants. And this time she was absolutely pressing charges. She was way past playing nice.

She turned back to the door and looked past the dripping letters as she waited for Will to come on. Her car was parked in the center of the garage, undisturbed, exactly as she'd left it. But the used paintbrush and can of red paint sitting on the stool she'd left near her father's old workbench were new.

Sam's gaze shot back to the letters painted on the pane. Her heart pounded a staccato rhythm against her ribs. Slowly, she ran her finger over the letters.

Nothing but cool glass touched her skin.

Her throat closed. No longer caring about fingerprints, she reached for the door handle and turned.

It didn't budge.

"Sam?"

Sam's heart rate spiked, and Will's familiar voice over the line did little to stop the icy fingers of fear from rushing down her spine.

Because someone had been in her locked garage. Someone could be *inside* her house right this very second.

# CHAPTER TWO

Ethan McClane needed a freakin' cigarette.

No, needing and wanting were two very different things. He *wanted* a cigarette. What he needed was a sharp smack upside the head for agreeing to this stupid idea in the first place.

He popped a cherry Life Saver into his mouth, one that did little to kill his nicotine craving, and glanced toward the aged bricks of Hidden Falls High School. From the safety of his BMW, it didn't appear that a whole lot had changed, but then he hadn't expected much. The yard was still wide and barren but for a couple of oak trees that were bigger than he remembered. A few kids lingered outside, chatting in the late-afternoon sun. Shouts resounded from the adjacent field where the football team practiced.

The familiar scene seemed calm and peaceful, but Ethan's stomach tightened with a crap ton of nerves. Almost twenty years later and the thought of being in this placid town in northwest Oregon still made him sick as a dog.

*Get a grip. Remember why you're here. It's not personal this time.*

He tugged off his sunglasses and tossed them on the console. As soon as Judge Wilson had called him about this case he should have figured a way out of it. He ran his own private practice now. He didn't work for the state anymore. Didn't have to evaluate or treat juvenile delinquents if he didn't want to. But he'd owed the craggy old judge for being lenient on one of his kids. And if he thought about it hard enough, he had to admit that he'd thought taking this case pro bono might be good for him. That it might force him to face his own demons so he could put the past behind him once and for all.

Of course, that was before he was actually here.

Man, he needed a smoke. And a freakin' lobotomy.

He pushed the BMW's door open, grabbed his bag from the passenger seat, and climbed out of the car. He'd only met Thomas Adler once. Just after the kid had been picked up for B&E in Portland. Thomas's rap sheet was long—theft, assault, vandalism—but instead of tossing Thomas in detention for his last run-in, Judge Wilson had decided that what Thomas really needed was a change of scenery and counseling. Now, Thomas was living with his estranged grandmother in the small town of Hidden Falls, and Wilson had asked Ethan to help the kid acclimate to his new surroundings.

Ethan wasn't naïve. He knew from his years working with the state that some kids were beyond help. He just hoped Thomas wasn't one of them.

The crisp, early-November breeze blew newly fallen leaves to rustle across his path while rich scents of ripe apples from the adjacent orchard and freshly turned earth greeted his senses. As he approached the building, he forced a smile at a teenage girl eyeing him cautiously from her spot on the stoop. She shifted out of his way, leaned close to the boy decked out in goth black sitting at her side, and whispered something Ethan couldn't hear.

Friendly.

Frowning, he pulled the heavy door open. Old wood, industrial cleaners, and ink scents greeted him as he stepped into the building. A long display cabinet filled with trophies graced the left side of the lobby. He scanned the display, reading names on plaques. When his gaze landed on a picture of the state championship basketball team, he tensed.

"Can I help you?"

Ethan glanced toward the office door to his right where a gray-haired woman stood eyeing him as if he were about to steal something. A pathetic smile toyed with the edge of his lips. One even he knew looked forced. "Yeah. Ethan McClane. I have an appointment with Principal Burke."

The secretary pushed her red-rimmed reading glasses back up her nose. "Ah yes. You're the psychologist." Disdain dripped from her words as she turned, gesturing for him to follow. "Have a seat here and wait. Mr. Burke is in a meeting."

*Extra friendly.* There had to be something in the water.

Muttering "Thanks," Ethan followed the secretary into the cramped outer office. A high counter occupied the middle of the space. To his right, three chairs were pushed up against the wall.

Since the secretary sat and went back to work on her computer, not the least bit interested in chatting, he dropped his bag on the chair and studied a bulletin board with news and announcements about upcoming activities at the school. The door behind him opened before he finished reading about the winter musical.

"I don't know how you expect me to do my job with the measly budget you've allocated for expendable supplies," a female voice complained.

"This isn't the private sector," a man answered. "And I don't have time to argue with you right now. I've got another appointment."

Footsteps sounded, then a man appeared in the open office doorway, frustration lines clearly evident on his face. He was average height, late forties, with dark hair slightly gray at the temples and a full beard, and he looked toward Ethan as if *he* were the one who wanted to run screaming from the building, not the other way around. "You must be Dr. McClane. David Burke. Come on in."

*Gladly.* Ethan grabbed his bag.

"When will you have time to argue with me?" the woman asked from inside. "I'd like to put it on your calendar so you can prepare your canned rebuttal."

The principal sighed. "How about tomorrow? I'll even come in early so you have plenty of time to rant. Does that work for you?"

The woman didn't immediately answer, and as Ethan moved into the office, her gaze snapped his way.

She was younger than he'd expected from the sound of her voice—late twenties maybe. Her dark, curly hair was pulled back and clipped at the base of her neck. Her cheeks were high, her nose straight, and she wore very little makeup that did nothing to hide the dark circles under her eyes. But even with the scowl and obvious exhaustion, she was a looker. And those eyes . . . they were mesmerizing. Like warm, melted chocolate sprinkled with honey. Eyes that screamed *look at me*, even though she'd obviously tried to downplay her appearance by wearing the ugliest gray pantsuit Ethan had ever seen.

Ethan smiled—really smiled—and for the first time since agreeing to this case, thought coming here might not have been such a bad decision. Not if this was the view he could look forward to each day.

The woman's gaze narrowed, and curiosity sparked in those spellbinding eyes. But instead of asking the questions Ethan knew were circling in her mind, she refocused on Principal Burke. "If you suddenly forget a meeting or conveniently fall ill, David, I'll show up on your front porch."

"I don't doubt that," Burke muttered as the woman walked out of the office. She didn't spare Ethan another glance, just swept by him as if he weren't even there. But as she passed, the sweet scents of lavender and vanilla drifted Ethan's way, sending a quick shot of heat straight to his belly.

Muffled voices echoed from the outer office, followed by the main door slamming shut. As the sound dissipated, Burke reached for a file from the corner of his desk and sighed. "Sorry about that. Annoyed teachers are often worse than disgruntled postal employees."

"That bad, huh?" Since the principal didn't sit, Ethan set his bag on one of two chairs across from the desk and tucked his hands into the pockets of his slacks.

"You don't know the half of it. Woman's not happy unless she's got my balls in a vise on a regular basis."

Ethan chuckled. Oddly, with her, that sounded painful and pleasant all at the same time. "Lucky you."

Burke handed him the folder. "I hate to cut and run, but I've got a meeting at the district office in fifteen minutes. We're all set for tomorrow. So long as you're not a disruption, we'll do whatever we can to cooperate."

"I know how to blend." Ethan flipped open the folder and scanned the top paper. "These are Thomas's behavior evaluations from the staff?"

"Yeah, only one missing is Sam Parker's."

"And he is . . . ?"

"Chemistry teacher." Burke shrugged on his suit jacket and lifted his chin toward the door. "You already met her."

"Ah." One side of Ethan's lips curled. "Disgruntled staff member. Yeah. I think I remember." As if he could forget the girl with the glittering eyes.

"She was heading back to her room. You can probably catch her if you need her evaluation before tomorrow."

Ethan didn't. Not really. He had enough here to get started. But the thought of seeing those eyes again was a nice distraction from reliving all the shitty things that had happened to him in this town. He tucked the folder under his arm and shook the principal's hand. "Thanks."

Burke fixed his jacket collar and stepped toward the door. "Annette will get you a copy of Adler's class schedule and a map so you don't get lost. If anything comes up, let me know. I'll see you in the morning."

Ethan said good-bye to the principal, gathered a campus map and visitor pass from Annette, the salt-and-pepper-haired secretary who continued to eye him as if he had a second head, and strolled down the long hallway with its scuffed walls and dinged lockers. Posters advertised the upcoming dance. A banner hung from the ceiling, reminding students to dress up for spirit week. At the end of the corridor, a janitor wearing headphones pushed a broom across the floor. The man looked up as Ethan approached, narrowed his eyes, then quickly turned away.

Another friendly resident. This place just got more and more welcoming.

He glanced at the map, continued down the corridor, and took the next right. Halfway down the hall, he spotted the chemistry teacher, standing next to a curvy blonde wearing a short skirt and ice-pick heels no woman in her right mind could possibly stand on all day.

They must have heard him because they both turned to look as soon as he rounded the corner. And the second Sam Parker's mesmerizing eyes locked on Ethan's, something hard and tight gathered right in the center of his gut.

Man, those eyes seriously needed to come with a warning label.

The blonde paused midsentence, and swept a heated look over Ethan. "You look lost, handsome."

Ethan glanced from the ostentatious diamond ring on the blonde's left hand to the staff ID badge clipped to her waist. Margaret Wilcox. English department, if he remembered correctly from the files he'd scanned earlier. "Actually, I'm not. I was looking for Ms. Parker."

Margaret flicked Sam a look. "Well, that has definitely got to be a first."

Ethan didn't miss the mocking tone, or the animosity shooting like sparks between the two women. Definite story there. One he shouldn't be interested in but nonetheless ignited his curiosity.

Sam Parker's eyes narrowed. "Did David send you down here, Dr. McClane?"

She knew who he was. No big surprise there. He tried a smile, but her stone-faced expression proved she was resistant to male charm. Or maybe just his. "I was wondering if you had a chance to finish the behavior assessment on Thomas Adler."

"Ah, that explains it," Margaret Wilcox said next to him. "I didn't think you were her type."

"Behavior assessment. Right." For a swift second, Sam closed her eyes and pinched the bridge of her nose. "It's in my room."

Margaret chuckled. "Translation? It's not done. You might be waiting awhile, Dr. McClane. Sam never finishes anything. You get bored, you come find me." With a last leering look, she turned and left, her heels clicking like cannon fire across the cement floor.

"Nice lady," Ethan said when she was gone. "Friend?"

"Black widow." Sam stared down the hall after the blonde. But before Ethan could ask what she meant, her expression cleared. She turned to look up at him. "So you're the shrink the state sent to spy on Thomas."

"Therapist," he corrected, catching her contempt.

"Right."

Ethan worked to keep his expression neutral. The woman might have pretty eyes, but she had a definite chip parked right on her shoulder, and he didn't have the energy to spar with her right now.

"Your evaluation is on my de—"

The sharp crackle of glass shattering cut off her words. A loud thump echoed down the corridor, followed by more glass breaking. Eyes widening, Sam headed in that direction.

"Ms. Parker. Wait."

She didn't seem to hear him. Her gaze was fixed on the door at the end of the hall. Closing her hand over the knob, she pressed her hip against the solid wood and muttered, "Dammit." She fished a key ring from the front pocket of her baggy slacks, slipped the metal into the catch, and turned.

Behind her, Ethan glanced through the long rectangular window in the door. A shadow streaked across the dark room.

His adrenaline spiked. He reached for her slim shoulder. "Hold on."

The door gave with a pop. She shrugged off his grip, but Ethan pushed between her and the open door before she could take a step. The shadow darted behind a lab station.

"Hey!" Sam yelled, stepping out from behind Ethan.

Shoes squeaked on the tile floor. Ethan dropped his bag and darted for the intruder. The kid or adult—Ethan couldn't tell which—parted the closed drapes and slithered out an open window. Swiping aside the heavy fabric, Ethan closed his hand over a denim-clad ankle. In the fading light of dusk, all he could make out was jeans and a hooded sweatshirt, pulled high over the person's face. The intruder kicked, broke free of Ethan's arm, then dropped to the ground outside with a thud. Footsteps echoed back through the window as he raced away.

Sam moved to the right side of the windows and pulled open the drapes. Dim light spilled through the glass. "Shit."

Ethan turned to see what she was looking at. Large, black-topped tables were overturned. Chairs lay on their sides, stools tipped upside down around lab stations. Broken glass and shredded papers littered the floor while a putrid chemical scent hovered over the entire room.

"What is that?" Ethan asked, wrinkling his nose.

The chemistry teacher darted toward the front of the room. "Gas line."

She knelt behind a long counter. While she fiddled with the main valve, Ethan popped open windows to let in fresh air. A ventilation fan in the ceiling clicked on, the low whir cutting through the silence.

"That should do it," she said, pushing to her feet.

Ethan wasn't so sure. "We should call somebody. Hazmat, the gas company—"

She turned a slow circle, surveying the damage. "The valve wasn't on that long. It should clear out in a min—"

She froze, and curious about what she was seeing now, Ethan followed her gaze toward the whiteboard. Large red letters spelling out the words "TAKE THE HINT."

A whisper of foreboding rushed down Ethan's spine, followed by a memory from nearly twenty years before. A frigid, moonless night. The roar of the falls. The slap of water again and again. Icy-cold liquid filling his lungs. And laughter, eerie and malevolent, echoing from the shore.

That whisper turned to a roar in his ears. But he reminded himself the words weren't meant for him, that no one in this town knew who he was. So long as he kept his mouth shut, no one would ever know the truth.

His gaze drifted Sam's way, and the haunted expression in her eyes shifted his concern from him to her. He stepped toward her, but before he could ask if she was okay, she turned away, then stilled.

Ethan glanced over his shoulder and spotted the open door along the back wall that gave way to nothing but darkness.

"Dammit." Sam stepped over chairs and shattered test tubes.

"Hold on." Ethan reached for her but she bypassed his grip. "You don't know if anyone's still in here."

Her shoes crunched over broken glass as she disappeared into the darkness. Ethan quickly followed. Just as he crossed the threshold, a light flicked on, illuminating a storage closet lined with shelves of chemicals, most of which—thankfully—were still standing upright.

"Thank goodness," Sam muttered from somewhere inside. "I was afraid they trashed this too."

Ethan moved deeper into the supply closet that was smaller than his master bath at home. A locked glass cabinet filled with bottles and tubes marked "Dangerous" sat to the right of the door. A few canisters were knocked over on the open shelves, but nothing appeared broken.

He righted a plastic bottle filled with pink crystals. "What kinds of things do you keep stored in—"

The door slammed shut with a loud crack.

Ethan glanced toward the sound. "What the—"

"Shit." The sexy teacher brushed past him and reached for the handle. "That can't—"

Darkness descended as the lights went out, and a chuckle echoed from the other side of the door. A dark, ominous chuckle that slithered through the crack and sent the fine hairs along Ethan's nape straight to attention.

One he was almost certain he'd heard before.

Eighteen years before to be precise.

# CHAPTER THREE

Sam rattled the door handle but the knob wouldn't turn.

"Sonofabitch." She kicked the steel door as hard as she could and slapped her hand against the smooth, cool surface. "You asshole! When I find you, you're gonna wish I hadn't!"

She didn't need this today. She'd had enough last night with that . . . whatever the hell it had been. She didn't even know anymore, because after coming back from the police station with Will in tow, the words she'd seen on her door had been gone.

She'd stayed up all night trying to figure out if those words had existed or if she'd only imagined them, if she was slowly going crazy or if someone was messing with her. But now she knew the words *had* been real. As real as that message out there on her whiteboard. As real as the bastard who'd locked her in this closet.

She swore again and gave the door another hard kick.

Pain shot from her toes and spiraled up her leg. She shifted her weight and hopped on her good foot. Rubbing her injured toes, she finally gave in to the urge and screamed.

"You're going to break your foot before you do any damage to th door."

Sam froze. And a heartbeat passed before her eyes slid shut.

Crap. She'd totally forgotten she wasn't alone. As if her life couldn't get any worse.

In the darkness at her back, paper tore. "Life Saver?"

She drew in a calming breath that did little to settle her raging pulse. "No, Dr. McClane, I don't need something in my mouth to shut me up, thank you very much."

A low chuckle echoed in the darkness. And too late she realized how suggestive that sounded. She suppressed a groan. Shit, she'd been wrong. Her life *could* get worse. Way worse, apparently.

"Not trying to shut you up, Ms. Parker. Just thought it might help."

"Help?" Sam turned his way and glared into the dark, even though she knew he couldn't see her. "It's close to five o'clock. Help is long gone by now."

"Hopefully not." A green light flicked on, one she realized had come from his phone screen. One that illuminated the angles and planes of his attractive face while he looked down and dialed. Rubbing her foot, Sam tried to avoid glancing at him. She might be on the edge of losing it, but she was still a woman. And upon first glance she'd noticed immediately that Dr. McClane was a thousand times hotter in person than he'd been in those pictures she'd pulled up last night.

Which only pissed her off more.

His brow furrowed as he studied the screen. "Damn."

Sam fought the burgeoning *I told you so*. "Let me guess. No signal."

When his gaze slid her way, she turned back for the door and jiggled the handle again. "This whole school's like a giant dead zone. No e gets a signal here."

ammit, she did not want to be stuck in here with this guy all
e slapped her hand against the door again. "Kenny!"
g but the whir of the ventilation fan in her classroom met

enny?"

Pounding on the door was as useless as wishing she'd never come home to Hidden Falls in the first place. "Janitor. But he's probably on the other side of the school, and even if he's not, he always wears those stupid headphones when he's working."

"What about the other teachers?" Dr. McClane stepped up next to her, and his fingers brushed hers against the door. Warmth spiraled across Sam's skin. She quickly stepped out of the way, then bit her lip to keep from crying out when the pain in her toe spiked.

"Have you never been in a school before?" she asked as the pain subsided. "Most teachers cut out as soon as four o'clock hits. I guarantee there's no one left."

And why the hell had she just said that? Okay, she was *seriously* going mental. She'd just told a complete stranger—a guy who looked like he outweighed her by at least seventy-five pounds and who obviously worked out—that no one would be coming for them. That no one even knew they were locked in here.

Yeah, that was smart. She moved back until her spine hit the shelving unit.

He flipped on his phone's flashlight app and shined the light across the door as he studied the lock. "What about that teacher you were talking with in the hall? The blonde black widow?"

Black widow. Great. She'd forgotten she'd called Margaret that in front of a shrink. She could only imagine what little nuggets of info he'd gleaned about her from that conversation.

She shook off the thought when she realized even Margaret would be gone. Most days she was the first out the door. She'd only stayed late today for an IEP meeting. But he didn't need to know that. "Um . . . she could be out there, I guess."

He turned toward her. And in the dim light she saw the way his green eyes narrowed. The way he was studying her like a lab rat, just as every other shrink had studied her.

Apprehension and fear gave way to anger. An anger that gave her strength. *Look all you want, head doctor. I'm not afraid of you.*

He broke the stare down, heaved a sigh, and sank to the floor, his back against the steel door, his long legs stretched out in front of him. Sam stayed where she was, but after several minutes of silence standing on one leg to keep weight off her bad toe, finally gave in and lowered herself to the floor too. Leaning against the shelving unit, she pulled her feet up next to her and rested her arms on her knees, watching him carefully for the slightest movement, just in case.

"I'm gonna flip the light off to conserve my battery," he said.

Sam didn't answer. The room fell dark. Her pulse picked up again as she waited for her eyes to adjust. But even when they did, she couldn't see more than the sliver of light coming from beneath the door. And in the dark, she was hyperaware of the cramped closet, of McClane's closeness, of the room's rising temperature.

McClane sighed. "So since we're stuck in here together for God only knows how long, why don't you fill the time by telling me who's got a grudge against you?"

Considering the trouble Sam had experienced lately, that could be a hell of a list. One she wasn't about to share with a shrink. "I don't know."

"You don't have any idea?"

"No, Dr. McClane, I have no idea who hates me so much they'd resort to this."

"Ethan."

"What?"

"My first name is Ethan."

Sam clenched her jaw. She didn't want to know his first name. She didn't want to know anything about him. And why was it so hot in here? She unbuttoned her jacket and fanned the tank sticking against her chest.

Silence settled between them. A silence that was both intimate and unnerving. She tried to shift farther away but whacked her shoulder against a shelf. "Dammit."

"Are you okay?"

"Fine." Sam definitely didn't like the concern she heard in his voice. Or the heat rushing over her skin that said he was closer than she'd thought. "Just stay over there on your side of the closet."

"I sense some animosity, Ms. Parker. I'm just trying to help."

There was that word again, "help." Why did everyone think she needed help? "That's what all shrinks say," she mumbled, rubbing her shoulder.

"Mind expanding on that?"

Sam stopped rubbing, thankful it was too dark for him to see her frustrated expression. "Look, it's not personal, it's just been my experience that most shrinks—"

"Therapists," he cut in.

"Fine, therapist. Most *therapists* end up causing more trouble than they set out to cure. I have issues with shrinks . . . therapists," she corrected before he could, "doling out advice when they don't have a clue what repercussions their words may have down the line."

"Ouch."

"And what does that mean?" she snapped before she could stop herself.

"Just means it sounds very personal."

Yeah, it sounded personal to Sam too. She cursed her short temper and quick tongue, especially when she was locked in here with a total stranger.

Paper tore again, and the sweet scent of cherry filled the room. Sam's stomach grumbled. She hadn't eaten breakfast because she'd been too stressed about the vandalism at her house last night. Had skipped lunch to help a couple of students redo a lab. And the handful of crackers she'd munched on after school wasn't cutting it.

"Okay, fine," she said after several moments of listening to him suck on his candy. "Give me one of those."

He chuckled. Seconds later, his fingers bumped hers in the dark, and heat spread across her skin just before the small, circular candy fell into her palm.

She pulled her hand back quickly, popped the candy into her mouth, and forced herself not to moan at the sweet cherry taste. That was all she needed to do. Moan in front of a hot shrink who obviously already thought she had issues.

"How long have you been teaching here?" he asked.

"Six weeks." Sam cringed at her quick answer.

"Only six weeks? Wow. How long have you been teaching in general?"

Couldn't they just not talk? Would that be too much to ask? Sam rubbed her throbbing forehead again, wishing for silence, but in the darkness she knew she was stuck. She had two choices: either keep quiet and tick this guy off by being rude, or try to ease the tension by attempting to be nice. He hadn't made any aggressive moves toward her. In fact, if she remembered correctly, he'd tried to keep her from darting into her classroom when she'd seen that intruder. He'd even warned her not to go into the closet when she'd noticed the open door, but like the moron she was, she hadn't listened.

A little of her apprehension eased. She could do nice. Even if he was a shrink—correction, *therapist*.

She moved the candy to the other side of her mouth and worked to keep the animosity out of her voice. "Yes, only six weeks. I was hired as a temp to fill a vacancy. The last chemistry teacher had a nervous breakdown."

Fitting, really. Good God, what was it about this school? This town?

"Nice. And you don't think taking someone's job is any reason for him or her to want you gone?"

Sam's brow lowered. She'd automatically assumed a kid had trashed her room and vandalized her house. Was it possible it was the guy she'd replaced?

Her mind ran back to the menacing chuckle they'd heard when the door had slammed shut, and a shiver raced down her spine. "Flip your flashlight app on. I have pepper spray in here somewhere."

The light flicked on, illuminating the room in a warm white glow. She pushed to her feet, stepped over his long legs, and found the stool in the corner. After dragging it to the back of the closet, she climbed up and pawed through a shelf.

"Now that makes me feel safe." He rose behind her. "A teacher with a dangerous weapon. I think I had nightmares about this in high school. What are you doing with pepper spray around kids?"

"David was concerned for my safety. The last teacher had a few run-ins with the police after he was let go. The pepper spray was a precautionary measure."

"I see. Just promise you won't use it on me. My teacher fantasies usually involve a ruler, a short skirt, and the occasional whip. Nothing as masochistic as pepper spray."

Sam couldn't help it. She smiled. Then nixed it quickly. "If you keep your hands to yourself, I promise. Ah, there it is."

She pushed up on her toes, reaching toward the back of the shelf. Her fingers grazed the canister. She could almost reach it. Grabbing the edge of the shelf, she rose higher. The stool beneath her feet rocked.

"Crap." Metal clanged. Air whooshed up Sam's back. Her fingers grappled for the edge of the shelf but the stool clanked to the ground. And then she was falling . . .

"Ms. Park—"

Sam hit the ground on her butt, and grunted. Pain shot straight up her spine. She looked up at the swaying shelving unit. Bottles and canisters rushed straight toward her.

Sam shrieked and shielded her head with her hands. The light went out. A crash echoed, but, surprisingly, nothing hit her.

She blinked several times, sure that shelf should be on top of her, and lowered her arms. "What hap—"

"That's gonna leave a mark," McClane grunted from somewhere above her. "Several probably."

Sam pushed up on her hands only to crack her forehead against something hard.

"Dammit," McClane muttered. "That's gonna leave another mark."

Sam winced and rubbed at her head. McClane was directly above her. She'd smacked her head against his. Two seconds was all it took to realize he'd put himself between her and danger.

"Hold still." Her hands and feet scattered bottles and cylinders along the floor as she scrambled out from under him where he was braced on his hands and knees.

Her fingers closed around the metal brace of the unit, and she strained to push the shelf back upright.

The unit clapped against the back wall, and Sam exhaled hard. Turning, she stepped McClane's way, but her sensible flats slipped in some kind of powder, and she wobbled. "Whoa."

"Don't move." McClane shuffled across the floor at her feet. "Let me find my phone."

Canisters rolled along the floor. Sam imagined him on his hands and knees searching for his cell, which could be anywhere in this mess. Just when she was sure he'd never find it a white light flicked on.

Sickness rolled through Sam's belly when she took in the broken jars and powders spilled over the ground. Luckily, there hadn't been any dangerous chemicals on that shelf, but her relief was short-lived when she spotted McClane.

"Oh my God. You're hurt." She stepped over a jar of powder to reach him. His white dress shirt was ripped at the shoulder, his hair covered in fine white powder, and something wet and black ran down the side of his face. She touched his forehead only to realize the liquid was warm and sticky. "Don't move. I have towels."

"Trust me. Not planning on it." He rolled back to sit on the floor. "Damn. My day is not improving."

"Mine either." Sam took the phone he offered so she could shine the light over the shelf. Grabbing a stack of towels, she knelt at his side and pressed the cloth against his forehead. "I have no idea how that happened. Those shelving units are bolted to the wall."

"Not so well apparently."

She pulled the towel away. That sickness resurged when she spotted the amount of blood on the white cloth. She pressed the towel against his forehead once more.

He hissed in a breath.

"Sorry." Sam gentled the pressure. "I'll try to be more careful."

"I'm starting to think you're a bad luck omen, Ms. Parker."

Sam grimaced because, yeah, she was starting to feel like a bad omen herself.

She checked him for any other injuries as he sat leaning back on his hands, his eyes closed. Colored granules covered his left shoulder, but thankfully he wasn't bleeding anywhere else. Her gaze skipped over the hard line of his jaw, the muscles in his arms and chest, and the thin tapered waist that disappeared into his slacks.

Warmth gathered in her belly. A warmth that came out of nowhere. But it was quickly overshadowed by the realization that he'd just protected her—again.

All the animosity slid from her veins as she moved the towel so a clean portion of fabric pressed against the oozing wound. "I'm sorry about being a bitch earlier. It's not you, it's—"

"Therapists. Yeah, I got that."

She checked the towel again, reminded herself head wounds bled a lot, but couldn't quite quell her concern over the fact that the blood wasn't slowing. "It's not just that. I like Thomas. He's trying hard to fit in. I know what it's like to be the odd man out, and I don't want him to have any kind of setback. Your being here could do that for him. I know he's had run-ins with the law, but I honestly believe he wants a second chance. He's a good kid."

Dr. McClane's hand brushed her forearm, and sparks of heat ricocheted across her skin, the kind that drew everything else to a stop. "I'm not here to cause problems for Thomas. As long as he stays out of trouble, my being here is just a formality. Trust me, no one believes in second chances more than I do."

Her pulse picked up speed. She barely knew this man, and considering what he did for a living, she had no reason to trust him. But something inside said he was telling the truth. And after the way he'd just put himself between her and danger, even when she'd done nothing but antagonize him, she knew he wasn't at all like her last therapist.

Her gaze locked on his, and in the dim light she saw something else. Something lurking in his eyes that told her even with all the horror and misery she'd experienced in her life, this guy knew way more about second chances than she ever would. And not just from clinical experience.

Electricity arced between them. An electricity that knocked her totally off-kilter. "Dr. McClane—"

"Ethan." A smile tugged at one corner of his lush mouth. A mouth that was a thousand times more tempting than it had been before. "My first name is Ethan. And since I just got my ass handed to me by your shelving unit, I think it's time we moved past the formalities."

"No."

His cocky grin faded, and she read the disappointment in his eyes, but her heart was suddenly thumping so hard she couldn't think straight. "Not because you got your ass kicked by my shelves. Because

I believe in second chances too. It's Samantha, but everyone here calls me Sam."

"Samantha," he said softly. "Want to seal our truce with something sweet?"

He held out his hand, and heat flared in her belly in anticipation of his touch. But the touch didn't come. And when one corner of his mouth curled in that sexy smirk again, she glanced down and realized he was offering her another Life Saver.

Her stomach growled. But this time not from hunger. At least not for food. This time it was from a sudden, wicked flash of something a whole lot sweeter sliding along her tongue. Something that would seal their truce in a much more satisfying way.

# CHAPTER FOUR

A heavy knock sounded at the door, and Samantha jerked back just when Ethan had thought things were about to get interesting.

"Sam?" a voice called through the door. "Are you in there?"

Samantha scrambled to her feet and muttered, "Thank God they found us." But Ethan frowned as she rushed toward the door and yelled, "We're in here!"

He definitely didn't want to get stuck in a cramped closet all night, but the heat in the sexy chemistry teacher's eyes when she'd looked at him a minute ago almost made him think she'd been about to kiss him. And even with the head wound and sore back and his crappy history in this town, he wouldn't have minded one bit if she had.

The lock turned, and the door hissed open, followed by light flooding the small room. Ethan blinked twice and averted his eyes from the blinding glare.

"What the hell are you doing?"

Burke. That was Principal Burke's voice. Wincing at the pain, Ethan held the rag against his head and slowly pushed to his feet.

"We were locked in," Samantha said. "Dr. McClane was talking to me in the hall when we heard the break-in. He followed me into the supply closet when I went to see if anything was damaged, and then someone locked us in."

Ethan stepped over cracked bottles and plastic canisters into the trashed classroom. Burke's gaze shot from Samantha to Ethan, focusing on the bloody rag against Ethan's forehead. "What the hell happened to you?"

Ethan opened his mouth to answer, but Samantha cut him off when she said, "The shelving unit came down. David, someone unbolted it from the wall. That thing never moves."

Burke glanced around the messy room and sighed. When his gaze swung back to Samantha, though, his expression hardened. "Sam, your arm's bleeding."

"I am?" Samantha looked down, and for the first time, Ethan noticed her jacket was torn, and that blood welled from a cut in her biceps.

Ethan's stomach tightened as she struggled out of her coat. Moving back into the closet, Ethan grabbed another towel, came back, and handed it to her.

Samantha took the towel and pressed it against her wound. "Thanks."

"Annette?" Burke pressed the phone on Sam's desk to his ear. "Get paramedics over here. Then call the police. We've had a break-in."

While Burke relayed what had happened, Ethan's gaze skipped over Samantha. Chocolate curls had slipped free from the clip at the base of Samantha's neck, framing her features in wisps and corkscrews. Some kind of white powder dusted her hair, and her face screamed of frustration and stress, but those eyes . . . they were just as mesmerizing as they'd been before. And even though his head hurt like a bitch, Ethan felt himself being sucked back under her spell all over again. "You wasted time tending my injury when you had one yourself?"

"I didn't feel it." One corner of her lips curled. And though he tried not to notice, he couldn't totally ignore the way her breasts pushed together under the thin white tank when she moved her arm to check the blood on the towel. "We make quite a pair, don't we?"

Yes, they absolutely did. "I—"

"Paramedics are on their way," Burke said as he hung up the phone. "Both of you head up to the office. Police should be here any minute."

"David, I don't need an ambula—"

Burke frowned. "Don't argue, Sam. You're covered in God only knows what, and you probably need a tetanus shot." Looking toward Ethan, Burke added, "Hell of a first day for you, Dr. McClane."

"Technically not even my first day." Ethan stepped around downed tables and chairs and followed Burke and Samantha toward the door. She'd draped her jacket over her forearm, leaving her shoulders bare and the tank molding to her curves, and he thoroughly enjoyed the view of her ass way more than he probably should. Especially knowing she'd been hurt.

He cleared his throat, focusing on Burke instead of the sway of Samantha's luscious hips. "How did you find us?"

"Janitor came in and saw the mess, called in the break-in. I rushed over from the district office."

Ethan nodded, happy they'd been found, but also disappointed he hadn't had more time alone with Samantha.

Their shoes clicked down the wide hall as Burke asked them both questions about what they'd seen when they'd first come into the room. By the time they reached the office, the ambulance was just pulling up out front in the darkening light.

Paramedics rushed in and ushered them toward the vehicles. Samantha continued to protest that she didn't need first aid, but when she pulled the cloth away and Ethan caught a glimpse at the gash on the back of her arm, he couldn't stop himself from muttering, "Let the poor guy do his job, Ms. Parker."

She shot him a challenging look but finally climbed in and sat on the padded bench.

Heat gathered in Ethan's belly while he followed and sat beside her. She was definitely feisty. And high-strung. And he liked both things about her. Liked them a lot more than he probably should.

The paramedic checked the wound on Ethan's forehead, and as another tended Samantha's wound, he took a good long look at her under the ambulance lights. The woman had great shoulders. Strong, toned, feminine. And the contrast between light and dark where her curly hair fell over her bare skin was more than captivating. But aside from her good looks, she was tough. He'd seen it in the way she'd rushed into her room during the break-in. Granted, that had been reckless, and she could have been seriously hurt, but she wasn't the kind of woman who backed down from a fight. And he couldn't help but be awed by that trait.

"You're going to need stitches," the paramedic told him. "I'm closing the wound with butterfly bandages until we get to the hospital."

Wonderful. A hospital. Just how he wanted to spend his evening. "I left my bag inside. I need to—"

"David will get it," Samantha said beside him as the EMT tending her moved out of the truck.

Ethan looked back at her, and like they had before, those eyes sent a jolt straight through him. The memory of the way she'd looked at him in the white light of that closet made him want things he knew he shouldn't. Things he had not come to Hidden Falls to find.

He tried to remember what they were talking about. His bag. Yeah, that was it. "There are case files in there that I—"

"Sam," a voice said from outside the open ambulance doors. "Are you okay?"

They both looked toward the blond man dressed in blue standing in a circle of light just outside the open ambulance doors.

"Will." Samantha's features relaxed. "Yes. I'm fine. I'm glad you're here." She nodded Ethan's way. "This is Dr. McClane. Ethan, this is Will Branson."

Ethan froze, and a knot formed in his stomach. And everything else—the break-in, his injury, what the hell he was doing in this town, even Samantha Parker's hypnotic eyes—fell to the wayside.

Because in that moment he wasn't thirty-one anymore. He was thirteen and trying hard to fit in with a group of kids that had altered the course of his life.

———

Sam sat on the side of a bed in an emergency room bay and waited while the doctor finished stitching up her arm. She'd had to argue until she was blue in the face that she didn't need a shower. The chemicals that had fallen on her and Ethan were mostly harmless ones, such as sodium chloride and ammonium sulfate. She kept the really dangerous stuff locked in a separate cupboard.

She had no idea what was happening back at school, and part of her didn't want to know. All she wanted to do was get home, see Grimly, and fall asleep for a week. Oh, and make sure Dr. McClane—no, *Ethan*—was okay.

Her pulse ticked up at just the thought of him. Beside her, the doctor looked down at her arm. "You okay?"

Her cheeks heated when she realized he must have felt it too. "Yeah. Fine. Just anxious to go home."

The doctor applied the last bandage and finally let go of her arm. "Try to keep it dry. I'm writing a script for antibiotics just in case. If you have any problems, call your primary care doctor or come back and see us if it's after hours."

She thanked him, climbed off the bed, and reached for her jacket. Cringing at the burn in her arm, she slid her arms into the sleeves and was just fixing the collar when footsteps shuffled from the doorway.

"All done?" Ethan asked.

Sam's stomach flipped. He'd obviously argued his way out of a shower too, because his hair was still dusted in fine white powder, making him look more gray than dark. A bandage covered the right side of his forehead, and the left shoulder of his white dress shirt was stained pink.

For a moment, worry rippled through her as she mentally cataloged what had been on those shelves. Then she realized it had to be sodium nitrite. Pink salt. Definitely safe. She breathed easier. "Yeah. Just. You?"

He slipped his hands into the pockets of his slacks and rocked back on his heels. "Good to go."

She was suddenly aware of the width of his shoulders, the way he filled the doorway to her room and seemed to suck up all the air in the space. And her nerves tightened when she remembered leaning over him in that closet, the way he'd looked up at her, the sincerity in his eyes, and how much she'd wanted to kiss him in that moment.

Which—she knew now—was completely and utterly insane and only went one step further in proving she was walking on very shaky mental ground.

She pulled her sleeve down and averted her gaze. Reminded herself to be smart. "How many stitches?"

"Six."

"You got me beat. I only needed four."

She stepped toward the door. He eased back to let her pass, but their shoulders brushed, and heat slid all along her skin where they touched, sending tiny tingles through her whole body. Tingles she liked way too much.

"I was wondering if you wanted to split a cab back to the school," he said. "I'm guessing your car's there?"

A cab ride alone with him in the dark? Where they'd talk more, and she'd find out he really was a nice guy, not the slimy shrink she wanted him to be? If she were a normal woman, she'd say yes. He was hot, and she was picking up all kinds of interested vibes. But she wasn't normal, and killing this wild attraction was the best thing she could do. For both of them.

"I—"

"Sam." Will's voice down the corridor drew Sam around, and relief spread through her at the perfectly timed interruption.

"Will," she said. "Hey."

Concern furrowed his blond brow. "Everything okay?"

"Yeah. Just a couple of stitches. No big deal."

Will nodded, but the concern in his eyes didn't lessen, and Sam's anxiety ramped up in the silence that followed. He wasn't just the chief of police; he'd been her brother's best friend when they were kids, and that made him her oldest friend too. In fact, he'd done more for her over the years than anyone in this backward town, even her mother, which made him the one person she knew she could depend on when things got rough. And she'd done just that for the last few days. Probably more than she should have, because lately she'd been getting the feeling he wanted more. And she didn't know how to handle that knowledge.

Feeling awkward, Sam turned toward Ethan. "We're both okay."

Ethan didn't answer, but Sam noticed his suddenly tight jawline and narrowed eyes. Eyes that only a minute ago had been deep emerald pools.

"I need to ask you both a few questions," Will said before Sam could ask Ethan what was wrong.

They stepped back into her room, and she waited while Will pulled a pad of paper from his back pocket, switching from concerned friend to chief of police. "We're running fingerprints, but you had a hundred kids in that room today—"

"Closer to two hundred," Sam clarified.

"Right. Which means prints aren't going to tell us a whole lot. We're also conducting a locker check but don't expect to find much as the break-in happened after hours. Tell me what you saw when you went in the room."

Sam relayed for Will what she and Ethan had found and how they'd ended up in the closet. Will jotted notes. But when he looked up at her, his hazel eyes softened, as if he were speaking to a child. "Sam, honey. There was nothing written on your whiteboard."

"*What?*" Sam's gaze snapped to Ethan, then back to Will. "It was there. I swear. I didn't make that up. It was there, just like the window."

Ethan glanced her way. "What window?"

Sam's stomach tightened, but before she could answer, Will said, "Sam's had some kids harassing her at home. Pranks. Nothing serious."

"Breaking into my house is not a prank."

Will sighed as he tucked the notebook in his back pocket. "There was no sign of B&E at your house last night, Sam."

"That's because whoever did it washed the window before you got there. Just like they obviously wiped the board after they locked us in that closet."

When Will didn't answer, incredulity spread through her. He was supposed to be the one person left on her side. "Are you implying we locked ourselves in that closet? Trashed my room just for the fun of it? Is that what you're saying to me, Will?"

Will rubbed a hand down her good arm, placating her. "No, that's not what I'm saying at all. I just think with everything going on, you might not be remembering clearly and—"

"I saw the note on the whiteboard," Ethan said. "It was written in red and said 'take the hint.'" He looked Sam's way with concerned green eyes. "What hint?"

Sam's pulse skipped. What was it about this guy that affected her so? It had started when he'd walked into the office as she'd been arguing with David and only seemed to be growing stronger. "I . . . whoever's been coming by my house spelled out the word 'leave' in white plastic forks last week."

Ethan's gaze shifted back to Will. "Leave? And you don't think that's related to the break-in at the school?"

Will's jaw tensed. "I didn't say it wasn't related. I said it wasn't breaking and entering."

"What about the teacher she replaced? The one who had the nervous breakdown?"

A vein in Will's temple pulsed, and the animosity on his face said he didn't like being told how to do his job. "I've got an officer on the way out to his place right now. If he's involved we'll find out soon enough." His gaze swung back to Sam, effectively dismissing Ethan. "I want you to make me a list of any kids you've had issues with lately. And I know you're tired, but I need you to go back up to the school and walk through your room with me. We need a detailed list of anything that's missing."

Sam's shoulders slumped. There went her plan to sleep for a week.

The phone on Will's hip went off. Tension radiated from his shoulders as he lifted it to his ear, then pulled the receiver away from his mouth and said, "I need to take this. I've got an officer out front ready to take you back up to the high school."

He flicked Ethan another hard look, one Ethan returned, then turned away.

Sam stepped past Ethan, more frustrated than she'd been all day, and headed for the parking lot. Ethan followed, and in the silence Sam knew she needed to say something, but she didn't know what. Wasn't sure what to think either. Had those words really been there? Was she making it all up? She couldn't be. This wasn't just in her head. Ethan had seen them.

"Are you sure you're okay going back to your house alone?" Ethan asked.

The tingles spreading up her arm made Sam realize Ethan was touching her, and she stopped and looked up at him. "What?"

"Someone's obviously trying to send you a message."

Yeah, someone was. But she wasn't about to let some stupid kid push her around. And, oh man, his hand felt really good. "I'm fine."

"Samantha—"

God, she liked the way he said her name. Her full name. No one called her by her full name here. No one anywhere ever really had. She'd always been Sam, or Sami, or—in the case of her students—hey, you.

*He's a shrink*, a voice whispered in the back of her head. *Be careful.*

"I'm fine," she said again. "If Will thinks the previous teacher is involved, he'll take care of it. He's got someone on the way out to his house. I'm not worried."

But a tiny space deep inside was worried. And she knew that worry was going to trigger her nightmares and keep her from sleeping again tonight.

Something hardened in Ethan's expression as he looked back toward the emergency room doors. Sam wondered if the look had to do with Will or being around cops in general.

Not her problem, she told herself as she forced a smile she didn't feel. The sooner she got away from Ethan McClane and this combustible heat brewing between them, the better off she'd be.

Through the glass doors, she spotted the police car waiting out front. "We should head back so you can get your car."

He nodded, and they moved toward the main double doors. But just as they reached them, Will's voice called, "Dr. McClane."

They both turned, but this time Will was focused only on Ethan.

"Yeah?" Ethan said beside her.

"I need you to come with me."

"What for?"

"Officers found a key in Thomas Adler's locker. Your kid. Looks to be a copy of the key to Sam's classroom."

*Oh shit.* Sam's stomach lurched into her throat. *Not Thomas . . .*

Will's jaw clenched down. Hard. "They just picked him up for questioning."

———

Bitter fingers of denial clawed at Ethan as he stood in the interrogation room, staring down at Thomas. This day was turning into a never-ending nightmare. Two days ago, if someone had told him he'd be working with William Branson, in any way, he'd have said they were flippin' nuts. The reality that he was now voluntarily helping the man sent an acidic burn straight through his gut.

*You're not helping Branson, you're helping Adler.*

He was. Or was trying to. Though at the moment "helping" was a generous term. Thomas Adler's grandmother had refused to come to the station, and Ethan hadn't been allowed in when they were questioning the kid. Now, several hours later, Branson, frustrated by Thomas's lack of cooperation, had finally let Ethan have a crack at him. Ethan knew they weren't alone. Branson and a handful of other cops were undoubtedly listening and watching through the one-way glass, but he was too pissed that he was back in this damn police station again to care. Once was way more than enough in one lifetime. And the fact that it was possible his kid was the one harassing Samantha Parker left him seeing red.

"I didn't do anything wrong," Thomas finally said, staring down at the table, his shaggy light-brown hair falling over his eyes.

"Then you have nothing to worry about. Tell me about the key."

"I don't know anything about a key. I don't know anything about the break-in in Ms. Parker's room either. I like her. I wouldn't do nothin' to cause her trouble."

Ethan wanted to stay mad, but he knew he needed to remain professional. According to Thomas's case file, the boy wasn't aggressive. The few instances of assault on his record had been provoked. Judge Wilson believed he'd acted in self-defense. Was Thomas prone to bad choices? Sure. Did he come from a shitty family? You bet. He'd been orphaned as an infant after his mother was killed. His file didn't give a lot of details, but it was clear there was no father figure in play. Two years ago, the aunt who'd raised him had died in a car accident, and he'd bounced from foster home to foster home before Judge Wilson had tracked down his grandmother in Hidden Falls. Did any of that make him violent, though? Only if Ethan had missed something big.

He pulled out a chair and sat. "Tell me about Ms. Parker."

Thomas picked at a spot on the table. His nails were chewed down to the quick, and he was too thin. Thinner than he'd been only a few weeks ago when Ethan had met him in Portland. Ethan made a mental note to have children's services take another look at his grandmother's home. "She's okay."

"You didn't get upset that she flunked you on a test a few days ago?"

Thomas glanced up. "How'd you know about that?"

"I know everything, Thomas. Don't try to snow me."

The kid lifted a shoulder and dropped it. His gaze slid back to the table. "Didn't care. Didn't even try."

Full of attitude, defiant, and a loner. But that didn't necessarily mean he was guilty. It didn't mean he was innocent either. "I can only help you if you're honest with me. That police chief? Principal Burke? They're ready to pin this on you whether you did it or not. The judge gave you a freebie last time by only assigning you to counseling. The next time you get charged, you and I both know you'll be looking at probation, if not detention. You've got a history with the law. You're new around here. Nobody's going to think twice if you take the fall."

"I didn't do it!" Thomas folded his arms protectively across his middle. "Go on. Don't believe me. You're like all the rest."

Ethan studied Thomas's tense face, the eyes shimmering with tears the kid wouldn't let fall. If he were inclined to go with his gut, he'd say the teen was telling the truth. But he'd learned over the years that his gut was sometimes wrong. And he definitely didn't trust it in this town.

"Then let's start at the beginning. Tell me everything you did today, where you went after school, and who the hell you could have possibly pissed off. Because if you're telling the truth, then that means someone's trying to frame you. And I'm possibly the last friend you've got, kid."

———

The doorbell rang later that evening, sending Sam's nerves right through the roof all over again.

She pulled the door open and looked into Will's drawn face. "Well?"

"Adler didn't admit to anything." Will strolled into her house, shoved his hands into the pockets of his jeans, and turned to face her in the entryway of her mother's old house. "No surprise there."

Sam closed the door behind him. From his spot by the fireplace in the living room, Grimly groaned and rolled to his side. "Do you really think he did it?"

She was still struggling with the idea that Thomas could be involved in any of this. He'd never once acted hostile toward her. But what did she really know about him? Not a lot. Just that he was a bright, quiet teen with a questionable past who, in some ways, reminded her of her brother.

"I don't know," Will said with a shrug. "Any dumbass can break into a locker these days. McClane doesn't think Adler's involved, but that doesn't mean much. He's on the kid's side."

Sam's thoughts spiraled back to Ethan, just like they had several times over the last few hours. After walking through her room and finding nothing of significance missing, she'd given the police a list of kids she'd had confrontations with over the last week. When she'd finally headed out to the parking lot, only a handful of cars had been left, and she'd wondered if one was Ethan's. Since then she couldn't stop thinking about where he'd gone.

Had he returned to Portland, an hour away? Or was he staying the night somewhere in town?

"Sam?" Will asked. "You okay?"

"What?" She looked up at him, refocusing on their conversation. "Yeah. Fine."

His eyes narrowed, and she knew he didn't believe her, but before she could reassure him, those familiar eyes softened, and he took a step her way. "Look. About earlier. I wasn't trying to imply that you're—"

"Losing it?"

A sheepish look crossed his features, and because she knew he hadn't intentionally tried to make her feel foolish, she let go of the lingering hostility. "I know that wasn't your intention, Will. But I know what I saw."

Now, thankfully, someone else had seen it too. Again she thought of Ethan. And her chest warmed the way it had when he'd stood up for her at the hospital.

Will rested both hands on her shoulders and squeezed gently, drawing her attention back to him. "I have to go on the facts, Sam. It doesn't mean I don't believe you. But I am worried about you."

She focused on his familiar hazel eyes and waited for that burst of excitement she used to feel when she was ten and he'd come over to hang out with her older brother, but it didn't hit. Time and distance had changed more than just her schoolgirl heart. It had changed her entire life. She wasn't ten anymore. Seth was dead. And right now the attraction coursing through her wasn't for Will but for a therapist she shouldn't be thinking about.

She looked down at his blue shirt. "I know you are, but I'm fine. You'll figure out whoever's doing this, and everything will get back to normal. I trust you."

His hands lingered, and she sensed he wanted her to step into him. But she couldn't. Because he wasn't the one she wanted.

After several long seconds, he finally let go and moved back. "The Crawford place is empty."

Sam looked up at the mention of the teacher who'd held the teaching position before her. "It was?"

Will nodded. "He moved up to Hood River about a month ago. Cops there questioned him. He's got a lock-tight alibi for the day. And for each of the instances when you were harassed."

It wasn't the former teacher. Relief slid between Sam's ribs, allowing her to breathe a little easier. That had been her biggest fear. "So it is just a kid."

"Looks that way. But to be on the safe side, I'll have an officer do some drive-bys. In the meantime, if anything comes up, be sure to call it in."

"I will. Thanks."

Will glanced down the hall, past the boxes stacked against the wall near the kitchen, then back at her. "I could stay tonight. If you don't want to be alone."

She saw the hope in his eyes. And not for the first time, she wondered why the heck she couldn't be attracted to him. He obviously cared for her; they had a history. He was handsome and kind, and everyone in town liked and admired him. But the chemistry just wasn't there. And she couldn't force herself to fall for him anymore than she could stop herself from having those nightmares.

"Thanks for the offer, but I'll be fine. I'm so tired I'll probably just pass out anyway."

"Okay. If you're sure." Will stepped back toward the door and reached for the handle. "Oh, I meant to ask you something."

"What?" She held the door open for him as he moved onto her front porch.

"Adler's shrink. McClane. Have you ever seen him before?"

Ethan's attractive face flashed in Sam's mind, and her stomach tightened at the memory of their time alone together in that closet. Of the way his body heat had surrounded her. Of how much she'd wanted to kiss him. Warmth rose in her cheeks. "No. Why?"

"I don't know. There's something familiar about the guy. I just can't figure out what."

Sam leaned against the door. "Maybe you ran into him in Portland. David said he used to work as a counselor for the state. I'm pretty sure he used to treat troubled kids."

"Maybe." But something in Will's voice didn't sound convinced. "It'll come to me." He flashed a smile and winked before stepping outside. "Lock your doors, Sam. You know I wouldn't be able to live with myself if anything happened to you."

# CHAPTER FIVE

"Workin' late tonight, Sam?"

Sam glanced up from the stack of labs she was grading and tried to hide her annoyance at the interruption. Ken Saunders pushed the broom around her classroom. His sandy-blond hair was in serious need of a cut, his dirty sneakers squeaked against the floor, and his keys jangled from the waistband of his worn jeans. "Trying to get some things done before the weekend, Kenny."

"It's almost six o'clock on a Friday night. Everyone else has already gone home." He paused, leaned on the end of his broom, and studied her over the lab tables. "You're either dedicated or way behind."

He had no idea. Sam shifted uncomfortably under his steely gaze and glanced back down at her papers. She'd come in early this morning to get her room back in order, then spent the day putting out rumors over the break-in. There was no word from Will on the investigation, and she hated that she was agitated over the fact that she'd only seen Ethan for a few minutes when he'd been observing Thomas in her class. So she hadn't gotten to talk to him. Big deal. Did that mean she had to think about him? Every hour?

Irritated with herself, she flipped a page and made a mark. She was obviously spending too much time with teenagers and their raging hormones.

"Sam?"

She jumped at the nearness of Kenny's voice and looked up. He stood in front of her desk. "Yes?"

"You okay? You look kinda lost."

Lost. Great. Like she needed the janitor thinking she was nutso too? *No way.*

"I'm fine. Just a lot on my mind. I have a few more papers to grade, then I'll be out of your way."

"Don't mind me. I got other rooms I need to clean first. Take your time." Kenny tugged his headphones back on and pushed his broom across the floor. The faint sounds of whistling drifted from the hall as he left.

As soon as he rounded the corner and disappeared out of sight, Sam dropped her head against the desk. Six o'clock on a Friday night and she was here, at school, with the janitor. God, her life was pathetic.

Okay, two more labs, then she was out of here. She went back to grading and made another mark. She didn't want to take this work home with her on a long weekend.

The lights flickered, hummed, and went out.

"Dammit. Can't one thing go right?" Sam pushed back from her desk and headed for the hall. "Kenny?"

The stupid breaker had a habit of going out when Kenny was running machinery in the other wing. She didn't have enough money in her budget for decent supplies, and David was skimping on the electrical system, but the football team had spiffy new uniforms every year.

*Great new career you picked, Sam.*

When Kenny didn't respond, she stepped into the darkened hall, missing her old lab at the pharmaceutical company she'd worked for before coming home. Unfortunately, there were no pharmaceutical companies in Hidden Falls, and the only job she'd been able to find that she was even remotely qualified for was the chemistry position at the high school.

Where the heck was Kenny? Frustration morphed to agitation. Unable to find him in her wing, she headed for the front of the school. The breaker box was in the office. A flip of the switch would fix the problem so she could finish her work and get the heck out of here.

Her sensible flats clicked along the dim passageway. The janitor's closet sat open halfway down the hall. She paused at the door and scanned the wall for the flashlight Kenny kept strapped to a charger just inside. She didn't particularly want to go in. Dark places had never been high on her list, and after being trapped in a closet just yesterday, she wasn't excited to repeat the event.

*You're being silly. No one's here.*

Sam looked up and down the hall to make sure she was really alone, then reached in and fanned her fingers along the Sheetrock. The scent of strong cleaning chemicals cut through the darkness. Her hand passed over the flashlight, and she exhaled a relieved breath.

She'd been through too much in her life to be scared by some stupid kids playing pranks on her. Flicking on the flashlight, she headed for the office.

A loud noise echoed from the direction of the gym just as she rounded the corner. Sam's heart rate jumped. She slowed and glanced that way.

Just Kenny. He'd probably tripped in the dark and hurt himself. But as she stepped toward the gym door and peered through the darkened rectangular windows, apprehension curled in her stomach.

She'd be stupid to walk into a pitch-black room alone. Especially after everything that had recently happened. Common sense drew her back a step.

Something brushed her shoulder. Her adrenaline spiked. She whipped around, swinging out with the flashlight.

"Whoa, relax." Ethan eased back and held up his hands.

"Oh my God." Sam pressed a shaky hand to her stomach. "You scared me. What are you doing here?"

"I saw your car in the parking lot after my meeting. The front door was unlocked. What are you doing at school so late?"

A thrill shot through her at the knowledge that he'd stopped back by because of her. Followed by a host of nerves.

*He's still a shrink regardless of how hot he is.*

"Um." She turned back for her hallway. "Finishing up some work."

"In the dark?"

From the corner of her eye she could just make out his sexy little smirk, and her heart raced faster. God, it had been months since she'd been attracted to anyone. Why him? And why now?

"The lights only went out a few minutes ago. I was on my way to the office to flip the breaker." She flicked the flashlight over the floor, growing more annoyed with herself by the second. "At least I'm not skulking around a building I shouldn't be."

"You missed me."

She huffed out a laugh that sounded more like a snort. *Beautiful.* "You read a lot into one little sentence."

"I read between the lines. I'm a trained professional. That's what I do."

She was all too aware of that fact. And knew for certain she didn't want to know what he'd "read" between her lines.

Change jingled behind her as she moved. She could feel his gaze at her back, knew his hands were in his pockets, that he was probably studying her like he did all his cases. Did he think she was as crazy as Will did? Ethan was nothing to her, so why did it matter so much what he thought?

"I consider lights-out a sign it's time to call it a day," he said in that sexy shrink voice of his. "Have you had dinner yet?"

Sam nearly tripped over her feet. And hoped it was too dark for him to notice. "Are you for real?"

"Me? Always."

She stopped and faced him. He was too cute for his own good. And dressed in crisp slacks and a white dress shirt rolled up to his forearms, he was currently looking at her in the low light as if *she* were all *he* could think about, not the other way around.

Her resistance wavered.

"I'm not . . . " She bit her lip and focused on the pocket of his shirt. Dammit, how did she explain this? "I'm not the best of company, Ethan."

"For me or Will Branson?"

She huffed in exasperation. "If I were interested in Will Branson I wouldn't be wasting all my time thinking about you."

His eyes widened.

Oh crap. Now she'd done it. Given away everything she'd been trying to hide. Her cheeks burned.

His thumb grazed the back of her hand where she held the flashlight, and she knew she should move away, but she couldn't. Because heat seared her skin under the gentle touch. A heat that felt way too good.

"Well," he said softly. "That's something at least, huh?"

He was too close. Too enticing. Too real. All the things she wanted but knew she didn't need. At least not now, when she was trying so desperately to get out of this town. "What are you even doing here, Ethan? It's Friday night of a long weekend. Surely you have someplace better to be."

"Honestly? There's nowhere else I'd rather be right now."

Oh man. Those deep-green eyes were going to be her undoing. That crescent-shaped scar above his eyebrow just begged to be traced. And though it was reckless and insane, her fingers itched to do so.

"Come on," he said. "It's late, neither of us has eaten yet, and I'm hungry."

"Ethan—"

"It's just dinner, Samantha. Tell you what, we'll go casual. Just two friends sharing a meal. After the bruises I took for you yesterday, it's the least you can do for me, right?"

She heard the teasing in his voice. Saw the spark of humor in his eyes. And felt the heat rolling off him in waves. The same heat which was rolling off her, but she tried hard to ignore.

"I don't know." She bit her lip. "Do you really think this is a good idea?"

"You and me having dinner? Why wouldn't it be?"

"Because I'm Thomas's teacher, and you're his . . . " She closed her mouth before she used the word "shrink."

He smiled that sexy grin all over again. "I guarantee we aren't breaking any shrink rules by having dinner together. And if it makes you feel any better, I won't ply you for information about Thomas's day. In fact, we won't even discuss him. How's that?"

That was great. That was exactly what she wanted. But she still knew it was a terrible idea.

A terribly tempting idea.

She didn't know how to respond, but when he brushed his fingers across the back of her hand again, sparks shot from there to her belly and lower. And in a rush she realized her resistance was dangerously close to breaking.

"Come on," he said again. "You know you want to say yes."

A smart girl would say no. Better yet, she'd say, *hell, no*. But Sam had never been a smart girl where men were concerned. And part of her just didn't want to say no to Ethan tonight.

"Okay," she heard herself say, even though she knew she shouldn't. "But just dinner."

"Just dinner," he echoed with an even wider grin. "For now."

———

Kenny watched from the front office window with narrowed eyes as Sam and the shrink headed out to the parking lot.

Anger slithered through him as he reached for the phone on the secretary's desk and dialed. He was tired of waiting around for Sam to get a freakin' clue. Was he the only one who could see this wasn't working?

The line clicked, and he didn't bother to wait for a greeting. "She doesn't strike me as a girl who's overly concerned about her safety. Power was out, creepy noises, and she still goes out searching the building by herself. That doesn't scream scared to me."

"Kenneth," the voice said calmly. "You're not taking matters into your own hands now, are you? We have a plan."

Kenny bit back the *fuck you* lingering on his tongue. Swearing wouldn't help the situation. If there was one thing he'd learned over the years, it was that staying calm was the only way to get what he wanted. "No," he lied. "I wouldn't do that."

"Hm," the voice hummed in a disbelieving tone.

Kenny ground his teeth and worked to stay calm, even though he felt the blood rushing to his head. "And what about this shrink, this McClane? He showed up here tonight. Out of the blue. Whisked her away like some knight in shining armor."

If it hadn't been for McClane, Sam would have stepped into the gym, and Kenny could have done some real damage. Forget this trying-to-scare-her crap. *It wasn't fucking working.* Couldn't they see that?

"McClane is not a concern."

"I know I've seen him before."

"I guarantee you don't run in the same circles as McClane, Kenneth."

Kenny's vision turned red. He was so tired of being treated like shit. Of being told what to do and when to do it. It had been going on now for more than eighteen years, and it was time for it to stop. It was time for him to take a stand and show the others he was in control. It was time for someone to finally do *something*.

"Stick to the plan, Kenneth."

Stick to the plan. Except . . . Kenny had a sinking feeling he was about to get fucked in this plan. He wasn't sure how, but he could feel it coming. "And what if Samantha Parker changes the plan?"

"Then *I* will take care of her. But not you. You're not to touch her. Do you understand?"

"Yeah," Kenny lied again, looking back out the windows toward McClane's taillights, dimming in the distance. A dozen different ways he *wouldn't* touch her floated through his mind. "I understand loud and clear."

———

Sam shifted in the passenger seat of Ethan's BMW. "When you said dinner, I erroneously thought you meant a restaurant."

Ethan glanced across the car. A bag of takeout sat in her lap, a six-pack of beer on the floor at her feet. The worry lines wrinkling her forehead weren't only cute but sexy as hell. Especially with all that curly hair flitting around her shoulders. He'd been happy when she'd pulled the clip from the nape of her neck after climbing into his car. More pleased than he'd let on that she'd said yes to dinner with him in the first place.

"Picnic." He grinned. "More fun."

And more relaxing—away from probing eyes, a chance to get a few minutes alone together. He hadn't been able to stop thinking about her all day, even during his meeting with Thomas. Maybe he should have gone home but spending the evening with her was way better than stressing over seeing Will Branson again and wondering if the man had any recollection of him. Or thinking about everything still happening around the investigation into Samantha's room and Thomas's possible connection.

He pushed thoughts of Thomas and Branson aside as they passed the high school again and told himself to focus on the right now.

Samantha sat up straighter. "Where are we going?"

"It's a surprise."

He drove onto campus and pulled into the parking lot near the dark football field. The team had an away game tonight, and the place was empty. Surprise flickered over Samantha's features as he eased through the open gate and parked near the edge of the track encircling the field.

"Groundskeeper must have forgotten to lock the gate," he said.

"Yeah." She glanced his way with narrowed eyes. "Like that ever happens."

Smiling, he reached behind her into the backseat and grabbed a football and two sweatshirts. "Come on."

He popped the door open and climbed out, keenly aware of the way she watched him through the windshield as he walked around the front of the car. When he reached her side of the car, she sighed and pushed her door open.

"What, exactly, are we doing here, Ethan?"

The warm glow from the car's headlights spilled across one end of the field, illuminating the yardage lines and goalpost. "Having a picnic. Here." He handed her a sweatshirt. "It's a little chilly."

A bemused expression crossed her pretty face. "On the football field? Are you nuts?"

"No. Trust me, I'd know." He tugged on his sweatshirt. "I'm a trained professional, remember?"

The smile she tried to hide warmed his blood. Walking out onto the field, he tossed the ball in the air and caught it as it came down. Samantha stared after him for several seconds, then finally pulled on her sweatshirt and followed him onto the grass. "I don't see a blanket or even a picnic basket."

The shirt was way too big for her. The hem fell to her hips, and the sleeves covered all but her fingertips. But she looked cute as hell in his clothes, and he wondered if it would smell like her when she took it off. He sort of hoped it would. "Ever play football?"

"Of course. Who hasn't?"

He pitched her the ball. She caught it with wide eyes, then furrowed that cute little brow all over again. "I'm not playing catch with you."

"Why not?"

"Because these are hundred-dollar shoes, that's why not."

A practical woman. He liked that. "Kick 'em off."

She eyed him like he'd completely lost his marbles. Several seconds passed, but she finally toed off her shoes and sighed. Hot-pink-painted toenails peeked out from beneath her blue linen slacks.

Ethan hadn't pegged her for pink, but he sure did like it. And that glinting silver toe ring that made him wonder what other surprises she had hidden under all that fabric.

They tossed the ball back and forth, and he stepped away a few yards at a time, widening the throw. To his surprise, she had a strong arm, not weak and girly like most.

"Did you play in school?" she asked.

"All four years."

"What position?" She stepped to the side and caught the ball with two hands.

"Quarterback. Alec, my brother, was wide receiver."

"You have a brother?"

"Two." He jumped to catch the wild toss she threw over his head. "And Rusty was a running back."

"Three boys? Your mother had her hands full."

"And one girl. There are four of us."

"Correction, she's a saint."

"Not quite, but close."

"Who's the oldest?"

"Me. By one month." When her brow wrinkled, he shrugged. "We're all only a few months apart."

She caught the ball again but this time held it. "Really? How—?"

"All except Kelsey. She's a couple years younger. We're all adopted."

"All of you?" When he nodded, she seemed to ponder that a moment, then said, "Did your parents plan it that way?"

"Plan on three rowdy teenage boys and a skittish ten-year-old girl? Not exactly."

Her curious expression said she wanted to know more, but instead of asking, she passed the ball back to him.

"What about you? Any siblings?"

"Nope. What you see is what you get."

Something about her quick answer made him think there was more to it than that. But the way she suddenly wouldn't make eye contact told him to be careful what he asked at this point in their relationship. Family, apparently, was a sticky subject.

Lightening the mood seemed like the best idea all around. He underhand pitched her the ball. "Okay. Try to get by me into the end zone."

Her lips curled up at the edges. And the sparkle he'd seen earlier—when he'd shown up at the school unannounced—flashed in her eyes once more. "You do not want to take me on."

"I deal with juvenile delinquents on a daily basis. Trust me, I can handle one little chemistry teacher."

She pursed her lips. Tucking the ball under her arm, she darted to the right. He blocked her path near the ten-yard line, and she skirted left. When she tried to brush by, he grabbed her around the waist, picked her up, and twirled her in a circle.

Sweet, feminine laughter echoed from her chest, warming his chest in a way he hadn't expected.

He dropped her on her bare feet and stepped back. "Try again."

Smiling, she eased back to the ten-yard line and started over. This time she made it to the three before he grasped her.

"My turn," he said, releasing her.

"No way. Third down. You're trying to jip me here."

"Okay, fine." He waved her back. "Try again."

A devious smile curled her mouth. Her top teeth sank into her bottom lip as she contemplated which direction to go. Finally, she darted to the right, but he anticipated the movement and blocked her path. She swiveled the other direction like an NFL pro before his momentum could correct itself, and sailed past him into the end zone.

Samantha spiked the ball into the grass, lifted her hands above her head, and did a little victory dance that sent a wicked shot of arousal straight to Ethan's groin. Muscles flexed in her thighs beneath the linen slacks as she turned in a slow circle. And even through the baggy sweatshirt she wore, he could see the swell of her breasts pushing against the gray fabric.

Damn, but he wished she'd get hot and take off that sweatshirt so he could see the rest of her. Wished he could take off what was below it as well.

Clearing his throat, he somehow managed to say, "My turn."

"Twenty-yard line." She picked up the ball and pitched it to him, that cocky grin of hers lighting up her entire face. "No cheating."

And, oh man. Yeah. He was in trouble here. Because he *really* liked that commanding teacher voice of hers, telling him what to do.

Ethan eased back, slapped the ball, and took off running. Samantha shifted forward, shuffling to the side to block him. Out of nowhere she charged, lowered her shoulder, and hit him square in the chest.

The air whooshed out of his lungs. He sailed back and hit the ground with a grunt. His hands fell out to his sides. The ball rolled from his fingers across the cool grass.

"Oh my God." Her adorable laughter echoed in the air. She crawled across the grass until her face hovered just above his. Tantalizing curls tickled his cheeks while the arousing scents of lavender and vanilla floated around him. "Are you okay?"

His mouth opened, but no sound came out. He felt like he'd just been hit by a truck. A really sexy truck.

"Ethan?"

"Am I . . . dead?"

"No. Do you feel dead?"

"I'm not sure. Angels are supposed be gentle." He blinked several times. Was pretty sure he could see stars, and not just from getting the wind knocked out of him. "They aren't supposed to knock you on your ass."

"The blow obviously didn't knock that charming wit out of you." She eased back and reached for his hand. "Here, let me help you up."

Her palm slid against his, and warmth encircled his fingers everywhere she touched.

"Sorry," she managed between victorious giggles. "But I warned you not to mess with me."

She had, hadn't she? His gaze swept over her face in the lights from his car. This woman was reorganizing his priorities, making him think of things other than the reason he was in this town. And even though something in the back of his mind said that might not be a good thing, he didn't want to listen. He just wanted to get to know her better.

"Next time I'll listen." He pushed up off the grass. "I think I need to rest and reclaim my manhood. You hungry?"

She rose and followed him across the field toward the car. "I think I worked up an appetite."

Ethan opened the driver's side door and flipped on the stereo. Music wafted through the open windows, the strum of a guitar drifting in the air. He grabbed the bag of deli sandwiches, popped the top off two beers, and joined her near the hood.

Her cheeks grew pink as he handed her a bottle. "We can't drink on school grounds."

That shocked and prim voice, in direct contrast to the domineering teacher voice he'd heard her use earlier, sent heat careening through his whole body. "I won't tell if you won't."

He took a long pull from the bottle, set it at his feet, and handed her a sandwich as he leaned against the car, waiting for her to join him.

"I could get fired for having alcohol on campus."

He glanced around the empty field and parking lot. "I don't see anyone but you and me." When she only continued to stare at him, he tipped his head. "Ever cheat on a test in school, Samantha?"

"Of course not."

Of course not. Silly question. "Sneak out of your parents' house late at night?"

She shook her head.

He couldn't help but smile. He'd never been attracted to a woman as straightlaced as Samantha Parker. "Get caught buying alcohol with a fake ID?"

When she pinned him with a look, he laughed. "Honey, you're with the wrong guy."

"You did all that?"

"And way worse. I was a class-A juvenile delinquent. Why do you think I'm so comfortable around kids like Thomas?"

She leaned against the hood next to him. He didn't miss the fact that she set the bottle at her feet, as close to being under the car as possible should anyone venture their direction.

"You look like you turned out all right."

Her face was cast in shadows as she took a bite of her sandwich, but her eyes danced in the dim light. Something in his gut tightened under her watchful gaze, something other than lust. He lifted his beer for a deep drink. "I was reformed. A lot of kids like me don't get a second chance."

"Is that why you became a juvenile counselor?"

"Partly." Ethan debated how much to tell her. He didn't want to scare her off, but at the same time, if he wanted her to open up to him, he knew he needed to take the first step. "I told you my siblings and I were each adopted. My father's a psychiatrist; my mother's an ER doctor. I don't know if it was their need to help others or what, but when they couldn't have kids of their own, they decided instead of adopting a baby, they'd help some of the kids they see walk through their doors on a daily basis."

"Did one of your parents treat you at some point?"

"Sort of. I met Michael McClane after I got into some trouble. I'd kind of bounced from foster home to foster home before that. He was the first person who actually gave me a chance."

"Huh." She looked down at her feet.

"What?"

"Nothing, it's just . . . your background sounds a lot like Thomas's."

It did. Ethan knew that was probably the reason Judge Wilson had asked him to take this case. There was just one minor difference. Thomas hadn't gotten himself into the same kind of trouble Ethan had. Not even close.

He wasn't ready to explain that whole ordeal to Samantha—wasn't sure he ever would be—so he decided to change the subject. "The other reason I'm a child psychologist is because I like working with kids. Keeps me young."

A wry smile toyed with the edge of her lips. "They definitely keep you on your toes. The kids are the one part about my job I really like."

"Where did you teach before?"

"I didn't. I was a research scientist for a pharmaceutical company in California up until a few months ago."

"Really?" When she nodded, he said, "What brought you to Hidden Falls?"

"My mother was sick. I came home to help take care of her. It was only supposed to be temporary. Some things . . . " She looked out over the football field, her gaze growing distant. "Some things just never go as planned, you know? I guess all you can do is adapt and move on."

The emptiness in her voice touched him in a way he hadn't expected. She was an intricate puzzle, feisty one minute, sweet the next, reserved and outspoken and mysterious all at the same time. And he wanted to know why. Wanted to know what had happened in her life that had shaped her into the woman she was today. Wanted to know everything about her.

He took the sandwich from her hand and set it on the hood of the car. She glanced up with wide eyes as he grasped her hand and pulled her away from the vehicle.

"What are you doing?"

"Enjoying the moment." He slid one arm around her waist and drew her close. From the speakers, some country singer's deep voice crooned about the lost days of youth. Soft rays from the headlights washed over them as he turned her in a slow circle.

"I don't usually dance."

"You should," he said. "You're not half bad. You haven't stepped on my toes once."

She frowned up at him. "We've only been dancing for fifteen seconds."

"And I'm already mesmerized."

She shook her head, but the smile on her lips said she liked that. Liked him the same way he liked her. And even though it was crazy, considering where he was and all that had happened to him in this town, he only wanted to see her smile like that for him again. As many times as he could.

"You're a charmer, aren't you, Dr. McClane?"

"No, I've been charmed. By a beautiful chemistry teacher I didn't expect to meet."

Her pulse picked up, he felt it where he held her hand in his, but something darkened in her eyes just as her feet stopped moving. "Ethan, I'm not good at . . . "

"At what?"

"At this. Relationships, dating, any of it." She sighed and backed out of his arms, and though he only wanted to go on holding her, he let go because he didn't want to push too fast too soon. "My track record with men is shit."

"I'm sure it's not that bad."

She huffed a sound that was both humor and disgust. "It is. I have the inherent ability to get involved with all the wrong sorts of men at the most inopportune times. Did you ever watch *Seinfeld*?"

"Sure. Who hasn't?"

"Well, you know how Jerry always found something wrong with every woman he dated? That's me. I *always* manage to screw things up." He smiled, but she only frowned up at him. "I'm completely serious. I've never been in a relationship that's lasted over a month. My last therapist called it a fear of commitment."

He reached for her hand. "Maybe you just haven't met the right guy, Samantha."

"Yeah, well, it certainly wasn't the therapist. I broke it off with him when I found out he was married."

She'd been involved with her doctor? That explained her animosity toward Ethan's profession the first day they'd met. "Holy crap."

She grimaced. "See. Told you. Really bad judgment."

Things she'd said, the way she'd acted . . . it was all starting to make sense. He slid his fingers around her other hand. "Not all guys are like that, Samantha."

And that particular guy should be shot for taking advantage of her.

"I know. I've even managed to get involved with some nice ones along the way. My ex-husband can attest to that."

His mouth fell open, but he closed it quickly, realizing he probably looked like a fool. Of course she could have been married. Why not? She was gorgeous and smart and absolutely entrancing.

"Shocked, huh? It lasted all of three weeks before I managed to screw that one up."

"Recently?"

"No." She sighed and looked toward the car. "Back when I was in college. He was a great guy. It wasn't his fault. I'm just not relationship material."

For some reason, he sensed that wasn't the least bit true. "Sam—"

"I'm not trying to brush you off, Ethan. I'm completely serious. And I like you—more than I probably should—which is why being honest is the best way to go at this point. I'm damaged goods."

The fact that she was admitting she was attracted to him set off an odd fluttering in his stomach. But knowing she didn't think she was worth taking a chance on made something deep in his chest tighten. "No, you're not. You're cautious."

"Emotionally crippled."

He moved closer and slid one arm around her waist. "Prudent."

She didn't fight him when he lifted her arm and drew her back into a slow dance. "Completely insane."

His whole body tingled as hers brushed his in the dim light. "You're definitely not that. I think you're just afraid. That's normal."

Her gaze drifted to the collar of his sweatshirt, and she sighed. "I love the way you say my name. Nobody calls me by my full name anymore."

Warmth seeped through his chest and circled his heart.

She looked up. "But I don't need or want a relationship right now, Ethan."

Those words were too easy. He'd said the same to himself a thousand times. But now, here with her, he didn't want to let fear or worry or even common sense control what was happening between them.

"So we'll just be friends who dance in the moonlight now and then." When she pushed her lips out in a sexy little pout, he slipped his other hand behind the small of her back and drew her even closer. "Let's not label it, Samantha. Let's just see where it goes."

Her eyes softened, a look that called to something in his soul. He'd always had a weakness for wounded animals, maybe because he was one himself. And there was definitely something in Samantha Parker that yearned to be healed. The therapist in him suddenly wanted to help. But the man in him wanted to be the one to jump-start that healing—and in some insane way, maybe help him through his own ongoing recovery.

"I don't think I can do that," she said. "I'm not a fly-by-the-seat-of-my-pants kind of girl. That's always gotten me into trouble."

"Trouble doesn't always have to be bad."

The look in her eyes said she didn't agree, but when he pulled her closer, she didn't fight him. He moved again to the beat of the music, and as she rested her head against his chest, his heart turned over.

He wasn't looking for a relationship either. Not with someone in this town, not when he didn't know how long he'd be around. But he wasn't about to pass up something that might just be amazing.

It was crazy. It was reckless. It made absolutely no sense. But if nothing else, maybe he could show this amazing woman she was worthy. And maybe, somehow, he could learn to believe the same thing about himself too.

# CHAPTER SIX

A cool November breeze blew across the valley the following Wednesday. The weather forecast called for a slight chance of snow—almost unheard of at this early-November date. Sam's kids were in an uproar about it, hoping for a day off from school, and she had to admit, she was too.

"Settle down." She turned from her Chem I class and picked up her marker. Keeping them on track was a constant struggle, especially with Misty Sloane wearing the hot-pink, skintight number she'd picked out today. The boys in the room were practically sweating.

"Kristen, explain the difference between atomic mass and atomic weight." Sam jotted numbers on the whiteboard, and glanced back at her students.

"One's how big it is, and one's, like, how much it weighs?"

Clever. Smashing her head against the board would be easier than explaining this for the umpteen-millionth time. Sam's gaze swept over the room, searching for any student who might have been paying *any* sort of attention during the last half hour. She paused when she reached the far side of the room.

"Thomas?"

Thomas looked back from the window where he seemed to be daydreaming. "Atomic mass is the total of protons and neutrons in a specific atom. The atomic weight is the average mass of all the isotopes of an element."

Definitely not daydreaming. Or if he was, he already knew this subject matter. "Thank you. Atomic weight is an average, which explains why it's generally a decimal." She turned back to the board. "I'm putting your homework up here."

Groans resounded behind her just as the bell rang.

Papers rustled while pencils scribbled furiously to get the last of the problems. Footsteps shuffled toward the door.

"I'll be on prep for the next hour if anyone needs help on yesterday's lab," Sam called over the hum of activity.

She filtered through the rush of exiting students and dropped into the chair behind her desk. Thankful for some peace and quiet, she reached for her water bottle.

She hadn't seen Ethan since their impromptu date on the football field. He'd given her his number before they'd said good night and told her he was leaving it up to her as to where they went next. She'd thought about calling him over the weekend but couldn't actually bring herself to do it. What would she have said if she'd called? That was fun, let's do it again? She was in no position to get involved with anyone when her goal was to get out of Hidden Falls as fast as humanly possible.

If she was being honest with herself, though, she had to admit that she'd expected to see him this week at school doing observations, just as she'd expected this whatever-it-was between them to work itself out. But by Wednesday, he still hadn't shown back up at school, and part of her was starting to wonder if he was ever coming back.

"Ms. Parker?"

Sam blinked twice as Thomas strolled into the room. "Oh, hey, Thomas. What can I do for you?"

"Mr. Elkins said I could cut PE and come down to get some help on my lab."

"Sure." She rose and rounded the desk, happy for something to think about besides his supersexy shrink. "Let's see what you've got there."

They moved to one of the lab stations, and she studied his paper a second before saying, "Here. Your equation isn't balanced correctly. Check your coefficients and subscripts."

His brow wrinkled, and he picked up a pencil, working through the problem.

She leaned back as he worked. He was an attractive kid—slightly-too-long light-brown hair, dark eyes, good skin, and a long, lanky body that would one day fill out and probably drive the girls crazy. Sure, he was quiet, but from everything she'd observed, he was also respectful and considerate of those around him. If she hadn't known he had a troubled past, she wouldn't look at him any differently than she did any of her other students.

He frowned. "Like that?"

She glanced back down. "Yes. Better. Now look at your work, compare it to your observations, and write up your results."

He flipped his notebook closed. "I hate that part."

"Everyone does. If it were just about mixing chemicals and watching reactions, mine would be the most popular class."

He bit his lip, as if he had something else to say.

"Thomas?"

His fingers clenched around his pencil. "I didn't take that key. And I definitely didn't trash your room."

"I didn't think you did."

"You didn't? Why not? Everyone else does."

"Call it a gut reaction. You're too careful with the materials in here, and any idiot knows you don't leave evidence behind in your locker. You don't strike me as an idiot, Thomas."

"Mr. Burke thinks I did it. Even Dr. McClane's been giving me a hard time about it."

"Has he?"

"Yeah. He thinks I know who did."

"And do you?"

He hesitated just long enough to make Sam suspect the same thing. "No."

He didn't trust her enough to confide in her. Not yet at least. The fact he was sitting here though made her think someday he might. "I spend a lot of time in Mr. Burke's office myself."

"You do?"

"Mm hmm. When he's not worried I'm going to blow up the school, he's jawing at me for leaving my keys lying around, or because I'm being difficult and unyielding in staff meetings." She smiled. "I've only been here a few weeks, and I'm already on his bad list."

"Does he have a good list?"

"I'm not sure. Mr. Ralston seems to be on his good side."

"Ralston-Purina? Man, kids chew him up and spit him out for lunch. He spends more time snoozin' in class than he does teaching. Manny Burton's talking about getting him one of those cedar dog beds and leaving it in his room as a joke. Even I could teach calculus better than he does, and I hate the stuff."

Sam couldn't stop the laugh that slipped from her lips. Reginald Ralston looked suspiciously like an old basset hound. Sounded like one sometimes too. "Don't let Mr. Burke hear you. They're related."

"Really?"

She nodded. "I think it's his uncle. Did you ever try to tell an older relative what to do? Doesn't usually work."

The laughter died from his eyes. "I don't have many relatives."

Sam was immediately sorry she'd mentioned family. She knew what it was like to be alone. In that respect, she and Thomas were alike.

He rose quickly and grabbed his papers. "I gotta get back to class. Thanks, Ms. Parker."

He darted for the door before she could ask why he was in such a hurry. Just as he reached the threshold, Margaret Wilcox appeared and shifted to the side. "Whoa. Watch where you're going."

"Sorry, Ms. Wilcox."

"You should pay closer attention to where you're going, Adler."

"Yes, ma'am."

Thomas rushed out the door. Sighing, Sam pushed to her feet, wishing she could follow. "Hey, Margaret."

Margaret wound through lab stations with a perturbed expression. "Freaky thing, that boy. Aren't you worried about being alone with him?"

"No." Sam drew in a calming breath. She always needed a calming breath when dealing with Margaret. "I'm here for the students, and he needed help on an assignment."

"Well, I'd tell him to find it somewhere else. That kid's strange."

Of course Margaret thought he was strange. She thought all kids were strange. Not for the first time, Sam wondered why Margaret remained in education.

"What do you need, Margaret?"

Margaret picked up a glass paperweight shaped like an atom from the corner of Sam's desk. "Where's that sexy doctor who's always hanging around in here?"

Sam's stomach tightened. He wasn't always hanging around in her room. He'd observed in her class two, maybe three, times tops. "Dr. McClane?"

"That's the one." Margaret leaned a hip against Sam's desk. "I'd let that one analyze me all he wants. Yummy."

Since Margaret was married, Sam decided to ignore that comment. "I don't really know."

"Oh, come on now, Sam. Rumor is you're seeing Dr. Delish."

"Who told you that?"

"I don't remember. David, Kenny, someone who saw you together. So are you?"

Sam's face grew hot as she looked back down at her papers. "Am I what?"

"Doing the delectable doctor?"

"God, Margaret. We're at school."

"That answers that question." Margaret rolled her eyes. "Get a life, Sam. Ninety-eight percent of the student body's having more sex than you." She set down the paperweight and eased off the desk. "If you need some pointers, just ask."

Right. Like Sam was about to go there with her archenemy. Margaret didn't care about Sam. She was digging for info on Ethan, though why, Sam didn't know. "What do you need, Margaret?"

"Nothing. Just wanted to let you know that Jeff and I are having a little get-together at the house Friday night."

Sam would rather pull her eyelashes out one by one. "Gee, that's awfully nice of you to invite me, but—"

"I'm not inviting you. Jeff is."

Margaret didn't try to hide the ice in her voice. God, the woman could hold a grudge. Ten years later, and she was still pissed her husband had taken Sam to Sam's senior prom. Forget the fact that Margaret had already been off at college, sleeping with half the baseball team at the time, or that she hadn't even developed an interest in the gangly guy until years later when he'd become a successful lawyer. Just knowing he and Sam were still on friendly terms grated on the woman's nerves to no end. And was the root of the reason she and Margaret didn't get along.

"It's really nice of him to offer, but I can't."

"Your mother made a sizeable contribution to Jeff's campaign before she died. He'd like you to be there. Seven o'clock at our house." She turned for the door, brushing off Sam's excuses. "And bring that sexy doctor with you. I'd love to spend some one-on-one time on his therapy couch. Or mine. Either works for me."

As soon as Margaret disappeared out the door, Sam's head hit the hard surface of her desk. She needed to come up with a life-threatening illness between now and Friday. Since she only had two days, odds weren't in her favor.

———

Ethan tapped a pen against his thigh and glanced across the table toward Thomas. The minute hand on the wall clock of the school counselor's office moved to the right, a low din reverberating through the room. They'd been at it for fifty minutes, but Thomas's eyes kept darting toward the clock, judging the minutes to freedom.

Shifting in his seat, Thomas let out a sigh. "We done yet?"

"Not quite. Let's talk about friends. Hanging out with anyone?"

"Not really."

"A few teachers mentioned they've seen you around campus with Manny Burton."

"Some. He's okay."

"Anyone else?"

"Not really."

"No girls?"

Thomas's face flushed. "None here I'm interested in."

Ethan nodded, not believing that for a second. "You going to the football game Friday night?"

"Might."

"How about the dance after?"

"Don't know. Not sure I can stay out that late."

Ethan made a note. "How are things at home with your grandmother?"

Thomas's shoulders tensed. "Fine."

"You two getting along okay?"

"Yeah. Sure."

There was more there. The kid's eyes were fixed on the wall as if it might just jump out and bite him. Ethan made a mental note to pay a visit to his grandmother.

"I'll be meeting with Judge Wilson sometime next week to discuss your progress."

"Yippie."

The minute hand of the clock snapped again. Thomas straightened and reached for his bag before Ethan even mentioned their time was up.

Sighing, Ethan closed his notebook and tossed his pen on the table. An hour-long session, a couple of words here and there from the kid, and a blistering headache. They were making progress.

"I'm going to be around tomorrow," Ethan said as he stood. "We'll catch up at the end of the day."

"Sure. Whatever." Thomas hooked his backpack over his shoulder. "We done now?"

"Yeah. We're done. Go on home."

When the door closed, Ethan rubbed a hand down his face. The kid wasn't blatantly defiant, but he wasn't exactly opening up yet either. They should be further along than this, but the speculation surrounding that theft last week had caused Thomas to shut down. He was still wary of everyone around him, including Ethan.

Ethan gathered his papers and stuffed them in his briefcase. He wanted this over. He wanted to get to a point where he only had to see the kid once a month—maybe. Since he'd had appointments in Portland earlier in the week, this was the first day he'd made it to Hidden Falls, and his anxiety had shot up as soon as he'd driven past the city limits. But he knew if he was going to make any kind of progress with Thomas, he needed to spend more time here, observing the kid and getting to know him better.

Which meant he should probably come back early tomorrow. Talk with some of Thomas's teachers before school about how he was doing, pay a visit to that grandmother Thomas seemed to be having issues with at home. Hell, he was already here. He should probably just find a hotel and stay the night.

Except staying in this town was so not what he wanted to do. Of course . . . his thoughts drifted . . . if he stayed tonight, he'd have an excuse to run into Samantha.

His pulse skipped, and warmth spread through his belly at just the thought of her. He'd hoped she'd call after their impromptu date on Friday, but she hadn't. He knew she was interested—he'd felt it when they'd danced—but something was holding her back. And, after five days, it was clear she wasn't going to be the one to take the next step, which meant if he wanted more, he had to be the one to take the initiative.

He headed out of the parking lot before he could change his mind. Checking the address he'd heard Samantha give the receptionist at the ER last week and had jotted down, just in case, he turned onto her street and scanned the houses.

Hers was the last one on the end of the quiet street, a rambling, two-story Queen Anne with steep gabled roofs, fronted by a "For Sale" sign. Weathered columns graced the large, wraparound porch. Chipped and peeling paint gave the house a gray, rather than white, appearance. An uneven brick path overgrown with moss led to the front door. But the towering maple trees in the yard gave the old house character. And the Douglas fir that rose behind the property promised privacy for someone willing to give the house a little TLC.

He parked along the street and climbed out, wondering what she'd think about him just stopping by. Hoped she'd be pleased. The harsh bark of a dog greeted his ears as he made his way up the front path toward the porch, and seconds later a large golden retriever bounded around the side of the house and jumped up, pressing wet paws against his chest.

Ethan jerked back, but the dog only wagged his tail and slobbered—no threat at all—so he scratched the brute behind the ears. "Hey, there, big guy."

"Grimly, get down."

Ethan looked up when he heard Samantha's voice, and a smile curled his lips as he took in her curly hair pulled back at her nape, the slim jeans on her long legs, and the baggy sweater that hung to her hips. "Hey."

Surprise flickered in her eyes. Followed by a hint of panic.

Panic was good. If he'd seen annoyance or frustration, he'd be turning right around. But panic meant she was interested.

"He's just a big oaf. Don't worry, he's harmless." She grabbed the dog by the collar and pulled him away. "Grimly, quit."

The dog barked once, then sat at Samantha's side and wagged his tail.

"Um, so, this is a surprise." She smoothed the flyaway curls away from her face in a nervous gesture while Grimly flicked her hand with his nose to get her to rub his head. "What are you doing here?"

Nervous was also good. "I probably should have called. Sorry. I just finished up with Thomas and thought I'd stop by to see how you were doing before I head over to find a hotel room."

"You're staying in Hidden Falls tonight?"

He nodded. "Most of the staff was already gone by the time Thomas and I were done. I need to meet with several of them in the morning before school starts. Easier to just stay over."

"I wasn't sure if you were coming back."

Did he sense disappointment in her words? That was also good. Really, really good. "I had cases I needed to see to in Portland. This was the first time I could get out here. But I was definitely coming back."

"Oh. Well, that's good. For Thomas, I mean."

The relief passing over her features made him relax. No, not good for Thomas. For her. He hadn't misread what he'd felt the other night on the football field. And stopping by unannounced was definitely not a mistake. That low pulse of arousal beat through him, the same one he felt whenever she was close. "Not sure what you've got planned for the evening, but I was hoping maybe you'd want to get some dinner."

The edge of her lips curled, just enough to tell him she was . . . oh yeah . . . very pleased. "I was just about to take Grimly for his walk."

"Now?" He glanced toward the sky. "It's about to get dark."

"I know. But he'll be hell to live with if he doesn't get some time outside. He usually runs ahead and leaves me in the dust anyway, but it's good for him."

"Mind if I tag along?"

Her smile spread across her whole face, making her dark eyes absolutely sparkle. "You got a coat?"

"Yeah, let me grab it from the car."

"Okay, I'll meet you out back. I have to get mine too."

By the time he made his way around the side of the house, Samantha was already standing on the back stoop, zipping her jacket. The backyard was unfenced, stretching to the forest behind her house. A low rose hedge at the side of the drive separated her property from the neighbor's. "This is a great place."

Grimly barked, looked at them, then took off running. Samantha stuffed her hands in her pockets and met him on the grass.

"Yeah. It was my mother's. I'm in the process of boxing up all her stuff. It's a mess inside. My mom was a pack rat."

"I saw the 'For Sale' sign. You're selling it?"

"It's too big for me, and once I leave, I don't want to deal with the hassle of trying to find renters."

"I didn't realize you were planning on leaving Hidden Falls."

They headed along a path toward the trees. "As soon as I can."

"What about your job?"

"I only took it to help with expenses when my mother's health went downhill. I always planned to leave when she got better, but then she passed, and I found myself stuck here dealing with her estate. Once the house sells, there's really nothing holding me here. I'll miss the kids, but I'm sure they'll be able to get someone else after I'm gone."

"You don't like teaching?"

She stepped over a downed limb. The forest was dimly lit, rays of late-afternoon sunlight flitting through the trees. The rich scent of musty earth greeted Ethan's nostrils, along with the sweet scent of Samantha's perfume. The houses disappeared from view. Moss and lichen graced the tree trunks. Sword fern littered the forest floor.

"I like the kids. I'm not wild about all the politics. To be honest, I never taught before taking this job. Districts have leeway in hiring if there's a high need. Chemistry's pretty specialized, and the last guy had his nervous breakdown just before school started, so they were desperate to hire someone. It was really just a right time–right place kind of thing."

"Why didn't you leave as soon as your mother passed?"

"Because of the house. Because I promised David I'd give him at least until Christmas to find someone else. But I'm definitely not staying."

Relief rippled through him, knowing she wasn't married to Hidden Falls. Though it was short-lived when he thought about her heading back to California.

Not that he was about to share that with her, though. She was already skittish. He definitely didn't want to do anything to scare her off when she was finally relaxing around him. "So you grew up here?"

"Pretty much. I left for a while to live with my dad after my parents split up but came back when I was in high school."

"Where's your father?" He pulled his jacket tighter around his shoulders. The forest was cold, his breath visible in the chill air. He'd like to move closer to her, use body heat to keep them warm, but he wasn't about to push things. Yet.

"Um, last I heard he was in Florida somewhere."

"Last you heard?"

"Yeah." She waved a hand. "We don't really get along. I haven't seen him in years. Talked to him on the phone after my mother died, but he didn't come home for the funeral."

"How long have they been divorced?"

She glanced around the forest. "Gosh, probably seventeen years. I think I was around eleven when they finally called it quits." She looked up at him. "They didn't have a happy marriage. It was better all around when they divorced. I wish they'd done it sooner. I really don't know why they stayed together as long as they did."

The blunt way she said it made a tiny place in his chest ache. She really didn't have anyone. No family to speak of. No close friends in this town. He knew what it was like to be alone. He couldn't imagine what it would feel like to be alone at this point in his life, with absolutely no one to lean on.

"I'm sorry," he said softly.

"Don't be. I'm used to it. To be perfectly honest, I'll be happy when the house sells. One less thing to worry about."

"What will you do if it sells before Christmas?"

"Not sure. Probably find an apartment in town, have a huge garage sale. What about you?"

"Me?"

"Yeah, you, Mr. Observer. Where did you grow up?"

Ethan tensed. "Northeast Portland."

"I hear that's turning into a nice area."

"Wasn't when I was there," he mumbled.

She'd opened up to him, and he figured he needed to give her a little more back. He wasn't ready to share some of the really awful stuff.

Wasn't sure he ever would be. Not everyone could handle it. But he definitely wanted her to know more about him so they could see where this—whatever it was between them—was headed.

"I told you my siblings and I were all adopted, right?" When she nodded, he said, "I was the first. Fourteen years old. Michael McClane was my counselor at Bennett."

Samantha stopped on the path and stared up at him. "The juvenile detention center?"

He nodded, watching her eyes closely for fear, apprehension, revulsion. What he saw was genuine curiosity, and in some strange way, that put him at ease. "My mother died when I was five. Drugs. My dad was an alcoholic. He passed from complications of cirrhosis when I was seven. I flitted from foster home to foster home after that, always managing to get myself into some kind of trouble. When I was thirteen, I got wrapped up with the wrong crowd. It was a stupid mistake, but it landed me in Bennett for about a year. After, I was placed with a family that already had four other foster kids. Michael came to check in on me one day. Saw it wasn't a great situation. He arranged to take me in instead."

"Just like that?"

"No. Not like that. It was highly irregular. But a guy in social services owed him a favor, and he arranged it."

She turned up the path and kept walking. "And the others?"

He fell into step beside her again. "Alec was a street kid. Got himself into some trouble and wound up at Bennett as well. We knew each other briefly there before I got out. Michael was also his counselor. After I'd been with the McClanes about three months, they brought Alec home. Figured I probably needed a sibling. They had no idea how, or even if, it'd work. But it did. My other brother, Rusty, came from a pretty screwed-up family. He ended up in my mother's ER one night after a pretty horrendous incident. She took one look at him and figured he needed a home too."

"Wow." Samantha stared ahead at the trees around them. "Your parents really are saints."

"Crazy is more like it. We were at each other's throats the whole first year. By the time we stopped trying to kill each other, those teenage hormones kicked in. It was one thing after another with us."

One side of Samantha's lips curled. "I bet. And what about your sister? You did say you have a sister, right?"

She'd been paying attention the other night. "Yeah. She came along a few years later. She was ten. She'd bounced from foster home to foster home too, got into some trouble, and wound up in counseling."

"With your father?"

"No. A colleague of his. I guess Mom always wanted a girl. She got one. A freaked-out ten-year-old who had to learn to fend for herself in a house with three rambunctious boys."

"I think I understand why you each feel such a tie to one another."

"When you're given something you've never had before, you realize how special it is. It sounds crazy. Like it never should have worked. But it did. I can't imagine my life without those lunatics in it."

"You're lucky." Her voice softened, and she glanced down at the path.

Ethan's chest tightened, and he gently gasped her arm, tugging her hand from her pocket. "Samantha." Their feet stilled. His fingers slid down to hers, and warmth radiated from her skin, sending tingling sensations straight up his arm. Sensations he knew she felt too by the way her pulse skipped against his hand. "You don't have to keep things locked up so tight. Sometimes letting them out can really help."

Her mesmerizing eyes narrowed. "That sounds like the counselor in you."

"Maybe. But it's also the man in me wanting to get to know you better."

She drew in a sharp breath. "Why do you have the innate ability to make me feel like I'm a teenager again?"

A sizzle of heat spread through his whole body, and he smiled. "Is that how you feel around me?"

"Yes. And it's really irritating."

He stepped closer. "It's also arousing."

Their eyes held for several seconds. Her gaze dropped to his lips. And as her breathing picked up, the desire he'd been fighting since the day he'd first heard her voice flared hot and strong.

He leaned down to kiss her.

Grimly barked, and she jerked back.

"Where did that stupid dog run off to?" She stepped around Ethan. "Grimly?"

Ethan sighed. They were always getting interrupted just when things were about to get interesting.

He followed her up the path before she could get too far ahead. "Samantha?"

Rounding a bend, he spotted her, standing on the edge of a clearing. Blue-green mountains lingered in the distance. The faint rush of water whispered through the trees.

Ethan slowed as he drew up beside her and looked around the forest. Déjà vu trickled through him, leaving his skin prickly and hot. And not in a good way.

"I used to play up here when I was a kid." Samantha pointed. "My friends and I built a fort in the trees through there. On the other side of that ridge is a waterfall and swimming hole where we used to cool off when it was really hot."

Ethan knew all too well about the waterfall. His pulse picked up, and he fought the growing sickness in his stomach.

He hadn't realized this was *the* forest. He'd been a kid when he'd been here last. Hadn't put two and two together. Hadn't once thought it could be anywhere near Samantha's property.

Samantha turned up the path and resumed walking.

Thankful she hadn't noticed, he drew a deep breath and followed. But his fingers curled into his palms to fight the sudden nicotine craving, and he wished he hadn't thrown away that last pack he'd kept hidden in his car.

His muscles finally relaxed when he realized they weren't headed toward the falls but into the trees again. Samantha wove around tree trunks, over downed logs on the sparse path. She was quiet as she made her way across the forest floor, and for the first time, Ethan didn't mind. She stopped again as they approached a small run-down cabin. The roof was patchy, missing in spots. The glass windows were broken out. Pinecones littered the front stoop, and the logs of the old shack were rotted and cracked in multiple places.

"I always end up here," she said softly. "I don't know why, but whenever I come this way, I always end up in this place."

Ethan didn't remember the cabin, but it had obviously been here for years. "Did you used to play here too?"

"No. I've never even been inside. But, I don't know, it always just seems to draw me up here. Like it's waiting for me."

She was quiet for a long time as she studied the shack, and a whisper of foreboding shot down Ethan's spine.

This time, he didn't hesitate to reach for her hand. Suddenly needed the contact. And something inside him sensed she needed it too.

She looked over as his thumb grazed the back of her fingers. "Weird, huh?"

"No, not really. Something about the place probably scared you as a kid. Childhood fears can last a long time."

"I have dreams about it." Her gaze slid back to the cabin. "There's a light on in the windows—a cold light that seems to spill through the holes in the glass. And I can hear voices—angry voices—and crying. But I can never get up the courage to go in. I've made it to the window, but I've never looked inside."

The blank look in her eyes sent a chill over Ethan that had nothing to do with the air temperature. Gently, he squeezed Samantha's hand, and something inside him sensed this cabin was not just part of a dream. Somehow it was tied to the haunted look in Samantha's eyes and the reason she kept herself closed off from those around her.

"Samantha," he said again softly.

She blinked rapidly. "Stupid, huh? Bet you could analyze the heck out of that one." She pulled her hand from his and started walking again. "Where's that darn dog? Grimly!"

Ethan followed Sam away from the shack. He wanted to know more about the cabin and her dream but sensed this wasn't the time. Samantha was already nervous around him. Just the fact she was opening up to him at all was a step in the right direction.

Grimly's incessant barking echoed through the trees.

"I sure hope he hasn't found a skunk again," she said. "I'm going to kill that dog if he went after one."

Ethan laughed behind her and slipped his hands into his pockets, relieved she sounded normal once more. "Yeah, me too. That'd seriously ruin my appetite, and my plans to hit on you later at dinner."

She smiled back at him. A big, gorgeous smile. One that brought the heat right back to his belly and made him forget that cabin, the waterfall, and everything else he didn't want to remember. "He loves to dig. The last time he disturbed a sleeping family of skunks, he reeked for a week. Trust me, it wasn't funny."

Ethan caught up with her and reached for her hand again. Her fingers were warm where they slid around his. Warm and soft and perfect. And once again those tingles spread up his arm and down into his chest. "Maybe we shouldn't chance leaving him alone. We should stay in tonight."

Amusement lit her eyes. "I don't cook."

"That's okay. I do."

He tightened his grasp on her hand, pulling her to a stop. Interest sparked in her eyes. Interest and excitement.

"You're just full of surprises, aren't you, doc?"

He reached for her other hand, lacing his fingers with hers. "I try to be. Wanna make out in the woods?"

She laughed. "It's cold out here."

"I know it sounds cliché, but I could warm you."

Her lips curved into a smile. A tempting, seductive, tantalizing smile. "I think you might be trouble, Dr. McClane."

When she didn't make any move to pull away, he let go of her hands and slid his arms around her back, tugging her body against his. Her hands flattened against his chest, and her hips drew flush to his, sending all those tingles straight into his groin. "The best kind, though, right?"

She laughed again, then drew in a breath as he lowered his head and kissed her.

Her lips were soft and cool, her mouth hot and oh so tempting when she opened. And the moment his tongue met hers and their kiss deepened, what was left of his anxiety slipped away, leaving behind only heat and need and a burning desire to get close to this woman in any way he could.

Grimly's bark interrupted their kiss, and Samantha eased back and dropped her forehead to Ethan's chest. "That dog has the absolute worst timing."

He did, but Ethan didn't really care. Because just knowing she was as disappointed as him made the interruption bearable.

"What do you say we go get him and head back?" He slid his hands to her arms, easing away just enough to look down at her glimmering eyes and cheeks flushed from their kiss. "Then maybe think about picking up where we left off."

"I—"

Grimly let out a sharp yelp, and Samantha jerked and twisted in the direction of the sound. "Grimly?"

She took off at a run and disappeared around a bend in the path, calling Grimly's name.

"Samantha, wait." Ethan's adrenaline shot up as he followed. Rounding the corner, he spotted Samantha drawing to a stop not far ahead. Past her, Grimly frantically dug and growled and whined at something he'd found in the earth.

"Grimly," Samantha yelled at the dog. "Stop that."

Grimly dropped and rolled over the dirt, then jumped up and dug again.

"If you found something dead to roll in, you're sleeping outside." Sam stalked toward the dog and grasped his collar.

"What is it?" Ethan called.

Samantha's feet shuffled to an abrupt stop, and her face went ashen. "Oh my God."

Grimly barked again and pulled at her hold.

"Samantha?" Concern shot Ethan's adrenaline up as he crossed the distance between them.

And he froze himself when he spotted the human skull.

# CHAPTER SEVEN

Flashlight beams dipped and bounced on the hillside behind Samantha's house. Standing at the kitchen window with his hands in his pockets, Ethan looked out into the darkness, watching the intense streams of light darting between tree trunks.

The kettle on the stove whistled, startling him, and he tore his gaze away from the window and the crime scene in what was basically Samantha's backyard. Flipping off the burner, he poured boiling water over the tea bag he'd slipped into a waiting mug.

Samantha sat in the living room, grading papers, where she'd been since they'd come back and called the police. He knew she was a mass of nerves, but she wasn't talking. After the police had arrived, Ethan had taken them into the woods and left her in the house with a deputy. When he'd returned, he'd found the officer on the porch with his phone and her hiding in her work. She'd completely shut down, blocked Ethan and everything else out. A self-defense mechanism, he knew, but still one that worried him.

A tap echoed at the back door. Ethan set the teapot down and pulled the door open.

Light from the kitchen cast shadows over Will Branson's face. Ethan's stomach lurched at the familiar face, but he stepped to the side. "Chief Branson."

"Dr. McClane. Officer Travers said I might find you here." Branson moved into the room and slipped off his cap. "Where's Sam?"

"Living room. Working."

With a nod, Branson ducked through the arched doorway and made his way down the hall. Ethan told himself to stay calm. This time it wasn't personal. The situation had nothing to do with Thomas and the reason Ethan was in town. Lifting the steaming mug of tea, he followed Branson into the living room.

Samantha glanced up as they both entered. Her legs were tucked under her on the recliner, papers scattered across her lap. Lowering her feet to the floor, she tossed her papers on the coffee table, slipped off her glasses, and set them on top of the stack. "Hey, Will. I didn't expect you to come by."

"Wanted to make sure you were okay."

"I'm fine." Samantha spared Ethan a quick smile as he set the mug on the end table beside her, then stepped back. "Peter already took our statement."

"Yeah, I know."

She pushed to her feet. "Are you done up there?"

"Almost."

"A little excitement in this boring town." She brushed the curls back from her face that had slipped free of the clip at the base of her neck, a nervous move Ethan had grown used to. "Peter seemed almost giddy. Any idea who it is?"

"We're checking missing-persons reports from outlying areas."

Samantha huffed and rubbed both hands over her face. "That body's been up there awhile."

"Sam—"

"I have a degree in biochemical sciences, remember? I took anatomy in college. That amount of decay? There was basically nothing left."

Branson sighed. "Yeah. I remember. You're not a forensic scientist, though, Sam. Leave it up to the experts. It's probably a vagrant, someone passing through who got lost in those woods years ago. Nothing more than that. You know how people get turned around up there."

She folded her arms in front of her and rubbed her biceps, as if she were cold. "There's only one missing person I can think of from around here."

"It's not her."

"Would fit the time frame, though," Sam said quietly.

Ethan glanced between the two. He didn't miss the tension radiating from Branson. Or the nerves vibrating in Samantha. "Who are you both talking about?"

"A teacher." Samantha glanced his way. "She taught science at the high school. Went missing, what, eighteen years ago, Will?"

Branson rolled one large shoulder. "Yeah. Something like that. It's not her, though, Sam. She left Hidden Falls."

"Not everyone thinks that. From what I remember, her sister said she never showed up in Seattle after she left here."

"Trust me. It's not her." Branson slipped his cap back on. "You sure you're going to be okay here alone tonight?"

"I'm fine." Samantha tucked her hands in the back pockets of her jeans. "Thanks for checking on me."

"Sure thing." Branson slanted a disapproving look Ethan's direction. "I'll let you get back to work."

Branson's footsteps echoed down the hall. When the back door opened then clicked shut, Ethan crossed to Samantha and ran his hands down her arms. "You okay?"

"Hmm? I'm fine." Stepping back out of his reach, she moved to the coffee table where she bent and straightened her papers. "I don't know why the two of you think I'm not. It's no biggie." A frown tugged at her mouth. "I mean, it is a biggie. But nothing that directly affects me, so I'm fine."

She was lying. Ethan could see it in her eyes, in the way she had to keep her hands busy and couldn't seem to hold still. Part of him wanted to wrap his arms around her and take away that haunted look she'd been sporting since they'd returned from their hike. Part of him wanted to run. Finding a dead body in that forest was too coincidental for his taste, and a thousand memories he didn't want to remember were running through his head.

"You don't have to stay, Ethan."

"We didn't have dinner yet."

"It's all right. I'm not that hungry now, and something tells me you aren't either. I really need to finish grading these papers, then I think I'm just going to head to bed. It's been a long evening."

He nodded. She wasn't going to let him in, confess what was really bothering her. And he didn't want to push at this point. He wanted her to open up when she was ready, and if he started prodding too soon, she'd never get there. Plus, she was right. It had been a long evening. And he needed some time alone to process what they'd found. "Okay. I should probably go, then."

He lifted the jacket he'd draped over the back of the couch and pulled it on. "I'll be at the hotel if you need anything."

He made it as far as the front door before she stopped him with a hand on his arm. "I'm sorry this ended up being such a bust. I . . . I wanted to call you over the weekend, I just . . . I chickened out."

He ran his thumb over her smooth cheek, reveling in the softness of her skin. "I get it. And what happened tonight is not your fault."

She glanced down at their feet. "Finding a body kind of put a damper on the whole go-back-to-my-house-and-make-out thing."

He smirked. "Kinda."

She bit her lip and looked up, wariness darkening her eyes. "I have a favor to ask. I have this . . . event . . . that I have to go to Friday night. A friend is running for political office, and he and his wife are having a little get-together. It's nothing fancy, and normally I'd find a way to blow it off, but I'm kind of stuck here. You're under no obligation, but I just thought . . . if you were free . . . that maybe you could save me from having to go alone?"

She really was adorable. She might not want his company tonight, but she wanted to see him again. And just knowing that made his heart skip a beat. "Friday, huh?"

"Yeah. We wouldn't have to stay long, and maybe we could try dinner after again."

"What time?"

She exhaled what sounded like a relieved breath. "Seven."

His blood warmed, and even though he wanted so much more, tonight he satisfied himself with a kiss on her forehead. "Okay. It's a date." He drew back and smiled down at her. "Be sure to lock up after me."

She gripped the door handle and pulled the door open for him. "I will. Thanks, Ethan. For everything."

He headed out to his car. But as the cool night air surrounded him, he knew he didn't want her thanks. He wanted a whole lot more. And considering everything he'd learned and found tonight, he wasn't sure how that would play out.

———

Sam watched the headlights from Ethan's car as he backed out of her driveway and disappeared around the bend. Closing the door, she dropped her head against the hard wood and drew in a shaky breath.

She'd been lying through her pearly whites. *Fine.* She wasn't fine, and if she said that one more time, she was going to seriously lose her slight grasp on reality. It amazed her that Ethan couldn't see through her veiled insecurities. Or maybe he just didn't want to. If he knew what a mess she was inside, he'd run for the hills.

She turned, braced her back against the door, and surveyed the entry of the old house. Scarred pine floors flowed down the narrow hall. The stairs swept up and to the right. Her mother's antique secretary sat against the stairwell wall, cradling bills and notes and to-do lists she didn't have time to get to. She didn't feel any emotional connection to the house or the things inside it. Didn't want to do anything but dump it and run. To her, it was a vast cavern of nothingness, much like her life.

Sam closed her eyes. She didn't want to be alone tonight. The house was too big, her mind too full of images and memories she didn't want to relive. But she couldn't really ask Ethan to stay. She didn't want to take advantage of him. And she knew she would have done exactly that if he'd stayed.

She probably shouldn't have invited him to Jeff and Margaret's party, but she'd wanted to do something to make up for this mess of a night. And taking him to the party would do that. They would be surrounded by people there. The setting wouldn't be intimate at all. They could mingle and have a few drinks, then she could take him to dinner in town—somewhere loud and busy. They could grab a bite to eat, and she could apologize for tonight. Then she could let him slip out of her life without another thought. Because, deep down, she knew she was not relationship material. After tonight, he had to realize that as well. From the way he'd kissed her forehead instead of her lips when he'd left, she sensed he already did.

A whisper of sadness rushed through her, but she knew it was for the best. Her life was nothing like his. He had a family, people who cared about him, and she was a loner. Plus, as soon as this house sold, she was heading back to California. There was no logical reason to start anything with anyone now.

Pushing away from the door, she made her way into the kitchen. After checking the locks, she left the kitchen light burning and climbed the rickety steps to her bedroom. She had to pick her way around boxes in the upstairs hall, reminding herself she still had a ton of packing and cleaning to do in the old house. That—if nothing else—would keep her busy this weekend and prevent her from thinking too much about Ethan.

She slipped into her favorite faded blue flannel pajamas, the ones with the little clouds all over them, and brushed her teeth. Making sure to leave the bathroom light on, she climbed into bed and pulled the plush comforter up around her neck. Then stared at the ceiling and prayed she wouldn't sleep.

Because as soon as she closed her eyes, she knew what she would see and hear. That weather-beaten cabin. The cold, eerie light shining through the windows. The blood-curdling cry for help that always paralyzed her. And, thanks to what they'd found tonight, the bones Grimly had uncovered in those woods.

Her mind would replay the dream, meshing the two together until she didn't know the difference. And, just like every other night, she'd once again be trapped in a nightmare of her own making.

———

Margaret took a long drag from her cigarette Friday night as Kenny continued to bitch into the phone pressed to her ear.

"This is all we freakin' need," he whined.

Margaret glanced toward the open door of her master bathroom. Dim voices echoed from the first floor where the party was already underway, and she hesitated to see if anyone was listening, but no sound came from her bedroom or the hallway.

"Relax, Kenny." She tapped her cigarette against the ashtray on her vanity. "You're making this bigger than it is. It's being handled."

"Bigger than it is?" Kenny's voice rose an octave. "That's a fucking dead body they pulled out of the woods! Don't tell me you aren't worried."

Margaret took another drag. Of course she was worried, but she wasn't about to let Kenny know that. "No. I'm not. As I said, it's being handled."

"By who?"

"Whom."

"What?"

"The proper grammatical pronunciation is, 'by whom.' And you don't need to know the answer to that question."

"Son of a bitch," he muttered under his breath. "Do you have any idea what could happen?"

"What's going to happen, Kenneth?"

"I don't know, but something bad. Samantha Parker found that body."

"And?"

"*And?* What if she was there—?"

He was getting worked up. Kenneth Saunders was only an asset so long as he didn't lose his shit. "She wasn't there that night, Kenny. End of story."

"But—"

Margaret was seriously losing her patience. She had guests waiting downstairs. He *knew* that. "It's been eighteen years. Don't you think Sam would have mentioned something about it by now if she had been there? Use your brain, Kenny. No one knows anything about what happened, and it's going to stay that way. Unless, of course, you start flipping out, in which case, people *will* take notice. And if that happens, I guarantee I won't let you drag me down with you."

Kenny grew quiet on the other end of the line.

There. That ought to shut him up for good.

Shuffling echoed from the doorway, and Margaret glanced in that direction, then sucked in a breath. He stood in the shadows of her bedroom. She couldn't see his face but instantly knew who he was. The same man she'd been waiting for. Her gaze slid across a hard chest and chiseled abs covered by a pressed white dress shirt, over slim hips encased in spendy black slacks, then finally down thick, powerful legs that knew just how to take control.

Arousal burst in the center of her body and radiated outward until heat was all she felt. Into the phone, she muttered, "I have to go."

"Wait," Kenny said.

"Remember what I said, Kenny. And don't be late tonight. It won't look good."

Margaret clicked off the phone before Kenny could whine again and pushed to her feet. The thigh-length black cocktail dress she'd slipped on for the event hugged every curve and showed off her best asset—her legs. She knew from the approval in his eyes that he noticed.

Anticipation and excitement rolled like fire through her blood. "You're earlier than I expected."

"I know. Was that Saunders?"

She nodded.

"And?"

"And he's not a problem."

"You'd better hope he stays that way."

A whisper of fear rushed down her spine. Fear mixed with lust and sin and temptation that only pushed her forward. "My husband's downstairs."

He didn't move. But his voice was like sandpaper and velvet when he held out his hand, drawing her to him like a moth to a flame. "Then, this time, you'd better not scream."

———

A light snow fell as Ethan pulled into Samantha's driveway Friday night. It wasn't sticking to the ground yet, but the kids at school had been beside themselves as the weather threatened all day.

Ethan hadn't been able to concentrate much either, but his distraction had nothing to do with the weather. Between lying awake all night thinking about Samantha and the remains they'd found behind her house, then catching glimpses of her at school between classes, all he could focus on was taking that worried look from her eyes and replacing it with the smile he'd seen when he'd kissed her in the woods.

That kiss still radiated through his toes every time he thought about it. Tonight he didn't want to talk about what they'd found. Didn't want to talk about the gossip he'd heard at school. Didn't want to do anything but take Samantha's stress away and have a good time. And kiss her again. Several times if she let him. He just hoped she wanted the same things.

He jogged up the front steps and knocked. The porch light illuminated small flakes floating in the air. Memories of snowball wars with his brothers filled his mind as the cool air enveloped him, sending a shiver down his spine. But when the door pulled opened, a whole other kind of winter fun seeped into his head.

Ethan's mouth went dry and fell open.

A strapless black jumpsuit nipped in at Samantha's waist, accentuating her cleavage and showing off her curves. Some gauzy, sheer overlay puckered around her waist and flitted down her hips, showcasing the wide cut of the leg, making her look like a sinful mermaid. The sheer black scarf she'd wrapped around her neck peeked out from behind the mass of curly hair falling down her shoulders, emphasizing the long, sexy line of her throat, making him want to use it to pull her in and never let go.

"You're letting in the cold, Dr. McClane." She tugged him into the house and closed the door at his back.

Maybe, but heat was suddenly all he felt. "And you're gonna freeze dressed like that."

Not that he'd mind. If she got cold, he was more than willing to offer his body heat to keep her warm.

"Tell me something, Ms. Parker." He watched the sexy sway of her hair as she turned to grab her jacket from the coat tree in the entry hall. "Do you always dress like sin when attending political parties?"

Approval lit her eyes as she shrugged into her coat. "No. But I rarely get to dress up. Looks like I made a good choice."

"Did you ever." His gaze swept over her, from the top of her curly head to the tips of her hot-pink toes peeking out beneath the black fabric in her strappy black heels. "How the heck did you get into that thing?"

She fluffed her hair from the collar of her coat. "Very carefully. I'll probably have to peel it off when the night's over."

A heavy tingling shot through his body, and he tipped his head to the side. "Stop. You're torturing me here."

Laughing, she grabbed her purse. "No, torture is where we're headed next. Let's go so we can get out of there and get on with dinner."

When they were on the road, she shifted in her seat, then smoothed her hair back from her face in that nervous way he'd come to anticipate. "I should warn you that we're going to Margaret Wilcox's house."

"The English teacher?"

She nodded. "Her husband's going to announce his candidacy for the Senate tonight. He wanted to do it here, in their hometown, first, just a small local deal. I don't think it's going to be a big party, but there will probably be a few reporters hanging around."

Light from the dash illuminated her face and made her hair look even darker. "You and Margaret don't seem to get along that well. Why are you going?"

She relaxed against the leather seat. "Because Jeff asked me to be there. Trust me, if Margaret had asked, I'd have said no. My mother contributed a hefty sum to Jeff Kellogg's campaign, and we've been friends for years."

Ethan sucked in a breath. Jeff Kellogg. He'd already suffered through Will Branson and Ken Saunders. Now he had to face Jeff Kellogg? Son of a bitch. His situation was just getting better by the day.

"Margaret will do anything to make me feel uncomfortable. So just be prepared. I have no intention of staying long." She pointed. "Take the next left."

He wanted to whip the car around and get the heck out of Hidden Falls for good, but being the responsible adult he'd worked hard to become, he turned where she indicated.

They drove up a long paved private road flanked on both sides by gnarled oak. Just as they turned the last corner, a large house came into view, a tower of stone and glass and wood. Warm light spilled through the massive windows. Alternating rooflines framed broad balconies and intimate verandahs. As Ethan continued up the drive, he spotted a circular drive complete with trees decked out in white twinkle lights and an illuminated waterfall. A parking attendant dressed in a black suit beckoned them closer.

Ethan's nerves were shot by the time he pulled to a stop. Beside him, Samantha reached for the door handle. "One hour. I promise we won't stay a second longer."

The attendant opened her door before Ethan could stop her from getting out. Closing his eyes briefly, he drew in a calming breath, then let it out. Did it again until he felt like his lungs weren't about to explode. Part of agreeing to Thomas's case had been about facing his own demons, right? If he could make it through the next hour, he'd have done that. Then maybe he could let go of the past once and for all.

The attendant walked around and opened his door. Ethan climbed out and handed the man a five. The attendant thanked him, took the keys, then climbed in and drove off with their getaway car.

Samantha eyed him warily as she pulled her coat tighter around her. "Everything okay?"

"Fine." Ethan knew she'd noticed his strange behavior, but at the moment he couldn't even muster up a smile. And there was no way he could tell her why. Especially here. Placing a hand at the small of her back, he ushered her up the wide stone steps. "Let's just go in so we can get this over with."

"Okay," she said softly. "Thanks for coming with me."

His stomach twisted tighter. She wouldn't be thanking him soon if Kellogg recognized his face.

Nerves bounced through every inch of his body, but to keep himself distracted from the horror that waited on the other side of that massive double door, he tried to remember the lesson Samantha had taught that day in class. Something about chemical bonding—sharing electrons, stealing electrons. Crap, he couldn't remember. Why wasn't his brain working?

They reached the top step, and Samantha leaned forward to ring the bell. Voices and laughter echoed from inside the house. The right side of the enormous mahogany door opened seconds later, and a woman in a black maid's outfit gestured them in. She took their coats and pointed down the wide hall toward the back of the house.

Samantha scanned rooms as they passed. "You're a saint, Ethan. You know that? And I owe you big for this."

He didn't feel like a saint. He felt like a fake. A giant fake who was about to be discovered.

The great room was crowded when they reached the threshold. People chatted in small groups, sitting or standing around plush furnishings. Waiters mingled with trays of food and drinks. Wide, two-story windows looked out to the backyard and the lit-up verandah while soft music echoed from the ceiling and firelight flickered in the enormous stone fireplace to their right.

Samantha smiled at the woman on her left and turned to speak with her. Ethan heard his name but couldn't focus on what Samantha was saying. Because ahead of him, three men stood in quiet conversation near the windows.

Three men dressed in slacks and dress shirts and ties. Three men he'd never expected to see together again in this lifetime.

———

Something was up.

"Ethan?" Sam said his name again. He still didn't answer, just stared straight ahead. Growing worried, she laid a hand on his arm.

Ethan startled and looked down. "Yeah?"

His eyes were a little dazed. His focus distracted. Did he not like crowds? He'd seemed fine at school. "This is Pearl Hamilton. She owns the café on Main Street."

Ethan offered a tight smile, one Sam had never seen on his face. "Nice to meet you." Releasing the sixtyish woman's hand, he leaned toward Sam and whispered, "I need a drink. Do you want anything?"

"No. I'm fine."

She watched him walk toward the bar and swipe a hand over his brow. An odd tingle spread down her spine.

"He's sure handsome," Pearl said, drawing Sam's attention back to the gray-haired woman who stood at only four foot ten. "Is he from around here?"

"No. Portland."

"Hmm." Pearl's gaze followed Ethan as he reached for his drink from the bartender. "He looks familiar. How long have you two been dating?"

"Oh, we're not dating. Just friends."

"Too bad." Pearl sighed and tugged on the shawl around her shoulders. "That man's a looker. And he has big hands. You know what they say about big hands."

Sam's cheeks heated as she glanced back at Ethan. But the flutter in her stomach had more to do with the word "friend" than Pearl's comment. Especially because saying it made her immediately remember that kiss in the woods and what she'd been ready to do to that so-called friend before Grimly had changed their plans with his wild barking.

She watched the muscles in his shoulders bunch and roll as he lifted his drink and tossed it back. Being friends was good, right? Friends was safe. She was nuttier than a Snickers bar on a good day. Someone like him would figure that out sooner rather than later. It was better to be friends and let him down gently tonight when they had dinner alone, rather than allow him to get close and see too much.

*If you only want to be friends, then why did you wear this supersexy outfit?*

Sam frowned, mentally cursing her subconscious.

"Sam?"

She turned at the sound of Will's voice and realized Will and Jeff were heading her way. Leaning toward Pearl, she said, "It was great to see you. I'll catch up with you later."

"Good to see you as well, dear." The older woman laid a hand on Sam's arm before she could step away. "Oh. I wanted to tell you how sorry I was to hear about that nasty business out near your place. I sure do hope we get some news soon. If you hear anything, be sure to let me know."

Pearl wandered off to another group, but just the mention of the body in those woods sent Sam's anxiety inching up all over again.

"Hey." Will took her arm and moved in for a hug. "Don't let that old biddy ruin your night. She's just looking for gossip."

Sam hugged him back. "I'm not." Though inside she was. She was afraid she knew exactly whom they'd found in those woods—everyone in town did, they were just too afraid to say the name out loud.

Turning toward Jeff, she hugged him too, taking in his crisp black slacks, white dress shirt, and Armani jacket. "Hey, you. All set for your big announcement?"

He smiled, perfect white teeth against tanned skin, his short, dark-blond hair expertly styled as if it didn't dare fall out of place. Jeff Kellogg was as calm and poised and professional as always, and she had no doubt he was going to get elected simply based off his presence alone. "You know me. I'm always ready for the cameras."

Sam didn't agree with all of Jeff's politics, but she knew it would be a boon for this town to have something good to talk about instead of something bad. And sending one of their own to the Senate would put Hidden Falls on the map. Every business owner in town was contributing to his campaign in the hopes it would help their bottom line.

"I, for one, can't wait to hear your speech," Sam said. "And I know my mother would have wanted to hear it as well."

"Any bites on the house?" Will asked beside her.

Sam sighed. "No. Not yet. I'm still doing some of those repairs the realtor said would make the place irresistible."

Will grabbed a beer from a passing waiter's tray. "Well, if you need any help, you know where to find me. I'm happy to lend a hand."

Sam's stomach tightened, and her gaze immediately shifted to Ethan on the other side of the room, speaking with David Burke and several others. Will's offer was nothing but friendship, but he wasn't the one she wanted lending her a hand—doing repairs or not.

"I still say there's something familiar about that guy," Kenny Saunders said.

Sam dragged her attention away from Ethan only to realize Kenny had joined their conversation. He stood across from her, between Will and Jeff, but Sam's back tingled just the way it always did when he was near. Tonight, at least, he'd combed his hair and was wearing slacks and a white dress shirt, even if it was wrinkled and rolled up to the elbows. "Which guy?"

"McClane." Kenny nodded toward the group where Ethan stood. "I know I've seen him somewhere before."

Will had said the same thing. And Pearl. Sam looked back at Ethan, deep in conversation with Principal Burke. Three people recognizing him was more than a coincidence. Had he passed through town once before and not mentioned it to her?

Will brushed a hand down Sam's back, angling her back toward their group. "I'm sure he's just one of those guys who has one of those faces."

Kenny took a long pull from his bottle and snorted. "I don't know, man. I'm just sayin'. Strange things have been happening around here lately. The stuff at Sam's house, the break-in at the school, that body up in those woods. McClane's new. Who's to say he doesn't have something to do with it all?"

Will shot Kenny a warning look and tightened his hold on Sam. "For all we know, that was a vagrant up in those woods. And the stuff at Sam's house was teenagers, nothing more." He glanced down at her. "You haven't had any more trouble lately, have you?"

Heat seeped from him into her where they touched, but it wasn't the good heat. It wasn't Ethan's heat. And Sam fought the urge to pull away. If she did, it might upset him, and she didn't need any more drama tonight. Especially when her head was suddenly swimming.

Could Ethan somehow be involved with everything that had happened lately?

No. That was ridiculous. He hadn't even come into town until the day her room had been ransacked. He hadn't been here when her house was vandalized. There was no way he could have locked himself and her in that supply closet, and he certainly hadn't been in Hidden Falls when that person in those woods was killed. The remains they'd found had been buried for a very long time.

"No." Sam hated that she was even entertaining the idea Ethan was somehow involved. Kenny was just trying to throw her off. For all she knew, he could be the one causing problems as of late. "Nothing. Everything's been fine recently."

"Good." Will's hand slipped down to her waist and gently squeezed, then released. "You be sure to let me know if it isn't, though."

Sam stiffened, but forced herself not to pull back. She was grateful for Will's help. He'd been a good friend to her since she'd been back. And he was just being a friend now.

*Friend . . .*

As the three men launched into a conversation about Jeff's campaign, Sam's thoughts rushed right back to Ethan, and she turned to watch him across the crowded room once more. Heat gathered in her belly when she remembered the way he'd looked at her in the entry of her mother's old house. Heat and need and a burning desire she was afraid she wouldn't be able to contain much longer.

Because she didn't want to be friends with Ethan no matter what common sense told her to do. She wanted more. She was just deathly afraid of the fallout when he learned her darkest secrets.

# CHAPTER EIGHT

All Ethan wanted to do was escape.

Standing in the Kelloggs' great room, surrounded by several of Hidden Falls's finest, all he could think about was making a break for the verandah and bumming a cigarette from another guest.

David Burke had introduced him around, and even though his mind was one giant tornado, Ethan had managed to catch a few names. The gray-haired woman to Ethan's left, Dot Appleton, owned a local bookstore. The bald, middle-aged man beside her, Lincoln Jenkins, ran the newspaper. Burke's wife, Cynthia, the bleach blonde aerobics instructor, stood to the principal's right, eyeing Ethan like fresh meat.

He seriously didn't want to be here. Why had he agreed to this nonsense? And why the hell wasn't his brain working? He couldn't even think up a pithy excuse to get out of the monotonous conversation.

Dot grasped his arm, startling Ethan out of the exit plan swirling in his mind, and looked up with wide gray eyes. "Oh my goodness. You're the one who found the body, aren't you, Dr. McClane?"

Shit. There went his anonymity in this backwater town. And his plan for a quick break. "I think 'body' is a questionable term considering the circumstances."

"Terrible discovery," Jenkins said, tapping his finger against the glass in his hand. Ice clinked in the bottom. "Whole town's sick over it."

Wrapping a hand around her neck, Cynthia shivered in a way that made her breasts jiggle in the extremely low-cut top. A move Ethan knew was planned. "Just makes me ill to think a dead body's been up in those woods all this time." Her voice lowered. "You know, people are saying it's Sandra Hollings."

Dot's lips pursed. "Serves her right."

"Dot." Jenkins's sharp gaze darted in her direction.

"Oh, hush. You and I both know that woman was the devil." Dot glanced at Ethan as if she were confessing a terrible secret. "You're not from around here, but let me tell you, the devil's just what she was. Why, she was a teacher up at the high school, a teacher who had one thing on her mind, she did. Caused all sorts of trouble in this town. Flitting around with another woman's husband, flaunting herself in front of those boys in class. I'm not the only one who was happy to see her go."

"Now, Dot," Burke said, slipping an arm around his wife's waist. "That was a long time ago."

"Long time ago." Dot huffed. "I have a memory like an elephant, I do. I remember what that woman was like." She glanced up at Ethan again. "We were all thankful when she disappeared. Especially poor Will over there."

"Chief Branson?" Ethan glanced across the room, his interest suddenly piqued. But when he caught sight of Branson standing with an arm wrapped protectively around Samantha, his stomach clenched.

He didn't want Branson's hands anywhere near Samantha, but he couldn't go over there and warn her off the guy without explaining what he knew. And doing that meant opening up a part of himself she wasn't ready to see.

"His daddy was the one she'd taken up with," Dot said. "Henry Branson was mayor of Hidden Falls at the time. There was a big scandal when it all came out. Cut that family in two, that evil woman did. Why, Eileen Branson committed suicide over it."

Will's mother? Ethan looked back down at the older woman.

"Dot." Jenkins sent her another warning glare.

"Can't say I was sorry in the least to see that Hollings woman leave," Dot went on, ignoring Jenkins.

"I thought someone said she went back to Seattle?" Ethan asked.

"She did," Cynthia replied. "But she came back. Alan Kendall saw her at the gas station, what, six or seven months after she took off?"

"Something like that." Dot waved a hand, then leaned closer to Ethan. "Alan's not always the best with details." She tapped her head. "But he's sure he saw her. None of the rest of us did, but I, for one, tend to believe him."

Jenkins frowned. "Let me get this straight. You think she left, came back because she missed the place, and then someone killed her? Why would she come back? You already pointed out that no one in town liked her. That's a little out there, even for you, Dot."

Dot's lips pursed when she turned toward Lincoln. "I don't know why she came back, but I'm sure she did. She had her talons in the Branson family, that's for sure, and she was none too happy about leaving in the first place. She was practically forced out of here. I think someone murdered her, that's what I think. Someone who was sick of seeing what she'd done to those people, to this town, for that matter."

"Oh Lord." Burke rolled his eyes. "We're all suspects now."

Ethan's gaze drifted back toward Samantha, still standing way too close to Will Branson for his taste. If what Dot Appleton said were true, then Sandra Hollings hadn't been missed when she'd left Hidden Falls. And the Branson family had reason to see her disappear forever.

"Well, I don't really know what to believe," Cynthia said, drawing Ethan's attention back to her and her heaving breasts. "It just creeps me out knowing someone died up there. Especially since that's the same forest where the Raines boy was murdered. What if the same person killed them both?"

Every muscle in Ethan's body contracted.

Dot waved a hand in a dismissive gesture. "That was a completely different situation. They caught the juvenile delinquent who drowned poor Seth. Some whacked-out kid from the city. Why politicians think good country folk should be responsible for rehabilitating scum like that is beyond me."

Dot's words echoed through Ethan's mind, but the tightness growing in his chest was all that held his focus.

"It was a pleasure to meet you all," he managed, interrupting Dot midsentence as she went on about the problem with social services programs in the United States. "If you'll excuse me."

"Certainly." Dot folded her hands over her small purse. But as he stepped away, Ethan heard her mutter, "Interesting fellow, that Dr. McClane. What do you know about him, David?"

Ethan wanted nothing more than to grab Samantha and run, to get as far away from this house and its inhabitants as possible, but he couldn't. Because he wasn't about to make a scene for her. There was still just enough preteen fear in him, though, to push him right out the patio door toward freedom and fresh air.

His heart pounded in his chest. Sweat slicked his skin. Clenching and unclenching his hands at his sides, he wove through the crowd on the verandah and cursed his stupidity for agreeing to come to this party. In his desperate attempt to spend more time with Samantha, he'd ruined their entire night. And his plan hadn't even worked, had it? She wasn't anywhere near him. She wasn't talking to or flirting with or touching *him*. She was with Branson. And Kellogg. And Saunders.

He moved past potted trees lit up with twinkle lights and groupings of people chatting and drinking on the verandah. Beyond the balcony, snowflakes wisped through the air, landing without a sound on the grass below. Heaters were strategically placed to keep the area warm, but

Ethan didn't need heat. He needed a dark corner where he could pull himself together before he gave in to the urge and ran.

He finally spotted it. Just past the last heater. A space at the end of the deck where he could be alone with his thoughts. Bracing his hands on the railing, he looked out at the darkness and drew in steady breaths.

"You look like you could use a friend."

Shit. So much for being alone with his thoughts.

He turned to find Margaret Wilcox slinking toward him, her black silk sheath dress clinging to her body, contrasting with her milk-white skin and blonde hair. She held one arm wrapped around her waist, while the elbow of the other sat perched on her hip, cradling a smoldering cigarette.

"Smoke?" she asked.

*God, yes. Right now.*

"No." He cleared his throat because it sounded way too desperate. "I quit."

One side of her blood-red lips tipped up as she moved closer. "Pity."

She took a long drag on the cigarette, then blew smoke all over his face. Ethan closed his eyes and breathed deep, ingesting as much nicotine as he could to keep from snatching it out of her grip.

"Self-control is overrated, Dr. McClane." Her voice dropped to a raspy whisper. "It's so much more enjoyable to be wicked."

He was not turned on by this woman. She smelled like a crowded bar, probably tasted like a dirty ashtray. There were reasons he'd quit smoking; most notably, he didn't find *this* attractive anymore. So why wasn't he moving back?

Because he was desperate for a hit. And right now he didn't care how he got it.

Her fingertips grazed the sleeve of his jacket, and he opened his eyes. Fine lines fanned out from her eyes at this close distance. Her skin was sallow and rougher than he'd originally thought. She hid it well with makeup, but she couldn't change the effects of years of smoking. She looked older than he remembered from school, worn . . . used.

"Why don't you let me give you a tour of the house? I'm sure we could find ourselves a nice, quiet spot to sit and get acquainted." Her finger slithered up his arm. "I could let you . . . probe . . . the inner recesses of my mind."

Ethan nearly laughed. *Not in a million years.*

"Ethan?" Samantha's voice rang out to his right. "I'm ready to leave."

Ethan looked her way, and when he saw her backlit by the warmth from the house, her curly dark hair falling around her shoulders and her lithe body wrapped in that sinful jumpsuit, the tightness in his chest eased.

"I am too." He stepped away from Margaret. "Really ready."

Margaret drew another long breath from her cigarette as Ethan moved around her. "Sam." The word was punctuated by a wave of smoke. "There you are. I'd almost forgotten you were here." She glanced at Ethan and grinned. "We weren't talking about you in the least."

"I'm sure you weren't." Samantha looked toward Ethan. "I'm ready anytime you are."

"Leaving before the big speech?" Margaret waved her cigarette. "Jeff will be so disappointed."

"Actually," Samantha lifted her brows, "he read me the speech privately when we were talking earlier. But I'm sure you'll enjoy it when he reads it for everyone else. Good night, Margaret."

Samantha turned and headed back into the house.

Ethan drew in a deep breath as he watched Samantha leave then looked back at Margaret. "Thanks for the hospitality."

"Anytime." Margaret puffed on her cigarette again and sent him one last lusty look. "We'll finish this some other time, *doctor.*"

Not if he could help it.

Samantha was already halfway through the great room by the time Ethan caught up with her, and one look at her tense back told him she was ticked.

He waited while she said good-bye to David Burke, did the same, and followed her toward the front of the house. Thankfully, Branson, Kellogg, and Saunders were nowhere to be seen, but at the moment he barely cared. All he could focus on was the fact that Samantha's shoulders were tight as a drum and she refused to speak or even look his way as they retrieved their coats and moved out the front door.

Shit. She thought there'd been something going on between him and Margaret.

"Samantha." He handed the valet his ticket when he reached the bottom step and waited while the man hurried off before he turned to her. "That wasn't what it looked like."

Snowflakes dotted Samantha's hair and cheeks and nose. "It was exactly what it looked like. She had 'wanton slut' written all over her, and you fell right into her trap."

A wisp of panic spread beneath Ethan's ribs. He reached for her arm. "I'm not interested in Margaret Wilcox."

"Do I look like an idiot? I know you're not." The valet pulled the car to a stop in front of them. As soon as he popped the driver's side door, Samantha tugged free from Ethan's grip and rounded the hood. "And I hate to burst your bubble, Ethan, but she doesn't want you, she's just using you to get at me."

The valet sprinted around the car to grab the door for her. More confused than before, Ethan watched her climb in and tried to figure out what was going on.

She wasn't the least bit jealous? He'd been jealous as hell when he'd seen her standing with Branson. Wanted to punch something every time he pictured the guy sliding a possessive arm around her waist as if he owned her. And just the thought of her alone with Jeff Kellogg, getting a private reading of his speech, made him see red.

He waited for the valet to come back around, handed the guy a tip, and climbed into the driver's seat. Had he missed something? Misread her? Sure, she'd pulled away from his kiss in the woods, but he'd thought that was because of Grimly. And tonight, she'd worn that sexy jumpsuit for their date. But had the outfit been for him? Or someone else? Someone at the party? A knot formed in his belly when he thought back to the way she'd leaned into Branson. And in a whir he realized she hadn't greeted Ethan with any kind of affection like that when he'd arrived to pick her up, just a smile.

The BMW's headlights bounced along the slick pavement and reflected off tree trunks lining the long drive. While they'd been inside, the snow had picked up, and a fresh layer of white now covered everything, even the road. Reality trickled in as he gripped the wheel. If he didn't get out of Hidden Falls soon, he might not make it home tonight.

That was all he needed after this horrendous day. To get stuck here one more night. He turned onto the highway. Snow barreled toward them. The windshield wipers snapped back and forth, filling the car with a rhythmic *whup, whup, whup* as he licked his wounded pride and reminded himself he'd walked right into this one. Samantha Parker had told him point-blank that she wasn't interested in any kind of relationship. And he hadn't listened.

"I cannot stand that woman." Beside him, Samantha rested her elbow on the windowsill and rubbed her forehead. "I swear to God she's got horns underneath all that hair. Did you see her? Oh my God. Did you see her? Her husband is just inside, and she's practically throwing herself at you out on the verandah. And there were reporters there. My God, she is the biggest slut I've ever met."

Great. She was worried about Jeff Kellogg? That was all Ethan needed to hear. He gripped the steering wheel tighter.

"She's been pulling crap like this my whole life. If I have something and she doesn't, she makes a point of worming her way in. She still can't get past the fact Jeff and I went out."

"You dated the guy?" The words were out before Ethan could stop them.

"Not really. I mean, he took me to my senior prom. We went out a few times after that, but it wasn't serious or anything. Margaret wasn't even interested in him until she found out. I don't even know why the hell he married her."

Ethan's jaw clenched, and he forced himself to refocus on the road.

"And she knows I showed up with you," Samantha went on. "That's why she was out there coming on to you."

Large white flakes flitted in front of the vehicle's headlights, the snowfall thickening, cutting down the visibility. His pride took another direct hit. "Nice to know it had nothing to do with me."

Samantha glanced his way, the first time since they'd climbed into the car. "I didn't mean it that way. She thinks you're hot. She mentioned it way before we started . . . " She looked back ahead. "Well, you know."

The lilt to her words caused Ethan to look at her. She smoothed the hair back from her face in that adorable anxious move that did weird things to his blood. "Since we started what?"

Samantha frowned. "You know."

"Dating?"

"I was going to say hanging out."

That little bit of hope he'd felt crashed and burned. Ethan frowned and refocused on the road.

"Look. I'm really not in the mood for a noisy restaurant anymore. Can we just head back to my house?"

"Sure." Ethan tried to hide his disappointment. Maybe it was for the best. It was a stupid idea to get involved with anyone from Hidden Falls.

She was silent during the rest of the drive, her gaze focused on the snow falling around them. When he pulled into her driveway and stopped the car, she climbed out before he could walk around and get her door.

He held her at the elbow as they crossed the snowy yard so she didn't slip in the strappy heels. Once they were on the covered porch, he let go of her and checked his watch. It was a little after ten. If he left now, he could be home and parked in front of ESPN in as little as ninety minutes.

Samantha turned the key and pushed the heavy door open with her hip. Grimly's nails clicked along the hardwood floor as he barked and rushed toward her, his tail wagging wildly. Samantha bent to rub his ears.

"So I'm gonna head on out," Ethan said.

"What?" Samantha turned quickly. "No, you're not."

"I'm not?"

"No." Grasping the sleeve of his coat, she tugged him into the house and closed the door at his back. "I don't want you to leave, Ethan. I'm just not in the mood for a lot of people."

She pulled the scarf from around her neck and tossed it on the bench by the front door. Her coat followed. Peeling his jacket from his shoulders, she threw it on top of hers before heading down the hall toward the kitchen. Grimly followed with a bounce in his step.

Ethan stared after her, seriously confused. The woman was sending him all kinds of mixed messages. Or maybe he was just reading them wrong. He rubbed his forehead.

"Aren't you coming?" she called.

He closed his eyes and drew a deep breath. Like he was leaving now. Just the sound of that sexy schoolteacher voice made him lose all common sense.

She stood at the kitchen counter pouring a shot of bourbon as he entered the room. Lifting the glass to her lips, she threw back the shot, licked her lips, and eyed him over the glass. "Don't look at me like that."

"Like what?" God, she was gorgeous, and he bet she didn't even know it. Light from the lamp across the room cast shadows on her smooth skin, accentuating her movements. He loved the way she moved. Jerky sometimes. Smooth at others. Unsure when she was around him, which he really liked. He could watch her for hours.

"Like I'm an alcoholic. I'm not. I rarely drink. But that woman . . . " She lowered the glass and filled another shot. "I swear, she knows just how to push my buttons. Do you want one?"

Why the hell not? It'd been a pretty shitty night so far. He stepped into the kitchen. "Sure."

She grabbed another glass from the cupboard, poured a shot, and handed it to him. Lifting her glass, she said, "Cheers."

The golden liquid warmed his throat as it went down, a hard punch to the gut where it settled. Heat slowly spread through his limbs, warming his muscles one by one.

"I should have warned you about Dot Appleton," Samantha said. "I saw she had you cornered."

He leaned against the counter and crossed his arms over his chest. "I'm a big boy. I think I can handle one nosy bookseller."

"She's the town gossip. I'm sure you got an earful."

More than. "Word spreads fast around here."

Sam shook her hair back and ran her fingers through the curly locks, looking more relaxed with each passing second. The movement accentuated the swell of her breasts, the arch in her back. Either the alcohol was working or her temper was settling. At the moment, he didn't really care which. He was just glad they were alone and that she seemed to want him around.

"Do you remember this Sandra Hollings?" he asked.

"Not really. I was just a kid when she lived here. I know she taught high school, and I remember hearing rumors about her, but I was, like, ten. I didn't pay attention to anything important back then."

He nodded. The name was vaguely familiar to Ethan, but he couldn't place a face with it. So many of his memories from Hidden Falls were a blur, that one night overshadowing everything before it.

"I think I have a yearbook photo of her somewhere." Pushing away from the counter, Samantha wandered back down the hallway.

Ethan followed her into what he could only imagine was a home office. At the moment it looked like a war zone. Boxes were stacked four high at every angle. A few sat open, half-packed. The large cherry desk near the window was littered with files and papers and the oldest computer Ethan had ever seen. To its left, a floor-to-ceiling bookshelf cradled old, dusty books and various knickknacks.

Samantha's heels clicked on the hardwood floor as she stepped over a box in the middle of the room and reached for another near the window. Muscles flexed in her trim arms as she lifted it from the stack and set it on a pile of papers scattered across the desk.

"What happened in here?"

"My mother happened in here," she said, rummaging through the contents. "She saved everything. I'm trying to figure out what can be sold and what should just be burned for good measure."

Dark, curly tendrils fell across her cheek, her posture accentuating her luscious cleavage in the strapless outfit. The soothing scents of lavender and vanilla wafted on the air, sending heat straight to his belly.

*Tonight is not about sex. She's keyed up. She probably just wants to talk and "hang out." Don't get any ideas.*

Ethan cleared his throat. "What are you doing with a yearbook from eighteen years ago?"

"Um . . . my mother dabbled in photography."

She didn't elaborate, but the question was lost when she pulled out a black leather book from the box. "Here it is. I knew it was in here."

She opened the book and flipped pages. Skirting the desk, she stepped over a half-packed box in the center of the room. "I remember she was really young. Right out of college."

Ethan stepped toward her, but his shoe hooked the edge of a wooden chair he hadn't seen sticking out from behind a box, knocking him off balance.

"Ethan!" Samantha reached for him. He grappled for something to stop his downward momentum, but his hand knocked into another stack of boxes. He hit the hardwood floor with a crack. Just behind Samantha, he saw the stack tip and sway. He lifted his arms just as they crashed to the floor.

"Oh my God, Ethan." Samantha frantically swiped boxes away and climbed over him. "Are you okay?"

He blinked twice and looked up into her worried dark eyes. Silky curls hung around her face and tickled his cheeks, bringing his skin to life, making him acutely aware of her thighs brushing the outsides of his, of her heat and that sweet, sweet scent he remembered from when she'd been close like this in the supply closet of her classroom. "I'm . . . not sure."

"I am so sorry." She pushed the last box away with her hand and kicked one more at her feet. Thankfully, most seemed empty, or at least only partially filled with paper. Judging from the sharp ache in the back of his head, though, Ethan figured his skull was another matter. "How do we always end up on the floor?"

He didn't know, but right now he wasn't complaining. God, she smelled good. And this close, all he could think about was how soft her lips looked. How warm her mouth had been when he'd kissed her. The throb in his head faded. Maybe it was the bourbon, dulling the edges, or maybe it was just her, calling to him like she'd done since the first moment he'd met her.

"I don't know." His hands slipped to her thighs, braced on both sides of his hips, and he ran his fingers up the silky soft fabric of her jumpsuit. "But being on the floor does have its advantages."

Her breath caught. It was a very subtle movement, but he heard it. And just knowing she was as aware of him as he was of her awakened places inside he knew only she could bring to life.

"Ethan," she breathed.

"Yeah?" He slid his hands up to her hips. Felt the pulse beneath her skin speed up. Inched his fingers higher.

Her breath quickened. Several heartbeats passed before she said, "Where does it hurt?"

His fingers stilled their slow movements, and he looked from her lips to her eyes. Her mesmerizing, smoldering eyes. Blood surged straight into his groin. "My head."

She rested her weight on one hand and tipped his head to the side with the other. Leaning close, she pressed a kiss to the base of his skull where he'd smacked it against the hardwood. "There?"

His throat grew thick. "Um. Yeah."

She eased back and rested her hand on the ground again. But this time a mischievous twinkle sparked in her eyes as she looked down. "Where else?"

Holy hell. Was she going to kiss every one of his injuries? This could get interesting. "My forehead."

She leaned forward and brushed her lips above his left eyebrow. "Anywhere else?"

"I think a box might have hit me on the cheek."

Her tongue darted out, wetting her bottom lip, making the blood in his groin absolutely throb. With slow motions, she kissed his cheek.

"No." He might as well milk it for all it was worth. "The other one."

Her grin widened, and she kissed the other side. "Is that it?"

"I think here too." He tapped one finger against his mouth.

A sexy smile pulled at the corners of her lips. "We definitely don't want you to be hurt there, now do we?"

He smiled, but when she pressed her mouth to his, all humor fled. Heat infused him the instant they touched. Heat and need and a desire he knew he should keep in check. But when her mouth opened over his, and her sweet little tongue swept between his lips, all he could think about was tasting her again, taking everything she was offering and losing himself in her for as long as she'd let him.

He slid his hands up to brush her hair back from her face, stroking into her mouth with slow, gentle sweeps. And when she lowered her weight onto his, any pretense he had of holding back slipped right out of his grasp. He moved one hand to the back of her head, trailed the other to her waist, and pulled her tighter as he kissed her deeper.

She drew her mouth from his way before he was ready to let her go and pressed soft wet kisses to his cheek, his jaw, working her way over to his ear. His eyes slid closed, and he groaned, flexing his hips so she could rub against him, loving her mouth on his skin, wherever she could reach. "Samantha . . . "

"Mm . . . ?" She nipped at his earlobe then sucked it between her succulent lips.

*Oh God* . . . If she kept that up he was gonna come, right here in his pants.

"I, um . . . think maybe we should slow down."

She dragged her tongue over the soft skin behind his ear. "Getting cold feet, Dr. McClane?"

He chuckled, loving the feel of her against him, loving her mouth and that wicked rocking she was doing with her hips. "Not at all. But you've been drinking. And the first time I take you, I don't want you to have any regrets."

"The first time?" She pushed up on her hand and looked down, cheeks flushed with arousal, lips plump from his kisses. Absolutely delicious. "Does that mean you've been planning for this?"

"Hoping is more like it."

"Me too," she said softly.

Excitement surged inside him. But he held back. Barely. "When it happens, Samantha, I want you all in. No inhibitions."

She leaned back, her knees locked tight against his hips, the heat between her thighs pressed right over his erection. Flashing a wicked grin, she reached for his belt buckle. "I have none now. I'm not wasted, Ethan. I want you."

It was all he could do not to grab her and take her, right there on the floor. Instead, he searched her eyes for any indication she was inebriated. He didn't see it. He saw heat and need and lust. The same lust boiling in his veins, overriding every other thought but her.

She slipped his belt buckle free, leaned forward, and whispered, "I want to feel you inside me now, Ethan. Right now. Please don't make me wait any longer."

And when she kissed him, the last of his resistance finally disappeared.

# CHAPTER NINE

"Hold on to me, Samantha."

Ethan's rough voice swept over Sam, sending shivers of anticipation straight down her spine. His arms closed around her waist, and he pushed to his feet, lifting her off the floor. Wrapping herself around him, she found his mouth again and kissed him with every bit of excitement pulsing through her veins.

It wasn't the alcohol. This overwhelming need had been building since the day they'd been locked together in her supply closet. A tiny voice in the back of her head warned her to be careful, but she ignored it. She didn't want to play things slow and cautious right now. She just wanted to feel as much as she could.

He lifted her over the box at their feet, his tongue sweeping into her mouth in a fast, hard, demanding kiss that kicked the fire deep in her core from smoldering to full-on flaming. When he reached the hallway, he drew back long enough to ask, "Which way?"

Her head was light. Her skin on fire. The couch was closer, but she wanted him in her bed. Threading her fingers up into his hair, she kissed his cheek. "Up . . . stairs."

He turned toward the stairs, claiming her mouth once more, and she groaned as he deepened the kiss, his tongue scraping her teeth, tasting and exploring every part of her mouth. Tightening her fingers in his hair, she kissed him again and again, the way he was kissing her. Moved to the corner of his lips. His jaw. Kissed her way to his throat, memorizing the lines and angles of his body while she tasted the sweetness of his flesh.

"Samantha . . . " Her name came out on a groan. Her feet hit the steps. The stairwell wall brushed her back while pictures swayed above. But she didn't care, doubted she'd even notice if they crashed down around her. Nipping her way across his throat, she finally reached his ear and drew the soft lobe between her teeth.

It wasn't enough. She wanted skin. Needed to feel every part of him. Her hands streaked down to his waist as he found her mouth again, kissing her until she was dizzy. She pulled at his shirt, jerking it free of his slacks, and made quick work of the buttons as their tongues tangled in a frantic kiss. Groaning into his mouth, she tugged the sleeves down his muscular arms and tossed the shirt away, then found the hem of the white T-shirt he wore under his dress shirt and pulled away from his mouth long enough to wrench it up over his head.

She had a quick flash of chiseled abs and toned pecs, but before she could take a closer look, his mouth was on hers again. Desire roared through her all over again, and her fingers moved over his skin, exploring every dip and angle and play of bone. But it still wasn't enough. She kissed him deeper, harder. He groaned, and his hands streaked over her shoulders, down her back, and around her sides, sending those tingles into overdrive, making her want even more. Heat. Skin. Everything. *Now.*

Ethan broke their kiss. "Tell me how to get this damn thing off of you."

"It's Lycra. Just peel."

The words were barely out of her mouth before his fingers darted into the tight fabric at her breasts. With one swift movement, the stretchy material slid down her body and hit the floor.

She gasped as cool air washed over her bare skin. But that gasp turned to a moan when she saw the heat in his eyes as his gaze swept over her and the small black thong she'd worn under the jumpsuit.

"God, you're beautiful." He dropped to his knees on the stairs and pressed his mouth against her belly. His fingers slipped under the edge of her thong, tugging it down.

*Oh yes . . .*

She held on to his shoulders, dug her fingers into firm muscles as he wrapped one arm around her waist. His broad hand swept over her hips and down to graze her inner thigh. His lips paved a path of fiery kisses down her abdomen. Sensations overwhelmed her. She closed her eyes and dropped her head back against the wall. Then his tongue was there, flicking over the sensitive nub between her legs, making her moan in pure pleasure.

The room rocked and swayed. She lifted one hand to the back of his head, trailing her fingers through his silky hair as she pressed against his mouth. That tempting tongue circled and swirled. His fingers brushed her stomach, then inched up to pinch and squeeze her nipple.

"Oh, Ethan . . . "

Shards of electricity shot from her breasts to her center. His tongue moved faster. She rocked her hips to the sweet, hypnotic rhythm of his mouth. Her heart beat fast and heavy. Blood pulsed in her veins. Her breaths grew heavy and labored with every skillful stroke of his tongue, with every tantalizing touch of his fingers, but all she could think was *more*. And then it came out of nowhere. A release so strong, it crashed into her like a sneaker wave, dragging her down and under when she least expected it.

Every muscle in her body clenched, and she cried out as her knees buckled. His arm tightened around her waist, holding her up so she didn't hit the floor while he drew out every last bit of pleasure from her body.

Tingles still ricocheted through her limbs as Ethan's lips skimmed her stomach, moving higher until they closed over one breast. His tongue darted over and around her taut nipple, bringing desire raging right back to the forefront.

"Wrap your legs around me," he said.

His husky voice made her stomach bunch with need all over again. One orgasm was not enough. Not even close to enough. "Hurry."

He lifted her off the floor and quickly moved up the rest of the steps, then turned down the hall. "Where?"

"Last door. End of the hall." Her hands fisted in his hair, tugged hard until his mouth opened, then she kissed him crazy all over again, tasting her desire and his all mixed together as one.

Boxes were stacked randomly through the hall. He continued to slide his tongue over hers while he maneuvered her around them. She rocked her hips into his erection, wanting, needing, craving every inch of him. He stumbled, and her back brushed cardboard. She lowered her hand, searching for the button on his slacks.

Her legs slipped free of his grasp. Her high heels hit the hardwood floor with a *thunk*. Without missing a beat, she dropped to her knees, yanked his pants open, and shoved his slacks and boxer briefs straight to the floor.

"Samantha . . ."

She wanted to give him exactly what he'd given her. But before she could close her hand around his steely length, he grasped her by the shoulders, pulled her up, and kissed her again.

"No," he mouthed against her when she tried to pull away. "I want to be inside you the first time."

Oh, she wanted that too. Right here, right now.

She opened to his kiss and ran her hands down his spine to clasp his firm, tight ass. Her tongue flicked wildly against his. Shifting one hand around to his front, she closed her fingers over his erection and squeezed.

"Shit." He gasped. "Not gonna make it to a bed."

He pulled her to the floor and kicked free of his shoes and slacks. Sam immediately rolled on top of him, pressing her body against all his strong, hard heat, then leaned down and kissed him again.

"Wait." His hand streaked out to the side. "Pants. Wallet."

She sat up and reached back for his pants. "Don't you dare go anywhere."

"Like I could," he breathed.

Dim light spilled from the end of the hall, washing over his firm body as she straddled his thighs and pulled the wallet from his slacks. God, he was handsome—even more so with his eyes full of longing, desire making his face flushed, his hair all tousled from her frantic hands. Warmth flowed through her whole body at the knowledge she was what he craved, what he needed.

Smiling, she opened his wallet and shook. Two condoms and a fifty-dollar bill dropped onto his chest. She picked up the fifty and fingered the bill. "You're not going to need this." She tossed the money, then reached for the condoms. "Might need more of these."

His deep laughter washed over her as she ripped open the foil packet, but it turned to a gasped breath when she rolled the latex over his arousal.

"Samantha . . . " Sliding his hand around the back of her neck, he pulled her mouth back to his and kissed her deeply. She straddled his hips. His hands shifted to her thighs. A shiver rushed down her spine as the tip of his erection brushed her slick core.

Tiny bursts of electricity sparked through her at the first touch. Bracing her hands against his chest, she lifted and lowered, just a fraction of an inch, working him over slowly, enjoying every slip and glide and tug and pull. Dropping her head back, she closed her eyes and groaned. "Oh my God, Ethan . . . "

His fingers dug into her hips. "You're killing me here, you know."

She blinked several times, smiled, and looked down at him. He was so sexy holding back, letting her take the lead. Muscles strained in his neck and face as he looked down her body to where they were just barely joined. "Then do something about it."

His gaze lifted back to hers, and his hand moved to the back of her head once more. And then he pulled her mouth down to his, and slid his wicked tongue into her mouth at the same time he thrust up into her body.

She gasped. Her heart rate quickened. He filled her in a way she hadn't anticipated, not just physically, but with a warmth she couldn't explain. Her breath grew shallow. He sat up, driving deeper inside her, and when he moved his hands to her hips and shifted her body into a rhythm with his own, all she could do was wrap her arms around his shoulders and hang on.

"God, you feel good." He kissed her jaw, trailed his lips to her ear, drew the lobe into his mouth, and sucked.

He felt good too. But she couldn't find the words. Couldn't get her lips and tongue and mouth to work together. Sensations rocked her as he nibbled at her throat, as he continued to drive into her again and again until everything but him faded to the background.

She dropped her head back. Slid her hands into his hair. Clenched around him with every thrust. He shifted to the other side of her throat, nipped at a sensitive spot. Pain arced through her. Then he suckled, running his tongue over her skin until there was nothing but pleasure. And the combination—his thick, heavy thrusts along with the sweet tantalizing suction of his mouth—pushed her right over the edge. A hot, fast punch of ecstasy made her cry out, made every muscle in her body shake with her release.

He groaned against her neck, and in an instant she was on her back, cool hardwood pressing against her spine, hard, firm male at her front.

"One more time." His mouth found hers again. He braced one hand on the floor near her head, used the other to push one knee back so he could drive deeper.

Sam groaned. Held on. Sweat slicked her skin. Mingled with his. The fire built again with every plunge, with every wild stroke of his soft tongue against hers.

"Come with me," he mouthed against her.

She didn't have a choice. His muscles flexed, and she closed around him, tighter. And when he let go, she went with him, feeling the pulse of him so deep inside, she was sure he had to be touching her heart.

They collapsed against the floor. His hot breath washed over her shoulder. Slowly, she became aware of his weight against her, pressing her into the hardwood, but it didn't hurt. If anything, it felt good. Perfect. Right.

Her fingers streaked up into his hair, twirling the ends of the silky locks as the last threads of pleasure trickled through her.

God, she could get used to this. Ethan McClane didn't just make love. He made a woman completely lose sense of time and place and purpose.

"I'm hurting you, aren't I?" he said against her shoulder.

Wrapping one leg around his so he couldn't get away, she sighed. "Not at all. I like this."

"Good, because I don't think I can move just yet."

A smile tugged at her lips. She loved that she'd wrecked him just as hard as he'd wrecked her.

Her fingertips slid over his shoulders as he relaxed into her. Sliding her foot down his calf, she held on to him, enjoying the moment. But her toe hit something rough, and she blinked several times, watching the aged ceiling dotted with water stains come into view. A giggle moved through her when she realized what she'd found.

"What's so funny?"

"You're still wearing your dress socks." She lifted her head and twisted to the side to see over his shoulder. "Very sexy, Dr. McClane."

He trailed one hand down her side, sending shivers all across her skin. "And you're still wearing those ice picks, Ms. Parker. Now that's sexy."

"I'm glad you approve. They made the outfit, don't you think?"

He pushed up on one hand and looked down her naked body. "Oh yeah."

Her skin warmed under his heated stare, and desire hummed in her veins all over again. She drew in a slow breath. "I don't know what you're doing to me, Dr. McClane, but I think I like it."

His gaze lifted to her face, and one corner of his lips tipped up in a sexy smirk. "If memory serves, I think you liked it more than once."

"I'm pretty sure I liked it three times, which, for me, is a first."

His grin widened. "Is that unusual?" Pleasure arced in his green eyes. "It's purely chauvinistic of me, but you just made my day. We'll have to think about giving you four next time."

Her heart skipped a beat. "Does that mean you're staying tonight?"

"Do you want me to stay?"

Want him to rock her world again? Absolutely. Want him to spend the entire night? That was something altogether different. Nerves rushed in, replacing all that sultry heat.

There was a reason she didn't get involved in relationships. Ethan thought it was fear holding her back, but it wasn't. It was self-preservation. If he stayed, and she had one of those horrendous nightmares, he'd see it. She risked opening herself up, baring her soul, and she didn't want to do that. But she wasn't ready for him to leave yet either.

Maybe she'd get lucky. Maybe sleeping in his arms would protect her from the dark.

Or maybe she could find a way to stay awake all night instead.

Decision warred inside her as she ran a finger along the crescent-shaped scar near his eyebrow. And though common sense urged her to be safe, desire—tonight at least—was stronger. "I want you to stay."

Relief swept over his features. "Good." His hand closed over hers, and he brought her knuckles to his lips for the softest, sweetest kiss. "Because there's nowhere else I'd rather be."

Her heart turned at the gentle touch. And she knew right then that if she didn't keep this casual, she was doomed.

"There's just one thing," she said, working like hell to steady her voice so he didn't see her fear.

His eyes twinkled as he gazed down at her. "Anything."

"Lose the socks."

A wide, wicked, ravenous grin spread across his lips. "Done."

———

A soft brush against his leg roused Ethan in the dark of night. Eyes closed, he ran his hand down Samantha's hair where she lay sleeping against him, her cheek pressed to his chest, her fingers resting over his heart.

They'd finally made it to her bed, where she'd continued to taunt and tease and drive him wild with those clever hands, with that tantalizing mouth. Every muscle in his body felt wrung out, and he knew he was going to be sore tomorrow, but he didn't care. It would be a good sore. The best kind of sore.

Her hand moved against his chest, causing Ethan's eyes to flutter open. Streetlights outside reflected off the snowy sky, casting an eerie orange light through the thin curtains.

He closed his eyes again, but his thoughts drifted to the party. To seeing Saunders and Branson and Kellogg all in the same room together. To watching Samantha stand so close to them. She didn't have a clue what the three were capable of. At some point he needed to warn her, but he didn't know how to do that without unleashing a firestorm he wasn't ready to explain.

Her leg grazed his again. Her fingertips brushed his chest. A low moan slipped from her lips.

Realizing he'd tensed and that she must have felt it, he forced his muscles to relax and brushed a hand down the length of her hair.

Her arm twitched. "No," she mumbled against him. "Don't want to look."

"Shh." Ethan smoothed his palm down her arm and kissed the top of her head. "I didn't mean to wake you. Go back to sleep."

Her knee jerked upward, and, reflexively, Ethan shifted so she didn't knee him in the groin.

"They're hurting her," she whispered. Against his skin, her pulse jumped. "Can't you hear it?"

Ethan wrapped both arms around Samantha and pulled her close, hoping to soothe her back to sleep. "There's no one here. You're okay."

"Make them stop." Her breaths quickened. She pressed against his side and shoved hard, backing away from him on the mattress.

"Samantha." Ethan eased his hold and sat up.

Her eyes flew open. Only they weren't the sexy, playful eyes he'd looked into earlier. These were wide, unfocused, and a little bit wild. In a tangle of arms and legs, she kicked out and scrambled off the bed.

"No. No. No." She darted into the shadows in the corner of the room and sank to the floor.

Ethan's heart beat hard as he stared at her trembling in the shadowy corner.

Slowly, so as not to spook her, he eased out of the bed and carefully crossed the floor. She sat slumped against the wall, her knees drawn up, her head buried in her hands, her naked body shaking in the dark.

He knelt in front of her, careful not to touch her just yet. His brothers had dealt with their fair share of nightmares in the past, and he'd witnessed some pretty bad ones growing up, but none had been like this. "Samantha, it's okay. It's just me, Ethan. You're in your room. You're completely safe."

A tiny sob echoed from the corner. And the agonizing sound was all Ethan could handle.

"I'm going to touch your arm," he said softly. "I'm not going to hurt you."

Cautiously, he reached for her. And the second he made contact, the muscles in her arm flexed and went rigid. But as he ran his thumb over her skin, she slowly relaxed.

"You're okay," he whispered. "It's just me, Ethan. You're totally safe with me. I'm not gonna let anything hurt you."

Her hand turned over and closed around his. But she didn't lift her head from her knees. "Ethan."

"Yeah. It's just me. You're okay, Samantha."

She turned into his arms in one quick movement, burying her face against his chest, and holding on for dear life. Her body trembled against his, her skin cold and slicked with sweat. He held her tighter, hoping to transfuse some of his warmth to her, hoping to alleviate her fears. Hoping to alleviate some of his too.

What was she remembering? He had a sickening feeling this wasn't just a nightmare, that it went deeper. Something terrible had backed her into that corner like a frightened animal.

Warm, wet tears fell against his bare shoulder, and she whispered, "Don't let go of me, Ethan."

His heart contracted. "I've got you. I'm not going anywhere. I'm staying right here with you."

She shifted in his arms. Lifted her head. And then her mouth was on his, drawing him into a hard, swift kiss that seemed to come out of nowhere.

"Make love with me," she whispered against his mouth. Her fingers slid into his hair, and she rose to her knees, pressing her body closer to his. "Just make me forget."

Ethan was willing to do anything to take that haunted sound out of her voice. He pulled her to her feet, then swept her off the floor and carried her back to the bed, kissing her as he moved.

He laid her out on the sheets. She immediately wrapped her arms around his shoulders and pulled him down to her, not giving him any chance to draw away. Lifting her mouth to his once more, she whispered, "Don't let go."

Ethan let her drag him with her into bliss, afraid it was already too late for him. He was pretty sure he couldn't let go even if he tried.

———

Steam swirled in the bathroom as Sam bent at the waist, ran a dry towel over her head, and shook the water from her hair. Straightened, she rubbed her wrist across the mirror to clear the condensation and gazed at her reflection.

Damp curls hung around her face and bruises marred the skin beneath her bloodshot eyes. She looked like she hadn't gotten a wink of sleep, which wasn't far off the mark. Between Ethan's delicious touch and that horrendous dream, she was pretty sure she'd slept an hour, tops.

Her eyes slid closed, and mortification rolled through her. She never should have let him stay. She'd been foolish to think she could keep the nightmares away. And now that he'd seen what a hysterical mess she was firsthand, it was no wonder he'd already left. By the time she'd dragged her eyes open, his clothes, his coat, even his car had been gone.

Mortification shifted to a blistering disappointment, one that grabbed hold of her heart and squeezed hard. This was why she didn't get involved in relationships. Because men didn't like needy, hysterical women. They wanted fun, carefree girls with zero baggage. Not ones who cried and begged and freaked out over something as stupid as a dream.

Lifting her hands to her face, she drew a deep breath and told herself it was all for the best. Life was simpler without a man. She was better off without the sexy shrink. She just hoped someday soon she could believe it.

The scent of frying bacon drifted in the air, forcing her eyes open. Sam dropped her hands and looked toward her bedroom. She didn't have bacon in the house.

Tossing her towel on the bed, she pulled on jeans and a long-sleeved T-shirt. Tiptoeing across the upper floor, she reached the banister, moved halfway down the stairs, and peeked through the railing into the kitchen. Ethan stood at the stove, dressed in the wrinkled slacks and dress shirt he'd worn last night, flipping bacon in a pan with a fork.

Her heart rate ticked up. He hadn't left. Not for good, at least. He'd gone to the store and come back.

She bit her lip, thought about going back up to her room and hiding, but quickly decided against it. She needed to face this head-on, no matter the outcome.

Ethan looked up and smiled as she rounded the corner into the kitchen. "Good morning, sleepy."

"Hi." Nerves vibrated, and she clasped her hands behind her back so he couldn't see. His dress shirt was open at the collar, his sleeves rolled up to his forearms. A shiver of awareness rushed over her at the memory of those strong hands sliding along her body, but she beat it back so she wouldn't make a fool of herself yet again.

"Hungry?"

Her gaze skipped to the eggs that were almost done frying, the bacon he was lifting out of the pan, and the toast he'd already buttered. Oh man, he'd come back because he felt sorry for her. "Yeah. I guess."

"Coffee's ready. Why don't you pour yourself a cup while I plate this all up?"

*And* he'd made coffee. He *really* felt sorry for her.

Stepping quickly past him, she moved for the counter on the opposite side of the kitchen, grasped a cup from the cupboard, and opened the fridge for the creamer. Then stilled when she peered inside.

Fruit, cheese, several containers of yogurt, and a gallon of milk graced the top shelf. Below sat a couple of steaks and beside them, bags of fresh veggies.

Sam's eyes widened. "You didn't just run to the corner market."

"You need to eat better, Samantha. Coffee, wine, and a container of something that looks like one of your science experiments is not a healthy diet."

"It was Chinese. From last week."

"Honey, the Chinese wouldn't eat that. Trust me."

Warmth circled Sam's heart, and she smiled the same way she always smiled when Ethan teased her. And, in a rush, all those nerves she'd been trying to contain relaxed.

Moving to the counter, she poured cream into her cup, then replaced it in the fridge. By the time she stirred her coffee and turned, Ethan was already filling two plates with the breakfast he'd made.

"Sit," he said.

Sam slid into a chair at her mother's old dinged-up table and tucked one leg under her while Ethan set a plate of food in front of her.

"Better than week-old Chinese." Sitting in the chair next to hers, he lifted his fork and nodded at her plate. "Dive in."

Sam reached for her fork as he started eating, but a lump formed in her throat before she could take a bite, and her gaze drifted toward his strong, square jaw and his sexy tousled dark hair.

God, she liked this. Liked spending the night curled in his arms, liked finding him in her kitchen at dawn. She liked his easy, gentle nature, liked the way he made her feel safe, liked everything about him. But most of all she liked that he had this innate way of calming her. She could be ready to bounce off the walls, but one smile from him settled her in a way nothing ever had before.

He glanced up. "You're not hungry? After last night you *have* to be hungry."

Sam's cheeks heated with the memory of his body moving over hers, *inside* hers, but she bit her lip, still unable to eat.

After several seconds of silence, she couldn't take it anymore. "Why are you still here, Ethan? Any sane person would have cut and run at first light."

He reached for his coffee. "I have to tell you a secret, Samantha."

Her eyes widened, and she held her breath while he took a sip, almost afraid to hear what he had to say.

He set his mug back down on the table. "I'm not entirely sane. Every shrink I've ever met—and I say this from a clinical perspective—teeters on the tightrope of sanity. We're just really good at hiding it."

The breath she'd been holding whooshed out, and she closed her eyes and smiled because he'd just done it again. Eased every bit of fear and anxiety inside her with one look.

"I'm telling the truth. Ask any shrink."

Sam laughed. "You said you weren't a shrink. You corrected me with the term 'therapist.'"

"I'm a professional. I'm able to use whatever label suits me."

Still smiling, Sam shook her head, but the smile turned to a frown when she realized he was making this too easy. She opened her eyes and looked up. "You aren't even going to ask, are you?"

"No. I figured if you wanted to talk about it, you would. And for the record"—he laid his hand over hers on the table—"I stayed because I wanted to stay. Because last night was amazing. A thousand times more amazing than I'd imagined. One bad dream doesn't change that."

There he went. Making her feel normal when she was anything but.

"That wasn't just a bad dream, and you know it. I don't have nightmares like that all the time, but when I do, they can be bad. I should have warned you. I thought with you here I wouldn't . . . " She shook her head because she knew she was rambling. "I should have known better."

His finger moved softly over the back of her hand. "When was the last time you had one?"

God, she liked his touch. More than she probably should. "I hadn't had one for a long time. But then after I moved home, they picked up again."

"Do you remember them?"

She nodded.

"Always the same, or different?"

"The same. Every time."

It was stupid. Talking out her nightmares with a shrink had always embarrassed and humiliated her, which was part of the reason she'd thrown in the towel and decided never to see one again. But with Ethan she didn't feel either of those things. She felt safe. She always felt safe with him.

"It's always the same. I'm on the outside looking in. Someone's being hurt, and I can't do anything about it. I can't even bring myself to look through the window to see what's going on. I can just hear it." She frowned. "Dr. Adams, my last therapist, said it had to do with feelings of inadequacy from childhood. Not being able to control my environment."

"Like what?"

"Like my parents' divorce."

Ethan eased back in his chair, his hand still covering hers on the table. "When was that?"

"Seventeen years ago, I guess. When I was eleven."

He didn't say anything, but she saw the skepticism in his eyes. "You don't think so, do you?"

"I don't know. Did your parents have a rocky marriage? Any abuse you know of?"

Her parents had argued routinely. Sam remembered numerous nights when she'd climbed into bed with Seth so he could tell her a story to distract her from their yelling. But things hadn't truly crumbled until her brother had died.

Pain clawed at her chest. The same pain she always felt when she thought about Seth. The same pain she had trouble talking to anyone about, even now.

"No abuse." Reaching for her coffee so he couldn't see, she lifted it to her lips and sipped. "My father didn't even like to set mousetraps. Couldn't stomach a living thing suffering. But my parents were never truly happy together, if that's what you're asking."

"I don't specialize in dream interpretation, but feelings of loss, being unable to control your surroundings, generally those types of dreams aren't violent. And the fact you're on the outside looking in. That's a completely different issue."

She nodded. She hadn't expected him to cure her. Hadn't expected him to even be here, but he was. For whatever reason, he wanted to help her, and maybe it was time she let someone try. God knew, dealing with it all on her own wasn't working.

She bit her lip. Contemplated. Finally decided to ask. "So what do you think?"

"I'm not sure, yet. I can do some research on it if you want."

"You don't have to do that."

His hand tightened around hers. "I want to. For you. It's your call, though. You don't want me to touch it, and I won't."

Her heart thumped wildly as he gazed at her. She'd never told anyone as much as she'd just told him, and to her utter amazement, he wasn't looking at her as if she were completely nuts. He was looking at her like he still wanted her.

And she wanted to kiss him. Wanted to drag him up on this table and show him with her hands and mouth and body just what that meant to her. But before she could move, he let go of her hand and reached for his fork.

"You need to eat, Samantha. And then I need to think about heading home."

Home. He was heading home. Leaving, not staying and making love with her like she wanted.

Disappointment came back swift and consuming, pressing like a heavy weight against her chest. "Oh. Sure."

He scooped up a bite of eggs. "I have some paperwork I've been putting off but need to finish."

Sam gazed down, her appetite long gone, and tried not to let her disappointment show. "Yeah. I have some term papers I should probably get busy grading."

"Good. Then I won't feel so guilty when I have to work. After you eat, go get your stuff together and pack a bag."

Her gaze lifted. "What?"

He glanced over, then his expression softened and he lowered his fork and reached for her hand once more. "You didn't think I wanted to go back to my empty house alone after last night, did you? I'd stay if I had fresh clothes and my case files. Since I don't, and there's already four inches of snow outside, I think it'd just be easier if you came with me. We can spend the weekend at my house. I have to be back in town on Monday, so I'll drive you back before classes start."

Sam looked to the windows and the blanket of white covering everything outside. She'd been so wrapped up in her thoughts and neuroses, she hadn't even noticed the snow. "Oh. Um. I have Grimly."

"He can come too."

At the sound of his name, Grimly groaned, pushed up to his feet, and wandered over from his spot by the heater. He plopped his big butt down between them on the hardwood floor and wagged his tale with that I'm-so-dumb-I'm-cute look on his face.

Ethan nodded down at the rangy beast. "See. He and I are already good friends."

Tendrils of excitement and relief pumped through her.

"Don't say no, Samantha." Ethan tugged gently on her hand, met her over her eggs, and brushed a gentle kiss against her mouth. "I've got a big fireplace, plenty of food in my fridge, and a nice, soft bed. I'll make it worth your while. I promise."

Her gaze skipped over his handsome face. Oh, she could so easily get lost in this man. She didn't want to be alone after last night either, but she was still afraid of what would happen if she went with him. "Ethan, I have nightmares wherever I go."

"In case you didn't notice, I don't scare easy. Besides"—he brushed his thumb over her lips, sending shards of heat straight to her belly— "I kinda liked the way you grabbed on to me last night. Made me feel special."

"You are."

His eyes darkened, and he leaned in and kissed her again. Only this kiss wasn't brief and chaste. This one was deep and filled with so much passion she absolutely melted.

She was taking a big risk here, opening herself to him. More than likely, she'd end up hurt in the end. But when he drew back and smiled, even that wasn't enough to stop her.

"What do you say?" he asked.

She nodded.

"Good." He let go of her and went back to his meal with a wink. "Eat up, beautiful. You're gonna need all your energy for this weekend."

# CHAPTER TEN

Ethan pulled to a stop in front of the run-down trailer on Monday morning. Sunlight glinted off the metal exterior, while tall weeds overpowered a dead lawn that looked as if it hadn't been mowed in years. A few patches of snow still lingered from Friday night's storm, but for the most part, it had melted in the weekend's afternoon sun.

He tossed his sunglasses on the front seat, then climbed out and tucked his keys into the front pocket of his slacks. His body was loose and relaxed from an incredible weekend with Samantha. A smile twisted his mouth as he headed across the cracked cement path toward the front door, remembering the snowball fight they'd gotten into when they'd taken a walk along the river behind his house, then the way they'd warmed each other on the carpet in front of his fireplace. But that smile faded when he thought about the fact that he wouldn't be seeing her tonight.

He'd dropped her off at work this morning, then spoken to the school counselor about Thomas before heading to the Adler home. Since he had appointments in Portland that afternoon, he was headed back to the city after this meeting, which meant he wouldn't be around to pop in and tempt her. He'd tried to talk her into driving to his house for dinner tonight after work, but she'd declined, saying she had papers to grade and work she needed to do around her house. And even though his body was still vibrating from that incredible weekend, a tiny place inside him was worried.

There was something she wasn't telling him. He'd sensed it when they'd had breakfast Saturday morning at her house. Something with her family. Every time he brought up her parents, she changed the subject, as if talking about them was too painful.

Ethan knew all about the terrible things some parents did to their kids. He'd lived it until the age of seven when his alcoholic father had finally died. He'd seen the scars on his brother Rusty's skin. He heard about it every day in his job. But he had a strong hunch that whatever Samantha was keeping secret had nothing to do with abuse. It was something else. Something he couldn't quite piece together. Something that kept her from forming attachments to other people. And that, he worried, was a problem. *That* might eventually make her pull away.

Thoughts of her rolled through his mind as he moved up the three rickety steps toward the dirty metal door. A rotten pumpkin occupied the second step, a dead potted plant the third. Ethan took in the stains across the exterior of the trailer and the dingy curtains in the window. Memories of his own childhood flickered in the back of his mind, pulling his thoughts away from Samantha. His back tightened as he lifted a hand and knocked.

Footsteps echoed just before the door opened. A sixtyish woman with curlers in her hair, wearing a dull-yellow housecoat, peeked one eye around the edge of the door. "I know you?"

"I'm Dr. McClane, Mrs. Adler. We spoke on the phone briefly last week. I was hoping you had a few minutes to talk about Thomas."

The older woman frowned in an obvious sign of disgust. When she pulled the door open farther, he saw the cigarette smoldering in her right hand.

Great. Just what he needed. He hadn't had a nicotine craving all weekend, and in a minute he'd be enveloped by smoke that would cling to him for the rest of the day.

"Don't know why you want to talk to me." She turned, leaving the door open. A black cat mewed and slinked between the woman's bare ankles. "Come in 'fore you let in all that cold air."

Ethan pulled the screen open and stepped into the small room. Stale cigarette smoke filled his lungs. A ratty green couch was pushed up against one wall. A recliner covered by a brown-and-orange afghan took up an adjacent space. Dark wood paneling void of any kind of pictures graced the walls, while dull-brown carpet stretched across the floor. There were no personal mementos, no photographs in frames, nothing that made the house a home. And absolutely no sign a teenage boy lived here.

Thomas's grandmother wandered toward the kitchen and pulled a mug from a cabinet above her head. "You want coffee?" she asked above the sound of the excited applause echoing from the TV as a contestant spun the wheel on *The Price is Right*.

"Sure." Ethan didn't really want any, but he figured it had to be better than inhaling her secondhand smoke.

She filled a mug, didn't bother to ask if he wanted cream or sugar, handed it to him, and sank into the frayed recliner with a harrumph. Picking up the remote, she flipped it to "Mute," then said, "Go on and say what you came to say. I got a schedule, you know."

Oh yeah. Definitely a happy home. Just like the one Ethan remembered from his childhood.

Ethan set his cup on a torn copy of *Reader's Digest* on the scarred coffee table and sat on the end of the couch. "How are things with Thomas here at home?"

Deep lines creased the skin around Mrs. Adler's mouth as she puffed on her cigarette. "Sleeps in that room there." She pointed down the hall with the cigarette in her hand, smoke billowing around her. "Grumbles at me in the mornin's. Always got his nose stuck in some book he shouldn't be reading. Doesn't talk much. Weird child, that boy. Then again, I always thought he was a strange one, even when he was little."

There definitely wasn't a lot of love radiating from the older woman's raspy voice. In fact, she sounded downright put out that she'd had to take Thomas in. "Did he talk to you about what happened at the school?"

"The vandalism thing? Yeah, he done tol' me. Principal called too." She lifted the cup and sipped. "'Spect I'll be hearing from more than just them before long though. That boy can't stay outta trouble. Not sure why they thought the country'd be good for him. You ask me, the country's just gonna make him bored. And bored's gonna make him do somethin' way worse than just a little vandalism."

Ethan shifted, growing more uncomfortable by the second. "About what happened at the school. You weren't present when Thomas was questioned regarding the break-in."

"No. And I don't plan to be if it happens again, neither. He gets himself into trouble, he can just get himself out of it. I give him a roof and food. I'm doing my Godly duties, but don't go 'specting me to do any more. Evil's in that boy." She narrowed her eyes and pointed at Ethan, the cigarette smoldering between her fingers. "Created in sin, he was. His mother was a she-devil, pure and simple."

Oh hell. Social services had dumped Thomas here? Yeah, they'd done a great job.

He tried to remain calm and professional, but inside all he wanted to do was shake the old woman. "Are you speaking about your daughter?"

She shot him a disgusted glare before taking another deep drink of her coffee. "No way that woman was my daughter, thank the good Lord." She puffed on her cigarette again. "She was my sister's brat. Girl done got herself knocked up, then dropped that baby like a dirty habit and hightailed it out of here faster than a hooker runs from the police. Always was like her to be irresponsible and inconvenient. I knew that baby was cursed—I could see it in his eyes—but my daughter, Maria, thought she could try to save him."

Mrs. Adler shook her head and blew out a long breath of smoke that swirled through the room. "Boy done ruined her, that's what he did. Got into all that trouble up in the city until my girl was so full of stress over what he was up to, she wasn't paying attention and got in that car accident." Her voice dropped, and her eyes filled with a vacant look as she focused on something across the room. "She done died because of that boy, and he could care less. Has no conscience. No remorse. He killed her, same as if he'd shot her with a gun."

Ethan leaned forward to rest his elbows on his knees, clasping his hands so he didn't reach over and wring the older woman's neck. No wonder Thomas hadn't wanted to come back here. And no wonder he had a perpetual chip on his shoulder. "And you're his last known relative."

She drew a puff from the cigarette. "Only one will admit to it. Don't know where his mother is. Probably dead." She stabbed the cigarette into a full ashtray on the dinged-up table to her left. "Good riddance. I done the Christian thing and did what the state asked me to do. I took the boy in. I'll give him a place to live so long as he stays out of trouble. But next year when he turns eighteen, he's gone. He won't infect me with his evil."

Her eyes narrowed on Ethan, and she wagged her finger in front of him like a parent scolds a child. "You'd be better off to request another shrink for this boy, Dr. McClane. You mark my words, only bad things happen around him. He can't help it. It's inside him. His life started in sin, and it'll end that way. God will protect me. But what about you?"

"I think I'm pretty safe, Mrs. Adler. Thomas is just a regular kid, one who's had a little more trouble than others, but not, as you put it, evil."

"You think, but you don't know." Her gaze narrowed to hard, sharp points of darkness. Ones that made Ethan wonder just what she'd seen.

And knew. Or was holding back. "In the back of your mind, though, you just ain't sure. If I were you, Dr. McClane, I'd run while I still can. I'd run long and fast, and I'd never look back."

———

Sam walked around her classroom Monday afternoon, picking up pencils and scraps of paper students had left behind. A folded scrap on the floor caught her attention, and she reached down for it. Pink and purple cursive jumped out at her when she opened the note.

*Manny Burton is such a hottie.*

*No, way! Check out the ass on Greg Warsaw.*

Each "i" was dotted with a heart, the penmanship flowing and artsy like only teenage girls can do. Sam recognized the handwriting, done by two girls who sat in the back of her Chem I class. They obviously hadn't been paying attention to the day's lecture on the specific gravity of elements.

She couldn't really blame them, though. She hadn't been too interested in the lecture herself, and she'd been giving it. Her mind had kept running back to her weekend with Ethan—playing in the snow, cuddling in front of the fire, making love in that big bed of his. Butterflies twirled through her stomach all over again just at the thought, but she went back to picking up garbage from the floor and reminded herself not to read too much into their weekend.

Yes, they'd had a fabulous time together, and, yes, she wanted to see him again. But reality had greeted her as soon as she'd awoken this morning. Once her mother's house sold, she was leaving Hidden Falls and going back to California. Back to San Francisco and her previous life. Her company wanted her back. They'd told her she had a job whenever she was ready to return. One incredible weekend with Ethan did not make a relationship. And even if it did, there was no way she'd be able to keep that relationship up when they were hundreds of miles apart.

Could she?

A chilly breeze blew through her open classroom door, distracting her from her thoughts. Realizing one of the kids must have propped the exterior door at the end of the hall open on his way out, she turned out of her room and headed down the corridor, dropping the note and her stupid fantasies in the trash can.

Patches of snow still lingered on the grass outside her room, but the majority had already melted. A few dry leaves skittered across the yard. She pulled the heavy door closed and brushed her hands together as she gazed out at the football field and the setting sun.

But what if they could somehow keep things going? She'd love to take Ethan to Fisherman's Wharf. Could just picture him riding a cable car. And based on the sports memorabilia she'd seen in his home office, she knew he'd probably love to catch a game with her at AT&T Park.

"Nice view."

Sam jumped and whirled toward the deep voice. Kenny leaned against the end of a broom, mere feet from her.

"Kenny." Sam pressed a hand to her chest. "I didn't hear you. You scared me."

A chill smile split his face, one that didn't reach his dull gray eyes. "Wouldn't want to do that, now, would I?"

She glanced past Kenny and down the empty hallway. Every other light was illuminated, the eerie red glow of sunset shining through the windows in the door behind her. Most of the staff had already left for the day. Which meant they were alone.

Unease skittered along her nerve endings. "Someone left the door open. I was just closing it."

He nodded, his gaze running down the length of her body like an intimate caress. But instead of stepping aside so she could pass, he moved a half step toward her. "Wouldn't want anyone to escape, now would we? That could be bad. That could be very bad."

Sam's instincts went on high alert. The look in his eyes, the cool tone of his voice, the way his gaze kept skipping back to her breasts . . . it all made her adrenaline shoot sky high. "Look, Kenny, I need to get back to my room."

"Why the rush?" He took another step closer, forcing her back into the corner. Something dark churned in his eyes. Something dangerous. He braced one hand on the wall beside her head. "You've got no one to meet there."

Sam's skin grew hot, and panic clawed at her throat. "Please step back, Kenny. I don't—"

"Miss Parker?"

Kenny's jaw hardened, and he stared at Sam a hard, scathing moment before dropping his hand. But he didn't move back.

"Thomas." Sam tried to keep her voice from quaking, but it didn't work. She darted around Kenny and stepped quickly away. "Are you ready to redo that lab?"

"Yeah, I'm ready." The kid had no clue what she was talking about, but he didn't miss a beat. And his narrowed gaze locked solidly on Kenny told her he knew exactly what had been going on.

A tense moment passed. Finally, Kenny picked up his broom. After another hard glare at Sam, he shoved his shoulder hard into the teen's shoulder, then swept his broom over the floor as he whistled and disappeared down the hallway.

Thomas turned and stared after the janitor. Sam reached for the boy's arm. "Let him go."

"I don't like what that guy was doing."

Sam's heart warmed. At seventeen, Thomas had probably reached his full height at just over six feet, but he was lean and gangly and had yet to grow into his stature. And even though he had three inches on

Kenny, she was sure he wouldn't stand a chance against the older man. But he was still standing up for her. "I'm fine. Nothing happened."

He frowned as if he didn't believe her.

Sam moved back toward her room. "So what are you doing here? Shouldn't you already be home by now?"

"I was down at the public library." He followed her into her classroom and hefted his backpack onto one of the black-topped lab tables. "Was hoping maybe you could look over my research project before I go any further." He pulled a handwritten paper from his backpack and handed it to her. "I, ah, would have done more, but I wasn't sure if it was good enough. I stopped by your house over the weekend to see if you could look over it, but you weren't there."

An odd tingle slid down Sam's spine over the fact that Thomas knew where she lived and had tried to visit her at home, but since he'd just saved her from an uncomfortable situation with Kenny, she kept the comment to herself.

She scanned the page. "Reverse osmosis for water purification. Hefty project."

He shrugged and looked down at his feet, kicking something on the floor with the tip of his dirty sneaker. "Yeah, it's not that hard."

No, for him it wouldn't be. She read quickly through his proposal, then handed the paper back to him. "Looks good. But then you already know that."

His gaze lifted.

"Don't look so surprised, Thomas. You could probably teach my chem class if you wanted, and we both know it. If you actually turned in your homework, you'd be getting an A."

"Homework's boring."

Sam smirked. "Yeah, it is. But it's important. You can't just skate through life without doing the work." When he didn't respond, she tipped her head to the side and studied him. Light-brown hair fell across his forehead, hiding his eyes, and for one split second he reminded her of Seth.

She blinked and refocused. There was obviously more on his mind than a science project he could probably do in his sleep. "What's up, Thomas?"

He was quiet for a minute, his shoe tracing a line along the floor. "You grew up here, right?"

"Yes."

"Did you know Chief Branson when you were in school?"

Interesting question. "Yes. Though he's a few years older than I am."

"So you were, like, friends?"

She couldn't quite gauge where this was going. "Yeah. You could say that." Sam's eyes narrowed. She liked Will, always had, but she hadn't missed the way he stiffened whenever Thomas's name was mentioned. Or vice versa. "Is Chief Branson giving you a hard time, Thomas?"

Thomas kicked at another spot on the floor. "Did you know that teacher everyone's talking about?"

So that's what this was about. Sandra Hollings had been the talk of the town ever since they'd found those remains. "Not really. I was in elementary school when she disappeared."

"But Chief Branson knew her, right? 'Cause he's older than you? He would have been in high school then."

"I suppose. I haven't really thought about that."

He reached for his paper and backpack. "I need to get home. Thanks for the help, Ms. Parker."

Thomas swept out of the room, leaving Sam to look after him and wonder what the heck that had been about. His discombobulated questions swirled in her mind, but before she could find a connection, she heard Kenny's whistling from the end of the empty corridor.

She'd lingered too long. Grabbing her purse and coat, Sam headed for the parking lot. Briefly, she thought about taking Ethan up on his offer of dinner, then dismissed it. As much as she loved spending time with him, he was getting too close. Her run-in with Kenny in the hall had reaffirmed one thing to her: she was not staying in this town. The sooner she sold her mother's house and got the hell out of Hidden Falls, the better. And as wonderful as it was to fantasize about spending time with Ethan in San Francisco, she knew long-distance relationships never worked.

Which meant he was a distraction she just couldn't risk right now. No matter how much she wanted to be with him.

———

Kenny watched as Sam rushed across the pavement, looking down at the keys in her hand. She bent at the waist to slip her key in the lock, giving him a nice view of that fine ass. Straightening, she pulled the Mazda's door open, and slid inside the vehicle. Seconds later, her engine roared to life, and she zipped out of the staff parking lot then disappeared around the bend.

"Quit ogling."

Kenny cut a glare at Margaret, sitting at her desk, scribbling a note. Man, he'd like to knock her on her ass. She'd been treating him like shit his whole life—because she had money and he didn't, because she'd gone to college and he hadn't, because she took pleasure in making people feel like crap.

He hated her, hated everything about her, from her bleached-blonde hair to her expensive designer shoes. He'd love to see Jeff beat the crap out of her, but he knew that wouldn't happen. The pansy-assed wimp had only married her to keep her from talking. The guy could barely stand her himself.

Someone needed to take control of fussy Margaret before it was too late. Even Kenny could see she was a time bomb waiting to go off.

Margaret leaned back in her chair and tapped a pen against the edge of the desk. "I want her out of here."

He didn't need to ask which "her" she was referring to. He went back to sweeping the classroom floor. "Tell me something I don't already know."

"You and I both know she's gonna fuck this up for us. It's up to you and me to make sure she doesn't talk."

"Who's she gonna talk to, Margaret?"

"Anyone. Jesus, Kenny, she's screwing that damn shrink. God only knows what he's gotten out of her at this point."

Kenny paused his sweeping. "What?"

"God, you're dense." Margaret rolled her eyes. "Use your brain. She showed up with him at my house Friday night. His car was parked outside her place all night long."

Kenny's muscles flexed at both her blasé revelation and her verbal put-down. He could just picture himself popping her right across the jaw, sending her sailing back into the desks in her room. He'd love to see the look of shock on her face. Just once.

"How do you know that?" he asked.

"I have my sources. It doesn't negate the fact she's a weak link we need to eliminate."

When he didn't say anything, her facial expression softened. She pushed out of her chair, rounded her desk, and stopped right in front of him. "Kenny, we need to stick together on this."

She rested her fingertips on his forearm, then moved them ever so slightly against his skin. He knew her well enough to know she was switching tactics. He'd watched her do it with other men too many times to count. But he didn't pull back. Yes, she disgusted him, but he wanted to see just how far she was willing to go.

"If we get rid of Sam," she went on, "things can go back to normal around here. She knows things, Kenny. Things she's either not saying or hasn't quite remembered yet. But she will. All this talk about Hollings is only going to make her remember."

Sam was a concern of his too, although he'd be damned if he'd admit that much to Margaret. She thought she was so smart, using him to do her dirty work. She didn't have a clue.

Her fingertips slinked up his arm and down across his chest. She tipped her eyes up seductively. "You know you have the most to lose here. Who do you think's going to take the fall when it all comes crashing down?"

"That won't happen."

"I can make sure it doesn't." She stepped closer, until her breasts brushed against his chest. And even though she churned his stomach, he grew hard. "All you have to do is help me with this one small problem."

She lifted to her toes, pressed her body against his, and whispered, "If you help me, I'll make sure no one blames you."

The tip of her tongue grazed his ear, and in the back of his mind, he knew she wasn't interested in him but that she was going to fuck him senseless just to get her way.

That was all the reason he needed.

He let go of the broom. It clanged against the tile floor. Grasping Margaret at the shoulders, he pushed her to her knees. Disgust rushed across her features, but she didn't pull away. And that only made him harder.

He reached for his belt buckle. "Open that mouth and talk me into it."

# CHAPTER ELEVEN

Sam checked her watch as she made her way down the hallway the next day. With her prep period and the lunch break combined, she had roughly an hour and a half before she was due back in class.

She peeked into the office and frowned. Annette wasn't at her desk. Rounding the corner, she knocked on David's office door. He grumbled a terse "Come in."

"Hey, David. I need to run home. I left a few supplies there I need for this afternoon's labs."

"Great. Wonderful." He reached for the phone. "All I need is another teacher out of the building. Just promise you'll be back before fifth period."

When he rubbed a hand across his forehead in a sign of obvious frustration, Sam stepped forward. "What's wrong?"

"Margaret didn't show up today."

She glanced at her watch. "Is she sick?"

"Who the hell knows? Annette just left to drive out to her house and find out what's going on. It's not like Margaret to be late and not tell anyone."

"I'm sure she's fine. Maybe she just went back to bed and forgot to call in."

"She doesn't have any more sick days left. She's already used up hers and half of everyone else's." He waved his hand. "Go on. Just be back in time for your next class."

"Thanks." Sam paused by the door. "Is Thomas Adler absent today? He wasn't in third period."

"We're working on that one too."

Sam nodded and backed out of the office, a strange sense of unease swirling in her stomach. She pulled the keys out of her jacket pocket. Cool air surrounded her when she moved down the front steps of the building and headed for her car.

Margaret's absence didn't really bother her. She couldn't care less what Margaret did. Thomas, on the other hand, was another story.

She drove out of the school parking lot and headed across town, hoping Thomas hadn't gotten himself into some sort of trouble. That strange conversation after school yesterday aside, his grades were finally starting to come up, and he seemed to be making friends. If he was cutting classes with Manny Burton, though, he'd only get himself into a world of hurt.

Her house was quiet as she pulled into the gravel drive. Grimly was likely snoring on her bed. After jogging up the porch steps, she slipped her key into the lock and turned. A soft click echoed, and she pushed her shoulder against the old door.

It didn't budge.

Confused, Sam pulled the key out of the lock, checked to make sure she was using the right one, then slipped it back in the catch. Again, it didn't move.

She rose up on her toes and looked through the four rectangular windows at the top of the door. Couldn't see anything besides the hardwood floor running down the hall and the stairs that led up to the second floor.

"Dammit." She didn't have time for this. She needed to get her stuff and get back to school. She still had to clean up supplies from third period, then get her labs set up for the classes after lunch.

Muttering curses, she jogged back down the front steps and picked her way around the house. She used her key on the back kitchen door and turned the handle. The door gave with a pop.

Sam was immediately inundated with a rancid scent and winced. Something was definitely rotting in that refrigerator. Probably one of those healthy things Ethan had bought and left for her to eat.

*Do not think about Ethan. You don't have time for that now.* She definitely didn't. But she couldn't help remembering the disappointment in his voice when she'd told him she wouldn't be able to meet for dinner yet again tonight.

Backing away was the best idea all around, right? He had a life in Portland, family he was close to. He wasn't going to uproot and move to San Francisco for her. She was saving them both from heartache and angst by calling things quits now.

Right?

*So why don't you tell him that's what you're doing? Why are you leading him on?*

She wasn't leading him on. Was she?

"Grimly? Where are you?" Irritated with herself and stressed for time, she moved through the kitchen. Where was that darn dog? Why wasn't he barking? He usually went haywire when anyone came to the door, her included.

Her shoes clicked along the hardwood floor of the hall as she moved from the back of the house to the front. As she approached the entry, she finally spotted Grimly lying against the front door. There was the reason she hadn't been able to get in. His big-ass body had been blocking her entrance.

"Get up, lazy. I don't have time for your games right now." She glanced through the archway into the living room and spotted the box of supplies she'd left sitting on the coffee table this morning. "There it is."

She picked up the box and walked back into the entry, running through lists of materials she still needed to grab at school. Grimly continued to sleep. Frowning, she stopped beside him, then nudged his side with the tip of her shoe. "I said get up, you lazy dog."

Not a single muscle moved.

Several heartbeats passed before Sam realized something wasn't right.

"Grimly?"

The box fell from her fingers, landing with a thud against the hardwood floor. She dropped to her knees and reached for his furry head.

"Grimly?" His eyes were closed, his breathing slow and shallow. She pried one eye open to find dilated pupils. "Oh my God."

Sam's heart raced as she scrambled for the phone on her mother's antique desk at the base of the stairs. Grasping the phone book from the top drawer, she frantically searched for her vet's number.

Her fingers shook as she dialed. She pressed the phone to her ear and fought back tears as it rang. Running one hand over her forehead, she paced the hall and watched Grimly while she waited for the receptionist to pick up. Just after the fifth ring, a voice chimed through the line. "Hidden Falls Animal Hospital."

"Hi. Um, there's something wrong with my dog. He collapsed and isn't moving. He's a golden. Four years old. I'm not sure what to do."

"Is he breathing?"

"Yes. But not well. He just had a checkup two weeks ago and was fine. And he was acting normal before I left for work a few hours ago."

"Okay, what's your address so I can find him in the system?"

Sam turned a slow circle. *Please be okay, Grimly. Please be okay . . .* "2753 Inglebrook La—"

The words choked in her throat as she looked through the archway to the dining room, and she gasped as the phone fell from her fingers.

Because she wasn't alone. Margaret Wilcox's limp body lay on her dining room table, eyes open, gaze staring blankly toward the ceiling.

———

Sam dug her fingers into the cracked plastic bench in the veterinarian's empty waiting room while the unmistakable scents of animal hair and dog saliva wafted on the air. Closing her eyes, she blew out a shaky breath in an attempt to settle her rolling stomach, but just as they did every time she closed her eyes, images of Margaret lying still and lifeless in her dining room flashed in her mind.

She rose quickly before the sickness could claim her and paced the small room. The bell over the door jangled just as she reached the far side, and she turned.

"Hey." Will slipped the cap from his head and shot her a weak smile. "How are you holding up?"

"Okay." If there was one person who would understand any of this, it was Will. He'd found his mother's body all those years before. He knew what Sam was going through.

Her gaze darted around the sparse room, searching for anything normal to focus on. A dwindling ficus sat in the corner, fallen leaves littered around its base. Magazines lay scattered across a beat-up coffee table. A cat slinked behind a chair, his pathetic mew echoing through the room.

"Any news on Grimly?"

"Yeah." Sam brushed stray hairs back from her face. "They think he was drugged. Maybe poisoned." Tears welled again, and she closed her eyes quickly. Dammit. She was stressing out about her dog when she should be crying for Margaret. "There's some kind of internal bleeding . . . "

"Come here." Will's arms enveloped her, pulling her tight against his chest. She didn't fight the embrace. Didn't have the strength. Didn't want to. His familiar scent washed over her, reminding her of her youth, of her brother, of a time that was so much easier.

"You're okay," he whispered, gently rubbing his hand down her back.

She wasn't sure she was, though. And she didn't know what to do to feel okay.

"I'm fine, Will." Pushing out of his arms, she brushed the hair back from her face again. "What can you tell me?"

"Not a lot, I'm afraid. Investigative team is working the scene now. They'll probably be at it through the night. You can't stay there tonight, Sam."

She nodded and looked down at the floor. Wasn't sure how she'd ever be able to set foot in that room again.

"I don't think she died at your house. Crime scene's too clean. I'm not sure if that helps or not."

Died. Dead. Murdered. She couldn't believe he was talking about Margaret. Her stomach pitched again. "Am I a suspect?"

"You're a person of interest." When her gaze lifted, he added, "But I'm pretty sure you'll be cleared of that soon. Coroner estimated time of death to be between 5:00 and 8:00 p.m. Several people corroborated your story that you were at the gym on a treadmill, then getting dinner at McNulty's Pub during that time."

She had been. Working out in a stupid attempt to run away from her incessant thoughts about Ethan and what she was going to do about him. Them. This crazy relationship. Then getting dinner and working on her laptop at the pub because she didn't want to go home alone.

"We'll know more once we get the autopsy report back and finish combing your house." Will shifted his feet. "I need you to think back to any conversations you had recently with Maggie. Any people you can recall who might have had issues with the both of you."

Sam's mind spun with a new host of questions. If Margaret hadn't been killed in her house, then that meant that someone had broken in and placed her there on purpose. "You think this is a warning?"

"Possibly."

A warning for what? Who could hate her so much they'd try to frame her for murder?

Sam dropped her face in her hands and tried like hell not to lose it in front of Will.

Gripping her shoulders, Will kneaded the tight muscles. "I don't want you to worry. Hidden Falls is a small town. We'll get to the bottom of this. You and I both know Maggie wasn't the most well-liked person around."

She lowered her hands. "But you think whomever did this might have it in for me too."

"I didn't say that. But . . . maybe . . . "

"Maybe what?"

Will sighed. "Maybe you should think about going back to California now rather than later. You've had nothing but trouble here lately. The vandalism at your house, the break-in at the school, finding that body up in the woods, and now this? I'm not trying to scare you, but one of those is a lot for anyone to handle. All four? It's too much. As much as I like having you back in town, I want you safe more than I want you close. Someone—for some reason—has his sights set on you. The best thing you can do is distance yourself from this place and everyone in it, especially the new people in town, until we figure out what's going on."

*The new people in town.* He didn't say Ethan's name, but she knew Will was thinking about him. A whisper of panic rushed down Sam's spine. Ethan was definitely new in town, and strange things had been happening since he'd shown up. And she couldn't deny that she'd picked up odd vibes from him on more than one occasion, especially when he looked at certain people in Hidden Falls as if he knew them. But he couldn't be linked to any of this, could he?

No. She swallowed hard. He couldn't be. The way he'd comforted her after her nightmare . . . there was no way someone as gentle as that could be as brutal as the person who'd killed Margaret.

"Look, Sam." Will squeezed her shoulders again. "You're not doing any good sitting in this waiting room. Dr. Watson will call you if Grimly's condition changes. Why don't you stay at my place tonight?"

Stay at his place? She couldn't stay with anyone. Not tonight. Not when she knew the nightmares would strike again. After what she'd found today, there was no way she'd have a peaceful night's sleep. And she didn't want Will, of all people, seeing that side of her.

"Thanks, but I already got a hotel room."

"You sure? It's no bother. I don't think you should be alone tonight."

She wasn't sure she should be alone either, but Will wasn't the man she craved, and as much as she wanted Ethan's arms around her right now, she just couldn't call him. She'd already decided things were happening too fast with him, that a relationship between them would never work. If she called him, he'd rush right over, and in her vulnerable state she'd take advantage of his comfort and they'd wind up in bed. She couldn't sleep with him again. She couldn't lean on him any more than she already had. If she did, it would just make things harder for both of them when she eventually went back to California for good.

"I'm sure, Will," she managed. "I'm really tired. I'll probably fall right to sleep. But thanks for the offer."

His finger grazed her cheek. "I'd do anything for you, Sam. You know that."

She did. She just wished that could be enough.

"Come on," he said softly, dropping his hand. "I'll give you a ride to the hotel."

Seated on the couch in his living room, Ethan closed Thomas's file, tugged off his glasses, and rubbed at his tired eyes.

He'd wanted to reread Thomas's file after his meeting with the charming Mrs. Adler. Not for the first time, Ethan wondered how the kid had managed to make it to seventeen without landing in more trouble than he'd already found. Most kids, in his situation, would have been running with gangs and meth heads by the time they were twelve. Ethan still wasn't convinced Thomas was as innocent as Samantha believed, but a small part of him wanted to give the kid the benefit of the doubt.

The phone on the couch beside him buzzed, and he glanced down at the screen. Relief bubbled through him when he saw Samantha's number.

"Hey," he said, lifting the phone to his ear. He hadn't talked to her since last night. He'd called her earlier, but she hadn't answered, and he hadn't left a message because he didn't want to push. If she was having second thoughts about their weekend, he didn't want to give her any reason to run. Though it killed him—and he was dying to see her again—he knew she needed some space to put everything together in her head. "I was going to call you a little later. How was your day?"

"Hi, Ethan. It was fine. Long."

Her voice sounded odd. Tight. Strained. Concern tugged at him. "Is everything okay?"

"Fine. Why do you ask?"

"I don't know, you just sound . . . tired."

"I am. I've been grading papers most of the night, and Grimly wasn't feeling well so I had to take him to the vet."

Oh man. He knew how much she loved that dog. He dropped his feet from the footstool and leaned forward to rest his elbow on his knee. "Is he okay?"

"Yeah, he's fine. Sleeping now. He . . . he got into something he shouldn't have."

She was holding back. He heard it in her voice, felt it through the line. "Do you want me to come by?"

"No. I'm fine. It's after nine already, and I'm about to go to bed."

Three fines. A big red flag something was definitely *not* fine.

"I want to be there for you, Samantha. I could—"

"I called to let you know that we're doing testing tomorrow. Most of the school is, so if you're planning to observe Thomas or meet with him or any of his teachers, you might want to wait a few days."

His stomach clenched. "Okay."

"Okay," she repeated. Silence filled the line, then she added, "There's something else. Something you should know before you come by the school."

"What?"

"Margaret Wilcox is dead."

*Holy shit.* Ethan pushed to his feet. No wonder she sounded so off. As much as Samantha disliked the woman, they taught at the same school and had grown up in the same small town. "What do you mean? What happened?"

"I don't know exactly. Will thinks she was murdered, though. They don't have any leads yet."

Ethan raked a hand through his hair, still unable to believe the news. "Are you sure you're okay alone? I could—"

"I'm fine, Ethan. Really. Look, I wanted to tell you that I had a great time over the weekend. I really did. And I enjoy spending time with you, but I just don't think I'm in a place right now where it makes sense to start a relationship. I have too much going on, and . . . and I'm going back to California soon anyway. I don't think this is the right time for us."

Ethan's chest drew tight as a drum. She was making excuses. What they'd shared over the weekend had scared her. And the news about Margaret clearly hadn't helped. "I'm not asking for any kind of commitment from you, Samantha."

"I know. I just . . . this is too much right now. Too much, too fast. I can't deal with it. I'd rather we end things here before one of us gets hurt."

Too late for that. She was breaking up with him. Or calling it quits. Or . . . hell, he didn't even know what. One incredible weekend didn't make a relationship, he knew that. But he'd hoped it had been the start of something amazing. Now he knew he'd been fooling himself.

"You've had a really long day, Samantha. This isn't the time to—"

"This isn't about Margaret, Ethan. I've been thinking about this since before we spent the weekend together."

*Ouch.*

His hands grew sweaty, and he heard himself mutter, "Okay," before he could think of something else to say. "If that's what you want."

"It's what I want."

A hard, sharp ache took up space beneath his breastbone. It was crazy to feel this way so fast, but he couldn't help it. And he knew if he stayed on the line much longer, he was going to make things worse, so it was time he signed off. "I'll try not to bug you at school. Thanks for telling me about Margaret."

"Ethan—"

"Good luck, Samantha."

Ethan clicked "End" on his phone and stared across the room toward the burning fireplace. His chest hurt, more than he'd thought possible. If this was the kind of pain his brother Alec lived with on a daily basis, it was no wonder the man could be such an ass.

Shit. There was no way he was sleeping tonight. Turning away from the fire, he headed for the kitchen and the whiskey bottle with his name on it. Ethan wasn't much of a drinker, but tonight he planned to get shit-faced drunk. And maybe, in some small way, forget about Samantha Parker for good.

———

Sam felt like pure crap as the bell rang, indicating the end of third period. Her conversation with Ethan last night kept replaying in her head. She should have told him the specifics, where Margaret had been found and how, but she hadn't been able to get the words out. If she'd said them, he'd have come right over, and she couldn't let him do that. She was doing the right thing for both of them by calling it quits. Eventually he'd see that. She just hoped the pain near her heart would hurry up and agree.

The low din of conversation echoed through the classroom as students grabbed their books and shuffled toward the door. Sam waited until the last student left, until she heard the door click shut, then dropped her head onto her desk.

She should have taken David's advice and called in sick. She shouldn't be here today. Not after what she'd found yesterday. Not after the nightmare she'd had last night. Not after the one hour or so of sleep she'd finally gotten after crying over Grimly and Ethan and the mess that had become her life.

What she needed to do was march herself down to the office and tell David she was in no shape to teach today. The kids were all looking at her like she had a tumor growing out of the side of her head. Word had spread fast. Everyone on campus knew what had happened at her house.

But she couldn't do that. The investigators had left her house late last night, and if she went there she'd just obsess until she made herself sick. So instead she was going to buck up and act like a mature adult.

Yeah, right. Like that would ever happen.

Coffee.

She lifted her head. Yes. Coffee would help.

Before she could change her mind, she pushed out of her chair and made her way through the corridor. Unable to stop herself, she paused when she reached Margaret's open classroom door and glanced into the room. Henry Branson, Will's father, stood near the chalkboard, waving his hands as he discussed something with the class, his silver hair glinting under the fluorescent lights.

Henry glanced in her direction and shot her a sad smile. He was a nice man, and he'd been a pretty good teacher before he'd retired ten years ago. A much better teacher than mayor. The fact that he and Will didn't get along wasn't her concern. She tried her best to smile back and looked over the class. The few students who had bothered to show up seemed as shell-shocked as he did.

Her mind skipped to Jeff. She needed to go see him. She could only imagine what he was going through today. Her stomach pitched again at the thought. She really shouldn't be at school. This was a stupid idea.

She headed back down the hall, desperate for a caffeine rush. As she rounded the corner, she noticed the two police officers standing near the office door, legs shoulder width apart, hands on belts, eyes focused straight ahead.

Another officer stood just inside the office doors, reciting Miranda rights. Sam stepped to the side so she could see through the glass windows of the office. Her gaze skipped over Thomas, being handcuffed by another officer at his back.

"No . . . " Sam rushed past the small crowd of students who'd gathered outside the lobby. David stood near the office door, one arm across his waist, one hand covering his mouth as he spoke quietly with a police officer. Annette held a phone to her ear. Thomas's eyes were wide and scared.

"What's going on?" Sam asked when she reached David's side.

"Miss." The officer David had been speaking with stepped in her way. "You need to stay back."

Inside the office, a cop grasped Thomas's arm and turned him toward the door.

"Wait." Sam stepped toward them, but David pulled her back.

"Let them do their job, Sam," he said in her ear.

"I didn't do anything!" Thomas exclaimed. His eyes cut to Sam. "Ms. Parker. I didn't do anything! Tell them!"

Sam's pulse ticked up as she looked to David. "Tell me that isn't what I think."

"It's not our concern. The investigators found evidence. Let them do their job."

"What kind of evidence?"

Sam took a step after Thomas and the police, but David hauled her back again. "Sam. There's nothing you can do for him. He was trouble before he even came here. The fact he'd go after Margaret just proves he was more trouble than any of us could have imagined."

No. They couldn't possibly think . . .

Thomas couldn't have been the one to hurt Margaret. He wasn't violent. He helped other students when they were lost in her labs. He was careful with her equipment and respectful when he spoke. He'd come to her rescue when Kenny had cornered her. A violent person didn't do those things.

"No." She shook her head. "That's wrong. They're wrong, David. They're wrong."

"If they're wrong, they'll figure it out. Let it go, Sam. There's nothing you can do."

There was something she could do. She pulled her arm from David's grip and rushed back down the hall.

"Sam, dammit," David muttered. "Where do you think you're going?"

"I'm taking the rest of the day off," she called over her shoulder. "You were right. I shouldn't be here today."

She went right to her desk, unlocked the bottom drawer, and tugged her cell phone from her purse. Ethan picked up on the first ring, but before she got more than one word out, she realized it was his voice mail, not him.

She slung her purse strap over her shoulder and found her keys while she waited until she heard the beep.

"Ethan, it's Sam. Thomas is in trouble. The cops just hauled him out of school. He needs you."

# CHAPTER TWELVE

Ethan slammed the door of his BMW and jogged up the front steps of the Hidden Falls Police Department. Even though it was close to freezing outside, sweat slicked his skin, and a low vibration echoed through his bones.

Pushing the heavy glass door open, he stepped inside and scanned the lobby. A high counter opened to his right. Plastic chairs were pushed up against the wall to his left. A set of double wood doors locked off the squad room from the lobby, and a fan turned slow circles above.

"Can I help you?" A dark-haired woman in a blue officer's uniform rested both hands on the high counter and raised one brow.

"Yeah." Ethan fished his ID out of the pocket of his slacks as he stepped toward the counter. "I'm Dr. McClane. I'm here to see Thomas Adler. He was brought in earlier."

The woman glanced down at the computer screen on her desk. "He's being questioned. Have a seat, and I'll find out what's happening."

Raking a hand through his hair as the officer left, Ethan turned to look over the empty room. He didn't want to sit. Wasn't sure he could. All he could do was hope whatever trouble the kid had gotten into had nothing to do with Margaret Wilcox.

Long minutes passed where the only sound was the clicking of keys, muffled voices, and a few ringing phones. Samantha's message had been brief, and when he'd tried to call her back he'd gotten nothing but voice mail. All he knew for sure was that Thomas had been arrested at school and was currently being questioned.

Will Branson's deep voice echoed from behind the double doors across the lobby, sending the hairs on Ethan's neck straight to attention. He turned in that direction just as the right side opened, and Branson stepped into the lobby with a younger officer at his side. The two were deep in conversation as they walked, but the second the chief spotted Ethan, his footsteps slowed. To the other officer, he said, "Joe, we'll talk more later."

"Sure thing, Chief." The officer nodded and brushed by Ethan. A whoosh of cold air bristled Ethan's skin as he exited.

"Dr. McClane." Branson stopped a few feet away. "I expected to see you at some point."

"What's happening with Adler?"

"He was arrested. He's meeting with the public defender."

"What are the charges?"

"I really can't divulge—"

"Bullshit."

Will's brow lifted, and he scratched the back of his head. "You can't do anything for him now. Kid got himself in big trouble this time."

*Fuck.* It was about Margaret. Disbelief and dread swirled through Ethan's gut.

The door behind him pushed open again before he could ask more, bringing another wave of cold into the room. Ethan glanced over his shoulder, and his heart rate kicked up when Samantha moved into the lobby.

Her skin was pale, her eyes red rimmed and bloodshot. Dark circles that screamed she hadn't slept in days marred the soft skin beneath her lashes, while curly tendrils hung around her face, dislodged from the loose knot at the back of her head.

He wanted to think she was distraught over what had happened between them, but something in his gut screamed her disheveled appearance had nothing to do with him and everything to do with the current situation.

She held Ethan's gaze for only a moment, then focused on Branson as if Ethan weren't even in the room. "Will, you made a mistake."

"Aw shit, Sam." Branson stepped toward her, grasped her arm, and turned her back toward the door. "You need to go home."

Ethan's stomach tightened into a hard knot. He didn't like Branson's hands on Samantha in any way. And that dislike had nothing to do with his feelings for her and everything to do with what he knew Branson was capable of. He took a step toward them.

Samantha pulled her arm from Branson's grip. "I'm not going home. Thomas didn't do this. He wouldn't hurt Margaret."

"We have enough evidence to prove otherwise. His prints were all over—"

"He was at my house," Sam said quickly. "Thomas stopped by my house over the weekend to talk about his research project."

Ethan stopped, and his gaze snapped right to Samantha's face. *Over the weekend . . .* She was lying. She'd been at his house over the weekend. They'd spent pretty much every moment together. And Thomas Adler definitely hadn't been anywhere close.

"Son of a bitch." Branson stared at her with hard, narrowed eyes. "I seriously hope you're joking right now. With all the rumors circulating about Hollings, you let a seventeen-year-old boy into your house? While you were alone?"

Samantha's back straightened. "What are you implying, Will?"

"I don't have to imply anything. Hell, half the town will be making up their own torrid version after they hear this."

Why the hell was she lying?

"Do you think I care what kind of gossip people spread?" Sam's eyes widened. "I don't. There's nothing wrong with me answering a few questions about a student's project. If you're only holding him on prints you found at my house, then you have to let him go."

*Prints at her house . . .*

Ethan glanced between the two, feeling as if he were playing catch-up on the conversation. "What does Samantha's house have to do with Margaret Wilcox's death?"

Samantha's mouth closed, and she looked down at her feet.

"Everything." Will clenched his jaw and glanced Ethan's way. "Since Sam found the body in her dining room."

*In her dining room . . .*

Ethan looked right at her, but she refused to glance his way. "When?"

"Yesterday afternoon," Branson answered.

Holy shit. She hadn't said a thing about finding a body when she'd called last night. Or that it had been in her house. She'd acted as if she weren't involved at all.

Samantha shifted her feet and zeroed in on Branson once more. "Will, he didn't do this."

"Dammit, Sam." Branson rested his hands on his hips in an obvious sign of frustration. Several tense moments passed before he said, "The kid isn't going anywhere if his story doesn't match yours."

Branson moved back toward the double doors that led into the station, and as he walked away, Samantha finally glanced toward Ethan.

Guilt reflected in her eyes. Guilt and something else Ethan didn't have time to deal with.

He stepped after Branson. "I want to speak with the public defender."

Branson typed a code into a keypad by the double doors. "I don't give a fuck what you want, McClane."

"Thomas has issues with law enforcement. You already know that. Your chances of getting anything out of him are better if I'm there."

Branson's hand stilled over the keypad, and he muttered, "Shit."

"McClane." The double doors hissed open. "Come with me. You," he glanced once more at Samantha, "go home and don't let any more teenagers into your damn house."

———

"Get in." Ethan climbed into his BMW and started the ignition in the fading light while he waited for Thomas to join him. Lights from the dash illuminated the interior of the vehicle and the clock flashing 5:07 p.m.

Warily, Thomas climbed in and latched his seat belt. As soon as it clicked, Ethan pulled out of the parking lot and pressed down on the gas. Thomas reached up to grip the safety handle above the door.

"Tell me," Ethan said, trying to keep his temper in check, "exactly why Chief Branson thinks you'd have anything to do with Margaret Wilcox's death."

"The chief doesn't like me."

Ethan glared at the kid as he turned down a side street without slowing. The force sent Thomas up against the door.

"Try again," Ethan muttered. He didn't care if he was being a hard-ass. When he'd been at the station, he'd gotten a pretty clear picture of what Samantha had found in her dining room, and right now he just wanted answers.

"Ms. Wilcox didn't like me much either."

Ethan gripped the wheel with both hands. This was a dead end. The kid was as closed-mouthed as Samantha Parker. "Did you go by Ms. Parker's house over the weekend?"

"Yeah."

Ethan darted a look toward Thomas. "Don't lie to me."

"I did. I swear. I needed help with my project. I just wanted to ask her a few questions."

"Did you go inside?"

Thomas sank down in the leather seat.

Ethan's jaw clenched again, and he looked ahead, making another turn. "I know for a fact you didn't see Ms. Parker last weekend. Wanna know how I know? Because she was with me all weekend. And I sure as hell would have remembered if you were there."

Thomas leaned toward the window.

Ethan whipped to a stop at the end of Thomas's street but parked far enough from his trailer so the crotchety old Mrs. Adler didn't see them. "Tell me why Ms. Parker would lie for you."

"I don't know," Thomas muttered.

"You'd better fucking know. She just put her career and her reputation on the line for you, so you'd better come up with something other than 'I don't know.'"

"She knows I didn't do anything wrong," Thomas said quickly. "She knows I wouldn't do that."

Ethan looked ahead at the barren trees lining the street. There was just enough panic in the kid's voice to make him wonder who was telling the truth.

"Then who did?" Ethan finally asked.

"I don't know."

"Shit." He glanced back at Thomas. "If I find out you lied to me—"

"I'm not lying. I swear."

Ethan forcibly gentled his voice. "Go home, Thomas. Stay out of trouble for one night. But you better believe we're going to talk about this tomorrow."

"Yes, sir." Thomas jumped out of the car and slammed the door. By the time Ethan glanced sideways, Thomas had already disappeared into his house.

Alone, Ethan closed his eyes and filled his lungs with one deep breath. He should leave well enough alone. She'd made it clear she was done with him. If he hadn't known it before, he knew it for sure after the way she wouldn't even look at him at the station. But he couldn't. Because she was risking everything for a kid who probably didn't deserve it.

Before he could change his mind, he pulled away from the curb and headed across town.

———

Sam dropped the book in her hands and rushed down the stairs as soon as she heard the knock at her front door. She'd been packing books and anything else she could find in a crazy attempt to keep from thinking too much, but she was going nuts at home waiting for news about Thomas.

She reached the entry, purposely didn't look toward the closed double doors that led into the dining room, and jerked the front door open. "Will, I—"

Ethan glared down at her in her porch light. "Wrong person."

Sam's heart rate shot up. His jaw was clenched, his shoulders tight, and the look in his usually soft green eyes was anything but friendly. "Ethan. I—I didn't expect to see you."

"Yeah, no kidding." He moved into her entry, perched his hands on his hips, and turned back to her. "What the hell do you think you're doing?"

Sam's pulse roared as she closed the door with a click and looked back at him. He was pissed. He had every right to be pissed. "Packing, actually."

"Don't be cute with me. I want to know what you think you were doing at the station earlier."

"Helping."

"You call that helping? I call that lying."

"I wasn't lying, Ethan. He did come by my house over the weekend. He needed help. He told me on Monday when he caught me after school."

"Did he come inside?"

Sam bit her lip and brushed the hair back from her face.

"Did he come inside?" he asked again, pinning her with a hard look.

Sam sighed. Lying to Will was one thing. Lying to Ethan was nearly impossible. "I don't know."

"Dammit, Samantha." Ethan's jaw clenched down hard. "You're putting yourself on the line for this kid. I got an earful at the station about what people are saying about Sandra Hollings. She was sleeping with her students. That's why she took off. And here you are lying that you let a seventeen-year-old into your house alone? It just takes one person to say—"

"To say what?" she snapped. "Do you honestly think I care what people around here say? Do you think I care about my job? I don't. The only reason I've stayed in Hidden Falls as long as I have is because . . ."

Her mouth snapped shut. She couldn't tell him he was the reason she'd started enjoying going to work. She was supposed to be calling things off. Not getting more tangled up in him.

"Because why?"

"Because I'm trying to sell my mother's house. I already told you that."

When he shook his head and looked away from her, a strange sense of panic told her she had to make him understand. "He didn't do it, Ethan. He's not capable of it."

"And how do you know?" Ethan glared at her again. "Have you read his file? Because I have. He's been in and out of trouble for years.

Not months, *years*. Assault, trespassing, possession, shoplifting. Not to mention all the trouble he's been in since he came here. Everyone knows he didn't get along with Margaret. His prints are all over your house, and he wasn't at school the day her body was found. And all you have to say is, you just know? That's insane."

He was making all the arguments she'd already heard, but she didn't care. "He didn't do it, Ethan. He couldn't. I don't have any proof, but I believe him. I've gotten to know him over the past few weeks, and I know he couldn't kill anyone."

"You've gotten to know what he *wants* you to know. Kids like this are good at hiding who they really are. It's how they survive."

"How do you know?"

"Because I *was* him, Samantha."

"Then you should understand that everyone deserves a second chance. You got one."

"That was different."

"How?"

"Because I didn't murder someone!"

Sam's mouth snapped closed as she stared at him. He really believed Thomas had done it. But as he dropped his head and raked his hand through his hair, she also realized he was struggling with that belief.

He didn't want Thomas to be guilty. As much as he tried to remain professionally detached, she knew he liked Thomas. But more than that, she knew he was here because he was trying to protect her.

Her blood warmed, and she took a step toward him. "Ethan—"

"Stay away from him." He looked down at her, his eyes just as hard and intense as they'd been when he walked into her house. "I don't know what he's up to and neither do you. But until the police figure it out, he's not someone you should mess with."

He stepped past her for the door, and that panic swelled when she realized he was leaving.

She moved quickly and slapped a hand against the door before he could open it. "Wait."

"What now?"

"I don't want you to go. Not like this."

"Why not? You already made it clear you don't want me around. I get it. I just came over to tell you to watch your back with Adler."

That panic intensified. She was about to lose him. Lose him because she was so incredibly stupid to think she could end things so easily. "I do want you around."

He huffed a sound that held no humor and pushed her arm out of the way. "Well, you've got a funny way of showing it."

His hand closed over the door handle. But before he could open it, Sam pushed her way between him and the door. "I panicked the other day, okay? Everything between us has happened so fast. I—I didn't know what to do. Haven't you ever done or said something you regretted?"

His gaze skipped over her face. In the silence she couldn't tell what he was thinking. Or feeling.

"I don't believe you." He reached for the door handle again.

"Well, believe this."

She gripped his dress shirt, rose up on her toes, and pressed her lips to his. He didn't kiss her back, just stared down at her with wide eyes. But she didn't let that stop her. She needed him to know she wasn't lying.

She pulled back but didn't dare let go of his shirt. "I don't want you to go, dammit. I want you. I want this, I want us, I wa—"

"Prove it."

Her heart stuttered. Prove to him she wanted him? Risk getting hurt by taking the first step?

Her heart picked up speed until her pulse was a whir in her ears. Yes. Yes, she could do that. Because he was worth it.

Letting go of his shirt, she grabbed the hem of her sweater and wrenched it over her head. The white cotton fell against the hardwood floor. His gaze dropped to her cleavage as she reached for the snap on her jeans and pushed the denim down her legs.

"I'm not good at relationships." She kicked the jeans away. "I told you that before. I always do something to mess it up. I don't want to mess it up with you anymore, though."

His heated gaze traveled the length of her body, over her white lace bra, down her belly, and across her matching panties, filling her with confidence.

She stepped toward him. "I'm sorry I didn't tell you about Margaret. I'm sorry I tried to push you away. I'm not good at leaning on people. But I want to work on it. With you. If you'll let me."

She slid her arms up his warm chest, then around his neck. Felt his body melt into hers as she rose on her toes again and kissed the corner of his mouth. This time softly. Gently. With all the emotion she hoped he knew was inside her.

"Dammit, Samantha," he whispered.

She'd hurt him. She hadn't meant to, but she had. She'd been so focused on her fears that she hadn't stopped to think about what he was thinking or feeling or how everything with Thomas was affecting him. She wanted to fix that. Needed him to know he mattered. Because something inside her knew he didn't think he really did.

"I want you, Ethan." She kissed the other side of his mouth, trailed her fingers into the silky hair at his nape, kissed his jaw. "Give me another chance to show you how much."

He didn't move, didn't speak, so she shifted higher and kissed his cheek. And just when she was sure he wasn't going to let her in, he groaned, wrapped his hands around her waist, and captured her mouth.

His tongue swept over hers, drawing her into a deep, passionate kiss. His arms slid around her lower back, pulling her tight against his hard, hot body. He pushed her back until her spine hit the door, then he lifted one hand to her face, deepened the kiss, and consumed her in a way only he could do.

This was what she wanted, just the feel of him next to her, the delicious sensations that overpowered her whenever he was close. She didn't want to think about Margaret, didn't want to think about Thomas, didn't want to focus on her fears or neuroses, or on anything else. She just wanted him. Had always wanted him. Since the first moment they'd met.

His tongue traced circles around her mouth, exploring soft surfaces, scraping firm teeth. Her skin tingled where his fingertips grazed her flesh. Every part of her body ached to be touched by him. Tipping her head, she kissed him deeper, rocked her hips against his, then swallowed the groan that echoed from his mouth.

*More, more, more* . . . They were the only words she heard, echoing in her head again and again. Dropping her hands, she made quick work of the buttons on his shirt, then pulled the garment free of his slacks and scrambled for the button at his waistband.

"Dammit, Samantha," he mumbled again as she shoved her hands into both sides of his pants. Only this time the words held no heat.

She loved the raspy sound of his voice. Loved that she had the power to push him to the edge. Pulling her mouth from his, she lowered to her knees, tugged off his shoes and socks, and unhooked the button on his slacks.

Ethan pressed a hand against the door above as she trailed her hands up the backs of his strong legs, pulled his wallet free, then yanked off his pants. "Samantha, I—"

His words morphed into a groan as she drew his erection into her mouth. He dropped his head back, flexed his hips forward, searching for more. Working him deep, she ran her tongue all around the head, then released the pressure and did it again.

She pushed him to the brink with her mouth, loving that she could give him this after all the heartache she'd caused him. Wanted—no, needed—him to know what he meant to her, even if she couldn't say the words.

"Samantha." His hands found her shoulders. "You have to stop." He pushed her away, then lifted her to her feet and pressed her back against the door. "I need you."

Sam's heart expanded as his mouth claimed hers again, greedy, hot, his probing tongue sending arousal pulsing through every part of her body.

She moaned when he pulled away, then shivered when she realized he was reaching for his wallet. A wrapper tore. His wallet hit the ground with a thud. Wrapping her arms around his shoulders, she hooked one leg around his hip and kissed him while he rolled on the condom. Then she trembled as he tugged her panties to the side and plunged deep.

Pleasure coursed through her. She lifted her hips, rocked to meet every thrust. Her hands darted into his hair, fisting the soft strands with a mixture of desire and greed she hadn't known was in her. Kissing him deeper, she took everything he gave, wanted more of this. Needed only him.

"Samantha . . . " He pulled back, rested his forehead against hers, braced one hand on the door as he held her up with the other and drove deeper.

Ecstasy teased her senses, but she held back, wanting him to come with her, wanting to watch his passion build. His features drew tight, his muscles hard everywhere their bodies touched. And as her gaze swept over his handsome face, she couldn't stop her chest from tightening to the point of pain.

She was going to get hurt in this. Worse than she ever imagined. Because they weren't just tumbling into a relationship. She was falling in love with him. In a way that didn't just leave her open and vulnerable, it scared her to death.

"Oh God so good . . . " He swelled inside her, plunged deep again and again. And when he groaned, his orgasm triggered hers, sending pulsing contractions to echo all through her body, even into her soul.

He slumped against her, his chest rising and falling with his deep breaths, his slick skin sticking to hers. And she loved it. Loved being close to him. Just wanted *him*.

He turned his head against her shoulder and sucked in a shaky breath. "I don't want to fight with you, Samantha."

"I don't want to fight with you either, Ethan."

He lifted his head and looked down at her, his face flushed from both pleasure and exertion. "I wouldn't be able to live with myself if something happened to you."

His green eyes softened with so much emotion that her heart sped up until it felt like it might fly right out of her chest. Forget *falling* in love with him. She already did love him. And she didn't have a clue how she was going to protect her heart now.

Swallowing hard, she looked down at the stray hairs dotting his chest and trailed her fingers over his collarbone. "Do you have to go back to Portland tonight?"

"No."

Relief was as sweet as wine. "I need to pick up Grimly from the vet, but I—I don't really want to be alone in this house tonight."

"Are you asking me to stay?"

She met his gaze. And knew there was no way she could protect her heart now. All she could do was hold on for the ride. And hope it didn't break her before the end.

"Yes," she whispered. "I want you to stay. If, that is, you want to stay with me."

"Samantha." He brushed a stray lock of hair behind her ear in a way that was so tender her heart filled all over again. "There's nowhere else I'd rather be tonight than right here with you. There's just one thing."

"What?"

"The next time you find a dead body in your house, call me. First."

He was making a joke. He always knew how to lighten the moment and make her feel better. Relaxing into him, she leaned toward his mouth. "I promise."

And she would. Because as she wrapped her arms around him and lost herself in his kiss once more, she hoped there was nowhere else he'd ever rather be.

# CHAPTER THIRTEEN

Sam stared at the aged ceiling in her bedroom and tried to stay still so she wouldn't wake Ethan beside her.

It didn't work. Her legs kept twitching, and she couldn't keep them still. She was exhausted beyond reason, but every time she closed her eyes, she saw Margaret's body, that cabin, had flashes of her horrible dream. And though she loved having Ethan next to her, not even wild sex had been enough to make her relax.

As quietly as she could, she tossed back the covers and eased out of bed. Not wanting to make noise looking for something to wear, she opted for Ethan's dress shirt from the floor and pulled it on. At the door, she glanced back to make sure he was still sleeping. Sure enough, he lay as still as he'd been since drifting to sleep, his bare chest rising and falling in a steady rhythm, his dark hair brushing his temples, and those insanely thick lashes skimming the soft skin beneath his eyes.

She couldn't remember a time when she'd ever looked or felt that relaxed. Really wished she knew his secret so she could stop her brain from spinning and finally get some rest.

Drawing a breath, she closed the door and made her way down the hall. At the bottom of the stairs she swept past the closed double doors that lead to the dining room and headed for the kitchen.

She was never going to be able to look in that room again. She needed to sell this house quickly. Of course, when that happened, there would be nothing rooting her to this town. She could quit her job and leave, as she'd planned, only running back to California didn't hold the appeal it had days ago. Because running didn't just mean leaving this town behind, it meant leaving Ethan as well.

Grimly's tail thumped against the blankets she'd made into a bed near the smoldering fire, pulling at Sam's attention as she stepped into the kitchen. She crossed toward him and sank to the floor at his side.

"Hey, buddy." She rubbed his ears. "How's my best guy doing?"

Grimly groaned, lifted his chin, and rested it on her knee.

"That bad, huh?" She scratched below his ear where he liked it best. "The vet said you'll be good as new in a day or two. Just have to give it time." When he groaned again, she moved to his other ear. "I know. You don't like being told what to do. But trust me, this will all be over soon, and you'll be chasing rabbits in the woods before you know it."

"Hey."

Sam glanced up at the sound of Ethan's soft voice. He stood in the doorway to the hall wearing nothing but wrinkled black slacks riding low on his hips. His eyes were sleepy, his dark hair mussed from her fingers. Firelight illuminated the muscles in his chest and the thatch of dark hair running down his abdomen that she'd traced earlier with her fingers and lips. And even though she was exhausted and stressed and still worried about Grimly, a burst of arousal singed her nerve endings, reminding her that he was the one shining light in the darkness of her life. Reminding her pushing him away had been the stupidest thing she'd ever done.

"Hey." She drew her hand down Grimly's back. "I tried not to wake you."

"You didn't." The old, scarred boards creaked under his feet as he crossed the room and settled on the floor behind her. He stretched both of his long legs around her and pulled her back into the heat of his body. Brushing her hair to the side, he pressed his lips against her nape and wrapped his arms around her waist. "It was the cold bed that got me up."

Tingles raced across Sam's skin wherever he touched. She tipped her head to the side so he could kiss her again, closed her eyes, and sighed. Yes, this was much better than stressing and worrying and pushing him away.

Resting his chin on her shoulder, he reached around her and rubbed Grimly's head. "What are you doing down here?"

"Couldn't sleep."

"You're exhausted, Samantha. You need to rest."

"I was worried about Grimly."

"He's going to be fine. You heard the vet earlier."

"Yeah." She rubbed a finger down Grimly's wet nose, her throat growing thick. "I know."

"You know, considering everything you've been through, it's normal to feel stressed and anxious. Anyone would."

He was right, and while her instincts urged her to agree and keep quiet, she didn't want to do that anymore. Not with him. He made her feel safe. He'd come back to her when he had every reason to walk away. And if she held back now, she knew she'd fall right back into the old trap of shutting down. She owed him more than that.

"I know they would. But this—what I'm feeling—it isn't just about Grimly or Margaret or even Thomas. I wanted to tell you about it all yesterday when I called, but I couldn't because seeing Margaret like that . . . " She shook her head and forced the image out of her mind. "It brought everything back up. The dream, the remains we found in the woods . . . " *Seth.* "I'm not sleeping because if I'm having those images during my waking hours, I can only imagine how horrible they'll be when I sleep."

He laid his hand over hers on her knee. Stared at her a long time as if debating something. And in the silence Sam was almost afraid to ask what he was thinking.

"How do you feel about hypnosis?"

That was not what she'd expected him to say. "Are you serious?"

"Completely."

She laughed for the first time in days. "I didn't know you were in the entertainment industry, Dr. McClane."

He frowned. "Hypnotic regression is a legitimate therapy tool used in psychiatry. Opening the unconscious mind is often the first step toward unblocking painful events that are preventing a person from enjoying a healthy, happy, and fulfilling life."

He wasn't joking. Her smile faded. "And you do this? With your patients?"

"Not me. I'm not trained in it. But my father is."

Her stomach flipped. He was dead serious.

He threaded his fingers with hers. "I think you have two choices. You can either go on the way you've been going, having these nightmares that keep you up all the time, or you can try to figure out what they're really all about."

"If it's a dream, it's just my psyche trying to freak me out. Horror movies give me nightmares. It's the same thing."

"I'm not so sure."

"What do you mean?"

"You were having those dreams before we found the remains in the woods and before Margaret was murdered. Dreams are another way the unconscious mind tries to process and explain events in our lives, especially ones that have left a mark on us."

Her chest grew tight with understanding. "You think the dream is real."

"Maybe." His fingers tightened around hers. "If that's the case, then hypnosis might be a way to draw it out so you can deal with it and move on."

Her stomach rolled. She'd heard her brother die. That had to traumatize a person, right? But sweat slicked her skin as a cold reality slapped her in the face. Never in all the years she'd been having this nightmare had she ever seen Seth's face. Not once had she felt like her dreams had anything to do with him.

Which meant she'd seen something worse that night. Something she hadn't yet remembered.

Her eyes burned with the sting of tears she did not want to let fall, and she closed them quickly and tried to hold them back.

"Hey." Ethan wrapped his arms around her and pulled her into the warmth and safety of his chest. "It's okay. We'll figure this out together. I promise."

Together sounded heavenly. But she was starting to wonder if anything would ever be okay again. Because if she'd really witnessed something so horrible her conscious mind had blocked it for almost twenty years, that meant what she'd seen and lived through the last few days was only the beginning.

———

Will dropped ice into his empty glass on the bar and looked across the Kelloggs' great room toward Jeff, seated in the leather chair, staring wide-eyed into the fire.

The man looked lost—bloodshot eyes, wrinkled clothes, hair he hadn't combed in two days. As Will filled his glass, he told himself this was why he was still single at his age. Because he'd seen too much shit in his life and knew all relationships crashed and burned at some point. He never wanted to be left broken and wasted like Jeff. Worse yet, like his own father.

He lifted the glass to his lips. Then again, there was a strong possibility it wasn't grief dragging that reaction from Jeff. It could very well be guilt.

"Funeral's Friday?" Will asked, setting the crystal topper back in the decanter.

"Yeah." Jeff continued to stare at the flames as if he were a million miles away. "Friday."

Will had to hand it to him. He played the grieving widower well.

He moved toward the fireplace with his whiskey, gripped the mantel, and studied a photo of Jeff and Margaret standing on a dock, which looked as if it had been taken a few years before. "Your poll numbers will probably go up. Sympathy vote's a pretty strong one."

"You think I care about the fucking election right now?"

Will glanced over his shoulder. "You'd be stupid not to. Somebody just did you a favor."

"She was *my wife*."

"Who you were forced to marry. We all know Maggie wasn't the easiest person to live with."

"Are you asking if I killed her?"

"Did you?"

"No! I loved her, dammit!"

The answer was too quick. Will turned away and frowned.

"I know you find that hard to believe," Jeff said behind him, "but I did. Maggie could be a real bitch when she wanted, but she had these . . . moments. Moments when she'd let down her guard. Do little things like rub my feet, or edit one of my speeches, or run her fingers through my hair and hum until I fell asleep." His voice grew thick. "She wasn't always all about herself. When no one was looking, she could be generous. And kind."

Will had never seen kindness in Margaret Wilcox. Maybe when they'd been kids, but not recently. Ever since Margaret and Jeff had moved back from Portland, she'd been shallow and self-centered. Will couldn't imagine her rubbing anyone's feet. Not even the Messiah's himself.

"I think Kenny did it," Jeff said quietly.

Will turned toward his friend. "What makes you say that?"

"They've both been acting strange lately. And I overheard her on the phone the other night. I think with him."

"You think they were having an affair?"

Jeff winced. "God, I hope not. No, I think Kenny was bugging her to do something about Sam. Kenny's been off his rocker since Sam came back to town."

Will's jaw hardened. Jeff was right. Kenny had been more paranoid than normal, and it had started around Sam's return. Will had talked Kenny back from a rage just a couple of weeks ago when he thought Sam was telling that shrink too much. And it was no secret that Kenny had both hated and desired Maggie in a way that was twisted and sick.

"Fuck." Jeff pushed out of his chair. "I need another drink." He slammed bottles against the bar. Bourbon sloshed from carafe to glass, spilling over the edge to pool on the hard surface.

Will stepped away from the fire. "I'll keep an eye on Kenny."

"If he did it, I don't want to know." Jeff tossed back the inch of amber liquid in his tumbler.

Interesting comment coming from the grieving widower. Unless he knew for a fact Kenny hadn't killed Margaret.

"Hey." Jeff eyed Will across the bar, looking half-sane for the first time all day. "What do you think about that shrink? McClane? The one Sam brought to the party?"

"Why do you ask?"

"I don't know. He just looks familiar. I can't place him."

A chill spread down Will's spine. He'd thought the same. There was something about McClane's eyes that was eerily familiar to him too.

"Mr. Kellogg?" The maid stepped into the room, cutting a cautious look between them. "Ms. Parker's here to see you."

"Sam?" Jeff's eyes brightened. "Send her in."

"Yes, sir."

As the maid disappeared, Will frowned. "Don't mention anything to Sam about Kenny."

Disdain crossed Jeff's features. "Then keep that fucktard away from her."

Relaxing the muscles in his face, Jeff stepped out from behind the bar as Sam passed under the archway. "Sam. It's so good of you to come by."

Sam stepped into Jeff's waiting embrace and hugged him. "I am so sorry. I would have stopped by yesterday, I just . . . I didn't know what to say."

Her grief-filled voice drifted toward Will, and he looked back at the fireplace. He hadn't changed his mind. He never wanted to be pathetic and vulnerable like Jeff. But he'd always had a soft spot for Samantha Parker. And right now he couldn't stand to see her in the arms of a possible murderer . . . friend or not.

"It's okay," Jeff said in a raspy voice. "I understand. How are you? I know this can't be easy for you either."

Fabric rustled, and Will glanced back, relieved they were done hugging. "I'll be okay. Do you know anything else?" She looked toward Will. "Do you have any leads?"

*Did he know anything else? Hell, yeah. He knew way too fucking much. More than he ever wanted to know.*

"No." Will rubbed a hand over the top of his head. "No solid leads yet. But we're still working on it."

"Okay." Sam's voice dropped. "I'm sure you'll find something soon. You're the best police chief in the county."

Instead of pride, guilt swept through Will. Yeah, he was some chief. He had two unsolved murders sitting on his desk from as many weeks, and he had a strong hunch he knew who had killed both victims. He just couldn't tell anyone or make an arrest, because then he'd be implicating himself in something he just wanted to forget.

"I know he will," Jeff said. "Are you okay at the house? I can't imagine staying there is easy."

"I'm fine. Don't worry about me."

"You're more than welcome to stay here. It's a big place." Jeff glanced around with that lost look again. "Empty now."

Will bit back a curse. If Sam fell for this sack of shit, he was gonna bust an artery. And then he was gonna hurt someone.

"That's sweet of you, Jeff, but the last thing you need is a houseguest." Sam reached for his hand. "I'm so sorry. I wish there were something I could do to make this better."

"Just seeing you helps." Jeff smiled weakly.

Will was pretty sure he'd puke if he had to listen to much more. "Kellogg, I gotta get back to the station."

Jeff tore his gaze away from Sam long enough to shoot Will an irritated glare that Sam obviously didn't see. "Yeah. Thanks for stopping by and giving me an update."

"Anytime." To Sam, Will said, "You got a few minutes? I have a couple things I need to talk to you about."

"Um. Sure." She looked back at Jeff. "You'll call me if you need anything, right?"

"Sure. You know I will."

Jeff hugged her once more, way longer than was socially appropriate, and Will had to clear his throat to get the moron to release her.

Sam eased out of Jeff's arms and followed Will across the foyer.

The door snapped closed behind them. A cool breeze blew across the yard, sending leaves skittering over the ground.

"God, he looks so sad," Sam said.

"He'll get by. He always does."

Sam sighed. "What did you want to talk with me about?"

He tucked his hands in the pockets of his jeans as he followed her across the paved drive toward her car. "Did Maggie ever hang out with anyone at school?"

"Do you mean with any of the staff?"

"Yeah."

She stopped next to her car. "Not that I know of. She was always the last teacher to arrive and the first to leave."

"What about that Dr. McClane?"

"Ethan?"

"I saw them getting cozy on the porch at Jeff and Maggie's party. And a few people mentioned that he observed in her room more than in some of the others."

Unease crossed Sam's face, but she masked it quickly. "He observed in a lot of rooms. Doesn't mean he was involved with her. As for that party, we both know Margaret liked to sink her claws into things that didn't belong to her."

He'd ruffled her feathers. There was definitely something going on between Sam and the doctor. And Will wasn't sure how he felt about that. Especially when he still couldn't figure out how he knew the guy.

"I'm just trying to cover all bases here. I've been thinking about what Kenny said the other night at the party. Strange things *have* been happening since Dr. McClane arrived in town."

"But he wasn't around when my house was vandalized."

"That doesn't mean he couldn't have been here and we just didn't see him."

Her face paled. "B-but those remains we found have been up there for at least fifteen years. He definitely wasn't here fifteen years ago."

Will rubbed a hand over his chin. Maybe, maybe not. But something in the back of his mind said Dr. Ethan McClane was somehow linked to this town in a way he hadn't yet uncovered. Or remembered. "As I said, Sam, I'm just trying to cover my bases. I'm sure you're right. It's my job to be suspicious, remember?"

"Yeah. Okay."

He reached for her car door and pulled it open. He didn't like scaring her, but in this case, scared could be good. Especially if it pushed her into leaving Hidden Falls once and for all. "Look, just be careful, okay? You got all the locks changed?"

She nodded.

"Good. Lieutenant Hanson's still keeping an eye on your place at night. We'll figure out whoever's behind this. Don't worry."

Sam nodded again as she climbed into her car. But when she gripped the steering wheel, Will saw the way her hands were shaking. "Bye, Will."

He closed her door and watched as her car pulled out of the circular drive and disappeared down the long treed lane. But instead of worrying about her, his mind rushed back over the years, trying to remember if he'd ever seen a younger version of Ethan McClane in Hidden Falls.

He came up blank.

Still, something inside screamed that figuring out Ethan McClane's real reason for being in town was important to everything.

———

*Strange things have been happening since Dr. McClane arrived in town . . .*

As much as she'd tried to get those words out of her head, Sam kept hearing them. They'd been spinning in her mind as she'd graded papers last night, as she'd climbed into bed and lain awake in the dark, as she'd showered and brushed her teeth this morning. And now, when she was running late for school because she was so exhausted she could barely move from not one but several nights of no sleep, they were still there, clawing at her subconscious until she wanted to scream.

It was a coincidence. Will and Kenny were both wrong. Ethan was not involved in any of the weirdness happening in Hidden Falls.

She jogged down the stairs and glanced at her watch, thinking about Ethan and the silly hypnosis session she'd agreed to tonight. Ethan had needed to go back to Portland yesterday for afternoon meetings and early ones this morning, so he hadn't been able to stay over again. She missed him already, and she had a feeling that was the reason she'd agreed to the hypnosis when they'd talked on the phone yesterday. She didn't have any great hope the session was going to cure her, but she was looking forward to seeing Ethan and spending the weekend with him again.

She hurried into the kitchen, poured fresh coffee into her travel mug, grabbed her bag and keys, and headed for the front door. Grimly trailed along at her feet, perky and annoying as always, thank goodness. "Sorry, bud. No time for a walk this morning." She rubbed his ears. "I'll take you this afternoon before we go to Ethan's. Promise. Be a good boy while I'm gone."

Juggling items in her hands, she yanked the front door open, then jerked back. Kenny stood just on the other side of the threshold.

Coffee sloshed over the rim of the cup. With the keys clenched between her fingers, she pressed her hand to her chest and sucked back air. "Kenny. Oh my God, you scared me."

She grasped the rim of the cup with her other hand, hissed as the heat burned her skin, and shook the hot coffee from her fingers. "What are you doing here?"

He didn't answer. Confused, she looked up, then stilled.

Something dark simmered in his eyes. Something dangerous. His gaze traveled slowly down the length of her body. It was the same look he often gave her at school, the one that made her stomach pitch. Only this time it was accompanied by a depraved twist of his lips.

Sam's adrenaline jumped, and perspiration dampened her skin. Everywhere.

"I'm really late, Kenny. Can this wait?" She gripped the door handle, pulling it toward her as she closed the gap between them and shifted back to shut him out.

"No, I don't think so." He slapped a hand on the door. "This has already waited long enough. It's time you and I got this over with once and for all."

*Trust your first instinct.* Her mother's advice just before Sam had left for college rang in Sam's head.

She didn't think, she reacted. Flicking her wrist, she tossed the hot coffee toward him, then shoved her hip against the door.

He screamed as the scalding liquid connected with skin. Before she could slam the door in his face, though, he shifted his foot in the jamb and pushed hard against the door with his hands. "You fucking bitch!"

Grimly growled at her feet. Her pulse went stratospheric. Whipping around so her back was to the old wood, Sam thrust her weight against the door until he had no choice but to jerk free before he lost a finger or a foot.

*Oh God, oh God, oh God . . .* She flipped the lock, latched the dead bolt, and jerked away from the door. He roared and pounded on the door with his fists.

"I'm gonna make you pay for that, you little whore!"

Sam scrambled for the phone on the antique secretary at the base of the stairs. Her fingers trembled as she punched in numbers.

"Nine-one-one," a voice echoed through the phone. "What's your emergency?"

Glass shattered in the sidelight. Sam shrieked and whipped toward the sound. Kenny shoved his hand through the hole in the glass, slicing his skin as he reached up and flipped the lock.

Sam gripped the cordless phone at her ear and raced toward the kitchen. "There's an intruder in my house. 2753 Inglebrook La—"

Kenny slammed into her from behind. The phone flew from Sam's hands. Her body sailed forward, and she hit the side of her head on the corner of the table. Sharp pain exploded across her face, blocking out everything else around her. She bounced off the hard surface and tumbled to the ground.

"You're a feisty one," Kenny growled, stepping over her and grasping her by the hair. "Maggie was feisty too."

He pulled hard, and pain ripped down Sam's scalp. She cried out as he picked her up by the hair and threw her to the side. She smacked into the cupboard and slumped to the floor. Spots filled her vision. Glass and pottery shattered. But all she could focus on was the pain echoing through every inch of her body.

"You just wouldn't take the hint," he sneered. "If you'd done what you were supposed to do, none of this ever would have happened. Maggie would still be alive, and I wouldn't have to be here."

Maggie . . . he was ranting about Margaret. Had he killed her? Sam wasn't sure, but she knew from the look on his face he was going to rape her. Probably kill her too.

She kicked out and slapped at his hands. He grasped her blouse at the shoulder and yanked. Fabric ripped. Sam scrambled to break free, clawed out. Her fingernails connected with skin, and she used every ounce of strength she had to rake them through his flesh.

He screamed, shifted, then smacked his elbow hard against her face.

Pain ripped through Sam's cheekbone, and she saw stars.

"I know you remember." Gripping both of her hands in one of his, he pinned them to the floor above her and locked her legs between his. "I told them you were at the cabin. I told them you were a problem. Right from the beginning. But no one ever listens to good ol' Kenny. Well, they're listening now." He lowered his weight onto her. "They're gonna fucking listen."

Remember . . . The cabin . . . A fresh wave of fear washed over her. What did he think she remembered about the cabin?

He grasped her blouse at her chest and yanked. Buttons flew across the kitchen. His gaze drifted over her white bra and cleavage and flared with both malice and heat.

*No, no, no.* Sam's whirling thoughts came to a grinding halt, and she struggled against his hold. She had to get away. She had to get free. But he was holding her too tightly. His weight was too heavy.

"Yeah, you're gonna listen now, aren't you, bitch," he growled, staring down at her breasts.

Sam choked on a sob, fought harder.

A growl echoed somewhere close, and Kenny jerked back and howled.

"Motherfucker!" Kenny screamed. He lifted his weight off Sam long enough to kick out. A thud sounded, followed by Grimly's whimper.

Sam's vision turned red. She struggled harder. Kenny laughed, an evil, malevolent sound—the same sound she'd heard from outside her supply room door the day she and Ethan had been locked in. He let go of her with one hand, reached for his belt buckle. The moment he relaxed his grip on her legs to free himself from his pants, she jammed her knee up into his groin as hard as she could.

He gasped. His eyes shot wide. His whole body stiffened, but he loosened his grip on her hands long enough so she could jerk free and jam two fingers into his eyes.

Kenny shrieked and rolled off her.

Air clogged in Sam's lungs. Blood ran down her hands as she scrambled to her feet. Broken dishes lay around her, and she slipped once as she took two steps toward the back door. Just as she reached the handle, Kenny's hand darted out, wrapped around her ankle, and yanked hard.

Sam yelped as her balance went out from under her, then grunted when she hit the floor with a thud. She tried to get up again, but Kenny tossed her onto her back once more and straddled her thighs. Blood and sweat trickled down his face, but his eyes were filled with so much rage, she knew this was it.

He grasped her by the neck, lifted her head an inch off the floor, then smacked it back against the hard wood. Pain stabbed through her skull. The edges of her vision darkened.

"You're gonna pay for that," he growled. "We were gonna have a little fun first, but I just changed my mind." His hands tightened around her throat, cutting off her air.

Sam gasped, clawed out, tried to pull his hands free. Her vision grew darker.

"Let her go, Kenny!"

Kenny darted a look over his shoulder but didn't lessen his hold. "What the fuck are you doing here?"

"Let her go," Will said again.

Tears filled Sam's eyes. She slapped at Kenny's hands. Kenny squeezed hard once, then growled and jerked off of her. Sam gasped in a breath, but the relief was short-lived. Because Kenny scrambled to his feet, grabbed her by the hair, and hauled her to her feet. Yanking her back against his body, he wrapped his forearm around her throat. "What the hell do you think you're doing, Branson?"

Will gripped a gun in two hands as he moved around a kitchen chair lying on its side. "Let her go. I'm not going to say it again."

"Maggie was right. She was right about everything. This bitch is a problem, and you know it." Kenny's voice grew fast and high as he tugged Sam back with him, deeper into the kitchen. Sam reached up to pull his arm free, but his grip was too strong. "You wouldn't dare shoot me."

"Don't tempt me, Kenny."

"There's no other way." Panic filled Kenny's voice. He reached out with his free hand and grasped a thick-bladed knife from the butcher block. "You know that."

"Drop the knife." Will's voice was low and even. He shifted the gun a fraction to the right.

"No." Kenny shook his head swiftly. "This time you're going to listen to me. You always had a soft spot for her. Goddammit." Kenny lifted the knife. "Put the gun down or I'll fucking cut her. I swear to God, I will. Right here."

Fear tightened Sam's chest until she couldn't breathe.

"We both know that won't solve your problem," Will said in that same low tone.

"She's my problem. You're my problem!" Kenny yelled. "You always have to be in control. Well, you're not this time! I'm in control. Do you hear me? I say when!" He lifted the knife toward Sam's throat.

Sam tensed. Will's finger tightened on the trigger.

A gunshot echoed through the kitchen.

Kenny's body stiffened at Sam's back, and his hold on her throat loosened.

Sam staggered forward and sucked in air as she turned. The knife slipped from Kenny's fingers and clattered against the floor. Blood trickled from a hole in his forehead. He swayed and reached out for Sam. His body hit the counter, then crumpled to the floor.

*Oh God. Oh God . . .*

The room tipped. Sam stumbled. Before her legs went out from under her, strong arms wrapped around her waist and hauled her against a warm, solid body.

"Stay with me," Will said from what sounded like somewhere far away. "You're okay."

Darkness descended. Sam wasn't sure where she was or what had happened. Then, slowly, it faded, and she opened her eyes to see Will's concerned face.

"Yeah, you're okay," he said. "Just stay still."

He pressed a rag against her cheek. Pain echoed from the spot, and Sam hissed in a breath, dazed and confused and unsure what Will was doing in her house when she was already so late for school.

"Sorry." Grasping her hand gently in his, he lifted it to her cheek, then closed her fingers over the rag. "Hold this here."

He pushed to his feet and stepped away. She didn't know where. Her head grew light. Glancing down, she realized her blouse was open, the buttons missing.

"Whoa." Will's arms darted around her before she could ask what was going on, and he pushed her back into the chair she didn't remember sitting in. "Don't quite have your bearings yet. That's okay." He moved her chair up against the table so she had something to brace against, then he took the rag from her hand—the bloody rag, she realized with a roll of her stomach—and wrapped it around a bag of ice before pressing it back against her cheek. "Don't let go of this."

Her fingers shook, but she held the ice against her cheek and swallowed hard to find her voice.

"You got it?"

She nodded. Something was wrong. Something had happened.

"You sure?" he asked. "I need to call this in. I don't need you falling flat on the floor."

That was a silly question. Why would she fall flat on the floor? "I-I'm okay."

His expression said he wasn't so sure, but he pushed to his feet again and tugged a radio from his belt. His deep voice echoed in her kitchen, some strange numbers she didn't understand and didn't have any desire to decode.

Her chest was tight. Why was her chest so tight? She drew a deep breath, unable to get air all the way into her lungs. Confused, she glanced around the kitchen, then spotted Kenny's lifeless body lying on the floor.

Oh God. Her stomach pitched. And in a rush, everything came back to her.

The room dipped and swayed. From far away, she heard Will swear. But blackness descended before she could do anything to stop it.

# CHAPTER FOURTEEN

Ethan's high-tops squeaked as he shifted left, pushed off the floor, and lifted his arm. The basketball tipped off his fingers and ricocheted off the backboard. A grunt sounded close by as his brother Alec leapt into the air. Ethan knocked the ball out of Alec's hand. It bounced out of bounds.

Panting, Alec jogged across the floor, picked up the ball, and shot Ethan a look. "Take it easy. We playin' rat ball now?"

Wiping the sweat from his forehead with the back of his forearm, Ethan scowled and turned toward the top of the key. "Just check the damn ball."

Alec tossed it at him. "You're in a mood."

He was. He knew it. He thrust the ball back toward Alec. A game of one-on-one was supposed to take his mind off Samantha and what was happening to her in that town, but so far it wasn't working.

He wanted her out of there. Wanted to warn her to stay away from Branson and Kellogg, but he knew if he did she'd just ask why. She was friendly with both, and it was a small town, but she didn't know the real them. Not the ones he'd seen. Could he tell her the truth? Could he tell her about the months he'd lived in Hidden Falls and what he'd done there? He wanted to, but he was afraid if he did now she'd bolt before he could explain. And after the other night, after she'd finally opened up to him, he didn't want to risk doing anything to make her pull back.

"You know," Alec said, eyeing him over the ball. "If I didn't know you better, I'd say you need to get laid."

Getting laid wasn't the problem. Sex with Samantha was off-the-charts incredible. It was everything else in that town that was the problem. Ethan pointed toward the net. "Play."

One corner of Alec's mouth curled in a knowing smile. "See. Told ya. Smart chicks are more trouble than they're worth."

Ethan rested his hands on his hips. "Just dribble the damn ball, asshole."

Alec chuckled, but his features sobered when he dribbled, faked left, turned right, and charged. Ethan jerked forward, lifted his forearms, then planted his feet. Alec hit the solid wall of his body, bounced off, and landed on his back with a grunt. The ball slipped from his fingers and bounded across the floor.

"I'm done," Alec croaked. "Enough, already."

Breathless, Ethan stepped up and held out his hand. "Sorry."

"Shit, man." Alec let Ethan pull him to his feet, then leaned forward on his knees to suck back air. "That teacher's got you tied in knots."

Ethan grimaced. Alec didn't know the half of it. All he'd told his brother was that he was sort of seeing a teacher linked to one of his kids. He hadn't mentioned where she lived or how he felt about her. He'd learned long ago that with Alec, less was more. But his brother had a sixth sense and seemed to figure things out without words. And now, obviously, he'd figured out just what was eating at Ethan.

Ethan moved for the bench against the wall and reached for the water bottle from his duffel. Other one-on-one games continued around them, the scents of sweat and rubber thick in the air. Shoes squeaked on the polished floor. Shouts resounded through the tall double gymnasium. Lifting the collar of his T-shirt, he swiped the sweat from his brow, wishing it would wipe away his foul mood, and let the cotton fall against his chest.

Alec dropped onto the bench at his side and took a deep drink from his own bottle. "Feel better?"

"No." Ethan watched a game on the other side of the court. If anything, he felt worse. And basketball hadn't killed his craving for a nicotine hit either.

"Sucks when you can't just fix it, huh?"

Ethan glanced toward his brother as Alec stood, pulled off his damp T-shirt, and wiped the sweat from his forehead. The four small letters tattooed into Alec's skin, just over his heart, caught the light.

*Shit.* Ethan looked away, feeling even worse. What the hell was he sulking for? His life could be so much worse.

"Sorry, man." Ethan said. "I didn't mean to—"

"Forget it." Alec took another long drink and dropped back onto the bench.

*Forget it.* That was Alec's answer for everything. He never talked about her. Refused to let anyone around him talk about her. Aside from that tattoo he'd gotten during one of his drinking binges, it was if she'd never existed.

Compared to that, Ethan's life looked pretty damn good. Leaning forward, he braced his forearms on his knees and raked his fingers through his damp hair. No, he couldn't just fix it. Couldn't fix anything. All he could do was wait and hope that when he did eventually confide in her, she'd be so head over heels in love with him by that point that she'd listen. And believe him.

"The way I figure it," Alec said, "you'll do one of two things."

"Oh yeah? What's that?"

"You'll either talk her to death until she runs off, or—"

Ethan frowned at his brother. "Or what, smart-ass?"

Alec grinned. "Or talk her to death until she agrees, just to get you to shut the hell up."

Ethan huffed and lifted his water bottle again. A lot Alec knew. Samantha liked talking to him. He was the one who was having trouble opening up.

"Aw shit, Ethan. I don't think I've ever seen you like this."

"Like what?"

"Whipped."

Ethan stiffened. "Say that again. Just once."

Alec laughed and pushed off the bench. "No way. The last time I took you on in a mood like this I got my ass kicked. Senior year. Julie Sparrows. Remember her?"

"I remember." Jet-black hair, short skirts, the sweetest ass at Columbia High. "Great legs." And nowhere near as nice as Samantha's.

"Ooooh yeah."

Ethan braced one hand on his thigh and glared up at his brother. "And you deserved to get your ass kicked for moving in on her when she was already going out with me."

"Minor technicality. She had the hots for the blond surfer god, not the moody, dark thinker."

"She had the hots for you and half the varsity football team," Ethan corrected. He hadn't cared about losing that girl. She hadn't meant that much to him. But losing her to one of his brothers had stung.

Only it was nothing compared to the sting he felt now at the thought of losing Samantha.

Ethan's cell phone buzzed. Wiping the depressing thought from his mind, he reached into his bag and pulled it out. Samantha's number registered on the screen, and relief trickled through him, easing a hint of his stress.

"Hey," he said, lifting the phone to his ear. "I was just thinking about you."

"Um, hi. Am I interrupting your work?"

"No, I'm between sessions."

Alec chuckled and muttered, "Between sessions, my ass. Told ya. Seriously whipped."

Ethan shoved a fist into Alec's side. Alec grunted and moved back but continued to laugh. Pushing to his feet, Ethan stepped away. "What's up?" A quick glance at his watch told him it was only 11:00 a.m. "Aren't you supposed to be in class?"

"I'm taking the day off."

Something in her voice sent a tingle along his spine. "Everything okay?"

"Not really—" Samantha sucked in a sharp breath, then muttered, "That burns. Warn me next time."

"Sorry," a second voice echoed over the line.

"Samantha? What's going on? Who is that?"

"*That* is the reason I'm calling. I was hoping maybe you could pick me up."

The tingle intensified. "Where are you?"

"The emergency room."

"*What?* Are you okay?"

"I'm fine. I promise. I just . . . " She swallowed audibly over the line. "Remember how you told me to call if I found another dead body in my house? Well, I'm calling."

———

Brisk air wrapped around Ethan as he slid from his BMW. He hadn't taken the time to shower, hadn't even grabbed a sweatshirt, and the cool breeze now tickling the dried sweat on his back chilled his skin, but he barely cared.

He jogged across the hospital parking lot, heading for the ER. The automatic doors opened with a swish. Scanning the waiting room, he searched for Samantha. She'd been interrupted by a doctor during their conversation and had to turn her phone off. All he knew was that something had happened at her house, she'd ditched school, and she was now in the ER.

The waiting room was nearly empty, only a handful of people sitting in chairs. A kid coughed. The woman along the wall to his left lifted her dark head. Ethan kept scanning only to jerk back when he realized the woman was Samantha.

She stood, grabbed the bag at her feet, and headed toward him. One whole side of her forehead was bruised, her left eye swollen and black. A thin bandage stretched across the upper part of her cheek.

"Holy mother of God," he muttered.

"It's not as bad as it looks," she said, stopping in front of him.

His heart pounded hard as he carefully cupped her chin and turned her face toward the light so he could get a better look. "What happened?"

"I . . . " Samantha looked over the waiting room and the curious eyes angled their way. Grasping his hand, she pulled him toward the door. "I'll tell you outside."

His chest squeezed tight. As soon as they were on the sidewalk, he tugged her to a stop and gently turned her to face him. "Samantha—"

"I'm okay," she said quickly, reading the panic in his eyes. "I just got knocked around a little. The doctor said it's just bruises. They'll be gone in a couple of days."

"How . . . Did this happen at school?"

"No. Before. Kenny showed up at my house just as I was getting ready to leave for work."

"*Saunders?*"

She nodded and pulled him out of the way so a woman could pass through the doors. "He was acting crazy, ranting about Margaret, about me remembering something. I locked him out and called nine-one-one, but before I could get out of the house, he broke through the sidelight. I tried to run, but he grabbed me and threw me across the kitchen." She brushed a finger over the bruises near her eye. "That's how I got this."

Ethan's vision turned red. He was gonna kill the son of a bitch. "What happened then?"

"Will showed up. He was on my side of town when he heard the nine-one-one call. I don't remember a lot. Just that Kenny had a hold of me by the neck, and then Will shot him."

Ethan's gaze shot to Samantha's neck. Fingerprint bruises marred her soft skin, and the sight stretched his chest tight as a drum. He ran a hand over his face, tried to settle his roaring pulse, tried to stay calm for her sake. But the images branded his brain. Branson with a gun in her house. Saunders attacking her.

She was okay, though. She was alive. She could have been killed, but she wasn't.

"Once for sure," Samantha went on. "I think I sort of passed out after that."

A new sense of fear rushed through him. "What do you mean you passed out? With both of them there?"

"It's okay, Ethan." Her hand closed over his, hot against his suddenly frigid skin, and squeezed. "I passed out from seeing the blood, that's all." She swallowed hard. "Kenny's dead. And Will called the paramedics and got me right over here. I'm fine."

She might be fine, but he wasn't. Adrenaline pumped hard and fast through his body as he wrapped his arms around her and pulled her in tight. Just thinking about what she'd been through when he'd been playing basketball made his chest cinch down so hard it hurt to draw air.

"You're coming home with me tonight," he said into her hair.

"Okay."

No argument? She was more shaken than she was letting on.

"And you're not working this weekend." He drew back and looked down at her.

She nodded. "No work."

He hadn't been there. He hadn't been the one to save her. Branson had saved her. And as much as Ethan hated the son of a bitch, all he could think about was how grateful he was that Branson had gotten to her in time. "Do you need anything from your house?"

"Just Grimly. He's a little banged up too."

"Okay." His gaze darted over her features and settled on the bruises around her eye.

He could have lost her, just like that. Before he'd figured out what she meant to him. Before he'd told her. Before he had a chance to find out how she felt. In a matter of minutes, he could have lost everything he'd never known he wanted.

That ache pushed its way back up into his chest. Losing her now, when he'd finally found her, wasn't a thought he was willing to entertain.

He brushed his thumb across the edge of her bandaged cheek instead of grabbing on and holding tight again like he wanted to do. That would only scare her away, and right now he needed her close. Always needed her close. "Let's go get him."

She nodded, and, together, they headed for his car. Glancing sideways at him as they walked, she said, "Did you forget to get dressed for work today?"

"I was at the gym with Alec when you called."

"Oh, really? I can't wait to meet him."

He pulled the car door open for her, helped her in, and walked around to the driver's side. She was talking about the future, about meeting his family, and he should be happy about that, but all he could think about was Saunders in her house attacking her.

Ethan didn't want her to see how freaked out he was by it all, though, so he fought back the rush of fear and anger and climbed in beside her. He reached for his phone on the console.

She snapped her seat belt. "What are you doing?"

"Calling my dad." He hit "Dial" and pressed the phone to his ear. "Telling him not to come over tonight."

"What? No." She plucked the phone from his hand and clicked "End." "Don't do that."

"We don't need to do this tonight, Samantha."

"Ethan, I'm fine. Your father already made plans."

"He's not going to care." And the last thing she needed after everything she'd been through was a trip through her own living nightmare.

"No." She slipped the phone under her far leg so he couldn't reach it. "You talked me into this. We're doing it tonight."

"Samantha, listen—"

"No. You listen." She turned toward him, but this time her eyes weren't soft and weary. They were insistent and a little bit wild. And for the first time since he'd seen her bruised and battered face, he knew she wasn't nearly as fine as she'd tried to make him believe. "I don't want to wait. I want to get it over with. I think Kenny may have killed Margaret. And I think it has something to do with me. He said I knew too much, that I saw something. I don't have a clue what he was talking about, and I can't ask him now because he's dead, but I have a feeling it has something to do with my nightmare and that cabin. And I'm not going to let it go on any longer because I just want it to be over. If you don't want to help me, I'll call your father and—"

"Okay." He gently placed a hand on her arm and rubbed. "We'll do whatever you want."

"Don't placate me."

"I'm not. Trust me, I'm not. But I don't want to fight with you either. You scared the crap out of me earlier, Samantha. I'd give you just about anything you asked for right now."

Her voice dropped to a whisper. "Don't do that."

"Don't do what?"

"Don't be nice to me when I'm irrational and inflexible."

His heart pinched. He couldn't help it. He loved her. He'd realized it as soon as he'd heard she was hurt. He loved her, and he couldn't fathom the thought of anything happening to her.

But he knew she wasn't ready to hear that yet. Didn't want to do anything to spook her into running. Carefully, so he didn't hurt her, he slid his arm around her shoulders and pulled her into his chest. And told himself . . . soon. Soon he'd tell her. He just hoped by then she felt the same way. "Come here."

He held her close, drawing in the sweet scent of her skin and savoring the way her silky hair tickled his face. But mostly he focused on the strong, steady beat of her heart mingling with his, the two thumping together in a way that chased away the chill and warmed him all the way down to his toes. "I happen to like irrational and inflexible."

She huffed out a sound that was half laugh, half groan. "Then I guess you got lucky. Because I am the queen of irrational inflexibility."

"I did get lucky. The day I met you. When I was completely spell-bound and you looked down your nose at me because of my profession."

She drew back and looked up. "I shouldn't have done that. I'm sorry. You're not like any other shrink I've ever met."

"I'm not?"

She shook her head, and her gaze dropped to his lips. "You're so much more. And I was spellbound too. I was just too afraid to let you see. But I'm not afraid now."

Heat brewed in the depths of her dark eyes. Heat and the same need he always felt around her. And when she pressed her lips against his, every nerve ending in his body tingled with awareness and hope.

Whatever was happening in this town, whatever its link to her, they could get through it. As long as they were together, they could get through anything. He just hoped she still believed that after he told her the truth.

———

Sam tossed the magazine onto the coffee table, unable to concentrate on the words or pictures she'd been staring at for the last twenty minutes. Clenching her toes around the soft threads of the carpet, she leaned forward and brushed the loose hairs back from her face, then blew out a slow breath.

A shower had helped her feel human again, and the fire was warm, but she still couldn't shake the chill. The severity of the attack hadn't hit her until Ethan had taken her home to grab some clothes. The minute she'd seen the busted-in front door and the mess that used to be her kitchen, it all came crashing in.

She was trying to hold it together for Ethan's sake. She'd seen how rattled he was at the hospital. But every time she closed her eyes, she smelled the blood, she heard the gunshot, and she saw a montage of Kenny's dead body lying next to Margaret's and the remains she and Ethan had found in the woods.

Pushing to her feet, she paced to the dark windows and back again, breathing slowly through her nose. In. Out. One breath at a time. The shower stopped upstairs, and she glanced toward the ceiling and thought about going up to let Ethan's hands and lips and body chase away the rest of her anxiety, but she knew she wouldn't do it. He was already touching her as if she were a china doll about to break. Even if she begged him to make love to her now, she was pretty sure he'd say no.

Tonight probably wasn't the best night to try to tackle the whole hypnosis thing, but if she didn't figure out what she'd repressed, she was afraid she'd go mad. Kenny had mentioned the cabin. If he hadn't, she might have thought he was just ranting, but Ethan was the only person who knew about her nightmare. And ever since Kenny had brought it up, Sam hadn't been able to stop wondering if his voice was one of the voices she heard nightly in her dream.

The doorbell rang, jolting her out of her jumbled thoughts. From his spot on the blankets near the fire, Grimly groaned.

Sam waited several moments for Ethan to come down, but he didn't. And knowing she couldn't let his father stand out in the cold, she headed for the entry.

She pulled the door open and faltered. An attractive man with dark hair slightly gray at the temples and a woman with a sleek auburn bob stood on the porch looking back at her.

"You must be Samantha." The man extended his hand. Fine lines fanned out from light-brown eyes, warming a face that was angular and strong. "I'm Michael McClane, and this is my wife, Hannah."

*Shit.* Sam's nerves kicked into high gear. He'd brought Ethan's mother. Her gaze skipped to Hannah's smooth skin, whiskey-colored eyes, and pleasant smile. This wasn't supposed to be a meet-the-parents kind of thing. It was supposed to be work. Or therapy. Or . . . crap . . . she didn't know what it really was.

"Um, hi." Sam shook Michael's hand, followed by Hannah's, and pulled the door wider for them to enter. "Ethan's in the shower." Dammit, that sounded like they'd just had sex. "I mean, he had a basketball game earlier, I think. With Alec." Great. Now she sounded like an idiot. Closing the door quickly, she added, "He should be down any minute."

He'd better be. Or he was in serious trouble.

She turned back to face them, and gasped as Hannah caught her in a quick hug.

"It's great to finally meet you," Hannah said. "Ethan's told us so much about you."

Wonderful. She'd have to quiz Ethan on just what he'd shared.

Michael slipped off his coat and took Hannah's when she let go of Sam, then hung them in the closet. "Basketball with Alec, huh? I'm sure that was a physical game."

Sam darted a look between the couple. "Do they not get along?"

Hannah waved her hand, then looped her arm through Sam's and turned her toward the hall that opened to the back of the house. "They're boys. And brothers. And they like to pound on each other when they're frustrated. Besides which, knowing Ethan, he could be awhile yet. When he was a teenager he used to take thirty-minute showers and use up all the hot water. Kelsey used to throw a fit. Michael had to finally install a timer on the hot water heater."

Michael chuckled. "First time the timer went off and he got a blast of cold water, I thought he'd come through the wall."

Hannah smiled. "I didn't realize my boy knew such colorful language until that day."

"Clearly picked it up on the streets," Michael said, behind them. "Or from Alec. Because he definitely didn't get those words from me."

Hannah laughed and glanced over her shoulder. "Right. Because you are Saint Michael. As the swear jar in my kitchen clearly states."

To Sam, Hannah said, "So, how are you feeling?"

Sam's stomach tightened as they stepped into the great room with its soaring ceiling, flickering fire, and wide windows that looked out into darkness. "Um . . . " She didn't know how much Ethan had told them. "Fine."

Hannah let go of her. "Did they give you pain meds at the hospital?"

"No. Ibuprofen seems to be doing the trick right now." Michael moved up on Hannah's side, and as Sam glanced between the two, she decided not to avoid the elephant in the room. "I guess Ethan told you about today."

"Yeah, he called earlier." Michael wrapped his arm around his wife's shoulders. "I'm with him on this one. I think tonight might not be the best night for this."

Hannah turned toward her husband. "Why don't you go turn some cold water on your son and get him out of that shower?"

Michael smiled. "Good idea. If he goes through the wall, it'll be his Sheetrock he's destroying, not mine."

As Michael moved up the stairs, Hannah stepped into the adjoining kitchen and pulled two sparkling waters from the refrigerator. "How many stitches?"

"Four." Sam reached for the drink. "It looks worse than it is."

"Four or forty, still had to be a scary experience."

Sam's fingers tightened around the plastic bottle. She really didn't want to remember what had happened, or talk about it. Not yet. "I'm okay. Really. You're not going to give me the look too, are you?"

Hannah's eyes brightened, and she tipped her head. "What look would that be?"

"That therapist look. The she's-too-stupid-to-know-what's-good-for-her one Ethan's been giving me all afternoon long."

Hannah grinned. "He learned that one from his father. I've been on the receiving end of it enough times to feel your frustration." Her amber eyes softened. "You know he's just worried about you, right?"

"I know." Sam ran her fingers over the label on the bottle in her hand. "But he doesn't need to worry. I'm really fine. The police showed up before things got out of hand."

"You're not used to people caring, are you?"

The unexpected question brought Sam's head up.

"Ethan wasn't either," Hannah said. "Not for a long time. Getting him to open up to us, to trust us, took a tremendous amount of effort. There was so much he had to work through first. It doesn't happen overnight. But it does get easier, especially when you're around people who love you."

Sam's pulse quickened. Ethan loved her? She knew he cared about her. Knew he was crazy about her. Knew she was already in love with him. But he hadn't told her he loved her yet. And while the knowledge sent a burst of excitement through her chest, it also frightened her.

Hannah reached out and clasped Sam's hand across the island. "Are you okay, Samantha? You look a little pale."

Of course she was pale. Because suddenly hypnosis wasn't the most frightening thing she had to look forward to tonight. No, making sure she didn't say or do anything to mess up the best relationship she'd ever had was now all she could think about.

# CHAPTER FIFTEEN

"You decent?" Michael's muffled voice echoed from the open closet door.

Tugging the thin sweater over his head, Ethan called, "In here."

Footsteps sounded across the floor, and seconds later Michael leaned against the doorjamb of Ethan's walk-in closet.

His father's face was cast in shadows, the gray at his temples barely visible in the dim light. Tucking his hands into the pockets of his loose jeans, Michael said, "That the sweater Kelsey picked out?"

Ethan glanced down at the cream-colored knit with two green horizontal stripes across his chest, then bent to pick up his shoes. "Yeah."

Michael turned as Ethan brushed past him and sat on the end of the bed. "Your sister's got good taste."

Ethan pulled on his socks. "You come all the way up here to talk to me about Kelsey and her fashion sense?"

Michael chuckled. "No. We both know she's got more of that than all of us put together. Your mother banished me from the kitchen."

Now that made more sense. Ethan tied his shoe. "Girl talk."

"Any reason you're up here and she's down there?"

"I was sweaty." When Michael lifted his brow, Ethan frowned. "Not what you think."

Michael nodded and pushed away from the doorjamb to cross toward the window. "How is Alec?"

"Okay." Ethan tied his other shoe, a small part of him relieved they were chatting about something else for the moment. "He's taking off on an assignment right after Thanksgiving. Iraq, I think."

"Dammit." Michael ran a hand over his hair. "He's an incredible photojournalist. He could get plenty of work stateside if he wanted."

Alec could. No one doubted that. He didn't travel because he needed the work, though. He traveled to run from his memories. And the guilt. "Holidays are tough on him. You know that."

"I do, which is all the more reason he should stick close to home."

Ethan moved to the dresser and snapped his watch on his wrist. Compared to Alec's problems, Ethan's seemed minor. Samantha was safe. She was a little banged up right now, but she'd heal. Alec, on the other hand, had no idea if his daughter was alive or dead. "He's been sober for three years. Cut him some slack."

"You and I both know three years is nothing. Alec could find a bottle of Jack Daniel's in the middle of the Sahara if he wanted it bad enough. And I seriously doubt there'll be many redheads in the Middle East to take his mind off the reason he's burying himself in his work."

Wasn't that the truth? "Fine. You talk him out of it when he's here for dinner next week. I'd love to hear that one."

Michael frowned. "I will. He does listen to me, contrary to what you all think."

"Yeah, right. Keep on foolin' yourself with that line of thinking, old man."

Michael picked up a book on the small table, glanced at the cover, then lowered it again. "Samantha gonna be here for Thanksgiving dinner?"

Ethan's shoulders tensed. "I don't know." He closed the dresser drawer. "I didn't ask her yet. Things have been a little strange lately." And he wasn't sure how she'd react to a big family dinner. She didn't like to talk about family, and he didn't even know if she'd still be around by Thanksgiving.

"Are you sure she's up for this tonight?" Michael asked.

"No. But she's determined to go ahead with it. I tried to talk her out of it, only, she's not budging."

"She looks worn out."

"I know. It's more than just today. I don't think she's been sleeping much. Whatever this nightmare is she keeps having, I think it's linked to what's happening in that town."

Michael's eyes narrowed. After several heartbeats, he said, "Okay. We'll take it slow. We can always stop if it gets to be too much."

"I want to be there when you put her under."

"I'm not sure that's a good idea."

"Dad, I'm a professional."

"I don't think so, son. I've heard the way you talk about her."

"What does that mean?"

"It means you're attached. And your objectivity is shot." When Ethan frowned, Michael stepped forward and squeezed his shoulder. "That's not a bad thing, Ethan."

They were the same height, roughly the same build. From a distance, most people would never know they weren't blood related. He'd picked up a lot of his father's gestures over the years, and he'd lived with the man long enough to know when he was holding back. "Just spit it out."

"Spit what out?"

"You're worried. And not about Samantha."

"I always worry about my kids. That's no surprise."

"Yeah, well, you don't have to worry about me. You know that."

Michael dropped his hand. "I didn't agree with your taking this case in Hidden Falls, but I understood why you did. All this other stuff going on with Samantha, though? Yeah, it worries me. You can't tell me it doesn't bring up memories for you."

"Sure it does. But this doesn't have anything to do with me."

Michael's brow lifted. "Are you sure?"

"What are you implying?"

"I'm not implying anything. I'm saying it clearly. Hidden Falls is a small town. You and I have talked about these nightmares of hers. If this turns out to be what we both think, there's a good chance you may know the people involved. And that worries me. You finally broke free of that town, Ethan. I don't want to watch you get sucked back in."

Memories of that dark night eighteen years before flashed in Ethan's mind. He didn't want to be sucked back in either. But at this point, it wasn't his choice anymore.

He drew in a deep breath and met his father's gaze. "I'm in love with her."

"I know you are."

Ethan's shoulders tightened. "And you're not happy about that fact."

Michael was silent for a long moment. Then he said, "It doesn't matter what I am, son. It only matters that you're happy."

Before Ethan could ask what the hell that meant, Michael turned for the door. "Come on. Let's go save Samantha from your mother."

"Happy" wasn't a word Ethan would use to describe his feelings at the moment. "Tired," "scared," "desperate," and "weak" all seemed a heck of a lot more accurate than "happy."

And in a matter of minutes, he had a sickening feeling he could add "disturbed" to that list.

Man, he needed a cigarette. He really shouldn't have tossed that last pack.

Tapping his hand against his thigh, he headed for the stairs and the answers trapped in Samantha's memories.

Feeling more than foolish, Sam slipped her hands into the back pockets of her jeans as she stood in the doorway of Ethan's home office.

"Have you ever been hypnotized, Samantha?" Michael wheeled Ethan's office chair around the desk so it sat opposite the leather couch pushed up against the wall.

"Once. In Las Vegas. Didn't work, but I got free drinks out of it."

Michael smiled and sat. "This will probably be a little different. Have a seat."

Sam's hands were damp as she lowered to the couch and gripped the cushions beneath her. She glanced once toward Ethan where he stood in the doorway watching her closely, then back at Michael. "So, um. You're not going to probe the deep recesses of my mind or anything, are you?"

"No. Don't worry." Michael grinned. "This is very directed. I'm going to talk you into a relaxed state, and if it works, I'll ask you some questions about your dreams. We'll try to zero in on what you're experiencing, nothing more. The first step toward healing is unlocking whatever's blocking you." He must have seen the nervous look in her eye, because his tone gentled. "No one's going to know what you did on your twenty-first birthday, I promise."

Sam exhaled and leaned back against the cushions. "Good. Because I was told what happens in Vegas stays in Vegas."

Michael laughed and reached for his pen.

Sam glanced toward Ethan, still standing near the door, watching her with that worried expression. "Are you just going to stand there?"

"That's up to you," Michael said. "Ethan can stay or go. Whatever makes you more comfortable."

Nothing could make her comfortable at this point. But her heart did that strange little bump thing again as she gazed at Ethan, calming her in a way nothing else could. "I want him to stay."

"Okay, then." Michael flipped on his tape recorder as Ethan sat on the opposite side of the couch. "If at any time you want to stop, just say so."

Sam nodded and tried to focus on Michael's warm brown eyes. Ethan was close, but not close enough, and she wanted to reach for him but didn't know if she should. "Will I remember any of this?"

"Yes. You'll be completely aware of everything that's happening."

She breathed easier. "Okay."

"I want you to sit back, close your eyes. Just listen to the sound of my voice."

Sam's eyes drifted shut. The relaxation exercises took a long time— longer than she'd thought—and twice she giggled because the whole thing seemed so serious and silly at the same time. But each time she broke focus, Michael would coax her back using imagery with his gentle voice, and soon she found her mind drifting. To thoughts of Ethan and what he'd been like as a kid. To how Michael hadn't just helped him but saved his life.

Ethan was that to her, though he didn't know it. His calming presence saved her every day. Kept her sane. Made her feel safe. And thinking about him at night, when she was alone, saved her from getting lost in her nightmares all over again.

She reached a hand across the couch cushions, searching for him. His warm, solid fingers closed over hers, relaxing her even more. Squeezing his hand, she held on, knowing that as long as he was with her everything would be okay.

"How do you feel, Samantha?" Michael asked softly.

Sam exhaled, relaxing her muscles one by one. "Tired."

"I want you to imagine you're lying down. Weariness is tugging at you. Your eyes are heavy. A soft pillow cradles your head. Your mind relaxes with every breath. In and out. One breath at a time. That's good. Keep breathing like that."

Sam's body melted into the couch as she floated along with Michael's voice.

"You're doing well," he said. "Now I want you to focus on your dream. To the start of your dream. What's the first thing you see, Samantha? Do you know where you are?"

"My bedroom."

"That's good. Is your bedroom quiet? Is anyone else with you?"

"Yes, it's quiet. I'm alone."

"Do you feel safe there?"

She nodded.

"Safe is good. I want you to think about how you feel right now, safe, warm, no fears. If you start to feel anxious, I want you to think back to this bedroom, okay?"

She nodded again.

"Good, now what does your bedroom look like?"

"Purple walls. A pink bedspread. My dolls are all over the floor. Mommy gets so upset when I don't pick up my toys."

"What time is it, Samantha? Can you tell?"

"Late. I'm supposed to be asleep. But they're fighting again."

"Who?"

"Mommy and Daddy. They don't think I can hear them."

"What are they arguing about?"

"That woman, the one who used to be at the school. Mommy doesn't like her."

"Why not?"

"Because she teases the boys. And because she's back."

"Back from where?"

"I don't know, but she's back." Her eyes tightened. "I don't want to listen to them fight anymore."

"No, you don't have to. What are you going to do instead?"

"I opened my bedroom window and climbed down the tree."

"There's a tree?"

"Yes. A great big oak. It's perfect for sneaking in and out."

"Do you sneak out through the window a lot, Samantha?"

"No. But sometimes."

"Is it warm or cold outside?"

"Cold." She shivered. "My sweatshirt's too thin. It rained today."

"Where are you going?"

"Into the woods. Rebecca's waiting for me."

"Who's Rebecca?"

"My doll. She doesn't like the dark. I have to get her."

"Did you leave her somewhere?"

Sam bit her lip and nodded. "In the clubhouse. I don't want the boys to find her. They pull her hair and throw her around. They're not nice to her."

"Are the boys at the clubhouse now, Samantha?"

She shook her head. "No. It's too late now."

"Do they always go to the clubhouse with you?"

"No. They climb trees and play war in the woods. Sometimes they go to the waterfall to swim. But it's too cold for that tonight."

Her brow wrinkled, and she tipped her head to the side.

"What's wrong, Samantha?"

"There's . . . there's someone in the clubhouse."

"How do you know?"

"There's a light. And I can hear voices."

"How many voices. Can you tell?"

"I don't know. Three? Maybe more."

"Tell me what the voices are saying, Samantha."

"I . . . I can't hear them. I'm too far away."

"Can you move closer?"

"I can't. I . . . " Her vision sharpened until the forest was all around her, and she jerked back. "Oh no."

And as Sam looked through the dark trees toward the glow coming from the small cabin, she covered her ears with her hands and screamed.

# CHAPTER SIXTEEN

*"Dammit. Hold her still!" a man yells.*

*Voices echo from the cabin. Sami's pulse soars. She isn't sure who screamed, them or her, but she has to look. She can't go back without looking.*

*Inching forward in the darkness, she eyes the run-down building as her heart pounds hard against her ribs. Shingles hang at odd angles. Dirt-covered panes of glass are cracked and broken. Shadows—monsters—dart back and forth behind the glass, breaking the steady stream of light, causing her heart rate to kick up harder in her chest.*

*Go home. Run. Turn away. The words spin in her head, but she can't go back because Rebecca's in there. Rebecca doesn't like to be alone. And Sami can't sleep without Rebecca.*

*She pushes shaking legs forward. Another scream rends the frigid night air. She jumps. Tingling fingers of panic race down her spine.*

*"I said to hold her still!" the man hollers again.*

*"I can't," someone else yells. This voice is younger than the first. It sounds like . . . like Seth's friend Kenny. "She's fighting."*

*"Let me go!" a female screams.*

*"Teach her a lesson!" another girl says.*

*A loud crack erupts, one that sounds like wood against wood, followed by a muffled sob.*

*Sami knows those voices. She's heard them before. Her stomach tightens as she presses her body to the side of the cabin and silently tries to figure out who's in there.*

*"Tie her arms down," the first instructs. "Then we'll teach her a lesson."*

*Footsteps sound. Then some kind of struggle. And a man says, "Son of a bitch! She bit me!"*

*"Oh, you wanna play rough, huh?" Another loud crack slices through the air.*

*Sami jerks back, and fear closes her throat.*

*Go back . . . Go back . . .*

*But she can't go back. Because Rebecca is still in there. She needs to make sure they aren't hurting Rebecca. Swallowing hard, she grips the window ledge and climbs with shaky movements onto the small pile of wood stacked outside.*

*The glass is dirty. She can't see through. Crouching lower, she peers through a hole in the pane.*

*Only she doesn't see Rebecca. She sees a woman with long dark hair and wide, frightened eyes. A woman she's seen before. At the school where Seth goes.*

*The woman is tied to a rusted bed frame and dirty mattress, naked. Blood stains her skin, and her makeup runs down her face in black tracks. And there are bruises on her skin. Nasty, angry bruises on her arms and legs and hips and ribs from things Sami doesn't want to imagine.*

*The woman sobs. "Please, just let me go. I won't tell anyone."*

*"No, you won't." A man steps in front of the woman. Sami can't see his face. Only his back. He's tall. Dark hair. He looks like an athlete. Something about the way he moves is familiar . . .*

*He loosens the belt from his waist and pulls it through the loops in his jeans. "Remember what we used this for?" he says to the woman. "Remember how much you liked it?"*

*The woman's eyes grow wide and frightened. She struggles against the ropes holding her down. To someone standing out of Sami's view, the man says, "Untie her."*

*Two people, smaller than the man, rush over and untie the woman's hands and legs from the rusted bed frame. She lunges to her feet. "You son of a bitch. I'll kill you. I'll kill you for this!"*

*The man lifts his arm and strikes her with the leather belt. A crack echoes through the cabin. The woman stumbles back and hits the wall. The man drops the belt, jerks forward, and grabs her by the neck before she falls to the floor. Shoving her back to the wall, he sneers, "No, you won't. You're not going to do anything ever again. You wanted to be the whore? Well, you got to be her tonight. How does it feel to be used the same way you used all of us?"*

*He grasps her throat with both hands. Lifts the woman so her feet dangle off the floor. The woman's face pales. Her eyes fly wide. She scratches at his hold, but he doesn't let go.*

*Sami's heart races. She knows she needs to run, but she can't look away. He can't hurt her. He said he was letting her go. He has to let her go . . .*

*"Hey, man," a panicked voice says from the shadows. "She can't breathe. Let go of her."*

*Muscles flex in the man's forearms, and he squeezes tighter. "No. She's not going anywhere. She's gonna pay for what she did. Aren't you, Sandy?"*

*His hands clench harder around her throat. Her eyes go bug wide. Her face turns red, then purple. She gasps and struggles, making a gargling sound.*

*"You're never going to torment another person in this town," the man yells. "Do you hear me, bitch? Never again!"*

*Another body slams into the man, knocking him away from the woman. The two fall to the ground and roll across the dirty floorboards. Vaguely, Sami can hear someone yelling to stop, that it's not right, that he didn't agree to this, but all she can focus on is the woman lying still and unmoving on the ground. Her eyes wide and lifeless.*

"*You fucking kid,*" the man yells. *In one quick movement, he shoves the smaller person off him and lurches to his feet.*

*Sami's leg shakes. She's dead. The woman is dead. They killed her. They—*

*She jerks back. Her foot slips on a log. Before she can stop herself, she crashes to the ground in a pile of wood.*

"*What was that?*" *someone asks from inside the cabin.*

Oh no. Oh no. Oh no!

"*I don't know,*" *another voice answers.*

"*Son of a bitch,*" *the man growls.* "*You two, go check what that was while I deal with this one.*" *The voice turns menacing.* "*You wanna end up like her, son? Think long and hard, because I'm way past fucking around.*"

*Footsteps boom across the cabin floor. Sami's adrenaline spikes. She has to leave Rebecca. She can't save her now. Tears choke her throat as pushes to her feet and runs.*

*A low branch lashes her face. She cries out, stumbles over rocks in the path. Her body hits the ground with a thud. Stones stab into her knees, slash at her flesh. The ripe scent of earth fills her senses, but she scrambles to her feet and keeps running.*

*She rounds a bend in the path, spots the lights from her house down the hill. Chokes back a sob, but safety is so close. She pushes forward. Strong arms close around her from behind, hauling her up off the ground.*

"*No! Let me g—*"

*A hand clamps over her mouth, muffling her words. She kicks out with everything she has, digs her fingernails into the soft flesh holding her tight, and flails.*

"*Shh! Sami, stop fighting me, dammit!*"

*Seth. That's Seth's voice. She slows her frantic struggling.*

*He lowers her to the ground and grips her shoulders as he drops to his knees.* "*What are you doing out here?*"

"*I . . . They . . . Rebecca . . .*" *Tears fill her eyes as she looks past him, up the dark path.* "*She's in there with them. I don't want them to hurt her like they're hurting that woman.*"

*Seth whips around and looks up the dark path. "They're there now? At the cabin? With her?" He shifts back to face Sami and grips her arms tighter. "Tell me. How many?"*

*Sami swallows the hard lump in her throat. Seth's familiar brown eyes look wild, and he's holding her so tight her arms hurt. "I . . . I don't know. I couldn't tell."*

*Seth pushes to his feet. "Go home, Sami. Run. As hard as you can. And don't come back up here. No matter what."*

*He lets go of her and takes a step up the path. Panic rushes in. Sami grips his hand to stop him. "You can't go up there. Something bad will happen. I know it!"*

*"Everything will be okay." He squeezes her hand tightly in his much bigger one. "I promise. Now go home."*

*"No!"*

*He disappears into the dark, leaving her cold and alone.*

*Sami shivers. She wants to chase him. Needs to follow. But she's scared. So scared she can barely move. Tears spill over her cheeks, track down her skin. An owl screeches above. Shivering, she backs into the brush and shakes.*

"Samantha."

*She looks up through the tears. Wipes a hand across her nose. Hope rushes through her. Seth has come back. He wouldn't leave her out here like this alone.*

"Samantha."

"Pull her out now!"

*But that frightened voice isn't Seth's. She ducks back into the brush. Shakes and squints to try to see clearer.*

"Samantha," a gentle voice says from a great distance away. "Listen to the sound of my voice. I'm going to count backward from five. When I get to one, I want you to open your eyes. Five . . . four . . ."

*No. She brushes the tears away with her forearm, peers through the trees toward the path. She wants Seth. She needs to find Seth. She has to go after him.*

"Three . . . "

*"No!" Her hands clench into fists.*

"Two . . . "

*"Come back!" she cries, pushing to her feet, but her legs don't seem to be working. Why can't she move her legs?*

"One . . . "

*A loud snapping sound echoes close. Blackness descends, blocking out the shadowy woods, the smell of pine and earth, even the cool breeze.*

"Open your eyes, Samantha. That's it. Deep breaths in and out. Remember your bedroom. Remember how safe you feel there."

*Michael.*

Over the sound of her racing heartbeat, Sam could just make out the tick of a clock somewhere close.

"Open your eyes, Samantha," Michael said again.

Her eyelids felt heavy. Her muscles like rocks. Drawing in several deep breaths, she focused on the soothing sounds of Michael's voice, and blinked several times.

"There you are." Michael smiled. "Welcome back."

"I . . . " Images plowed into her. Everything she'd just experienced. But one was stronger than all the rest.

*Seth.*

Her eyes snapped shut, and she groaned.

"This was a bad idea," Ethan said at her side. "We shouldn't have done it. I told you she wasn't strong enough for this tonight."

Dimly, she became aware of warmth covering her hand against the couch cushion and realized Ethan was holding on to her.

She turned her hand over and squeezed his, needing the connection. Needing him.

"A rush of emotion is normal after a session like this," Michael said. "Samantha, you're safe here. Nothing can hurt you. Can you tell us how you feel?"

*How she felt . . .* She couldn't tell them how she felt. Wasn't even sure how she felt. All she knew was that she needed air. Needed a moment to think. Needed out.

"I-I'm okay."

Her voice sounded scared and shaky. They had to hear it. Clearing her throat, she gently pulled her hand from Ethan's and pushed off the couch.

"Samantha." Ethan stood, worry darkening his eyes.

"I-I'm okay. Really. I think I need to get a drink and use the restroom."

Michael rose. "Can we get you anything?"

She stepped toward the door. The cool wood on her bare feet felt solid, real. Something she could focus on. "No, thanks. I'm fine. I-I'll be right back."

Hands shaking, she closed the bathroom door and stared at her reflection. Tears welled in her eyes, but she blinked them back. That was the last time she'd seen Seth. The same night he'd died. And it was the same night a woman had been murdered in that cabin.

She pulled herself together as best she could and opened the door. The hallway was empty. On shaky legs, she moved back toward the office and paused outside the door when she heard Ethan's tense voice.

"We shouldn't have done that."

"She'll be fine, son," Michael said.

"You haven't seen her in the throes of one of these nightmares. I have. This is just going to make them worse."

Sam stepped back into the room. Both men turned at the sound of her footsteps and looked toward her with expectant eyes. But Ethan's were worried. And she knew she had to put him at ease.

Crossing her arms, she moved to the desk and leaned back against the shiny surface. "It was Sandra Hollings."

"Are you sure?" Michael asked.

"Yes. I saw her face."

"What about the others?" Michael asked.

Sam rubbed a hand across her forehead. She didn't want to remember, to even think about it, but she had to get it out. "I'm not sure. I couldn't see them. Several were young. Teenagers, I think. And one man. But his back was to me. I'm not sure who he was."

"Think about the voices," Michael said. "Were any familiar?"

"Kenny. I heard Kenny's voice." Sam shook her head. "This morning, when he came after me, he was ranting about me being there. I . . . I didn't know he was talking about this. About Hollings." Her gaze drifted to Ethan. He stood near the couch, his muscles rigid, his arms at his sides. "Those remains we found weren't far from that cabin. I was ten when all of this happened. I know people didn't like her. I remember my parents arguing about her before she disappeared, but I never thought . . ." She swallowed hard. "I didn't think it would result in this."

Ethan's jaw hardened, but he didn't speak.

"How do you know how old you were when she went missing?" Michael asked.

*Because I was ten when Seth died.* Sam bit her lip, unable to say the words. Unable to think about Seth involved in any of this.

"Because I was ten when I lost my doll," she managed. "It was fall then. October. There was a full moon that night. I was worried we might get an early snowstorm. That's why I went up to the cabin that night . . . to find my doll. I didn't look for her again after that. Until tonight, I never really understood why I stopped searching for her. Now I do."

Michael and Ethan exchanged looks and something darkened in Ethan's eyes, but Sam didn't have the strength to guess what he was thinking. She just wanted to finish.

"There was a girl there too. With Kenny and the others. Egging them on. I think it might have been Margaret, but I can't be sure. The others, though . . . I didn't get a clear look at them. I don't know who they were."

"It's okay, Samantha." Michael squeezed her arm reassuringly. "If they were kids, you might never know. Voices change. You were talking to someone there at the end, though. Can you tell me who that was?"

Yes, she knew. But she still couldn't make her lips form his name no matter how much she wanted to, because his loss was like a knife to the heart, more painful now than it had ever been before.

She shook her head.

Michael eyed her for several long moments. Finally, he bent and pulled a small box from the bag at his feet. "Sleeping pills. These should help you tonight so long as you aren't still taking any pain meds from the hospital."

"Thanks."

"Do you want to talk more about it now in detail?"

*Yes.* She wanted to tell Ethan about Seth, but the words still wouldn't come. "Not tonight. I'm pretty tired."

He nodded. "Details might come back to you as you process it all. If you want to talk more, just give me a call."

Sam forced a smile she didn't feel. "Thanks."

He squeezed her arm once more, then let go and glanced toward Ethan near the doorway. "I should go tell your mother we're done down here."

"I'll help you."

Michael slung the strap of his bag over his shoulder. "Try to get some rest, Samantha."

"I will. And thanks. I know this is probably more drama than you expected to deal with tonight."

One corner of Michael's lips tipped up. "This is nothing. In this family, we're used to drama. You fit in well."

A little of Sam's anxiety eased. As awful as it could have been, she'd gotten through it, mostly because of Michael's gentle nature, but also because she'd had Ethan by her side.

She glanced Ethan's way as his father left, but instead of the gentle, warm eyes she expected to see, something hard hovered in their green depths. Something she didn't know how to define.

"I'm going to see them out." Ethan stepped toward the door. "I'll be back in a few minutes."

He turned without another word. And alone, Sam fingered the box of medication as she stared after him and tried to ignore the shiver rushing down her spine. He was just worried about her, that was all. She hadn't shocked him. She couldn't have. Because right now she needed his strength and comfort more than she ever had.

———

*Samantha at ten years old. October. Full moon. Eighteen years in the past.*

Ethan closed the front door as the thoughts swirled in his mind. His dad had caught it. Michael hadn't even needed to say the words, but Ethan knew his father was currently thinking the same damn thing Ethan was.

If Samantha's memory was correct, the night Sandra Hollings had disappeared was the same night Ethan had been arrested.

His chest drew tight as a drum. Turning away from the door, he moved through the hallway, trying to piece together shapes that didn't want to fit. If Saunders and Margaret Wilcox had been at the cabin that night, that meant Branson and Kellogg had probably been there as well. But how had they gotten to the waterfall? And who had Samantha been talking with there at the end? Ethan didn't want to believe it was Branson, but his gut thought otherwise. She considered Branson a friend. If she'd seen his face in that cabin or heard his voice, would she admit it? Whoever it was had seemed to show up to the party late. If she thought Branson wasn't involved in what the others had done, would she protect him?

Ethan hoped not. Because he knew Branson was not innocent. Branson and Kellogg had both been in the water that night at the falls.

"I like your parents," Samantha said from a stool near the island when Ethan stepped into the room.

He looked her way and blinked, working hard to separate past from present. "What?"

"Your parents. They were nice."

She was talking about meeting his parents. She wasn't flipping out like he expected her to do. Like he was doing.

"Ethan?" Her brow lowered as she pushed off the stool and crossed to him. "Are you okay?"

No, he wasn't okay. He was as far from okay as a person could get. "I want you to stay away from Will Branson and Jeff Kellogg."

"Why?"

"Because they're dangerous."

She frowned. "Why would you think that? Will saved my life today."

Branson had. Not Ethan. Ethan hadn't been there when she'd needed him most. She trusted Branson more than anyone in Hidden Falls. Maybe even more than she trusted the man currently warming her bed. "He and Kellogg were friends with Kenneth Saunders."

"That doesn't make a person dangerous. Lots of people were friends with Kenny."

"I saw them together at the Kelloggs' party. There's a freakin' picture of them on the same basketball team up at the high school."

"So what?" Sam's eyes grew wide. "David was on the same team with them. Are you saying that makes him dangerous too?"

He opened his mouth to tell her exactly what he knew about Branson but closed it when he caught the disbelief in her eyes. She wouldn't believe him. The knowledge was like a sucker punch to the gut. She'd known Branson since she was a kid, but she'd only known Ethan for a couple of weeks. It didn't matter that they were sleeping together. It didn't even matter that he loved her. When push came to shove, she'd believe someone she'd known all her life over someone who'd just shown up in town.

A deep ache filled his chest, but it was quickly replaced by a nicotine craving that hit hard and fast, making his mouth dry and his fingers itch for a cigarette. "There are things you don't know about him, Samantha."

"Like what? Ethan, you're jumping to conclusions. Will was not one of the voices I heard at that cabin. He wasn't involved in whatever Kenny was doing. I would have known. Look, I get that you're worried about me, but Will is the last person you have to be concerned about." She stepped toward him, closed her fingers around his, and squeezed his hand. "Let this go."

He wanted to, but he couldn't. Because something in his gut screamed that Will Branson was involved in ways neither of them understood. And he couldn't stand the thought that Samantha might turn to the man for help, now or in the future.

The nicotine craving intensified. He pulled his hand from hers, stepped back, and rested his hands on his hips. He needed to get out of here, needed to think, needed to try to come up with a way to make her see reason. Because if he stayed, they were just going to argue, and after everything she'd been through today, she didn't need that.

He turned for the front of the house. "I have to go out for a bit."

"What?" Panic filled her voice. "Ethan, where are you going?"

He grabbed his coat from the closet and pulled the door open. "I'll be back later."

"Wait. Why . . . " Her feet drew to a stop. "Ethan, please. Talk to me."

He couldn't. Because his thoughts and memories were so jumbled from what he'd seen today and heard tonight, he didn't know what to say . . . or what to do, for that matter. All he knew was that he was too close to all of this to think rationally.

And he had no idea what that meant for their relationship in the long term.

———

A soft click echoed as the front door opened and closed, rousing Sam from her spot on the couch. She'd been lying there for the last hour, thinking about Ethan, thinking about what she'd seen in that hypnosis session, thinking about her memories of finding Seth lifeless in the pool beneath the falls.

It had all happened the same night. She couldn't deny that any longer. The two events were related. She'd seen two people dragging Seth out of that cabin. Knew that the boy who'd drowned him had to have been one of them. Realized that he must have been involved in what they'd all done to Sandra Hollings.

She still didn't understand why she'd remembered finding Seth in the falls but had repressed what had happened to Sandra Hollings in that cabin. Maybe it was because she'd seen Sandra Hollings's murder but had only heard Seth's. Was that possible?

She wanted to ask Ethan but didn't know if she should. And since he'd run out on her and had yet to come home, she wasn't sure if she'd ever be able to.

Grimly pushed up from his spot near the fire and rambled down the hall. Sam blinked several times and lifted her head.

"Hey, big guy," Ethan said from the entry. "You waiting up for me?"

Nerves churned in Sam's stomach as she slowly sat up and blinked. Her heart urged her to jump and meet him, but after the way he'd left, she wasn't sure that was a smart idea.

She brushed the hair back from her face. Was it all too much for him? He knew she had major baggage now. Seeing the things she'd seen, living with them as long as she had . . . was he asking himself if he should cut and run?

Her throat grew thick. She wasn't sure what she'd do if the answer to either of those questions were yes. He'd made her fall in love with him even though she'd tried not to, and tonight of all nights she needed his arms around her.

Footsteps sounded in the hall, then stilled. And even though the lights were off and the fire was nothing but deep-red embers, she swiped at the stupid wetness on her cheeks so he couldn't see.

A long silence stretched over the room. She knew he'd seen her. Her stomach tightened with fear, and she held her breath, afraid to turn and look, afraid to move in case he was about to say it was time to call things quits.

His tennis shoes sounded across the floor, then quieted as he stepped onto the carpet. And when he stopped in front of her and looked down, she finally mustered up the courage to meet his eyes.

These eyes weren't the same hard, cold eyes she'd seen before he'd left, though. These eyes were a soft mottled green, and they were filled with so much regret, everything inside her broke. "Ethan . . . "

"I'm sorry," he whispered. Sinking to the floor, he wrapped his arms around her waist and leaned forward until his cheek pressed against her belly. "I'm so, so sorry. I shouldn't have left like that."

She still wasn't sure why he had, but she closed her arms around him and pulled him in close as tears—tears of relief this time—spilled over her lashes.

"It was just . . . I should have been there," he said against her. "It should have been me. I should have been with you today, only I wasn't. I was playing basketball with my stupid brother when you were . . . " His arms tightened around her. "And then hearing everything you saw in that session tonight, it just . . . It scared me, Samantha. There were other people involved besides Kenny. Others at the cabin that night, and we don't know who they were. And after everything that's happened lately, I can't think about you going back to that town without panicking. I don't know what I would do if I lost you. I can't lose you like that."

Her heart filled, and all those worries she'd stressed over after he'd walked out faded into the ether. As did every fear she'd ever had about opening her heart to someone else.

Cupping his face, she lifted so his gorgeous green eyes could meet hers. "Nothing's going to happen to me, Ethan. I'm not going anywhere. I promise."

"Samantha." Pain etched his features, and his eyes slid closed. "There are things you don't know. Things about me I haven't told you. Things that—"

"They don't matter."

He looked up at her again and frowned. "You don't—"

"Nothing matters except the way you make me feel, Ethan. I never would have agreed to that hypnosis without you. I couldn't have gone through it alone and come out on the other side sane. And for the first time in a long time, that's how I feel. Sane. Because of you. Just knowing you were there made me feel safe. You always make me feel safe. You're the only one who ever has. I've been running from people since I was ten because of that night. Because I was too afraid to let them get close and see the real me. But with you, I don't have to be afraid anymore. You've seen the real me, and you're still here. And I love you for that, Ethan. I love you because you make me feel alive. I love you because—"

His mouth covered hers, so fast she barely saw him move. And then he drew her into a kiss that rocked the world right out from under her.

His tongue swept along hers, and even though all she wanted to do was get lost in him forever, she pushed back. "Have you been smoking?"

He exhaled and rested his forehead against hers. "Five months and twenty-six days without a cigarette. Down the drain."

"Really? You never told me that."

"My nicotine addiction is not something I go around advertising." He lifted his head and looked at her. "Usually I can control it. Tonight, I lost the battle."

"Oh, Ethan. I don't want fighting with me to be your weakness. I'll stay away from Will and Je—"

"Samantha." He rubbed his thumb over her cheek, and shards of heat raced across her skin at the simple touch. "*You* are my weakness, and nothing you say or do can stop that. I knew you were my weakness the minute you danced with me on that football field, and I wouldn't change it for anything. I know I'm being irrational about Branson, but I can't bear the thought of anything happening to you."

Tears filled her eyes again. Tears and hope and a joy she'd always been too afraid to wish for.

"I'm not going to lose you, Samantha. Today scared the crap out of me. I can't go through that again."

She wasn't going to lose him either. She lifted her mouth to his lips, wrapped her arms around his shoulders, and drew him into her mouth, into her heart, even into her soul.

His tongue danced over hers, and she pulled him down with her to the couch cushions. His weight pressed against her, solid, warm, real. And then his hands were on her, streaking down to the hem of her sweatshirt, pushing it up her ribs and over her breasts, dragging it over her head as he broke the kiss and tossed the garment on the floor.

His gaze swept over her breasts, and the approval she saw in his eyes made her nipples pebble and her stomach cave in. "You're gorgeous."

He lowered his mouth to her breast, drew one nipple into his mouth, and suckled. Threading her fingers into his hair, Sam tipped her head back and groaned.

He moved to the other side, repeated the licking, sucking, and swirling with his tongue, then kissed his way down to her torso and flipped the button on her jeans. "I want these off."

She lifted her hips as he tugged her jeans and panties down her legs. Didn't try to hide herself as his gaze raked her most intimate flesh. Moaned long and deep when he lowered his mouth to her sex and licked right where she wanted him most.

The horror of the day drifted to the back of her mind. All she could focus on was him. On this. On them. She slid her hand into his hair as she lifted to his mouth, loving each and every stroke of his sinful tongue and the way he could make her forget everything but him.

Her orgasm built, growing in strength and intensity, teasing the edges of her control. Her hips flexed. She tightened her fingers in his hair.

"Oh yes, Ethan . . . " He licked faster, drove her harder to the edge. Sex with Ethan was like nothing she'd ever known. It wasn't just physical. It touched every part of her. It made her crave so much more. It left her spinning in a way that wasn't just satisfying but made her feel absolutely complete. "Right there. Just . . . there."

The wave crested, and she cried out as pleasure streaked along every nerve ending. And as it faded, she felt his lips kissing a soft, wicked path up her torso, around each breast, then higher until he reached her throat and suckled.

Desire rebuilt, hot and needy. She needed to show him, needed to be close to him. Framing his face with her hands, she pulled his mouth back to hers and kissed him until she was breathless.

"I want you, Ethan," she mouthed against him. "Just you. Now. Right now."

# CHAPTER SEVENTEEN

Ethan's heart swelled. He wanted her too. Just her. An hour ago, he hadn't known what to do. Now, the only thing that mattered was this, her, them.

He pushed up on his hand, reached back and fisted his cotton shirt. Her fingers tickled his bare chest as he pulled the garment off and tossed it on the floor, warming his torso and pecs, sending tingles all across his skin. She trailed her hands lower, unhooked the button on his jeans, and slid her hands inside his waistband. Lowering his head, he kissed her, desperate to taste her, to feel her, to be close to her. Her hands shifted inside his jeans and cupped his ass, pulling him into her heat just as she flexed her hips and lifted.

Blood pulsed in his veins and gathered in his groin, leaving him hard and hot and desperate. He kissed her deeper, toed off his shoes, then pulled away from her mouth so he could reach back for his wallet and find a condom. Breathing heavy, she helped him shove his jeans and boxers off while he fumbled with the condom, then wrapped her arms around his shoulders and pulled him back down to her. "Come here."

Her legs opened, and she lifted to his kiss, drawing him into her mouth and her body at the same time. He groaned at the tight, slick pressure, at her sweet, wet tongue tangling with his. And as their bodies moved in a rhythmic dance that was familiar, desperate, and new all at the same time, he knew everything that had happened in his past—even the most horrible things—had been worth it. Because they'd brought him to this moment. To being here, with her. To finding a love he'd never thought he deserved.

Every slip and glide and pulse and throb pushed him closer to his release, but he didn't want to crest without her. Levering up on one hand, he brushed the silky hair back from her face and whispered, "Open your eyes, Samantha."

Her body trembled. Perspiration dotted her skin and melded with his. Blinking several times, she looked up with warm, glossy chocolate eyes he was almost sure he could see forever in.

"That's it." He thrust deeper, moved faster. "Don't look away. Stay with me."

"Ethan . . . " Her fingertips dug into his shoulders, but she didn't look away. And then her whole body shook, and his name faded on a groan.

Her orgasm triggered his. Pleasure raced down his spine and exploded in his hips until there was nothing left but a shimmer of sensation that radiated outward and echoed through every cell.

He collapsed against her, his body slick with sweat, her chest rising and falling against him while she sucked back air. Trembling through the aftershocks, he pressed a kiss against her shoulder and rolled to his side on the couch so he didn't crush her. His arms closed around her as she laid her head against his chest. And as he ran his hands up and down her damp spine, he knew this was right. He knew they could make this work.

"You're the one, Samantha. The only one for me."

She sighed, pressed her lips against his throat, and held on tighter. His heart swelled even more, and he told himself . . . soon. Soon he'd find a way to tell her about his past. But not tonight. Tonight he just wanted to go on holding and loving her. Because tonight he didn't want her to have to worry about anything in their past or future. Tonight he only wanted her to focus on him.

———

Sam rolled to her side in Ethan's big bed and sighed in complete contentment.

Her muscles were sore from the most amazing night with Ethan, but she barely cared. She was so relaxed she didn't even care that she was alone because she knew he hadn't gone far. Shifting to her back, she stared up at the ceiling and smiled. He was probably downstairs making her breakfast or getting her coffee or juice. He was always doing little things like that to make her feel special. And she loved him for that. Loved the way he took care of her, loved the way he looked at her, loved everything about him. But mostly she loved the way he loved her, in a way no one ever had before. And she couldn't wait to see him again and show him just how much that meant to her.

She climbed out of bed, found a baggy sweatshirt in his closet, and pulled it on. After running her fingers through her hair, she brushed her teeth with a new toothbrush she discovered in his bathroom cabinet, then headed downstairs to look for him.

The kitchen and great room were empty. Moving through the house, she checked rooms and smiled again when she found him in his office.

He sat in the chair behind his big desk, his feet bare and perched on the dark surface, his strong legs covered by gray sweats while a blue Mets T-shirt stretched across his toned pecs. A file folder lay open in his lap, a soda can sat on the desk to his right. Tortoiseshell glasses were perched on his nose, and his hair was mussed as if he'd run his fingers through it several times. And even though Sam knew he wasn't trying to look sexy as he worked, a wicked hot burst of arousal coursed through her just the same.

"Hey," she said, stepping into the room. "Am I interrupting?"

One corner of his lips curled in a sultry smirk. "Not at all." Dropping the folder on his desk, he lowered his feet to the floor, pushed back, and held out a hand. "Come here, gorgeous."

Tingles rushed all over Sam's skin as she took his hand and let him pull her onto his lap. She relaxed against him, laid her head on his shoulder, and sighed as he wrapped his arms around her. Oh yes, she was definitely getting used to this. Could easily see herself here with him every day.

"How do you feel?" he asked softly, running his hand up and down her arm.

"Good. Tired." *Horny.* She traced a lazy pattern on his T-shirt. "I missed you this morning."

"Sorry. I couldn't sleep any more, and you looked too peaceful to wake."

There he went again, being considerate, making her feel special. She relaxed into him even more, loving the way she seemed to fit against him as if they were made for each other.

Her gaze strayed toward the can on his desk. "Is that how you get your caffeine in the morning?"

He chuckled. "No. That's how I get my caffeine at eleven a.m."

"Eleven?" Pushing a hand against his chest, she sat up and looked toward the sun slanting through the glass. "I didn't realize . . . " She glanced down at him. "Why didn't you wake me?"

"Because you needed the sleep."

"I didn't even take that sleeping pill your father left."

"I know. You can thank me for completely wearing you out later."

Smiling, she sank back against him. "I can't remember the last time I slept 'til eight, let alone eleven."

"You obviously haven't been out partying with my brother Alec."

"Late nighters, huh?"

"Let's just say I've been dive-bombed in some really interesting places because of Alec."

She trailed her finger over the logo on his T-shirt. It was silly. She usually shied away from family, but she had a burning urge to know more about his. "Maybe we should try it sometime. I'd love to meet him."

"Sorry. Alec gave up his wild ways a few years ago."

"That's too bad. We'll have to find another reason to stay in bed until 11:00 a.m."

Beneath her hip, his erection swelled. "I can think of several reasons to stay in bed until 11:00 a.m."

She laughed and turned her lips against his throat, loving this easy, lighthearted moment.

Unfortunately, though, it couldn't last. "I, um, need to go home today, Ethan."

He tensed beneath her. "I don't think it's safe for you to stay there alone right now."

"I agree."

"You do?"

The surprise in his voice made her push back. She nodded. "Until we figure out what's really going on, I think it makes sense to be cautious. I just want to go pick up a few things and fix the broken front door so the realtor can sell the place."

"Okay." He studied her with narrowed eyes. "I can take you."

"I was also hoping"—nerves bounced through her belly as she dropped her gaze to his collar—"that you might have some suggestions for where I can stay. In the meantime, that is. I'm not opposed to a commute to work each day so long as the place is nice. With, oh, I don't know . . . a fireplace, granite counters, a Jacuzzi tub, and a big soft bed."

His lips curled into a sexy, knowing smile, and his hand skimmed her thigh. "I think I know of a place like that."

"Oh yeah?"

He nodded and lifted to kiss her. "It's got a great couch too. The last woman who spent some time on it was thoroughly satisfied."

Desire surged in every cell. "Oh, yes, she was."

He leaned in and kissed her, and as Sam wrapped her arms around his shoulders she knew the decision she'd made this morning while brushing her teeth was the right one.

She drew back, resting her forehead against his, and toyed with the hair at his nape. "I'm not going back to California."

"You're not?"

She shook her head and leaned back. "You have completely rearranged my priorities, Dr. McClane. I want to stay right here. With you."

His hands captured her face, and then his mouth was on hers again, kissing away any lingering doubt. "In that case," he said when they were both breathless, "you might need to grab more than just a few things from your house."

"What kind of things?"

"All your things."

Sam's heart filled as she looked up into his gorgeous eyes. It was crazy. They'd only known each other a few weeks, but moving in with him felt . . . right.

He smiled, a sexy, mesmerizing grin that did wicked things to her blood. And sliding his arms around her waist, he lifted her out of the chair. "Wrap those gorgeous legs around me."

She obeyed, tightening her hold on his shoulders at the same time. "Where are you taking me?"

"Our shower."

*Our* . . . She sighed, loving how one small word made everything perfect. "You already had a shower, Dr. McClane."

"Yeah, but you didn't."

She laughed. "I have a feeling we aren't getting to my mother's house for quite some time."

"Now you're thinking."

———

Standing on Sam's front porch, Ethan braced a hand against a piece of plywood and hammered a nail into the wood, boarding up the broken sidelight by her door.

The happiness he'd felt earlier had trickled away as soon as they'd reached her house. He'd been so focused on getting what she'd needed yesterday that he hadn't taken time to survey the damage. Now it was all he could focus on. Every time he looked at her broken front door or the shambles that used to be her kitchen, he had flashes of Saunders attacking her, of Branson barging in midscene with a gun, and his vision turned red.

He should have been here. He shouldn't have left her alone. And the fact that she hadn't confessed how bad it had actually been made his chest burn. He hadn't yet asked her about the shredded blouse he'd found in her trash can. But he would. When he could think straight again.

"Hey, Dr. McClane."

Ethan turned and stiffened. "Thomas." Looking away from the kid, he pulled a nail from between his lips and knocked it into place. "What are you doing here?"

Thomas moved up the first step with a backpack slung over his shoulder. "Ms. Parker wasn't at school yesterday afternoon. I, uh, just wanted to stop by and make sure she was okay."

Warning vibrations zinged up Ethan's arm. The kid might be innocent of what had happened to Margaret Wilcox, but Ethan didn't like his budding fascination with Samantha. "She's fine. Too busy to see—"

The door next to him pulled open, and Samantha stepped out onto the porch with a dish towel in her hand. "Thomas." Her lips curled in a smile that was anything but suspicious. "What are you doing here?"

"Hey, Ms. Parker." He shifted his backpack and looked quickly away from her bruised face. "I, uh, I was on my way home from the library. Just wanted to stop by and see if you needed anything."

"That was sweet of you. I'm fine, though." She ran a finger over her bruised cheek as she stepped out onto the porch. "Word spread, huh?"

Unease passed over Thomas's face when he looked up at her. "Yeah. Manny Burton's dad works at the hospital."

"Ah." Samantha shot a knowing smile Ethan's way. "I should have guessed. Manny Loose Lips Burton."

Thomas chuckled, then kicked at something on the step with the toe of his sneaker. "He's not that bad. Not that good either, but don't tell him I said so."

Samantha chuckled.

Ethan gripped the hammer. Why the hell was the kid here? It wasn't normal for students to check up on teachers.

"You, ah, need any help here?" Thomas asked, looking up at the broken window.

"No," Ethan said quickly. "We've got it covered."

Thomas looked Ethan's way, and his gaze dropped to the hammer. His face paled, and he glanced back at Samantha before quickly stepping off the porch. "'Kay. If you need anything, Ms. Parker, I'll, uh, be around this weekend."

"Thanks, Thomas. I appreciate it."

He moved down the path, paused, and looked back. "You gonna be at school on Monday?"

"Should be. Midterms are coming up. I hear your chem teacher's a total hard-ass, so you'd better study for the exam."

"I heard the same thing." Thomas grinned. "Catch ya later, Ms. Parker."

"Bye, Thomas."

As soon as the kid disappeared around the corner, Samantha turned toward Ethan and lifted her brow. "What was with that look?"

"What look?"

"The one that scared the crap out of the kid and screamed, 'I don't trust you as far as I can throw you.'"

"I don't trust him."

Sam rolled her eyes and sat on the top step. Setting the dish towel on the wooden planks at her side, she frowned. "You worry too much, Ethan."

"That's because you give me reason to worry, Ms. Parker." Ethan dropped the hammer into the toolbox he'd found in her garage, wiped his hands on his jeans, and sank behind her on the step, sliding his legs around hers as he pulled her back into the heat of his body.

She sighed and laced her fingers with his against her belly. "He's a good kid, Ethan."

"Yeah, you keep saying that."

"Because it's true."

He didn't want to fight with her about this again. He'd much rather focus on her than the damn juvenile delinquent down the street. He nipped her ear. "Whatever."

She laughed and tipped her head to the side so he could kiss her. "I'm not stupid, you know. I know he's got a troubled past. But . . . " Her smile faded. "A lot of us do. That doesn't make him bad. And I know you believe that deep down as well."

He did. But when it came to Samantha, Ethan's objectivity was shot. And he wasn't willing to put her in any more danger simply because he wanted to believe the kid could be reformed.

"Fine." He kissed her neck again. "We'll just agree not to agree on this one."

She frowned as he kissed his way back up to her ear. "It's just . . . He reminds me of Seth. I think that's why I don't see the things you see."

Ethan's lips stilled against her ear, and for a heartbeat, nothing moved. Even the air seemed to come to a screaming halt.

"Maybe it's the light-brown hair or that quirky grin. I don't know." Sam sighed again. "I've always kind of thought he looked like Seth."

Ethan's heart picked up speed, and he lifted his head. "Who's Seth?"

"My brother."

The air caught in his lungs. "Y-you said you were an only child."

"I am. Now." She squeezed his hand. "I should have told you sooner, and I wanted to tell you last night, I just . . . I have a hard time talking about him." She drew a deep breath. "Seth was several years older than me, but we were very close. He died when I was ten. My whole life changed the day we lost him. My parents broke up, my dad moved away. Everything crumbled. The day he died was like . . . like the beginning of the end for my family."

Sweat popped out on Ethan's skin, chilling him down to the bone. It couldn't be the same Seth. Fate was not that cruel.

"How . . . " He swallowed hard, tried again. "How did he die?"

"He drowned. At the falls." Her voice hardened. "He was murdered. I'm pretty sure it happened the same night Sandra Hollings was killed."

*Mother of God.* Sam's voice turned to a jumble in Ethan's head. Tugging his hands from hers, he stumbled back onto the porch.

Samantha shifted and looked up. "Ethan?"

Bile rose in his stomach. He had to get out. He had to get out right now.

"Keys," he mumbled, turning a slow circle, patting his empty pockets. Where the hell were his keys?

"Ethan?" Samantha pushed to her feet. "Are you okay?"

He yanked the door open and walked through the house as fast as his shaky legs would carry him. Where had he left his damn keys? He fumbled through a stack of papers on the table in the kitchen, swiveled, and finally spotted them on the counter.

Samantha moved into the room. "Ethan? You're scaring me. What's wrong?"

"I, uh, I have to go."

He brushed past her, careful not to touch her in the process, unable to even meet her gaze.

"Wait." She trailed after him through the hall and toward the open front door. Grimly followed at her heels. "Ethan. I don't understand."

He jogged down the front steps on legs that felt like gelatin. The ground tipped and swayed. Air whooshed out of his lungs as he crossed the yard, pulled the car door open, and fell behind the wheel. One look up told him Samantha was standing on the porch, staring after him with wide and confused eyes.

And in that one look, his heart crashed against his ribs and shattered at his feet.

"I'm sorry, Samantha. God, I'm . . . " His throat grew thick, and unable to finish, he pulled the door shut and tore out of her drive.

# CHAPTER EIGHTEEN

Ethan stared out at the water beyond the dock on his parents' property, barely seeing any of it.

The small lake was surrounded by homes with big yards and towering trees. Those trees were mostly empty now as he sat on the end of the dock with his legs hanging over the water, a lot like his soul. Wind rustled fallen leaves along the bank, but he didn't turn to look. Couldn't seem to do anything but sit and stare and think about all the ways the past had come back to nail his ass.

"Put this on." Michael McClane's voice echoed from above just as a coat dropped in Ethan's lap. "Your mother's watching from the kitchen window."

Ethan looked down at the jacket, knowing it wouldn't do anything to warm the cold place in his heart. But for his father—for his mother—he slowly shrugged his arms into the sleeves.

Easing down to sit on the end of the dock next to him, Michael braced his hand on his thigh and stared out at the water. He didn't speak, didn't ask, but that was just like Ethan's dad. The man never pushed. Not once in all the years Ethan had known him had Michael McClane ever rushed anything. He let the problem at hand work its way to the surface. And considering he'd raised three juvenile delinquent boys and an emotionally screwed-up girl, there had been numerous problems. And altercations. Only, he'd never lost his cool, not once in all that time.

Not like Ethan was doing now.

"Samantha is Seth Raines's sister," Ethan finally said.

"Are you sure?"

No surprise. God, nothing rattled this man. Ethan's heart contracted, and he closed his eyes. "Yeah, I'm sure."

"Does she know who you are?" Michael asked softly.

"I don't think so. We were at her house today, and she started talking about Seth, and I . . . shit, I bolted like a freaked-out thirteen-year-old. I couldn't even breathe."

He opened his eyes and looked out at the water. "I knew, dammit. I knew there was something going on with her, but I was so focused on helping her get through those nightmares that I didn't even think it could be this. She changed her name, Dad. She never talked about her family. I mean . . . I was a kid then. I didn't know where the Raines family lived. I never in a million years would have gone out with her if I'd thought there was a chance she was Lynne Raines."

Michael placed a gentle hand on Ethan's shoulder. "You need to tell her."

"I know."

"No." Michael tightened his grip. "You need to tell her soon. I don't think you understand the ramifications of this."

"Ramifications?" Ethan looked toward his father. "What could possibly be worse than my telling her that I went to juvenile detention for killing her brother?"

Worry filled Michael's eyes. "I know that seems bad, but there's more to this, Ethan. At the end of the hypnosis session last night, Samantha was talking to someone. She said she didn't remember who that was, but I could tell she was lying. She knows something more, Ethan. She just wasn't telling us."

"Why would she—" Ethan's brow wrinkled. He'd assumed she'd been talking to Branson, that she hadn't wanted to say his name because she didn't want to implicate her friend. "You think she was talking to Seth?"

"I think there's a strong possibility. Whoever she was with at the end was someone she trusted. And you and I both think Seth Raines's death happened within days or even hours of this Hollings woman's disappearance. Samantha was distraught at the end of that session. It was something more than witnessing that attack on Hollings. If it was the last time she saw her brother . . . "

Ethan's gaze skipped over the lake again. "Then that means he was involved."

Michael nodded. "I think it's entirely possible that he either knew about or was a party to what happened to the Hollings woman. You said you never understood why those boys turned on him that night up at the falls. What if—"

"Oh shit." Ethan scrambled to his feet.

"Who else was at the quarry that night?" Michael asked, standing.

"Saunders."

"And he's dead now. Who else?"

"Will Branson and Jeff Kellogg."

———

Ethan was frantic to find Samantha and warn her.

His heart pounded hard as he pulled into the high school parking lot an hour later. He'd swung by her house first, only to find her driveway empty. Fear had nearly closed his airway as he'd driven around town in the fading light, searching for her. Until, that is, he'd passed the school and spotted her car in the lot.

He glanced at his phone, willing it to ring. Alec had dropped everything to help him but had yet to call with the information Ethan needed. Ethan knew the smart thing would be to wait and talk to

Samantha after he had all the facts, but he couldn't wait. He had to see her. He had to set at least part of this right. And, most of all, he had to make sure she didn't go within a hundred yards of Branson or Kellogg.

He pushed the car door open and crossed to the front of the school, only to find it locked. Skirting the building, he headed for Samantha's wing and stopped to peer through her classroom window.

His heart turned over when he spotted her seated at her desk, head bent, hand furiously moving over a paper. A lock of curly hair fell across her face, and she reached up, twirled it around her finger, then pushed it back from her flawless cheek.

Warmth spread through his chest. God, he loved her. Loved her more than anything. And in a minute she was going to hate him forever.

Swallowing the lump in his throat, he lifted his hand and tapped on the glass. She sat up straight and glanced toward the window. A heartbeat passed before she dropped her pen and motioned toward the hall.

Ethan picked his way through the brush along the edge of the building and headed for the back hall entrance. Just as he reached it, the door pushed open, and Samantha's familiar scents of lavender and warm vanilla swept over him, igniting a rush of memories of the two of them wrapped together at his house just last night.

"I'm a little surprised to see you here, Ethan."

She was hurt. She had every reason to be. "I went by the house. You weren't there."

She turned back for her classroom. "After you ran off, I decided to finish some grading."

She didn't want to be alone at that house. He didn't blame her. Steeling his nerves, he followed. "Where's Grimly?"

"At home. Sleeping." She turned into her room and crossed right to a lab station. Picking up a rag, she wiped down the counter, a nervous attempt to do anything to keep her hands busy and not look at him.

His heart pinched as he watched. He wanted nothing more than to pull her into his arms and reassure her that everything would be all right. But he couldn't, because he had to tell her the truth. Even if it meant watching everything she felt for him harden into a cold, dark cinder, he had to finally be honest with her. It was the only way he could keep her safe.

"I'm sorry about earlier," he said softly.

"It's fine." She lifted beakers out of the sink and placed them in the cabinet above her head.

"No, it's not fine." God, he hated this. "It's not anywhere close to fine. And it's all my fault."

"You're right, it's not fine." She moved test tubes into a rack. "It took a lot for me to open up to you, and you just ran off like it didn't mean anything."

"It meant everything, Samantha."

She huffed a sound that was both exasperation and disbelief. "Well, you have a funny way of showing it."

His heart stuttered, because she was right. "I'm in love with you."

Her fingers stilled against the test tubes, but she didn't look over. And he knew he deserved that too because she'd told him she loved him last night, and he hadn't said the words back. He'd wanted to say them, felt them all the way to the depths of his soul, but something had stopped him. At the time, he'd thought it was worry over her future and what she would do when she finally sold her mother's house. But now he knew that what had stopped him was fear. Fear that if he said the words and she found out about his past she'd run and he'd be left hurt and alone. But now there was nothing stopping him. And before he ruined this for good, he needed her to know how he truly felt.

"I am," he went on. "Head over heels in love with you. I have been since the day you knocked me on my ass on that football field."

She let go of the test tubes and finally turned to face him, hurt reflecting deeply in her chocolate eyes. "And you realized that today and couldn't get away from me fast enough?"

"No." He hated that she thought that. "I've known I love you for a while. I just haven't been able to tell you."

"Why not?"

"Because I was scared."

"Of what?"

His heart cinched down so hard that pain radiated all through his body. "Of this."

"Ethan, I don't—"

"You changed your name, Samantha."

"What?"

"Your name wasn't Samantha Parker, it was Lynne Raines."

Her brow wrinkled. "Lynne is my first name. It was my grandmother's name. I didn't change it, I just never went by it. Everyone has always called me by my middle name."

"And what about Parker?"

"I . . ." Her gaze skipped over his face in clear bewilderment. "I told you I got married in college and then quickly divorced when I realized it was a mistake."

"You never changed your name back? Why not?"

"Because I was lazy. Because . . ." She crossed her arms over her chest. "Having a different last name was like separating myself from everything that happened to Seth."

*Seth.*

A hollow ache filled Ethan's chest. Everything came back to Seth. Eighteen years later and Ethan's life was still being defined by that one horrendous moment.

"If I had known Seth was your brother, Samantha, I swear to God I never would have walked into your classroom. I'd have turned around and found someone else to handle Thomas's case."

Unease flashed in her eyes. "What do you know about—"

*Do it. Just get it out.* "You never asked me why I was sent to Bennett."

Several heartbeats passed in silence. "I figured you'd tell me when you were ready."

"You never wondered? A year is a long time for a thirteen-year-old boy to spend in a detention center. Only kids who've gotten into serious trouble get locked up that long."

"I—I didn't know that."

She gripped the counter behind her with shaking fingers, and he fought the urge to move toward her. "I don't usually take cases this far outside Portland. I told you I agreed to work with Thomas because a judge asked me to. That was part of the truth. The whole truth is that I took this case to put the past behind me. I thought it might be therapeutic." He drew a breath for courage. "Samantha, I used to live here."

"You did? W-when?"

"When I was thirteen. Social services dumped me with a foster family here in Hidden Falls after I'd gotten into some trouble in the city."

Her gaze skipped over the classroom. "I—I don't remember you."

"We never actually met."

She didn't look at him. Kept glancing over the desks. And he knew she was thinking back, trying to fit puzzle pieces together.

"I knew Seth," he said quietly.

Her gaze shot to his, and she gripped the counter tighter. But she didn't speak. And though it nearly killed him, he forced himself to finish what he'd started.

"He ran with a group of kids I'd started hanging out with at the rec center. They were older than I was, in high school. Back then, I thought they were cool. I just wanted to be a part of their group."

She still didn't say anything, just stared at him with wide, frightened eyes.

"Samantha," he said, desperate to get the words out, "I changed my name too. After I got out of Bennett. After I was adopted. My last name wasn't McClane. It was Coulter. James Ethan Coulter."

For a heartbeat, she didn't react. Didn't move. Didn't speak. Then her face paled, and she jerked to the side, sliding down the counter away from him. "No. That's . . . that's not possible."

"Wait." Panic rushed through him, and he stepped toward her. "Just let me explain."

"No!" She swatted at his hands so he couldn't touch her and stumbled backward. Tears filled her eyes as she covered her mouth with her hand. "Oh my God. Please tell me you're joking."

"It's not what you think. I—"

"Not what I think? You? You're James Coulter? Oh my God. I saw you. I was at the falls that night. I followed Seth. I saw you holding him under the water."

"No. I jumped in to help Seth. I—"

"You lie! You had marks all over your face where he fought back."

"The marks weren't from Seth. My foster father tore into me because I'd been ditching school. I was late getting to the falls because of him. By the time I got there, Seth was already in trouble."

"No." She shook her head, her eyes wild and shimmering with tears. "That's not right. That's not what I remember."

"I wouldn't kill anyone, Samantha. I had no reason to hurt Seth. I barely knew him. He was four years older than I was. You have to believe me. It was a misunderstanding. When I saw what was happening, I ran in to help Seth, not hurt him."

She stared at him as if she didn't know who he was. Tears rushed down her cheeks, forming tracks on her perfect skin.

She didn't believe him. He'd known she probably wouldn't. But part of him had hoped the love she felt for him would be enough to make her question what she'd seen. Knowing now that it wasn't sent burning pain straight through his heart.

She crossed the room and grasped her purse from her desk.

Panic coursed through him all over again. "Samantha, wait."

"No. I . . . I can't."

"There's more," he called after her.

She stopped at the door, gripped the jamb, but didn't turn.

"I think Seth knew what happened to Sandra Hollings," he said quickly. "Your dream, the cabin . . . it all happened on the same night."

She whipped around with horrified eyes. "How do you know? Were you there too?"

"No. God, no." But just the fact she had to ask told him just how far she'd slipped out of his grasp. "I swear to you I wasn't there. But I think Will Branson and Jeff Kellogg were."

She huffed a sound of disbelief. "And I'm supposed to believe you? After everything, I'm supposed to believe that two men who have done nothing but support me and my mother the last twenty years had something to do with the Hollings disappearance?"

"Yes," he whispered. "I would never lie to you. Samantha, you have to be careful around them. They were at the falls the night Seth died. They're involved with the Hollings disappearance. I know it."

"I don't . . . " Pain tightened her features. "I don't know what to believe right now. I just . . . " Shaking her head, she turned abruptly and rushed out the door. "I can't do this."

She was gone before he could stop her. Before he could push his legs into gear and run after her. And in the silence, his heart shattered into a million pieces beneath his ribs.

He'd lost her. Lost her forever because of one horrible night he could never change. Because of two men she thought were her friends.

His stomach twisted as his mind skipped to thoughts of Kellogg and Branson, and he pushed away from the table with a renewed sense of purpose. She might not love him anymore, but he was still determined to keep her safe. And he was willing to do whatever it took to make sure she stayed that way.

# CHAPTER NINETEEN

Ethan's cell buzzed just as he reached his car. One glance at the screen told him it was the call he'd been waiting for. Minutes too late. He lifted the phone to his ear. "Your timing sucks."

"And you sound like shit," his brother Alec said.

"Tell me something I don't already know." He looked around the parking lot as he slid behind the wheel. Samantha's car was already gone. She'd probably gone home. He'd catch her there, try to talk some sense into her, try to convince her to leave Hidden Falls for good and head back to California. "What did Hunt find?"

Hunter O'Donnell, Alec's friend, was a former Marine, now running his own PI and securities firm in Portland. The guy had connections all over the place, and when Ethan had called Alec and asked for help, O'Donnell had been at the top of his list.

"Sandra Jean Hollings . . . " Papers rustled. "Twenty-five years old. Put on administrative leave of absence looks like roughly eighteen years ago." He let out a low whistle. "Nice picture. Where the hell was she when we were in school? Remember Mrs. Kennedy who taught physics? Nasty. The woman smelled like Pine-Sol."

"Alec. Focus." Ethan reached for the pack of cigarettes he'd tossed on the dash, only to realize he'd already smoked the last one.

"Sorry. Okay, left Hidden Falls pending an investigation due to misconduct. Forwarding address listed a sister in Seattle."

"What was the outcome of the hearing?"

"Um . . . Here it is. School board terminated her employment in early February."

And if Samantha's memory from the cabin was even remotely close to Seth's death, that meant Sandra Hollings had returned to Hidden Falls in October. Eight months later.

"What kind of misconduct? Like with a student?"

"Don't know. Hunt's still looking for that info."

"There's got to be some mention of it," Ethan said. He knew how gossip spread in a small town. "Old news clippings, complaint filed by a parent, something. It had to have gotten out. You know how the press is, even small town press."

"Watch it," Alec said. "Those of us in the press don't appreciate jabs like that. And just so I don't forget, Hunt says you owe him."

"Irish whiskey," Hunt hollered from somewhere behind Alec, his voice muffled.

"You hear that?" Alec asked.

Ethan frowned. "Yeah. I heard him. And you better not drink any of it. Keep going."

"A case of Irish whiskey," Hunt hollered. "From the old country. None of that piss-ant crap you can get in the States."

Alec chuckled.

"What did she do after?" Ethan asked, trying to get his brother back on track.

"After getting canned? Doesn't look like much. Can't find any other employment records, if that's what you mean. There are a few medical files, though. And this you'll find interesting."

"What?"

"Couple of bills that were never paid to the family birth center of Cascade Valley Hospital in Arlington, Washington, just north of Seattle, from August, six months *after* she left Hidden Falls."

"She had a baby?"

"Can't find any birth certificate or any birth record. But why else do you go to a birth center?"

*Damn.* "Does Hunt have an address for the sister? Maybe she can help us."

"No luck there either. Tried it. Christie Hollings was reported missing by a neighbor about two weeks ago."

"Fuck." Ethan ran a hand over his head.

"Yeah. Convenient, if you ask me."

"What about the others?"

Papers rustled again. "Jefferson Davis Kellogg. Man, the guy just sounds slimy."

"He's a politician."

"Ah. That explains it. I knew I'd heard that name before. Let's see. Thirty-four years old, graduated with top honors from Willamette University, went to law school at Harvard. Straight-A student. President of the debate team. Varsity letter in tennis. I bet this guy's real fun on a Friday night?"

"What else?" Looking through Kellogg's transcripts wasn't helping the situation, and it didn't give Ethan any solid info to warn Samantha.

"Guy's clean as a whistle. Seriously. Too clean. No rowdy college behavior, no jilted lovers. It's almost as if someone's wiped his record spic 'n span."

That didn't surprise Ethan. He ran a hand over his face.

"Only thing that even raises a flag at all is his lightning-quick Vegas marriage to one Margaret Wilcox. No preannounced engagement. And judging from his family's well-to-do political status and Wilcox's shady upbringing, that couldn't have gone over well. Shotgun wedding?"

"No. Margaret didn't strike me as someone who'd get herself into trouble like that. I don't think he married her because she was pregnant."

"Blackmail?"

"Possibly." Though most people didn't blackmail others into marriage. In this case, though, it made a sick sort of sense. "What else?"

"Speaking of the dead. Margaret Anne Wilcox. Thirty-three years old, grew up in Hidden Falls. Was raised by her grandmother in a trailer park on the south side of town. Smart chick—got a scholarship to Portland State. Was working as an administrator at a high school in the city when she up and eloped with Kellogg."

"When was that?"

"About three years ago. She finished out the year, then moved home with her new hubby."

*Interesting.*

"Kenneth Saunders," Alec said, drawing Ethan's attention once more. "Man, this guy was a piece of work. Thirty-three, married right out of high school, two kids ages twelve and ten. Looks like Washington County Sheriff's Office was called out to his house numerous times for domestic disturbances."

"Any arrests?"

"No. Wife refused to press charges each time."

"Nice." Ethan's stomach rolled at the thought of Saunders alone with Samantha. "She's better off without him."

"Obviously. And I saved the best for last. William Branson. Thirty-four, son of Henry and Eileen Branson. Mother committed suicide when he was a teenager. Father was a teacher at Hidden Falls High. Elected town mayor, served ten years. Branson attended Oregon State Police Academy, worked as a lieutenant in Portland for several years. Moved back to Hidden Falls about three years ago when he was hired as chief of police."

"Why'd he leave Portland?"

"Don't know. Mayor of Hidden Falls hired him. Um, Lincoln Jenkins."

"I met Jenkins at Kellogg's party. Runs the paper here in town. I didn't realize he was the mayor as well."

"He chummy with Branson?"

"Not that I could tell. But everyone knows everyone in this town."

"Curse of the small towns," Alec muttered.

Ethan tapped his hand against his thigh. "The question is what happened three years ago to draw Branson back and to make Kellogg marry Wilcox."

"Good question. When did Samantha move home?"

"Just a few months ago. Whatever caused them to shift back here had nothing to do with her."

"You hope," Alec said. Voices echoed on the other end of the line. "Hey, Ethan. I'm gonna put Hunt on. He's got some info from the Washington County ME."

"Okay."

The phone crackled, and Hunt's deep voice echoed across the line. "Got a headache yet?"

"I've had a headache since I first drove into this town."

"That's got to feel good. Okay, I just got off the phone with Jill Bradbury. She's the Washington Co. ME. Your guy Branson? He told her not to rush the results of those remains you found up in the woods."

"Is that unusual?"

"Not for remains that old. Odds of identification without family of some kind offering dental records is pretty slim."

"Like a sister."

"Yep, like a sister. Bradbury also passed on some info from the Wilcox autopsy. The woman wasn't raped. ME found garrote marks around the neck, but there were no other signs of a struggle—no tissue under her fingernails, no other bruising, nothing. Body was completely clean—too clean, if you get my drift. She'd had sex before she died, but it looks like it was consensual. And judging from her dear husband's statement, it wasn't with him. He claims he was out of town the day she was killed. His staff is backing him up on that. This woman was a piece of work. She makes Alec's ex look like June Cleaver."

Ethan barely heard him. "Margaret would have fought back if someone had tried to kill her."

"That'd be my guess. Any woman would. Unless she didn't know."

"What do you mean?"

"Some people are into kinky shit," Hunt said. "It's called erotic asphyxiation. Heightened sexual awareness when the airway is—"

"Yeah. I've heard of it." Ethan rubbed the nape of his neck. He didn't need to imagine it to get the idea.

"I'm just saying, it could have been a sex session gone awry, or—"

"Or someone knew she was into that and took advantage of her. And by the time she figured out what was happening, it was too late. Shit," Ethan muttered.

"Yep. That'd be my guess. If it had been an accident, and the boyfriend simply wanted to cover it up, he would have dumped the body. He wouldn't have positioned it on your girlfriend's dining room table. That was a clear warning, if you ask me."

Ethan's chest tightened. Samantha wasn't his girlfriend. Not anymore. "Is the investigation still open?"

"No. Got word this morning that Branson closed the case. Report states he had enough evidence to prove Saunders killed her. Convenient, don't you think? Guy's dead now. Can't argue."

"Shit."

"Kellogg's holding a press conference about it tonight. He'll probably compliment the chief of police on his swift action. This bodes well for both of them. Branson gets credit for protecting the residents of Hidden Falls, and Kellogg gets the sympathy of his constituents. His poll numbers have skyrocketed since his wife's death."

"They're covering their tracks." Sickness gathered low in Ethan's stomach.

"Yeah. And doing it pretty damn well. Listen, I'm gonna dump all this with the Washington County Sheriff's Office. Jack Simms owes me a favor, but most of what we've found is pretty circumstantial. There's no hard evidence here to indicate Branson or Kellogg had anything to do with either the Hollings disappearance or the Wilcox murder."

And that was just what they wanted. Ethan wished for another cigarette.

"My gut thinks differently, though," Hunt added.

"Mine too."

"Safest thing for you to do is get your girlfriend out of that town. If she knows anything about what happened to that Hollings woman, and these two yahoos find out, odds are pretty good she'll be the next one to turn up missing."

Ethan reached for the keys and turned on the ignition. "That's where I'm headed."

He just hoped he could convince Samantha to leave before it was too late.

———

"Dammit." Sam pulled her car to the side of the road as steam billowed from the hood. Swiping her nose with her sleeve, she tried the starter again. It whirred once and puttered out.

She dropped her head against the steering wheel and drew a deep breath that did nothing to ease the hot sting behind her eyes. This was all she needed. The one time she wanted to run, she couldn't.

It had to be a nightmare. None of this could be real.

Memories bombarded her. Running after Seth that night when he'd walked away from her on the path. Hearing voices through the woods and chasing after them, afraid whoever had hurt that woman in the cabin was going to try to hurt him. Coming over the ridge sweaty, tired, and sore. Then seeing him lying lifeless in the water below as another boy held him under.

That boy had been Ethan. Her chest squeezed tight. She'd never seen him up close in court. The judge had let her testify in private with him and a counselor. She'd told them about the horrible boy who'd drowned her brother. About the splashes and screams she'd heard. They'd shown her a picture lineup of multiple suspects roughly the same age, and she'd identified Ethan. But . . . the Ethan she knew could never have done such a thing. He'd said he was a troubled kid, but could someone change so drastically? Go from evil to good in only a matter of years? She wasn't sure.

She closed her eyes tight. Focused on that memory. On the fight in the water. On Ethan holding Seth by the shirtfront. On the trees and shadows and voices echoing from the shore.

Her head came up, and she blinked several times. Others had been there. She'd never let herself focus on that part of the memory before. But now she was certain that Ethan hadn't been at the falls alone.

*I jumped in to help him.*

His words ran back through her mind. Could he have been telling the truth? Her heart raced as she sniffled and swiped at the tears on her cheek. She thought she'd been sure, but if there had been others at the falls, it was possible *they* had hurt Seth, and, as Ethan had stated, that he'd arrived late and tried to save her brother. And if that were true, it meant . . .

"Oh God." Horror swept through her, and she covered her mouth with her hand.

Her eyewitness testimony had been the evidence the court needed to send Ethan to that juvenile detention center. She was the reason he'd spent a year of his life in a prison for children. She'd altered the course of his life far worse than Seth's death had altered hers.

Sickness gathered in her stomach. Sickness and a frantic need to know whom else had been at the falls that night.

*Think, Samantha.*

A sharp tap at her window made her jump. Sam twisted and peered up at Jeff's worried face.

Pressing a hand against her heart, she rolled down the window. "Hey, Jeff. I didn't see you drive up."

"Everything okay?"

No. Everything was completely wrong. "My car died."

"Pop the hood. Let's have a look."

She wasn't really in the mood to play mechanic, but she was stranded out here and didn't have another choice. She pulled the hood release, pushed the door open, and stepped out. Tugging her cardigan tighter around her shoulders, she followed Jeff toward the hood and took his suit jacket when he handed it to her.

He was dressed in slacks and a tie, as if he were headed somewhere important, and a new sense of guilt stabbed at her. "I'm sorry. You're going to get all dirty."

"It's okay. I'd rather help a damsel in distress than meet with the press any day."

"You have a press conference?"

"Yeah." He checked hoses as he searched for the cause of her engine problems. "Will has some new info about Maggie's case."

Sam's stomach dropped, and she clutched his jacket to her chest, unsure what to say. Yes, her life was in shambles, but it could be so much worse. "Oh."

A crisp breeze blew across the highway, whistling through the woods on both sides. She glanced up and down the deserted road. She'd made it all of five miles out of town before her car had broken down. She hadn't even known where she was headed; she'd just wanted to get away. And right now she felt like a complete idiot because she was freaking out about something that had happened almost twenty years ago, and here was Jeff, looking like a rock after just losing his wife.

*Will Branson and Jeff Kellogg were at the falls the night Seth died . . .*

Unease trickled through Sam. Could he have been there? What if Ethan were telling the truth?

"Looks like you ran out of coolant," Jeff said. "Overheated and ruptured a hose."

Suddenly, Sam just wanted to get back on the road. Alone. "Oh."

He snapped the hood closed. "You're not going anywhere anytime soon in this thing. I'll give you a ride into town, and you can call a tow. Don't worry. It's an easy fix."

"I can just wait here for a tow. It's no big deal."

He frowned down at her, took her elbow, and turned her toward her car. "Don't be silly. I'm not leaving you out here alone. Not after what happened to Maggie."

Sam's pulse picked up speed, and her hands grew sweaty. Margaret had been at the cabin the night Hollings had been killed. Sam had heard her voice and others. Could he have been one of them? And if that were true, could he have killed her? His own wife? "Really, Jeff. I don't—"

He pulled her door open, grabbed her purse from the front seat and handed it to her, then maneuvered her around to the passenger door of his Lexus. "Stop arguing, Sam. I'm driving you home. End of story."

Sam swallowed hard as he pushed her gently into the seat and closed the door. She didn't want to make a scene. Didn't want to do anything to let him know she was suspicious. The best thing she could do was sit quietly, let him take her home, then get as far from him as she could.

He rounded the hood, slid behind the wheel, and started the engine. "You okay?"

She stared out the side window as he made a U-turn and headed back toward Hidden Falls. "Yeah. I'm fine."

But she wasn't. She was freaking the hell out. Was Jeff a murderer? Was Will?

His finger grazed her cheek. She jolted and glanced in his direction with wide eyes.

"Sorry. You had a little smudge of dirt there."

Her heart pounded even harder. "Oh. Thanks."

Her cell phone buzzed, making her jump. She fumbled inside her purse, grasped it with shaking fingers, and pulled it out. But in her haste, it slipped out of her hand and flew across the console to land on the floor at Jeff's feet. "Sorry."

Keeping his eyes on the road, Jeff reached down for it. "Slippery little bugger." He picked it up and glanced at the screen. "I'm sure—"

His foot shifted to the brake, bringing the car to a screeching halt. Sam shot forward and hit the dash, then bounced back. Groaning, she cursed herself for not latching her seat belt.

"Son of a bitch," Jeff muttered at her side.

Dazed, Sam pulled herself back onto the seat. "Jeff, what the—"

"Stupid fucking son of a bitch." He tossed her phone in her lap, then reached for his from the console, hit "Dial," and held it to his ear. The car whipped quickly around on the street, and he punched on the gas. "Yeah, it's me. I know I'm not supposed to call, but we have a major problem."

Icy fingers of fear rushed down Sam's spine. Hand shaking, she looked at her phone. A message from Ethan showed on the screen.

> Ethan: If Branson or Kellogg discover you were at the cabin that night, they'll come after you. Whatever you do, don't go near them, and don't tell them who I am. Just please, PLEASE go home and stay put until I get there. I would never hurt you, Samantha. All that matters is that you're safe.

———

Ethan knocked on Samantha's front door and waited. Grimly's muffled barking sounded somewhere upstairs, but nothing else moved. Turning a slow circle, he looked out across the front yard. Her car wasn't in the drive, but the fact she'd left Grimly at home meant she hadn't gone far.

He checked his phone again. Still no response to his text. Tapping his hand against his leg, he tried to figure out where she could be. A friend's house? Not likely. She wasn't close to anyone as far as he knew. The more logical explanation was that she'd gone for a drive to blow off steam and work through everything he'd told her. He just hoped she'd read his text and wasn't somewhere confiding in Branson or Kellogg.

Panic pushed at his chest again as he jogged down the porch steps and climbed into his car. Frustration, fear, and worry churned in his stomach as he stared at her house. He had two options. He could sit here and stress, or he could drive around and look for her.

He started the engine before he could change his mind and drove slowly through town, searching side streets for any sign of her car. When he turned onto Elm, his eyes locked on the Hidden Falls Library to his left. He pulled to the curb and looked up at the building.

He needed proof. Alec and Hunt hadn't been able to get it for him. If he was ever going to convince Samantha she wasn't safe in this town, he needed more than his word. He needed something concrete to show her.

He glanced at his phone again. Still no response. Indecision warred inside him. Branson and Kellogg didn't know she'd remembered anything from the cabin. No one knew but him. She wasn't in any immediate danger. He was letting fear and panic get the best of him when what he really needed to do was think. Twenty minutes wouldn't change anything, and hopefully, by the time he was done, she'd already be home and he could present her with proof that would make her believe.

He climbed out of the car. A brunette with a ponytail and thick glasses sat at the information desk with her nose buried in a book when he walked in.

"Need somthin'?" she asked when he stopped in front of her.

"Yeah. Do you keep past copies of the *Hidden Falls Herald*?"

She frowned like he were the biggest idiot on the planet. "Of course we do."

"Great. I'm looking for editions in a four-month span from this date." He jotted the month and year on a scrap of paper on the counter and slid it across to her.

"That's eighteen years ago."

"Yeah. It's research. For a town project," he added quickly.

She rolled her eyes, stuck a bookmark between the pages of her book, and shifted to the computer at her left. While she typed, he glanced at his phone to make sure it was still on.

Still nothing from Samantha.

The brunette picked up her book. "They're in the microfiche room downstairs." She pointed toward a small door without looking up. "Take the stairs."

"Thanks."

Ethan jogged down the steps and checked the time again. Fifteen minutes left. Thankfully, the woman manning the microfiche counter was more helpful than the one upstairs, and within minutes he had a stack of film ranging from January to May.

He settled into a seat at a viewer and put the first film on the slide. Spinning the knob, he scanned articles as quickly as he could, searching for anything related to Sandra Hollings.

Just when he was sure this was a dead end, he came across a small article on the third page of the February 21 edition.

*Science Teacher Released from HFHS.*

Like Hunt had told him, the article stated that due to teacher misconduct, the school board had released her from her contract. No legal action was being pursued from either party involved. No mention of any student or what the misconduct included.

Ethan sat back and frowned.

"Anything I can help you with, Dr. McClane?"

Ethan glanced up at the bald, middle-aged man standing just behind him, searching his memory for the connection he knew was there. "Jenkins, right?"

Lincoln Jenkins smiled. "Call me Linc. Everyone does." He grasped the back of a chair, pulled it up next to Ethan, and sat. "I came in to pick up a few books I put on reserve, and Molly told me you were down here going through old fiche of my paper."

Ethan ran a hand over the nape of his neck and looked toward the viewer. The tight-lipped Molly had suddenly become chatty. Nothing was secret in this town. Which meant there *had* to be info about Sandra Hollings somewhere. "Just doing a little research."

"Anything I can help with?"

"How long have you run the paper?"

"Goin' on thirty years now. Started right after I got out of college."

"So it'd probably be accurate to say you've had your finger on the pulse of the big stories here over the years?"

"On every single one." Jenkins grinned.

"What can you tell me about Sandra Hollings?"

Jenkins's expression sobered as he leaned back in his chair. "Had a feeling that's what you were looking up." He shook his head. "That woman caused a lot of trouble in this town. I understand the curiosity, but some things are best left dead and buried, Dr. McClane."

Interesting choice of words. "I'm a shrink. I'm not in the habit of letting things lie."

With a chuckle, Jenkins shook his head. "I like you, McClane. You say what's on your mind." His tone lightened. "What do you want to know? I'll see if I can help."

"For starters, why was she fired?"

"If memory serves, the school board felt it was in everyone's best interest if she found employment elsewhere."

"Just like that?" Ethan asked. "And she didn't fight it?"

"No, not just like that. By that time, her affair with Henry Branson was pretty well-known. Henry had been fairly stupid where Hollings was concerned. She was . . . " He looked away, as if trying to find the right words. "When she talked to you, she had a way about her that made you feel like you were the only person in the room."

"She was charming," Ethan stated plainly.

"She was more than charming, Dr. McClane. She was dangerous. More than one man in this town fell prey to her good looks and intoxicating voice. Henry was just the poor sap who got caught."

"By whom?"

"His son."

"Chief Branson?"

Jenkins nodded. "Way I heard it, the boy and his friends walked in on them in Henry's classroom one day after school."

"Ouch."

"Yeah. Traumatic for young Will. Henry broke things off after that, but three days later, Will's mother committed suicide. Poor Will found his mother's body hanging in their shower. Horrible thing for any kid to live through."

It would be. But it would also give Will Branson a motive for killing the woman who'd destroyed his family.

"Word spread through town," Jenkins went on. "People can be vicious when they gossip."

Ethan knew that to be true. "So Hollings just left after that? All because of the affair?"

"No. There were other issues with the board. That was just a big strike against her."

"Other issues," Ethan said, thinking about what Alec had told him. "Issues with a student?"

"I don't know. If there were, it was never made public. But . . . "

"But what?" Ethan asked.

"Well, there was talk that she'd been involved with one of her students. Some said it was her way of getting back at Henry for ending things, and at the school board for reprimanding her over their affair. No one knows for sure, though."

"Wait. You're telling me she was screwing around with a student, and the student's family didn't press charges?"

"None of that was ever proven. But that was the general consensus around here. My guess is the family didn't want to drag their child's name through the mud. People in this town don't forget anything either, Dr. McClane."

"I don't suppose you'd know who that student was?"

"Sorry. That I don't know."

But he sure had a guess and wasn't saying.

It had to have been Seth Raines. Samantha had mentioned she'd heard her parents arguing about Sandra Hollings before Seth had died. Ethan looked back toward the viewer. "So she had an affair with both a student and a teacher, and the school board kicked her out. She left in February and then showed back up here in the fall." After she'd had a baby. Did Jenkins know about the baby? "Why do you think she came back?"

"Beats me. And not everyone's convinced she did come back."

"You don't seem so concerned over the fact she just up and disappeared."

"That's because I don't think she did. Listen, Dr. McClane, you weren't here then, and you didn't know her. Sandra Hollings was the kind of woman who wanted attention. She loved that people were talking about her, scandal or not. She didn't care one iota that she'd damaged marriages or caused trouble in this town. She could wrap a man around her finger, and did, more than once, and when the well ran dry or she quit having fun, she moved on. She was always in control, and she loved it. Henry was the first one who slapped her down before she had a chance to dump him. And that grated on her."

Jenkins shook his head. "If she showed back up here like people say, then it was because she wanted to torment poor Henry—or someone else. I wouldn't put it past the woman. But I can't help you with that, because I didn't see her. I know people are talking like something awful happened to the woman, but from what I know, that's not the case. Odds are pretty good she's working on her fifth marriage somewhere, causing chaos for some other stupid sap who didn't have the good sense to get away from her when he could."

Jenkins's cell phone rang, and he glanced down at the number. "Sorry. That's my assistant. Step out for a minute and the place falls apart." He stood. "Look, I gotta get back to the office."

"Yeah." Ethan rose and shook his hand. "Thanks for the information."

"I'm happy to help. If you have any more questions, come by the paper and I'll see what I can do for you."

"I appreciate it."

"Anytime." He disappeared up the stairs.

Ethan sat and reread the article. Something didn't make sense. If Hollings had been a gold digger as Jenkins had insinuated, would she have come back after she gave birth to bleed money from Henry Branson? Or Seth Raines's family? Neither family seemed to have a lot of money. Not like the Kellogg family.

A quick look at his phone told Ethan he'd been at the library for more than thirty minutes. Urgency pushed him out of his seat. He still didn't have the definitive proof he wanted, but he printed a copy of the article anyway, gathered the microfiche, and headed for the stairs, hoping and praying the whole time that Samantha was back at her house and that he could talk some sense into her.

And if she wasn't, he'd camp out on her front porch and force her to listen when she finally came home.

———

A single sconce cast light over the small basement bedroom in Jeff's palatial house. He hadn't spoken a word to Sam on the drive, just dragged her in this room and locked the door.

Heart racing, Sam dug through dresser drawers, searching for anything to help her escape. Blankets and sheets filled the chest. Nothing she could use to pick the door lock. Slamming the drawer, she moved on to the next one, and the one after that, only to find them empty.

Frustrated, she turned and glanced over the sparse room. A bed, a dresser, a nightstand. No phone. No window. No way to out. Tightness pressed on her chest, making it hard to breathe. She fought back the panic, but her legs trembled, and she sank to the end of the bed.

Her nails dug into her palms. She told herself to stay focused, that she could figure a way out of this. She didn't know who Jeff had called from the car, but her gut said it had to be Will. If Ethan had seen Will that night at the falls, then Will really was involved too. He and Jeff had lied to her all these years. They'd had a hand in both Hollings's death and her brother's. And now, because she hadn't listened to Ethan when he'd tried to warn her, they knew who Ethan was too.

Panic came back, swift and urgent. She pushed to her feet and paced. She had to get out of here, had to warn Ethan. She knew for certain he hadn't been at the cabin. If he'd been there, she would have remembered. She knew his voice almost better than her own. But more than that, she believed in her heart that he hadn't killed her brother. He couldn't have. The man who had so gently and thoroughly cared for and loved her these past few weeks couldn't possibly be a murderer.

There had to be something in this room she could use to pick the lock on the door. A pen, a paperclip . . . anything. Moving around the bed, she tugged the nightstand drawer open. The lock on the door clicked, and her heart rate shot up as she whipped toward the sound.

Will stepped through the doorway, his face drawn, his jaw as hard as stone. "Dammit, Sam. I really wish you weren't here."

# CHAPTER TWENTY

"Dr. McClane!"

Ethan froze when he heard the voice. With one hand on his car door outside the library, he glanced over his shoulder only to see Thomas barreling right for him.

He took a step back and held up his hands to brace himself before the kid took him out. The article he'd printed fluttered to the ground. "What the—"

Face flushed, Thomas skidded to a stop mere inches away. "Sorry." Breathing heavy, he stepped back. "I've been looking all over for you. I saw your car at Ms. Parker's, but"—he sucked in a breath—"you left before I could catch you."

"I'm in a rush, Thomas. I don't have time to chat."

"I know. But it's important."

"Whatever it is can wait." Ethan jerked the door open.

"Oh shit."

The shock in Thomas's voice made Ethan glance over his shoulder. And when the boy lifted Ethan's paper from the ground, his face white as snow, a whisper of foreboding rushed down Ethan's spine. "Thomas?"

"Why do you have a picture of the Hollings woman?"

"You know who she is?"

Thomas nodded.

"How?"

"She . . . I'm pretty sure she was my mother."

"Holy shit." Ethan slammed the car door and focused in on Thomas. He hadn't put that piece together. Hadn't even thought the kid could be involved. "Start talking."

"I don't know much about her. Mary—the aunt I was living with in Portland—used to talk about her when she got drunk. They were cousins. Mary mentioned Sandra Hollings's name a few times, said how she didn't want me, how she'd only had me to get money out of my old man, but that it hadn't gone how she'd planned. I put two and two together."

The elderly woman's rant about how evil Thomas's mother had been suddenly made sense. "Your guardian knows?"

He nodded. "She doesn't let me talk about her."

"Who else knows?"

Thomas swallowed, but didn't answer.

"Don't think about lying to me right now. Who else?"

"Ms. Wilcox knew. When I started high school in Portland, she was the vice principal at my school. I wrote a paper in my English class about my birth mother. About how I was doing research, trying to find her. About how I didn't know where she was, I only knew her name. She called me into her office one day and asked a whole bunch of questions. After that, I started getting into trouble."

"What kind of trouble?"

Thomas shrugged. "Little stuff. At first I got blamed for things that went missing at school, graffiti on property. Got suspended a few times. Then one day the police came out to my aunt's house, asked a bunch of questions about who I was hanging with, what I was doing. Cops searched the house, found some stuff in my room that wasn't mine. Wouldn't listen when I said I never stole anything."

"You never did?"

Thomas looked away, then back again with a frown. "Not at first. After? Yeah. Why not? I was already getting in trouble for it. No one believed me."

They'd set him up. Ethan ran a hand over his face. Crap, he'd been wrong about the kid. As wrong as all the people who'd believed he was a murderer. "You recognize any of those police officers?"

"Yes. Chief Branson was one of them."

*Shit.* Thomas was the link that had brought them all back to Hidden Falls. He'd been digging up info on his mother, and Margaret and the others were afraid of what he'd find. "Who's your father?"

"I don't know. Mary always changed the subject whenever I asked."

"But you guessed."

Thomas shrugged again. "People talk. You just have to listen."

"What did they say?"

"That Sandra Hollings got around. That she was seeing another teacher up at the school." He looked away and bit his lip as if he didn't want to go on.

"What else?"

Frowning, he let out a breath. "People also said she messed around with one of her students."

"Seth Raines?" Thomas nodded slowly. "And you figured out Ms. Parker was his sister."

"Manny Burton told me."

Ethan rested his hands on his hips. "Why didn't you tell me any of this sooner?"

"If she'd been your mother, would you go bragging about it?"

Hell, no. He'd have kept quiet too.

Ethan ran a hand through his hair. The fact he, of all people, had been wrong about Thomas cut through him. He'd have to figure out a way to make it up to the kid. "Sometime I'll tell you about the woman who gave birth to me. We can compare war stories." He pulled the door open again. "But right now I have to find Ms. Parker."

Thomas grasped his arm. "Wait. That's why I was looking for you."

"What do you mean?"

"I saw Ms. Parker was with that politician guy. In his car."

The hair on Ethan's neck tingled. "Kellogg?"

Thomas nodded. "She was crying. I've seen that guy with Chief Branson. And with that janitor, the one who hurt Ms. Parker. It didn't seem right."

Fear clawed at Ethan's chest. He reached for his cell and dialed Samantha's number. "When?"

No answer. *Dammit, Samantha. Pick up.*

"About an hour and a half ago."

"Son of a bitch. Where did they go?"

"I don't know. They were headed out of town."

*Out of town . . .* That could be anywhere. She'd been alone with the guy for over an hour. If she'd told him about Seth, about what she'd remembered from the cabin . . .

Fear sliced through him.

"Do you have a cell phone?"

"Yeah." Thomas pulled a small phone from his pocket. "It's a pre-paid. Nothing fancy."

Frantic, Ethan grabbed it, then punched in Alec's number and handed the phone back to Thomas. "That's my brother. You tell him everything you just told me. Do it fast and then tell him I'm headed to Kellogg's to find Samantha. He'll know what to do. Then get yourself to Manny Burton's house and stay there until I find you again."

"Yeah, but Dr. McClane, what if—"

Ethan didn't hear the rest of Thomas's question. He climbed into his car and slammed the door. Then prayed he found Samantha before it was too late.

Sam's heart raced, and she moved back as Will stepped into the room and closed the door with a soft click at his back. Sad stone-gray eyes focused on her from across the room. Eyes she'd stupidly trusted all these years.

"I never wanted it to be like this," he said softly.

She eased back another step. "I don't know what you're talking about."

"Yeah, you do. You know too much. That's the problem."

"No, I don't. I don't know anything."

He shook his head. "I tried to keep you out of it, Sam. I did everything I could to get you to leave. Even after Kenny flipped out, you still wouldn't go. Do you know how hard it was for me to move that body? A normal woman would have seen that and run. But not you. No, you stayed, and now we're both fucked."

Sam's hands flattened against the wall at her back, and her pulse went stratospheric. She wasn't sure what he was talking about, but something in her gut said the body he was referring to was not Kenny's. "You . . . You killed Margaret?"

He pinched the bridge of his nose and sighed. "No. That was Kenny. I don't know what the hell got into him. Margaret must have been busting his balls about you. Kenny was always nervous around you, Sam. But I had to cover it up. Just like I've been covering up their bullshit for twenty years. I took her to your house so you'd see it and run. But you didn't."

Terror tightened her throat. "Will—"

He glanced toward the door and back, then lowered his voice. "Listen carefully. We don't have a lot of time, and the only way you're getting out of here is with me. They want me to take you to the cabin. They have something special planned. But I'm not going to let them hurt you."

His words circled around Sam as she stared at him. Confusion clouded her thoughts. Was he saying . . . he wanted to help her? "Y-you're not?"

"I'm so fucking tired of this shit. Of cleaning up after them. I made one bad choice, one terrible choice, and I've been paying for it my whole life. I didn't like the Hollings woman, Sam. I hated her for what she did to my family. And I wanted her to suffer. But I didn't want what they did to her. I tried to stop them. I really did. But it was too late."

Hope spread like fire through her chest. A hope she was almost too afraid to reach for.

"Did he . . . " She almost couldn't form the words, but she had to know the truth. "Did Seth hurt her?"

"No." Will's eyes turned sad. "I think in some small way, Seth felt sorry for her. I know there were rumors she was screwing around with him, but she wasn't. She was just a tease. She flirted with all of us in school, and Seth, well, you know how mature he was. I think he thought it was all an act and that he just wanted to help her in some way. But it wasn't an act, and she wasn't above using him to make the men in her life jealous. She spread those rumors about the two of them so that Jenkins and my father would fight over her."

"Lincoln Jenkins?" Sam's eyes widened. "Jenkins was sleeping with her too?"

"Jenkins was pissed when he found out he wasn't her only lover. Wanted to teach her a lesson. He came to the rest of us and convinced us he had a plan to scare her. Kenny and Jeff were more than happy to play along. They were ticked she wasn't flirting with them in class, and Maggie . . . well, she just couldn't stand not being the center of attention, you know?" He shook his head. "Being the center of Jenkins's attention didn't save her from Kenny, though."

"Are you saying Jenkins and Margaret were—"

"Yeah. On and off for years. She wanted money and power, and he had both, but he wasn't stupid enough to marry her, so he convinced Jeff to do it instead. That kept her quiet for a while, but when she discovered the Adler boy was Hollings's kid, she got antsy. I don't know if

Jeff knew about her relationship with Jenkins, but I'm pretty sure that's how Jenkins kept her from talking."

Connections and links Sam hadn't been able to piece together suddenly clicked. Thomas was Sandra Hollings's son. He must have learned something about Seth's connection to Hollings and found out Sam was Seth's sister. His coming to Hidden Falls had started a landslide that was still tumbling out of control.

"Me, though," Will went on. "Jenkins knew he had me all those years ago because of what happened to my mom. Sandra Hollings tore my family apart. I wanted her to suffer for that. I wanted her to pay."

Sam's hands shook against the wall. "But you said you didn't want what they did. You said it was a mistake."

"It was. I just wasn't strong enough to stop it. After it started . . . " A sick look passed over his face. "He had her by the throat, and I just . . . I couldn't stand back and watch anymore. I lunged for him, knocked him to the ground, but by then . . . " He shook his head. "By then she was already dead."

Sam's stomach pitched. Will was the one she'd seen fighting with Jenkins. He'd tried to save Hollings, but it had already been too late.

"I think he would have killed me too," Will went on, "but there was some kind of noise outside, and it distracted him. He stopped beating on me and sent Kenny and Jeff to see what it was. Shortly after that was when Seth arrived. I don't know how he knew something was going on, but he did. He went wild. Jenkins heard the commotion and came out. He told the others to take Seth to the falls."

Every muscle in Sam's body tightened. She'd heard the commotion. She'd followed Seth. Those were the memories she'd lived with all these years. "Wh-who killed my brother?"

Will's eyes darkened. "Jeff. Jeff and Kenny are the ones who dragged him out into the water, but Jeff's the one who held him under. I managed to get away from Jenkins and went after them, but I got there too late. When I tried to pull Jeff off, Kenny took me under. We wrestled.

Coulter . . . " He shook his head again. "Jenkins must have known he was a juvenile delinquent. He talked Kenny into recruiting him into the group, probably to frame it all on him at some point, I think. Kenny told Coulter to meet us at the falls earlier in the night and planned to take him to the cabin with us, but Coulter never showed. First time I saw him all night was when he saw what was happening and ran into the water to try to save Seth."

Sam's heart squeezed so hard she could barely breathe. She'd been right. Ethan hadn't killed her brother. He'd been trying to save Seth, as he'd claimed. And she'd run from him when she should have stayed and listened.

"No one planned what happened to Seth," Will said. "You have to believe that. Seth was my friend. What happened to him made me sick, and if I could go back and change it, I would. But I can't. When you fingered Coulter for the murder, Jenkins was thrilled. Seth's death took the focus off Sandra Hollings's disappearance and put it on the Coulter kid. I wanted to tell the cops what I knew, but I couldn't, because Jenkins threatened me and my dad. But I always owed you, Sam. It's why I tried so long to keep you safe. It's why I tried to scare you into leaving town. But you wouldn't go. You wouldn't go because of that shrink." His jaw tightened. "He's Coulter, isn't he? I knew he was familiar. I just didn't put it together until Jeff showed me that text message. Dammit, I wish he hadn't seen that."

Sickness swirled in Sam's stomach, a newfound fear for Ethan. "You can't—"

"Listen." Will's voice hardened as he stepped toward her. "They're upstairs. They're waiting for me to bring you up. I need you to act scared and to fight against me, to make it look like you want to kill me. If they suspect I'm on your side, we're both dead."

*On your side . . .*

Sam's head spun. Was he trying to help her? She met his steely gaze. Tried to see the lie or truth. He could be trying to spring a trap. But she knew for certain that one thing he'd said was fact. The only way she was getting out of this room was with him. She could figure out how to get away from him once she was free of these walls.

"O-okay. I can do that."

"That's my girl." Will's eyes softened. "I'm sorry, Sam. I'm sorry for all of this." He brushed a finger down her cheek, and she forced herself to stay still and not recoil. "I'll make it right. I promise."

She wasn't sure he could. Even if she got out of this, she could never look at him the same.

The door pushed open before they could take a step toward freedom. Will dropped his hand and turned. A gunshot exploded through the basement room.

The force of the bullet sent Will sailing back against the wall with a thud.

"Will!" Sam scrambled to grab him. Blood pooled from a wound in the center of his chest. He slumped to the ground.

"Will." Frantic, Sam pressed a hand against the hole in his chest, trying to stop the flow of blood. "Hold on, Will."

Blood pooled all around her hands, gushed onto the floor, wouldn't stop. Sam looked up, desperate for help. Jeff stood in the doorway, a handgun at his side, his eyes flat and cold.

"Do something!" she yelled.

"Stupid fucker," Jeff muttered. "He always had a soft spot for you. I told him it would kill him one day."

No. *No, no, no, no, no.* Tears burned Sam's eyes as she looked down at Will. "Just hold on, Will."

"Sam, I'm so—" But the rest of his words were lost as the life slipped out of his body. His hand landed against the carpet with a thud and his eyes stared off into nothing.

"Get up, Sam," Jeff said from the door. "You can't do anything for him now. And we have somewhere we need to be."

A blinding rage came over Sam. She scrambled for Will's gun from the floor, but Jeff crossed the distance between them and yanked on her hair, pulling her up and away before she could reach it. A shriek tore from her throat.

"I always knew you were trouble," he growled.

Sam struggled against him. "People will know. You won't get away with this."

"I already have. I'm Oregon's next senator. I'm the Hidden Falls golden boy. Besides which, McClane was behind the whole thing."

Sam's eyes flew wide as he jerked her up the stairs. "No."

"You explain it right, and people will believe anything. After all, he killed Seth. No one's forgotten that. All I have to do is say he was jealous. He wanted what Seth had. Hell, I spin this right, I bet I could even pin Hollings's murder on him and solve several cases at once. He came back here, met you, didn't realize who you were. When it all clicked, the guilt was too much. I figure a murder-suicide will get the point across."

Sam swayed as they reached the top of the stairs, and she realized just why they'd wanted Will to take her to that cabin. "Oh God."

"Not yet." Jeff pulled her toward the back door. "Wait to say your prayers until McClane shows up to save the day. Again."

———

Where the hell was she? Ethan sat in the front seat of Sam's broken-down car, looking for anything that might tell him where she'd gone. The hood was cold, indicating she hadn't driven in quite a while, and he'd already been out to Kellogg's. The place was empty.

Nerves danced all through his stomach.

He glanced up at the rearview mirror as a car approached. The pickup slowed to a stop behind Sam's Mazda. Ethan tensed, then relaxed when Lincoln Jenkins climbed out of the cab.

Jenkins's shoes crunched across the gravel on the side of the road. "You need help there, Dr. McClane?"

"No." Ethan pushed out of Samantha's car and closed the door. "It's not mine."

"Looks like Sam Parker's rig. That your shiny BMW across the street?"

"Yeah. Say, you didn't see Samantha in town, did you?"

"No. Not that I remember. She been having car trouble lately?"

"Looks like it." Crap, where was she? Ethan fingered the keys in his pocket. "If you see her, tell her I'm looking for her, okay?"

"Sure thing." Jenkins waited until Ethan crossed the highway. "Oh, Dr. McClane?"

He stopped with one hand on the car door. "Yeah."

"You know, now that I think about it, there was a car parked in her drive. Looked like Jeff Kellogg's SUV."

Ethan's chest constricted. "When?"

"Little bit ago. Saw it on my way out here. Betsy Murphy's cat had kittens. Each with eight toes. Headin' up there with my camera to take pictures. Should make for a good human-interest piece."

Ethan barely heard him. They were at Sam's house. Would Kellogg really be stupid enough to take her there? He stepped back toward Jenkins. "I need your help."

Jenkins's eyes widened. "Sure thing. What's up?"

"I think Samantha knows who killed Sandra Hollings."

"You're kidding."

"No. You got a piece of paper?"

Jenkins pulled a pen and pad from his shirt pocket. "I'm a reporter. Course I do."

Ethan took the paper and jotted a note. "I want you to call Jack Simms at the Washington County Sheriff's Office at this number and tell him to meet me at Samantha's house. You got that? The sheriff's office, not the HFPD."

"Sure thing, but why not our local cops?"

"I can't explain now." Ethan handed Jenkins the pad of paper and climbed into his car. "Just do it."

Dusk was settling over the valley as he parked in front of Sam's house. The drive was empty. No lights shone from inside. His heart dropped into his stomach as he glanced around the quiet street. Maybe she wasn't here. Maybe Jenkins had been wrong. Kellogg could have taken her anywhere. He killed the engine and knew he had to check, just to be sure.

The front door was locked. He jiggled the knob and tried to peer through the panes of glass at the top of the door. Grimly barked and tore down the stairs.

He picked his way around the house. A breeze blew across the yard, chilling his skin. The dark sky threatened rain. He tried the back door, twisted the handle, and found it unlocked.

His adrenaline ticked up. Samantha knew better than to leave her house open. Quietly, he stepped into the kitchen. Grimly barked and rushed forward, slamming on his brakes when he spotted Ethan.

Ethan dropped to his knees and rubbed the dog's ears. "Hey, buddy. Where's Samantha?"

Grimly looked up at him with big, brown, stupid eyes.

Ethan frowned. "It'd help if you could talk." But it was a good sign the dog was in one piece and not freaking out. Grimly was fiercely protective of Samantha. If someone had come into the house, he'd be acting funny.

The chairs were pushed up against the table. A few dishes sat in the sink. Sam's purse lay on its side on the counter. Ethan rifled through the contents—hairbrush, tube of lipstick, wallet, keys.

No cell phone.

A tingle ran down his spine. Turning, he checked rooms as he headed toward the front of the house. Nothing looked out of the ordinary, but still there were no other signs of her. He moved up the stairs, maneuvered around boxes in the upstairs hall, glancing inside bedrooms as he went. But the house looked exactly as he'd left it earlier.

When he got to Sam's room at the end of the hall, he turned the handle. Grimly plowed by and jumped on the bed, wagging his tail. On a groan, the dog dropped to the mattress.

"You're not supposed to be up there, big guy." With a frown, Ethan checked the adjoining bath, found that empty too, and moved back into the bedroom.

"Shit." He turned a slow circle. Every minute that passed felt like a hundred years.

A tree limb tapped against the window, drawing his attention to the darkness beyond. He peered out into the night. Muttered, "Samantha, where are you?"

A light flickered on the hillside.

*No way he'd take her up there.*

Rushing downstairs, Ethan scribbled a note for Simms, slapped it on the kitchen table, and tore out the back door. He paused when he got to the clearing, trying to remember which direction they'd gone when they'd taken that walk. An owl screamed above. The wind whistled through the trees as the first droplets of rain hit him. Closing his eyes, he envisioned the cabin from the day he and Sam had hiked these woods.

*Left.*

His legs seemed to move on their own. He jumped over a log in the path, rounded corners, and climbed the steadily rising hill. And finally slowed when the dim outline of the cabin came into view around the bend.

Sucking in air, he leaned forward and tried to quiet his breathing so he could listen. The forest was silent but for a woodpecker somewhere in the distance and the soft patter of rain on the ground. No lights shone from the windows. As quietly as he could, he eased through the trees toward the cabin.

Wood scraped against wood. A muffled grunt echoed from the building. Cautiously, Ethan moved past a tree and peered through the window. Then bit back a curse.

Samantha sat on a metal chair in the middle of the room, her hands hooked behind the back, struggling against the ties around her wrists. Lincoln Jenkins walked around her with what looked to be a whip in his hand.

Ethan's adrenaline soared. She was alive, but, if he didn't do something fast, not for long.

His body urged him to rush in there, but he held back. Jenkins . . . *Sonofabitch.* He'd confided in the fucker. The man had been playing him. He'd all but sent Ethan up here. Ethan had no doubt Kellogg and Branson were somewhere close. Which meant they'd staged this so he'd walk right into a trap.

It almost killed him, but he forced himself to move away from the cabin and back into the trees. When he was twenty yards away, he pulled his cell from his pocket and dialed.

Hunt answered on the third ring. "Ethan? Alec and I are at still ten minutes out."

*Shit.* He couldn't wait ten minutes. "They have her up at the cabin," he whispered. "There's a path that runs off the back of her property. Stay to your left. Samantha's inside. Jenkins has her bound."

A twig snapped somewhere close. His gaze shot to the side.

"We're on our way," Hunt said. "Alec's got Simms on the line right now. Listen to me, Ethan. Don't go into that cabin alone. You got it?"

His heart thundered. He couldn't just let her sit in there. Not with Jenkins. "Just fucking get here."

Another limb snapped to his left. Ethan turned toward the sound and sank back deeper into the trees. "I gotta go."

"Stay where you are, Ethan. We'll be there soon. Don't—"

Ethan clicked "End," shoved the phone in his pocket, and reached down for a thick branch on the ground at his feet. The crackling stopped a few feet away. He held his breath and peered through the darkness.

Rain ran down his wet hair, slid into his line of vision. The sliver of moonlight wasn't enough to see three feet in front of him.

Branches rustled to his right. Gripping the limb in his hands, he whirled around and swung. Wood connected with something solid. A muttered curse echoed from the darkness. Ethan's adrenaline surged, and he swung again, but the branch cut through empty air.

An elbow cracked against his cheek from the side, knocking him off balance. He stumbled back. A hard punch to his stomach pushed the air out of his lungs, and he gasped just before a body plowed into him.

He hit the ground with a thud. Rocks jabbed into his back. The branch fell from his hands.

"You just won't quit, will you, McClane?" Kellogg pressed a meaty forearm against Ethan's throat. "Branson should be doing this, but the son of a bitch always had a soft spot for Sam. I knew he was going to betray us. Guess it's time I took matters into my own hands, after all."

Ethan lifted his leg and jabbed his foot into Kellogg's groin. Kellogg jerked back and groaned. Closing his hand into a fist, Ethan threw a right hook across Kellogg's face, knocking the man off him.

He stumbled out from underneath Kellogg's weight and reached for the branch. Kellogg growled, rolled to his back, and pulled a handgun from his waistband. Ethan swung as hard as he could. The gun went off just as the branch hit Kellogg's arm.

A burning pain sliced through Ethan's shoulder, the force of the bullet thrusting him backward to slam against the ground.

A muffled scream echoed from the direction of the cabin. Water droplets slapped against Ethan's face.

Through a haze, Ethan watched as Kellogg scrambled for the gun. Ethan rolled quickly to his side, slapped out across the muddy ground, and closed his hand around the butt of the gun.

Kellogg roared and lurched toward him. Ethan rolled to his back and fired.

The bullet hit Kellogg in the thigh. He dropped to the ground and screamed, clutching his bloody limb. Pain ripped through Ethan's shoulder and chest, but he struggled to his feet and stumbled toward the cabin, desperate to get to Samantha.

His arm hung at an odd angle. Something warm dripped down his hand. Spots appeared in his vision, and he swayed as he moved onto the porch, but he had to get to her before it was too late. Had to save her . . .

He kicked in the door and lifted the gun in his good hand. Jenkins had untied Sam and now held her in front of him, one arm around her neck, the other resting on the top of her head.

"Drop the gun, son. Drop it right now or I'll snap her neck."

"Let her go." Ethan's vision blurred. "It's over. Cops are on their way. You're done, Jenkins."

"Ethan." Samantha's frightened eyes shot to Ethan's limp arm.

"I say when it's over," Jenkins yelled. "I make the news in this town. Do you hear me? I decide when something's over or not."

Ethan swayed. The gun shook in his hand. He was losing too much blood. In a few minutes he'd be on the floor. He had to do something fast.

"Drop it now or she's dead," Jenkins screamed.

He caught Samantha's gaze. And even though his vision was already starting to dim, he saw the resolve in her eyes. And the trust. She gave her head a small nod, then angled her eyes upward.

"Let her go," Ethan repeated, fighting to stay upright. "I'm not going to say it again."

"I—"

Samantha lifted her foot and stomped down hard on Jenkins's instep. The man howled and loosened his grip on her neck. Samantha shoved her elbow back into his abdomen, and he doubled forward with a grunt. She jerked out from beneath his arm. The second she was free, Ethan pulled the trigger.

Gunfire echoed. Jenkins grunted. Something hard hit the floor. But Ethan wasn't even sure where he'd hit the fucker, because his legs went out from under him and he slumped to the ground before he could look.

"Ethan!" Samantha scrambled to his side. "Oh my God, Ethan."

From across the cabin, Jenkins moaned, "You shot me!"

"Ethan, hold on."

Pressure landed against his shoulder, and Ethan realized Samantha had whipped off her cardigan and was pressing it over his wound. "Just hold on, Ethan."

Footsteps sounded somewhere outside.

"In here!" Samantha yelled. "We're in here!"

"I can't believe you fucking shot me," Jenkins moaned.

"Holy shit." Alec, that was Alec's voice, Ethan realized.

"He's bleeding," Sam said frantically somewhere above Ethan. "It won't stop."

"Keep pressure there. Ethan? It's Alec. Can you hear me? We're gonna get you out of here. Just hold on."

His vision came and went. "Kellogg . . ."

"Hunt's got him. Police are already on their way." Alec pulled something from his pocket, held it up to his ear. "Simms, we need EMTs out here right away. We've got three gunshot victims. Two don't look life-threatening, but Ethan's already lost a ton of blood. Yeah, okay."

Ethan rolled his head on the cabin floor. Through hazy vision, he spotted Jenkins slumped against the far wall, holding a hand against his side. Blood oozed from between his fingertips. The man leaned his head back and groaned.

"Ethan." Samantha's voice echoed around him. "Ethan, look at me. Just stay with me, okay? I'm here. I'm right here."

He stared up at her pretty face, already darkening at the edges. "Should have told you sooner."

Tears filled her eyes. "It doesn't matter. I don't care who you used to be. I know you didn't have anything to do with Seth's death."

Somehow, he found the strength to lift his good arm and lay his hand over hers against his chest. "Not . . . that. Should have told you sooner that . . . I love you."

"Oh, Ethan." Her tears spilled over her lashes.

He didn't want to close his eyes, just wanted to go on gazing up at her beautiful eyes, but he was suddenly more tired than he'd ever been.

"Ethan?" Samantha's frantic voice pulled at him, but he was already fading.

"Don't leave me," she whispered.

He didn't have a choice. Blackness descended before he could stop it.

# CHAPTER
# TWENTY-ONE

Sam's heart beat like wildfire as she stepped through the hospital's double front doors.

"Hey, Ms. Parker." Thomas laughed and flipped his hair to the side as he moved away from the chestnut-haired beauty at his side. "Cut that out," he said to Ethan's younger sister.

Beside him, Kelsey McClane dropped her hand and smiled. "Hey, Sam. I was just taking this mongrel for a haircut. Did you hear the good news?"

Sam had met Ethan's siblings yesterday when they'd all swarmed the hospital while he'd been in surgery. They were each very different, both in appearance and demeanor, but there was a bond between them that couldn't be broken. A bond formed by tragedies overcome. "He's awake?"

"Awake and grumbling," Kelsey said with a roll of her pretty hazel eyes. "Alec and Rusty are with him now. He was asking about you."

Nerves skipped through Sam's belly. She hadn't wanted to leave the hospital, but the police had needed her official statement, and she'd had to go down to the station this afternoon. She'd managed to put them off until she'd known Ethan was going to be okay, but the questioning had taken longer than she'd expected, and when Michael had called to tell her that Ethan was finally awake and coherent, she'd been desperate to get back here.

Her gaze drifted to Thomas, smiling in a way she hadn't seen the boy smile ever. He'd been at the hospital the whole time too, worried about Ethan and everything that had happened, and somehow in the time he'd met Ethan's siblings, he'd formed his own bond with them. "You're getting a haircut?"

"Only because she won't leave it alone." He ducked away from Kelsey's hand when she tried to ruffle his hair again, and his smile widened. "Stop that already."

Kelsey chuckled, tossed her long chestnut hair over her shoulder, and looked back at Sam. "Is Grimly at your house? We were thinking about swinging over and taking him for a walk. That okay?"

"Um. Yeah." A little overwhelmed, Sam fumbled for her keys, pulled her house key off the ring, and handed it to Kelsey.

"We'll be back," Kelsey said, stepping past her with Thomas.

As the two disappeared out the doors and headed off into the parking lot, Sam turned to look after them. Thomas laughed at something Kelsey said, and she smiled back, totally at ease, as if they'd known each other for years.

"He's a good kid," Michael said behind her.

Startled, Sam turned toward Ethan's father. Michael's salt-and-pepper hair was mussed, and his eyes were tired from being at the hospital all night, but they sparkled with warmth and acceptance, and as he watched his daughter and Thomas, she didn't miss the pride in his features.

"What's going to happen to him?" Sam asked.

Michael turned and walked with her toward the elevators. "Poor sucker's going to have to put up with us for a while."

"Really?"

Michael nodded. "His guardian agreed to relinquish custody. I just got off the phone with a friend at social services who's going to expedite the paperwork."

"Wow." Sam stepped onto the elevator. "Does Ethan know?"

Michael nodded and punched the button for the fourth floor. "It was his idea."

Sam's chest tightened. They still didn't know if Thomas was Seth's son, and she wasn't even sure how she felt about that, yet Ethan was already pulling the boy into the family, making sure he had a place and people who cared about him. Just as he'd always made her feel as if she belonged.

"Here." Michael pulled a folded sheet of paper from his back pocket and handed it to her. "I had Rusty bring this from the house. Thought you might want to read it."

Hesitantly, Sam fingered the paper. "What is it?"

"Just read it."

*Dear Mr. and Mrs. Raines,*

*I don't even know how to start this letter. Saying I'm sorry doesn't seem like enough. And the words probably don't mean anything to you at this point anyway.*

*The counselors here talk about owning up to the choices that brought each of us to Bennett. I think about that night every day. Not because I'm in here, but because I know I should have done things differently. If I could trade places with Seth, I would. If I could go back and try to set it right, I would.*

*I'd say I'm sorry a thousand times if it would make a difference, but it won't. I won't ever forget, though. No matter what.*

*J. Ethan Coulter*

Tears blurred her vision. "I never saw this letter."

"You weren't meant to. It was an exercise in forgiveness. It was never mailed."

"He didn't even do it."

"Doesn't matter. He still felt guilty for what happened."

She looked up. "You never questioned his innocence, did you?"

Michael turned toward her. "Ethan managed to get himself into a lot of trouble prior to that night, and that trouble didn't help him with the judge when Seth was killed. He was able to plead down from criminally negligent homicide to fourth-degree assault for what happened to your brother, but that prior trouble is really what contributed to his twelve-month sentence at Bennett. I knew after one hour with him, though, that he wasn't violent. He was conflicted. Some kids"—he shrugged—"you just know by looking at them."

Sam's chest pinched hard. "Like Thomas."

"Yeah, like Thomas. Ethan is one of the gentlest people I know. It's in his nature. When he was a teenager, even when he first came to live with us, he was always trying to nurse injured birds or chipmunks he found on the property back to health. What happened to Seth . . . " Michael shook his head. "It wounded him, but it also taught him the value of life. He's never killed anything or anyone. But he was willing to kill for you, Samantha. He was willing to do whatever he had to do to keep you safe."

A tear slipped down her cheek, and she swiped at it with the back of her hand. Ethan was the only person in her life who made her feel safe, and she didn't think she'd ever be able to get the image of him bleeding on the floor of that cabin out of her head. "What happened to Jenkins? And Kellogg?"

"Looks like they're both going to pull through."

For Ethan's sake, Sam was relieved.

"But they'll likely spend the rest of their lives behind bars," Michael added.

For Seth's sake, Sam was glad.

"It's finally finished," Michael said softly.

*Finished.*

Except, as the elevator doors opened, Sam was afraid it wasn't totally finished. Because she had no idea how she could ever make up for everything she'd put Ethan through.

Michael stepped off the elevator and turned to look back at her. "Aren't you coming?"

Drawing a deep breath for courage, she nodded and followed him toward Ethan's room.

———

Ethan couldn't get comfortable. Shifting in the hospital bed, he tried to find a better position and winced when his shoulder pinched.

It was no use. He hadn't been able to relax since he'd awoken and discovered Samantha was gone. His gaze shot to the door again, searching for any sign of her. His mother had said she'd left for the police station, but that had been hours ago. What if she'd run? What if she'd decided it was all too much and she'd gone back to California? He couldn't follow her in this freakin' hospital gown. Wasn't even sure she wanted him to follow her after everything that had happened.

"So Rusty goes in to make his move," Alec said with a smile, tipping his chair back next to Ethan's bed, "and the blonde with big eyes shoots him down on the spot."

"Yeah, right. Like you know." Leaning against the wall on the other side of the room with his arms crossed over his chest, Rusty tipped his dark head and shot Alec a condescending look. "You weren't even there, jackass. You were across the bar hitting on the redhead with the IQ that matched her cup size."

"Oh man." Alec's blue eyes took on a dreamy look. "She had the finest rack—"

"Alec McClane." He flinched at the sound of their mother's voice and dropped the legs of his chair to the floor with a sheepish grin. Hannah stepped into the doorway with a glare and a steaming paper cup.

"Caffeine," Alec said, pushing to his feet. "You read my mind."

Hannah smacked his hand when he reached for the cup. "Get your hand back. You want your own coffee, you can go down to the cafeteria. This is for Ethan." Her face softened as she stepped forward and set the cup on the bedside tray. "Here you go, honey."

"Thanks, Mom."

Alec held out his arms. "I gotta get shot to get some sympathy in this family?"

Hannah frowned. "Don't start with me." She looked back at Ethan. "How's the pain?"

Ethan shifted in the pillows again, desperate for some kind of comfort. "Fine."

*Liar.* He felt like shit, and not from the bullet wound in his shoulder. And his brothers' attempts to cheer him up were only making him feel worse.

"Lean forward a bit." Hannah fluffed the pillows at his back and helped him sit more upright. "We're going to work on some shoulder mobility after you drink your coffee."

Sometimes having a doctor for a mother was nothing but a great big pain in the ass. "I'd rather have a cigarette." *And Sam.*

"Not on your life," his mother said. "You want to kill yourself slowly, you're going to do it on your time, not mine."

Alec chuckled at the end of the bed. "Wuss."

"Total pussy," Rusty muttered.

Ethan leaned his head back and closed his eyes, wishing they'd all just leave him the hell alone.

"How's our patient?" Footsteps echoed, followed by his father's voice from the doorway.

Wonderful. More family fun time. Ethan exhaled a slow breath.

"Cranky," Hannah said with a sigh. "Well, hi there, Sam. All done downtown?"

Ethan's eyes snapped open. And excitement pumped through him when he saw Samantha standing in the doorway with his father, wearing jeans that molded to her long legs and a loose red sweater that brought out the color in her cheeks. Her hair was pulled back into a ponytail, and her eyes looked tired from lack of sleep, but to Ethan she'd never been more beautiful.

"Yes. All done," Samantha said, staring at Ethan.

"Sugar." Alec sidled up to Samantha and slung an arm over her shoulder. "I had a feeling you'd come back for me. No way you'd be back for him." He angled a thumb toward Ethan. "He cried like a girl when they wouldn't give him a cigarette."

Ethan glared at his brother.

"Like a little girl," Rusty added, leaning close on Samantha's other side.

"All right." Hannah stepped forward and waved her hands. "Stop tormenting your brother. You two. Out."

Alec let go of Samantha and chuckled as he moved out of the room. And for a second, Ethan thought he saw a smile crack Rusty's normally stoic face.

"I'm glad you were able to wrap everything up at the station." Hannah stepped past Samantha and squeezed her arm. "We'll be outside if either of you need anything." She gestured for Michael to follow her out the door, then said, "Have you talked to that boy about this trip he's taking?"

Michael frowned. "No. I was dealing with the details for the new addition."

"Thomas will be fine. It's the good-looking blond in denial out here that you need to worry about." She took her husband's arm. "Come on. I prefer when you're the bad guy."

"What if I want to be the good cop for a change?"

"With Alec?" Hannah huffed. "Right. You can play good cop with me later."

Their voices faded, and in the silence that followed, Ethan was almost too afraid to say anything because there was a nervous look in Samantha's eyes he didn't know how to read.

"I saw Thomas downstairs," she said when they were alone, stepping toward the end of the bed.

She wanted to talk about Thomas? That couldn't be good. Nerves replaced the excitement Ethan had felt only moments before. "Apparently my folks needed a new project. Four juvenile delinquents weren't enough. They needed five."

"I told you your parents were saints."

"Or crazy. Depends on how you look at it."

"Either way," she said softly. "I know I have you to thank for looking out for him. I have you to thank for a lot of things."

His heart squeezed. "Saman—"

"Ethan, I . . . " She moved around the side of the bed, but she stopped near his feet instead of moving closer as he wanted her to. "Ever since your dad called to tell me that you were awake, I've been trying to figure out what to say to you. Everything that's gone wrong in my life can be traced back to the night Seth died. My parents' divorce, my lousy track record with men, my inability to commit to anything. I've blamed you for all of that for eighteen years. And now . . . " She lifted her arms and then dropped them. "Now I know I was wrong. It wasn't you. Saying I'm sorry doesn't seem good enough. I don't know how to make up for that."

"You have nothing to make up for."

"Yes, I do." Pain reflected in her gorgeous eyes. "I ruined your life."

"How could you ever think that?"

"Ethan. If it weren't for me, you never would have gone to Bennett."

"You're right." Her eyes darkened, but he didn't let that stop him. "If it hadn't been for you, I wouldn't have gone to Bennett. I wouldn't have met Michael, I wouldn't have the family I've got outside, and I definitely wouldn't be the man I am today."

"But, how can you not hate me when—"

"If it weren't for you, I'd probably be in jail by now, or worse, dead. I was headed nowhere fast back then, but you saved me. In every way that matters. Hate you?" He shook his head. "Never."

Her eyes filled with tears. Tears that made his chest absolutely ache. Because she still wasn't moving toward him and he didn't know what she felt for him. Or if she still felt anything at all.

Long seconds past. Then softly, she whispered, "He would have liked this. Seth had a soft heart. He always wanted everyone to be happy. He would have liked that you and I found each other. It would have made him happy to know that the man I fell in love with was the same one who tried to save him, and in the process saved me as well."

Emotions filled Ethan's chest, so many he thought he might just burst. "If I have to bolt out of this bed to get to you, I'm going to rip my stitches. And if tha—"

She reached him in one step. He grasped her with his good arm and pulled her down next to him as soon as they touched, ignoring the pain in his side. Sliding his hand into her silky hair, he tugged her mouth toward his. "I love you. God, I love you, Samantha."

"I love you too, Ethan. More than you will ever know."

Their lips met, and as the healing power of her love swept through him, he grew dizzy and lightheaded in a way that had absolutely nothing to do with the painkillers he'd taken earlier and everything to do with her.

They were both panting when she drew back. And when she rested her forehead against his, he knew every moment of suffering he'd lived through had been worth it, because it had brought him here to her.

"You know, I still have issues," she said. "You're not going to try to get inside my head and fix me, are you?"

He chuckled. "No way. I love you just the way you are. Klutz and all." She laughed against him, and the vibration zinged along his nerve endings, warming all the places inside that had gone cold since he'd lost her. "Besides which, you're not the only one with issues. In case you haven't realized it yet, I don't have much of anything figured out."

"Ironically, that explains why you're a shrink."

"A damn good shrink."

She smiled. "The best one I know."

She climbed onto the bed next to him and laid her head on his good shoulder, exactly where he liked her best, and warmth encircled his heart when her body brushed his side. "What if I don't know what I want to do with myself now? I mean, I'm not sure if I want to stay in teaching or go back to research. I'm not sure of anything except you."

"I'll support you in whatever you want to do. But right now, I won't complain if you're focused solely on me."

She smiled. "I don't deserve you."

"Yes, you do," he whispered, looking down at her. "You deserve a hell of a lot better than me. But there's no way I can be noble and let you go. I need you too much, Samantha Parker."

Her fingers brushed the stubble on his jaw, and her eyes darkened with so much emotion, his heart turned over. "Nobody else ever needed me. You're the first, Ethan. The only one."

"You're damn right I am. Now shut up and kiss me before those lunatics come in again and interrupt us."

She smiled once more. And when her lips brushed his, he knew the past was finally buried, never to hurt them again.

# ACKNOWLEDGMENTS

Each book is a labor of love, time, and effort, and I wouldn't be able to write without the support and advice from several key people.

Special thanks go to Johanna Balascio, Probation Support Services Manager with Fairfax County Juvenile and Domestic Relations District Court, and Lauren Madigan, Assistant Director Central Intake Services, for their expertise translating juvenile sentencing codes and providing real-life advice for this book. Ladies, I owe you both a round of drinks the next time I'm in Virginia!

I also want to thank my writing girls—Skye Jordan/Joan Swan, Darcy Burke, and Rachel Grant for their help brainstorming and plotting this story. Girls, I couldn't have finished this one without our author weekends away! When's the next one?

Thanks also to my agent, Laura Blake Peterson, my editors, Anh Schluep, Christopher Werner, and Charlotte Herscher, and the entire team at Montlake Books for turning this story into a novel.

Finally, I want to say a big thank you to my husband Dan for his faith and support during the writing of this book and all the others. Living with a writer is not easy. Somehow, he manages to not only put up with me, but to act as if he's enjoying himself. Babe, I definitely got lucky the day I hit on you.

# ABOUT THE AUTHOR

Photo © Curtis Almquist at Almquist Studios

Before topping multiple bestseller lists—including those of *The New York Times, USA Today,* and *The Wall Street Journal*—Elisabeth Naughton taught middle school science. A voracious reader, she soon discovered she had a knack for creating stories with a chemistry of their own. The spark turned into a flame, and Naughton now writes full-time. Her books have received nominations for some of the industry's most prestigious awards, such as the RITA® and Golden Heart® awards from Romance Writers of America, the Australian Romance Readers Awards, and the Golden Leaf award. When not dreaming up new stories, Naughton enjoys spending time with her husband and three children in their western-Oregon home.